SANCTUARY:

Where Shadows Rise

Through Roads Between

When Worlds Collide

AMY LAURENS

OTHER WORKS

Find other works by the author at http://www.amylaurens.com/books/

SANCTUARY

Where Shadows Rise
On Roads Between
When Worlds Collide

NON-FICTION

How To Theme
How To Write Dogs
The 32 Worst Mistakes People Make About Dogs
How To Plan A Pinterest-Worthy Party Without Dying

Sanctuary:

Where Shadows Rise

Through Roads Between

When Worlds Collide

AMY LAURENS

AUSTRALIA

Hardcover ISBN: 978-1-925825-97-8
Paperback ISBN: 978-1-925825-79-4
eBook ISBN: 978-1-386027-21-8

Where Shadows Rise: 978-0994523808
Through Roads Between: 978-0994523815
When Worlds Collide: 978-0994523822

www.inkprintpress.com

National Library of Australia Cataloguing-in-Publication Data
Laurens, Amy 1985 –
The Complete Sanctuary Series
540 p.   cm.
Hardcover ISBN: 978-1-925825-97-8
Paperback ISBN: 978-1-925825-79-4
Inkprint Press, Canberra, Australia
1. Fantasy Fiction 2. Fairies 3. Shadows 4. Juvenile Fiction

Summary: Fairyland is not only real, it's in danger, and it's going to take all of Emma Tanning's abilities to save it.

First Edition: September 2018
Printed in Australia.

Cover design © Clare Williams.

CONTENTS

SANCTUARY - BOOK 1
WHERE
SHADOWS
RISE
AMY LAURENS

1

THE DOORBELL RANG. That doesn't sound exciting in and of itself, but let me assure you: it was the most heart-pounding thing to happen all week. It was my birthday, I was home alone, and because of the stupid witness protection business, I'd been stuck in the house all summer. I hadn't even been allowed out to see friends, because we'd arrived in town at the end of last year with only three school weeks to go—so I didn't have any friends.

Well. I had friends, but they were back in Melbourne, and I wasn't allowed to contact them for fear someone would track down our new location. Lucky me.

Anyway, it was my birthday, I was alone because Mum and Dad had gone to do something regarding birthday surprises and Anna had inexplicably chosen to go with them, and the doorbell had just rung. I stared at the closed door, heart pounding, while our chocolate Labrador, Veve, tried to chew it down. Was I going to open it?

Of course I was going to open it. The chances of it being a mobster were slim to none; for starters, a mobster wouldn't have rung the bell.

I opened it.

"Miss Tanning?" The deliveryman raised a questioning eyebrow and cocked a digital pen at me.

I nodded, heart flip-flopping, and scrawled a fair impersonation of my signature on the digital pad.

He handed over a small, brown-paper parcel with a handwritten address, and departed.

I closed the door behind him, throat dry, and stared down at Veve. On the one hand, yay birthday present. On the other, holy crap, someone had our address. That was *not* a good thing.

It became even less of a good thing when I noticed that the parcel was indeed addressed to a Miss Tanning: a Miss *Anna* Tanning, as in my sister, not me, Emma Tanning.

Anger bubbled up in my chest, hot and tight, and the parcel protested in my grip.

Veve whined softly.

"How could she *do* this?" I whispered to Veve.

I turned the parcel over. It was from Kade, Anna's frogging ex-boyfriend. Who apparently wasn't an 'ex' after all.

Urgh. I ground my teeth. "You know what?" I asked Veve.

She looked up at me with her liquid brown eyes, tongue lolling as she smiled.

"Screw it. If Anna can get interstate mail from people who aren't even supposed to know we exist anymore, you and I can go for a walk on my birthday. What do you think?"

They say dogs don't speak English, but Veve sure as heck knew the word 'walk'—though I think in her vocabulary it was something closer to 'Magical Trip To Disneyland' and less like 'Comparatively Bland Meander Through Trees'. She tucked her tail right under her butt and shot down the hall, whirling in frantic circles a few times at the end before pelting back as I retrieved her lead from the drawer in the front cabinet.

I rolled my eyes as I clipped her lead onto her collar. For my troubles, I got slimed right up the nostrils. "You're disgusting, you know that?" I wiped off the worst of the dog slobber on the shoulder of my shirt. She just grinned.

Out on the street, she leapt and twisted madly. "Hairbrain," I told her, snapping the lead to get her attention. "It's just a walk."

She just snorted—and stiffened. I followed her gaze to where a flock of corellas pecked their way through the dry grass at the end of the street.

"Veve!"

My shout was in vain: the lead burned through my fingers and Veve shot down the road, a chocolate bullet howling death and destruction for all things feathered.

I cursed her to the lower circles of doggie hell. Which probably involved, I don't know, a world devoid of birds, cats, people, sunshine, and walks, if Veve was anything to go by.

"Veve!" If the sight of the mad Lab-rat barrelling toward them hadn't scared the birds off, my shouts would have. "Come back here *now!*"

Predictably, she ignored me, pounding down the slope, through the fringe of gum trees, and down the narrow stairs between giant granite boulders that led to the river.

"Stupid frogging brainless beast of a stupid frogging dog," I muttered as I followed. "If Mum gets home before we do and freaks out, I swear, I'll pluck your tail hairs out."

Empty threats, obviously, but Mum's freak-out wouldn't be. Her thoughts would go straight to the day Anna nearly died—and I wouldn't blame her. I should have left a note. Urgh.

The stairs ended and I found myself on a track broad enough for two twisting along a creek the colour of bitter tea. Tussock grass clustered in spikes—where the eucalypts would let it—and hot summer sunlight glinted from the leaves. Somewhere to my right, downstream and in the opposite direction to the house, Veve barked. I exhaled like a whale coming up for air and set out after her.

Veve bounded out from the undergrowth in front of me, a dolphin leaping through water, tongue flapping with every bound. "Stupid mutt," I told her under my breath.

She didn't care what I thought (of course), and saved a leap for the last minute so she could plant muddy feet on my hips as I tried to catch her collar.

I straightened, about to insult her some more, and realised that she'd gone stiff again, ears pricked and mouth tight, listening down the path.

My neck prickled. Someone was coming. A second later, I heard footsteps in the gravel, and a low, male voice, humming, or maybe singing softly.

My chest constricted, and just as suddenly my hands were slick. Chances were it was just a stranger out for a midday stroll, but my stomach wound knots about my memories and I smelled the hot concrete and melting asphalt, old oil and stale urine of the Lilydale train station where the body had been hidden in a toilet stall, the body of the girl who'd looked like Anna.

I had to get off the path.

"Come on, Veve," I said, pulling her close, white-knuckled as I stepped into the undergrowth. The tea tree scrub protested, but I shoved my way through anyway, glancing over my shoulder as the humming grew louder.

I kept going until I couldn't hear footsteps any more, until the wind swallowed the hum that sounded too like the warning cry of a hive—danger, we're working here, come close and get stung.

I didn't want to get stung; visions of a blood-streaked face refused to be blinked away. Only Veve tugging brought me back to myself, and I realised firstly that I was holding the lead way too tight, cutting off Veve's air supply, secondly that the reason my cheeks were suddenly cold was because I'd been crying, and thirdly that I'd found the creek again, looping back parallel maybe fifty meters or so from the path.

Abruptly, I dropped Veve's lead and strode forward to kneel by the water. I dipped my hands in. A shiver slide through me at its chill, and I scooped it up to wash my face.

Flinging the excess water away, I gulped at the air, deep, calming breaths all the way down into my belly, and visualised a river washing away the blood from my thoughts, just like the police psych had taught me.

Once the space behind my eyes was calm and black, I drew in one last forceful breath, and opened my eyes. Perched on a rock by the creek, I hugged my knees to my chest as cool water lapped at my toes. Veve was a little upstream, just before the creek bent back toward the path, doggy paddling in circles in a deep spot where the water broadened to maybe ten meters across. In front of me it was broad but shallow, only ankle deep, its path torn to white foam by the rocks.

And—I gasped. In the middle of the stream, glittering in the sun like a piece of fallen sky, was the hugest butterfly I'd ever seen. Which was pretty huge; besides the fact that I grew up visiting the Melbourne Zoo with its impressive butterfly house every Christmas since I could remember, Mum and Dad had taken us up to Brisbane for a family holiday two years ago, and we'd seen giant tropical butterflies bigger than my hand.

This one, bright blue with black edging like a Ulysses, was bigger than both my hands put together.

And then it turned around.

Okay. I'd grown up reading fairy tales as much as the next person, and although I'd had a horse-crazy stage instead of a fairy-crazy stage like Anna had, I'd seen all her paraphernalia. Still, none of it prepared me for finding something that looked exactly like a fairy, standing smack in the middle of a creek in boring, backwater Nowra. I'm pretty sure my eyes were only hanging in their sockets by a thread.

And then it talked.

Her face lit up like a cloud had just uncovered the sun as she spotted me. "Hi there!" she said, fluttering over.

I just stared, heart pounding against my ribcage as though it wanted to run away from the absurdity of it all. "No," I said. "I'm hallucinating."

The fairy frowned. "I don't think so."

I shook my head. "No. No, things like this do not happen. Things like this aren't *real*." I stood, backing up a step.

The fairy sighed. "I promise. I'm quite real."

"You would say that, wouldn't you," I said, eyeing her. "Veve!" I waved at the dog and hopped from one foot to the other, trying to lure her in with the promise of play. "We're going now!"

Veve, adorable beast that she was, landed a little upstream and shook vigorously before trotting toward me. I backed hurriedly away from the bank, dancing to keep Veve's attention.

"Wait!" the fairy cried, wings snapping out and propelling her a couple of feet into the air. "You're a Traveller! I need to talk to you!"

"Uh huh, sure," I said as I wound the lead around my hand and set off back into the bushes. This was punishment for leaving the house, obviously. The universe was out to get me, reminding me forcefully that once you started disregarding some rules, who knew what other rules you'd end up flouting.

The rules of physics, for example.

I glanced back once, right before the bushes hid the stream altogether. Blue flashed, high up, but I ducked to get a better view and it was only the sky. I scowled. Stupid fairy. Stupid universe. Served me right for leaving the house in the first place. Urgh.

"Come on, Veve," I said, snapping the lead. "Even if the house is prison, at least it's *sane.*"

I was stomping so furiously as I burst out onto the path that when a figure rose from a stoop only a couple of steps away, I squeaked in surprise.

I scowled. People rarely surprised me; usually I could tell without trying that someone was near. I really must have been off in my own little world.

I glowered at the boy who lived to make my school life a misery. "What are you doing here?" I snapped. "Isn't it bad enough that I have to deal with you on school days? Which, by the way, don't start until tomorrow. You're ruining my holidays."

Okay, so maybe that was a little harsh, but come on. It was *Scott.* I'd arrived in town with three weeks left in the school year, and he'd spent every day of them humiliating me in front of his mates, and I didn't care for a repeat this year.

Scott eyed me warily, which was a strange expression on him. Usually he strode around like he knew without a doubt that he was too good for the world, and also—somewhere deeper, somewhere I'd only caught a glimpse of once or twice—that it had nothing left to throw at him that could hurt.

Occasionally, in my more generous moments, I wondered what had happened to make him look that way. Mostly, however, I just wondered why he was such a moron.

"What are you doing here?" he asked, voice dripping with accusation and suspicion.

My hands fisted of their own accord, and beside me Veve's hackles rose as she chimed in with a low-pitched, rumbling growl. I flicked the free end of the lead at her nose. "Nothing," I said, in a rousing blaze of wit. "What are you doing?"

He scowled. "You shouldn't be here."

For one heart-stopping instant I thought he meant out here generally, walking around, as if he knew what had happened and why I'd hidden away all summer. Then I realised he was nodding into the undergrowth. I rolled my eyes. "I might be a city slicker," I bit off, "but I'm not stupid. I made enough noise to scare off a herd of elephants, let alone any snakes that might have been lying around." The thought chilled me, though; I *hadn't* been thinking about snakes when I'd hurried off the path. One badly-timed footstep and a brown snake bite later, and I could be a dead body too.

But Scott had moved on, stalking off down the path. He had nice shoulders, I'd give him that much. Pity he couldn't derive his personality from them, instead of whatever dead weight it was he kept inside his head for brains.

Beside me, Veve growled again, louder this time, more urgent. I snapped the lead at her and stared after Scott's retreating form, trying to think of something cutting.

It was only when Veve growled for the third time that I realised she wasn't even facing Scott. Instead, she was looking back into the bushes—and something dark was flickering in there, deep in the shadows of the trees.

My chest squeezed in on itself and adrenalin shot through my body. Veve's growling grew louder until it broke in a bark, something midway between slavering and terrified, and I realised my tongue was stuck to the roof of my mouth. Carefully I peeled it away, unable to tear my eyes from the shifting darkness in the bushes. There was no discernible form, just shadow, darker than it should have been this soon after midday, and a pervasive sense of dread clamping down on me like an on-coming storm.

Veve began backing away, hackles prickling, growl rising and falling like thunder. I glanced down at her, back to the shadows— and they were closer, much closer than they had been.

I turned and bolted.

2

THE BUS PULLED up at school and I wondered if anyone would notice if I didn't get off. My roll call teacher, probably. Maybe. And then Mum when the school called later on to find out why I wasn't there.

I sighed and schlepped off the bus amidst the horde of student clones. Yesterday hadn't ended terribly; I'd been grounded for going out without permission, but as Anna had pointed out, grounding was hardly that much different to witness protection anyway. Plus, unlike Anna, I never broke rules, so Mum had pretty much forgiven me by dinner. We'd had cake and candles and curled up to watch a movie as a family, which was pretty cool. We hadn't done that in... a while. A long while.

But I was still having trouble deciding whether school was better or worse than being cooped up in the house. On the one hand, yay, no house. On the other... I surveyed the unkempt masses between me and my locker and sighed again.

It wasn't their fault. Not really. They had no idea that having travelled to Sydney 'that one time, for Christmas, with my parents' didn't amount to worldly wisdom, or that there were more important things in life than who had dumped who for other-who—like the fact that both whos were still alive, for instance.

I rubbed my hands over my forehead, set my shoulders, and marched on in. I'd survived nearly a month of school here at the end of last year, so I could survive this year.

Semester. Term. Okay, I could definitely at least survive the week.

As I entered H block and headed toward my locker, I downgraded that to 'day': Scott lounged against the lockers like some sort of drug lord (cue involuntary shudder) and eyed me as I approached. He was back in usual form, black hipster-glasses perched precariously on his perfectly-sculpted nose, blond hair gel-spiked to bedhead precision, tie-knot strategically loosened. Greeeat. Here we went again.

"Well hello there, Emma." Eyelash flutter that shouldn't look that natural on a guy, quirk of the perfectly sculpted eyebrow, fold of the arms across the chest. I knew those plays off by heart, thanks to that month last year.

"Scott, you're spreading your germs all over my locker. Move."

His eyebrows jumped suggestively. "Or what?"

"Or I'll go and get Mrs Johnston and have you explain to her why I couldn't access my books." Somehow he'd gotten it into his head that because I didn't immediately bow down and fawn over him when I'd arrived last year, he was in love with me. I would actually rather date dirt, but he just wouldn't take a hint. Or a clue-by-four to the head.

He leered some more. Seriously. It was like he *wanted* me to hit him. "Naw, you wouldn't do that."

I swung my bag off my shoulders and onto the floor at the foot of the lockers—and, somewhat coincidentally, the foot of Scott.

He winced. "Jeez woman, what are you carrying? Bricks?"

"Just for you." I smiled sweetly. "Move."

He looked like he was going to argue some more, but then an arm caught me around the shoulders and the fight went out of his eyes.

Gemma, now draped around my neck, beamed at Scott. "You were just leaving, were you?"

He scowled and disappeared.

I shrugged out of Gemma's half-hug and dove at my locker. "Thanks," I muttered.

Gemma was... Well, Gemma was also arrogant, but not like Scott. With Scott, you knew he thought you were beneath him. With Gemma, she just kind of forgot that other people had feelings that sometimes differed from her own. Her parents had money, and although I wouldn't go so far as to call her spoiled, she did kind of assume the world would revolve around her, lacking any evidence to the contrary. Rules were optional, not because she was naughty, but because she forgot that other people's rules weren't identical to hers.

I didn't like breaking the rules—any rules—because that kind of attitude got you killed. But hey. She was better than Scott, and I supposed she was also better than spending the next school year as a loner.

After stashing my bag and retrieving my books, I let Gemma shepherd me down the hall to roll call, and then when the bell rang ten minutes later, off to science.

"I checked your timetable this morning," she bubbled at me as we wove through the crowd. "We have all our core classes together. Isn't that awesome?"

"Of course we do," I muttered, before correcting myself: "I mean, of course it is. Yay." I managed some semi-enthusiastic jazz hands and a half-hearted smile.

We entered the science classroom and I hesitated for a moment. Gemma usually sat up the back somewhere; I was a front row kinda gal, and I wasn't about to change that for anybody.

Oh well. Sitting by myself wouldn't be *so* bad. I plunked into a front-and-centre seat and arranged my books at neat right angles along the front of my desk, placing a pen and perfectly-sharpened pencil atop them. Gemma pulled out the chair to my left and shot me a sunny smile. Tension I hadn't known was there melted from my shoulders, and I dared a tiny smile in return.

The back of my neck prickled, erasing my half-hearted smile. Cold, vast emptiness niggled at my consciousness, and I knew without looking that Scott would be standing in the doorway, surveying his domain. I stiffened, fighting the urge to turn around. Instead, I pretended to drop my pen on the floor, sneaking a glance under my arm as I bent to pick it up.

Yup, Scott. Oy. As he swept into the room girls paused in their conversations, straightening to emphasise their curves, eyes wide through luxurious curtains of hair.

Okay, okay: the entire room didn't stop just to watch him enter, but the way he walked you'd think the crowd would start offering him babies to kiss any moment now. And at least five of the girls up the back had major crushes on him, so they definitely did the stop-straighten-peer-through- hair thing.

Scott, of course, ignored them, heading straight for me. I wondered why for a brief moment as I replaced my pen on my neat stack of books, and then I realised: the only empty desk was right next to me. *Oh for crying out loud, Universe. Seriously?* I face-planted on the desk, wondering if thinking hard enough would let me melt straight through it and into oblivion.

"We meet again, Emma-my-love."

"Scott," I mumbled at the desk, "what have I ever done to deserve your unwavering attention?" He dropped into the desk to my left. "Please, tell me so I can stop."

"Miss Tanning." I snapped upright at the sound of Mrs Johnston's voice. "If you're quite ready."

I blushed. "Sorry."

Beside me, Scott snickered.

"Shut up," I whispered furiously. "I hate you."

"I'm wounded," he said, putting a hand dramatically to his chest. "What do I have to do to get you to like me?"

"Drop dead?" I offered as chills ran up and down my spine. Something about him really gave me the creeps, and my 'drop dead' suggestion was only *ninety* percent joking.

"Couldn't do that," he chirped. "Then you'd have to live with my death on your conscience, and I know you could never cope with that. Far too high and mighty."

"What?" I lowered my inappropriately loud volume mid-word and cut sharp eyes over to where Mrs Johnston was handing out worksheets on the other side of the classroom. "I am not high and mighty!" I muttered furiously at Scott. "How dare you judge me! You have no idea about my life!"

A worksheet slapped down on my desk, and I glanced up at Mrs Johnston's disapproving face. "On task," she said. "Now. If you think I'm not willing to hand out detentions in period one on the first day, you're wrong."

Frustration welled up as tears, and I blinked firmly. "Yes, Miss. I'm sorry, Miss."

"Mm." She pursed her lips before moving on.

Scott leaned over just long enough to whisper, "Maybe you shouldn't be the one judging me."

The rest of the day had passed with far less stress—turned out I only had to deal with Scott in science, maths and English—and no more disapproval from teachers, thank goodness.

After dinner I lay sprawled on my bed, in theory going through the snowdrift of paperwork I'd accumulated during the day, but actually just staring out my window. If my subconscious was going to magic something up to personify the anxiety I'd been having since the girl—Georgia, her name was Georgia, and the psych had told me that even though saying her name felt uncomfortable, it would help me process it faster—since *Georgia* had been murdered, then I could understand that. After all, it had thrown vivid nightmares at me every night for two months afterwards. It had been about a month since the nightmares had ceased, so probably I was due for some kind of relapse.

But why a fairy? That's what was really getting to me. The shadows I could understand: a vague, dark menace that I couldn't control, approaching from the shadows around me... That made sense. But a fairy? Seriously? I couldn't even begin to imagine what that might mean.

Idly, I punched holes in the paperwork and slid it all into my tabbed and colour-coded folder. Shadows made *sense*. A fairy was just bizarre.

A tap on my door interrupted my thoughts. I shook them away. "Come in, Anna."

She stuck her head into my room. "Hey, Edge," she said, using the nickname we'd made out of my initials, E. J. "How was day one?"

I shrugged. "Fine. I'm filing," I said, lifting papers as proof.

Anna rolled her eyes. "You are way too organised to be human, you know. It isn't normal."

I shrugged again. "Sure. How was your day?"

She grinned. "Oh, you know. The usual."

I raised a sceptical eyebrow. "Seriously? Day one and you were in the principal's office already? What did you do, strip naked in the quad?" It couldn't have been *that* bad; I'd have heard something if the school's newest year twelve student had done something *really* stupid on the first day back.

It was Anna's turn to shrug as she stepped into my room and closed the door behind her. "Actually I just wanted to ask about changing out of art."

"Really?" Both my eyebrows lifted this time. "But you know it's too late to change subjects."

She scowled. "Thus have I been informed. It's stupid. I had literally five minutes to choose my subjects when we arrived last year, and art's ridiculous; Mr Ridely's a joke. It's a complete waste of time, and I'm awful at it, and I wish they'd just let me switch out and be done with it." She slumped against the wall, arms folded tightly across her chest.

"Sorry," I said, shifting uncomfortably on my bed. "That's the system for you."

"Yeah, well, this system sucks."

"Yeah." It did kind of suck that we couldn't have at least stayed in the same state, but those were the rules we'd been given, and we had to stick to them.

Cogs turned. Fairies and rules, Anna and her stuff-the-rules attitude... I licked my lips. "Anna? Can I... Can I ask you something weird?"

She cocked her head. "Sure. Hit me."

My mouth felt suddenly dry. I swallowed a couple of times, heart racing as I tried to figure out how to verbalise my thoughts. "I... I mean you..." I took a deep breath and told myself to stop being stupid. "Why don't you care about the rules? Like, ever?"

Anger flashed in her eyes as she drew herself upright, and I hurried to forestall it.

"I'm not talk about the g—about Georgia. I mean generally. All the time. You never seem to care about what other people think or what you're meant to be doing and I don't get it. I'm just trying to understand, I promise, I'm not judging you. I just wondered..." *How you live with yourself. Why you're not the one seeing fairies. Are you seeing fairies? Anna, do you have hallucinations?*

I shook my head. "I don't even know what I'm asking. Sorry." I went back to my hole punching.

Anna eyed me thoughtfully—I could feel the weight of her strawberries-and-cream gaze out of the corner of my eye, hear the tiny clack-clack-clack of spider feet that I'd learned to associate with her thinking—then abruptly sank to the floor. She rubbed at the back of her neck and seemed to be searching for words.

"I don't know," she said in the end. "I'm not like you, or Mum, or even Dad. You guys just... It's easy, for you," she continued. "I mean, look at you. It's the first day of school and you're already doing homework, organising your notes within an inch of their lives. I feel claustrophobic just looking at it. Don't you ever just long for some space, for five minutes where you don't have to worry about doing the right thing and saying the right words, where you can ask questions of the universe and demand answers?"

I flinched away from the conviction of her gaze.

"No," she said more softly. "I guess you don't, any more than I like your rules and plans and organisation." She shrugged. "The universe is full of questions, Edge, and 'just because' is never a good enough answer." She unwound to a stand, long-legged, lithe like a lioness who knew how to hunt what she needed to survive. "How else do you know you're alive?"

Blood, crimson lines on porcelain-white tiles. I knew what she meant, a little. I'd never been so aware of *life* before I'd been confronted so violently by death.

I nodded. "Thanks." My voice was dry and raspy, and I couldn't bring myself to meet her eye.

She nodded back, though—"Welcome."—and disappeared back to the hall.

Shadows drifted down the hallway toward me, filling the doorway of my room like smoke before billowing over the threshold and into my room. I backed up in my bed until I pressed against the cold glass of the window.

A fluttering sort of tap made me turn, and against the window a bright blue bird hopped and scratched, trying to get in. Beyond it, more shadows mounted, frothing forth from underneath the prickly bushes that marched along the fence.

Something cold touched my hand, and I jumped. The bird. The bird had gotten inside, blue like the sky, wings stretched as wide as my two hands together, covered not in feathers but in tiny, iridescent scales—butterfly wings, edged in black.

Shadows slid toward me from my doorway, through the window, and I clutched the fairy tightly. She cried out, and I opened my hand to see nothing but red, a double-handful of sticky, crimson blood on hands so pale they seemed white.

The shadows whispered toward me. *Surrender. Surrender...*

3

I WOKE IN the morning sick and exhausted, vague memories of bad dreams hanging over me. I knew from experience that wallowing around the house all day would only make things worse, so I got up, got ready for school, and headed off on the bus, pretending I didn't twitch whenever I saw darkness in the corners of my vision.

The first two periods passed uneventfully enough—electives, so I had neither Gemma nor Scott to entertain or annoy me respectively—and after recess I had my first appointment with the school counsellor. It went about as well as I'd expected.

Back in the empty halls, I slammed my locker shut and leaned my head against it. The visits to the counsellor were compulsory for now, but I missed the awesome woman the police had assigned me back in Melbourne. I'd only spoken to her twice, but she'd been kind, and understanding, and gentle. The school counsellor was a little more confrontational than I'd have liked.

Okay, a lot more confrontational, and I'd left with a headache and anger bubbling away in my stomach.

"You need to let go, Emma," I mimicked cruelly. She had no freaking idea what she was talking about. I *wanted* to let it go. It wasn't like I *enjoyed* having nightmares and being twitchy and irritable.

"Hey there."

I jumped, bashing my elbow against the sharp metal corner of the locker. "Go away, Scott," I said, blinking furiously and hoping he wouldn't see the glistening on my cheeks.

He hesitated and out of the corner of my eye I saw his jaw working. "Are you okay?"

I closed my eyes and slumped forward against the locker. "Brilliant." A sudden sob forced its way through my throat.

Scott paused awkwardly, then put a hand on my shoulder. I tensed, cold seeping into my body. "Hey," he said softly. "It's okay."

I shrugged his hand forcibly away from me and glared. "No, Scott, it's not okay. Nothing is okay. I left my friends, my home, my *life...*" I trailed off as tears choked my words. I couldn't even *begin* to describe the nightmares of blood and shadow—not that I was supposed to mention them. As far as everyone here knew, we'd moved for Mum and Dad's work.

The bell rang.

Scott's lips twitched and I thought for a split second that he might speak again, and that it might even be something nice—and then the crowds poured out of the classrooms and he stiffened.

"Ooo, Scott and Emma, sitting in a tree," a boy taunted as he wandered past.

"Shut up, Mitch," Scott muttered, shooting him a look.

Mitch just grinned. "Aw, you know you wish it was true." He punched Scott's arm and hurried off.

It took me a second to recognise the half-concealed expression on Scott's face as embarrassment, and I softened a little.

Then he smirked, and my stomach dropped. "So Emma," he said far too loudly. "Finished crying over your old school yet?"

The blood drained from my face. "I hate you," I said tightly.

"I know you don't." Scott grinned, showing too much tooth. "Hey guys!" he called to the pack of derelicts he called friends. "Emma said she *looooves* me!"

His mates hollered and cheered.

I wanted to sink through the floor. Or smash him in the face. Or maybe both, in reverse order. Instead I spun away and tore my locker door open just for the satisfaction of hearing it clang. "I hate you, Scott Harden," I said furiously, not caring whether he heard me or not. "Don't ever come near me again."

A hand on my shoulder made me whirl back again, ready to punch him in the face—but it was Gemma, wide-eyed with concern. "You okay?"

"Brilliant," I snapped, tearing books from my locker like they'd personally offended me.

"Do you want to skip class and talk about it?"

I blinked. "Um, no?"

Gemma laughed, withdrawing her hand. "Wow, okay, it was just a suggestion. It's not like we'd miss much you know, and I doubt we'd even get into trouble."

I shook my head. "No. I'm fine." I gathered up my books and shut the locker. "Class is good." I tried for a smile that felt thin and brittle.

Gemma laughed again and tucked her arm through mine. "Fine. Well, I know something we can talk about to cheer you up."

I quirked a sceptical eyebrow at her. "Mm?"

She grinned. "The fact that I'm going to call you Jeanette for the rest of your life unless you offer me an alternative."

I stopped in my tracks, part playing along, part genuinely horrified. "You wouldn't." Jeanette, my middle name, had come from a great aunt who'd died not long before I'd been born. She'd probably been a lovely person and all, but I detested the name. *How* had Gemma found out my middle name? I shook my head and carried on walking. "What's wrong with Emma anyway?"

Gemma leaned her head awkwardly on my shoulder. "Because, dearest BFF of mine, it's far too close to Gemma. People will get us confused."

I took a moment to absorb that. On the right, Gemma, dark-haired, brown-skinned, beautiful and sparkly and confident of her place in the world. On the left... Well, me. Mousy hair, averagely tanned skin, and nondescript, still carrying a little baby fat around my hips and face—easy to ignore, made more for blending into the background than standing out in a crowd.

I sighed at the thought of anyone ever getting us confused. "I highly doubt that, Gemma."

"Gem," she responded brightly.

"What?"

"Gem! My nickname is Gem! Because you can't make anything else out of Gemma but Ma, and Ma is stupid. But it still doesn't resolve our problem, because Em is the obvious choice for Emma, and Gem and Em might as well be Gemma and Emma." She drew my arm to her side. "So, you know, unless you offer something else, I'll call you Jeanette."

I could tell by the wicked edge to her grin that she knew exactly what kind of a threat that was. Man *alive* but I'd love to know where she got her information. I exhaled dramatically as we reached the classroom, secretly grateful for the distraction.

"Edge," I pronounced solemnly, peering down my nose at her. "My name is Edge. It's from my initials," I explained in response to her obvious confusion.

"Ah!" She smiled and pulled my arm tight again, an odd sort of meld between a hug and a claim of ownership. "I like it," she said. "Edge."

I arrived home that afternoon to find Anna waiting for me, which was odd. Anna usually caught the last possible bus out of school so she go ride it looping through the suburbs—an excuse to spend longer with the friends she'd made within about three seconds of arriving last year, and to avoid the house as long as possible.

Today, though, I opened the front door and she bounded up from where she'd been sitting in the family room.

"Oh, you're home, are you," she said, sounding an awful lot like Mum.

I rubbed my forehead. "Anna, I've had a really long, sucky day, so if you have a problem, seriously, take a number."

"One," she said, clipping the word. She flourished a pearlescent envelope under my nose. "What *I'd* like to know," she continued, "is why, having made *such* a big deal about me getting a parcel from Kade, *you* seem to have gone behind all our backs and given out your address to some freak whose name doesn't even make sense!"

I caught Anna's wrist and forced her to hold the envelope still so I could read it. Adrenalin shot through the pit of my stomach: the letter was addressed to me. I snatched it from her and pushed past down the hall. "I have no idea who this is from," I snapped. "And I haven't given our address to anyone."

"Hypocrite," Anna called as I slammed my door. "I'm telling Mum!"

Heart pounding as though I'd run the whole way home, I dumped my school bag, kicked off my shoes, and plonked onto the bed clutching the pearly envelope like death. The front bore my name in big, loopy handwriting—and there was no stamp.

My pulse calmed a little at that; it must have been hand delivered, which meant someone local, rather than a stalker. Unless it was a local stalker. Ha ha.

Hurriedly, I flipped it over and scanned the address. Hmm. I could see what Anna meant. The address read like the definition of obscure: Quoise, The Lodge, Sanctuary.

Sanctuary. Maybe they meant Sanctuary's Point? That was a suburb a little way down the coast from here—too far to walk and a long trip on public transport, but it wasn't *entirely* impossible that someone might have driven over to deliver the letter. It seemed like a lot of effort, though; surely the post would have been easier?

I bit my lip. Fingers trembling, I tore the envelope open and pulled out the most beautiful invitation I'd ever seen. Even my cousin Kelly's wedding invitations hadn't been this fancy.

Thick, pearly cardstock bore silver and gold embossed letters in stunning calligraphy. It took me a moment to remember I was supposed to read the invitation, not just stare at it in awe.

I read it, and stared some more. It had to be a hoax—but who on earth would know I'd hallucinated a fairy down by the creek? No one had been there, and I hadn't said a word about it.

Well, Scott had been there, I remembered, frowning. But surely he hadn't known anything about the fairy. Unless I'd been mumbling about it as Veve and I had reached the track? I didn't think so; if I had been, Scott wouldn't have passed up the opportunity to mock me there and then. And sending an invite like this wasn't his style.

But who then?

I shook my head. It made no sense at all. I tucked the beautiful invitation back into its envelope and hid it between some books before grabbing my maths textbook out of my schoolbag.

But no matter how much I tried to remember what Gemma had explained about algebra, all I could think of was the invitation:

Dear Emma,
It is our great pleasure to inform you that you are a Traveller, able

to cross between worlds to Sanctuary, home of the fairies. We would dearly love to introduce you as soon as possible. Please meet your appointed fairy at your nearest crossing on Wednesday at five in the evening.

Kindest regards,
The Keeper,
On behalf of the Sanctuary fairies.

4

I'D SPENT MOST of Thursday distracted by the invitation, alternating between hope and despair—*Maybe it's real! Ridiculous, it's obviously a hoax. There's no such thing as fairies!*

Veve growled at the shadows as well, there was something in there... Rubbish, she was growling at Scott, and even if she wasn't, that's all the more reason not to go back there. Those shadows weren't exactly friendly. Besides. You're still housebound. You couldn't go down even if you wanted.

By the time I got off the bus with just two streets to walk to home, my head was whirling.

Mum greeted me the second I walked in. "How was your day?" she said from the kitchen, knife thudding on a chopping board.

"I survived," I said, kicking my shoes off in the hallway.

"I have some news from the police," Mum said. "But go get changed first."

I headed down to my room, stomach flip-flopping back and forth. Why the police? Mum didn't sound stressed, so it couldn't be *that* bad, but... I squeezed my eyes shut against visions of a blood-stained face. Would her—would *Georgia's* face ever stop haunting me? Urgh.

Out of my uniform, I hurried to the kitchen, snagging an apple from the fruit bowl as I passed and trying to act casual. "So, what's up?"

Mum looked up from the pumpkin she'd been chopping, an odd expression on her face. Puzzled, I slid onto one of the barstools.

"So you had a good day, then?" Mum asked.

"I wouldn't say 'good'," I replied around a mouthful of apple. *Come on, Mum. You're killing me.*

"Ah, well," said Mum, resuming her chopping. "And what's this about you receiving a letter?"

I squirmed. "Oh, it was just a note my friend from school dropped off." Guilt gnawed at me.

"Oh, that's lovely."

Colour me suspicious, but Mum was acting beyond weird. I realised where I knew her expression from—it was exactly the same expression Anna got when she was up to something. Curiouser and curiouser.

Mum set the knife down on the bench. "Well, the police called."

The apple froze halfway to my mouth. "Yes, you said that," I said, trying to contain my impatience.

Her eyes sparkled. "They've arrested someone in connection with the murder."

My stomach flipped. "What?"

"This doesn't mean it's over," she added hurriedly. "The gang was far too well connected for one arrest to make us safe."

My stomach flopped back the other way as I realised Mum's eyes were sparkling because they were filled with unshed tears.

"But it's a start. We still have to be careful—no gallivanting around town by yourself, no widespread sharing of our address, and, I'm sorry to say, no social media still—"

Bah and humbug to that.

"—but at the very least it means you can take Veve for walks around the neighbourhood if you like. Maybe down to the creek, she'd like to swim."

I slipped around the bench to hug Mum. "Thank you," I said, punctuating it with a squeeze.

Mum laughed and hugged me back, wiping at her eyes. "I knew you'd be happy."

Happy didn't begin to cover it. Mum was right. This definitely wasn't an end, but it was a very welcome start. "I'll bet you are too," I said, squeezing her again and breathing in the delicious smell of cookie dough that always seemed to linger around her.

"Of course." She clung to me for a few moments longer before untangling herself. "Anyway, I know you're technically grounded, but I thought, given the circumstances, you might want to celebrate. I hear Veve's itching to get out of the yard." She twitched her eyebrows at me and I laughed.

"Thanks, Mum." I headed out to the hallway to grab some shoes and Veve's lead. "I'll be back for dinner!"

"Take your phone!" Mum called back.

Out in the yard, Veve leapt like a mad fish at the sight of her lead, and I laughed. "We're free, girl! For a little bit, anyway."

I nearly had to sit on her to attach the lead, and her efforts to get me through the gate and down the street were enthusiastic to say the least. By the time we got to the stairs through the boulders, my hand hurt from holding her back. I tugged her to a halt. "Veve, *sit*."

She plonked her butt down next to me, tail wagging furiously, a silly, happy grin on her face.

I rolled my eyes, but if I was being truthful, my face was pretty much a mirror of hers. "All right, beast," I murmured as I unclipped the lead. "Don't run too far, okay?"

Veve tensed, waiting for me to release her, and as soon as I did she pelted down the steps.

I followed, shaking my head. As I reached the bottom I heard the splash of her totally inelegant entry into the stream. Now I just had to hope she wouldn't bounce some poor, unsuspecting stranger with her soggy wet feet. Veve pelted toward me through the trees, spray glittering in the afternoon sunshine. That was one advantage of brown dogs: you couldn't tell the difference between dirty and clean.

I set off up the path, slapping my thigh. "Come on, girl."

She snuffled my hand and bounded away again.

A flock of sparrows erupted into the sky and Veve leapt, trying to follow them. They wheeled away, squeaking angrily at the creature who'd frightened them.

Nerves flushed through my stomach. What if the fairy was real? Would Veve try to chase her like she had the birds? What if Veve caught her?

Nerves piled on top of nerves. I reached the place where we'd turned off the path last time and called Veve back, clipping her lead on just in case. I took a deep breath, heart pounding. What if the fairy wasn't there? What if she *was*?

I shook my head and pushed forward through the bushes. "Here we go," I muttered.

I didn't realise I'd been holding my breath until I emerged at the creek and saw the fairy standing with her back to me, bright blue wings glimmering in the sunlight as she stared at the opposite bank. Relief burst over me and I felt like iron bands around my chest had been cut loose. Not a hallucination. There really was a fairy.

Veve, however, was not relieved. She crouched in front of me, snarling as her hackles rose.

"No, Veve." I yanked sharply on the lead.

The fairy turned, face grave.

Veve barked, a throaty alarm call. Before I could brace myself, she sprang, and I had the familiar sensation of the lead burning through my fingers.

"Genevieve!" I screamed as she hurtled toward the fairy. "No!"

5

VEVE BOUNDED AT the fairy, snarling, and leapt into the air. The fairy squeaked and ducked, arms shielding her head. Veve sailed through the air toward her—and kept on sailing, landing with an almighty splosh in the creek. Had she completely misjudged the jump?

But she continued through the creek and up onto the opposite bank, and I collapsed to my knees in relief. The fairy and I stared as Veve dashed into the trees, hackles raised, barking madly.

She disappeared and I gasped—then promptly fell sideways on the ground, laughing hysterically. On the one hand, my dog had just disappeared in a snarling fit. But on the other, she hadn't eaten, bitten, trampled or otherwise mauled the fairy. And there was a fairy. A fairy!

The fairy stared after her. "I hope she's okay."

I wiped my eyes and sat up straight. "Why shouldn't she be?" But shivers rippled down my spine. The fairy was real. What did that make the shadows?

The fairy gave the opposite bank one last look before turning to me with a sigh. "I'm not sure. Does she usually come back?"

I frowned. "Of course." The shadows there still seemed thicker than normal, like last time, and the prickly, ominous feeling ran over my skin like oil. "What's she chasing?" I asked.

"How should I know?"

I watched the fairy closely. "You were staring over there when we arrived. I thought you might have seen something."

She glanced across the creek and resettled her wings. "No. I've no idea." Abruptly she fluttered over and perched by my knee. "Are you ready?" Her tone signalled the end of the discussion.

I frowned. Veve would be fine. They were just shadows, right? "I've no idea," I replied. "What am I even here for?"

The fairy laughed, a quicksilver sound like tiny bells. "Yes, you probably have some questions, don't you. First of all, I'm Quoise," she said, offering me her hand.

I reached for it, then stopped, wondering how to deal with the mechanics of shaking a hand the size of my pinkie's tip.

Quoise laughed again and shook my finger. "You're Emma. I found out that much already. But I haven't seen you around before. Are you new?"

Her voice was soothing, and her interest genuine. I smiled. "Yeah. My family just moved up here from Melbourne."

Quoise lifted her eyebrows in surprise. "That's quite a move."

"Heh. You're telling me."

"Okay," she said, settling herself on the ground and rubbing a small area clear of debris. "Let me start at the beginning then. Here." She pulled out something tiny and brown from her pocket, and held it up for me.

I put my palm out flat and she dropped the object onto it. "A seed," I said.

She nodded.

"What do I do with it?"

"First of all, you listen," Quoise said, leaning back on her hands and staring up at me. "What do you know about Sanctuary?"

"Honestly?" I said. "Nothing. I've heard of Sanctuary's Point, but I've never heard of a place called Sanctuary."

Quoise nodded. "That's quite normal. Sanctuary means refuge, you know that, yes? Well our Sanctuary, it's not a place of refuge from anything in particular, but it was created to be a refuge from everything, and from time itself."

"How can somewhere be a refuge from time?" I asked, glancing uneasily at the shadows across the creek. Veve would be back in just a second...

Quoise waved her hand dismissively, recapturing my attention. "That's not important quite yet. All you really need to know is that Sanctuary is a place created for you to use whenever you need it."

Across the other side of the stream, Veve's alarm bark rang out.

Nerves pooled in my stomach and I tensed. The shadows thickened. "Maybe I should go find her," I murmured, half rising.

"No." Quoise's tone froze me in place. "No," she repeated, softer. "I think it's better that you stay on this side of the stream for now."

"But Veve…" I said, gesturing.

Quoise shook her head. "I'll call her in a minute if need be. Listen." She pulled another seed out from her pouch. "Not every person can cross to Sanctuary. People who can are called Travellers, and they usually occur in families, though not always."

I wrenched my gaze back. Veve was a dog in the middle of suburbia, I told myself. She'd be perfectly fine. And Quoise had said she'd get her in a minute if she didn't come back by herself. Veve was perfectly fine. "So how can you tell who's a Traveller and who's not?"

Quoise looked smug. "We're fairies. It's our job to tell."

"Okay, so I'm a Traveller." And maybe also dreaming. "How do I travel to Sanctuary?"

"With a sacrifice," she said.

"A sacrifice?" A dead girl, skin bloody. White tiles, streaked with red.

I must have paled, betraying the direction of my thoughts, because Quoise smiled. "Death or life. Travelling between worlds is a gift, in a way; the world is giving you something by allowing you to travel across the borders, so you should give something back in return."

I nodded. That seemed fair enough. "And we give life…?" I prompted, hoping Quoise would elaborate further.

"Yes." Her wings gave a flap. "*Some* people offer death sacrifices, but death sacrifices will *not* get you into Sanctuary. And anyway,"—she brightened—"I don't think we have to worry about *you* attempting a death sacrifice."

My eyebrows quirked. "Hardly."

She glanced at the other bank again. Had the shadows grown even darker, or was I imagining it? "Ordinarily, I'd walk you through it yourself. But if it's alright, today I'll just give a demonstration."

I nodded and Quoise thrust her seed into the ground, murmuring as she did.

A sharp tingle raced up my spine. Somehow she'd planted the seed deep in the ground without leaving a trace. I stared, awed—and nothing else happened. "That's it?" I said, unable to keep the disappointment from my voice.

Quoise's lips quirked upwards in a fleeting smile. "I need you touching me so we can cross."

"Oh," I said. My gaze drifted to the other side of the creek again. Of course Quoise hadn't done anything yet. She'd wait a second until Veve got back before doing anything else.

A yelp echoed across the stream and I was on my feet in an instant.

"No!" Quoise zoomed up. "You can't!"

"That was Veve," I said. "She's hurt!" I stepped around Quoise.

"Emma, please!" Quoise hovered in front of me again at eye level, staring intently at me. "You have to listen to me. Call her as much as you like, but you *can't go over there*. You're a Traveller. Travellers are *not allowed to go over there*."

Veve yelped again and I ran to the stream. "Veve!" I yelled. "Veve, come here!" I wanted to plunge to her rescue—but I hesitated on the bank, transfixed by the lurking shadows. I definitely wasn't imagining it. Shadows shouldn't be that dark, not this early in the afternoon, not with the hot sun shining in a clear blue sky. Fear slithered between my shoulder blades and sweat broke out on my palms.

Something tugged my hair and I jumped around, pulse racing.

"You can't—go—over!" Quoise said, punctuating each word with a tug on my hair.

I grabbed her gently. "I'm not!" I said. "I'm not." I set her on my shoulder and turned back toward the opposite bank.

Something rustled through the bushes. "C'mon, Veve!" I called. "Here, girl!"

"Emma, we need to go," Quoise said behind me, voice suddenly fearful. "I know you're worried about Veve, but she's a dog, they're not after—" She cut off abruptly, the kind of full stop that meant she was too afraid to say any more.

I turned to her, hands fisting at my sides. "*Who's* not after dogs?"

"Nothing, that's not what I meant. Please, I think it's really important that we leave *now*." She rubbed at her upper arms, gaze darting to the shadows across the creek and back again.

"I'm not leaving without Veve," I said.

The shadows bulged. Surely they hadn't covered that rock in the stream a second ago.

"Emma, she'll be fine."

I froze, staring at the creeping shadows.

"Emma, I really think it's time to go now."

They crept farther.

"Emma? Emma, please get over here!"

I backed away from the stream, eyes wide, heart in my throat. *Veve*.

"Emma, hurry!"

The shadows deepened, making it hard to see where water ended and bank began. "I can't leave without her," I whispered. But I backed farther away without even meaning to; everything about the shadows shouted at me to run.

Quoise flew into my calf and I glanced down at her frustrated face, surprised to see that I'd reached the little clear patch in the dirt—and that a dandelion now bloomed in the middle of it.

"Emma, we have to leave. Sit down, please!"

Unable to think straight through the fear that licked at my chest, I crouched.

Veve exploded out of the undergrowth on the opposite bank, shattering my terror.

I lunged toward her, jumping a few paces into the stream. "Veve, come here!"

She bounded through the water and leapt at me, shadows flying in her wake.

"Hurry," Quoise called. "Grab her!"

I hauled Veve toward me, wrapping my arms around her neck and diving toward Quoise, reaching her just as the world faded away.

Then there was nothing but blackness, the beating of my heart, and Veve's warm, furry body huff-huff-huffing in my arms.

6

THE WORLD REAPPEARED—or *a* world did, at least. As my pulse slowly calmed, I noted that we'd arrived on lush emerald grass encircled by a white wall, which was broken just ahead by an archway.

Veve struggled out of my arms and slopped her tongue at my cheek. I giggled, and the tension broke.

Quoise laughed too. Veve turned to her, ears pricked and nostrils flaring gently as she sniffed.

I tightened my grip on her collar just in case, but instead she whuffed in delight and gave Quoise a slop of approval as well, covering her head-to-toe in drool.

"Veve!" I jerked her away. "You little snot."

Quoise held up her dripping arms. "Well," she said. "Nice as it is to have the approval of the guard mutt, that was one kiss I could have done without."

I laughed too loudly, sounding slightly hysterical. "What *was* that? The shadows, I mean."

Quoise shook her head. "Nothing." She flew upwards and performed a dazzling series of pirouettes, dog slobber flying off her in gobs and glops. "Come on," she said when she was done, heading for the archway.

I stood, brushing dirt from my knees and butt. "It wasn't nothing," I said. "You were scared. *I* was scared." A gentle glimmer in the grass caught my eye, and I realised a series of domed glass beads ringed the place where we'd been sitting.

"It was nothing," Quoise insisted. "Now come on. I want to show you something."

Right. Clearly discussing the shadows was a no-go. I joined her in the archway.

"This," Quoise said proudly, "is Sanctuary."

A vast meadow of grass lay before me, sloping gently uphill. Dense forest obscured our view to the right, craggy mountains rising above it in the distance. To the left, the trees were softer, sparser, and I caught a hint of water beyond them. Halfway up the slope ahead of us, a slightly ramshackle building perched like a mushroom in the grass. "Our destination," Quoise said, pointing at it before flying off.

As I followed, Quoise galloped off in the direction of the beach. "Will she be safe?" I called, jogging to catch up to Quoise.

Quoise smiled back at me over her shoulder. "Sanctuary, remember? Everything is safe here."

As Veve neared the trees, a flock of crimson and purple birds took flight. She jumped at the trees, barking with body-wriggling enthusiasm.

When the last bird had disappeared, she trotted back to me, head and tail high—because clearly scaring away the terrifying birds was something to be proud of.

"Yeah, good job, Hairbrain," I told her as she approached. "Real impressive."

She upended herself at my feet, tripping me to a halt, and obligingly I rubbed her belly for her.

"Come on," Quoise said. "I want to show you the best bit."

My heart fluttered in anticipation as we headed up the slope, our way lit by Sanctuary's strange, pervasive glow. "Where does the light come from?" I asked as we neared the stables.

"Everywhere," Quoise replied. "And nowhere. It just is."

"There's no sun?" I scanned the sky, which was the indeterminate grey-blue of a sky right before sunrise.

"A sun would mean that we were orbiting a star, which would mean Sanctuary was in the same plane of existence as Earth," Quoise said as she hovered by the stable door.

I blinked. "It's not?"

She laughed. "Well, it wouldn't make a very good sanctuary then, would it?" She twirled in the air. "No. Sanctuary is everywhere and nowhere, a portal to all worlds and all dimensions. You can get to anywhere from Sanctuary."

Wow. This was so not a conversation I'd ever expected to have in actual real life.

But the surprises kept coming: as we neared the little building, a familiar face appeared in the doorway. Adrenalin trilled through my chest. "Gemma?"

Her face split into a grin like the sun from behind a cloud. "Edge! You made it!" She swept me up in her trademark possessive bear hug. "I can't believe you're a Traveller too," she gushed. "Isn't this just the best thing ever?"

I couldn't move. Literally, because Gemma was squashing me tight, but also out of shock: fairies were real. Fairy *land* was real. I could travel there, and so, apparently, could Gemma. "I guess we have to be BFFs now," I said, mostly teasing.

She poked me in the shoulder. "Tragic."

We were still laughing when another fairy fluttered up, this one with wings the colour of blood, edged in silver. "Quoise," the red fairy said. Her tone sobered us in an instant. "I'm so glad you're here. There's something..." Her gaze flickered over Gem and me for just an instant. "I need to talk to you."

Quoise turned to me and smiled brightly—too brightly. "I'm sorry," she said. "I'll just be a minute. You go on inside and see the twins."

"Twins?" I asked. "What twins?"

Quoise's smile relaxed. "You'll see. Head right to the back. I'll join you in a second."

Gem tucked my arm in hers. "Come on. You'll want to see this."

I followed her into the dim building—a stable, the aisle lined with empty stalls. Something moved in the straw down the far end, and I headed over to investigate.

Gem held me back. I shot her a puzzled glance, but she pressed one finger against her lips and tilted her head toward the door. Brow wrinkled, I crouched with her as she lifted the flap of the door a little and peered out.

Over her shoulder I could see Quoise a little way off, conferring quietly with the red fairy. "What's going on?" I whispered.

She shook her head. "Later."

I couldn't hear everything, but the snatches I caught sent shivers down my spine. Shadows, darkness, something changing.

That sounded too much like what had happened back in the clearing.

I rubbed goosebumps from my arms. The train station had seemed safe, too. I'd have to be careful.

Gem mustn't have understood any more of the conversation than I did; after only a minute or two she stood abruptly, brushing her pants down and sniffing in disgust. "Later," she insisted, cutting off my questions before they could leave my lips. She strode away down the aisle.

I shrugged. "Come on, Veve," I muttered, and followed.

The main aisle was dim and rather dusty, and I sneezed at the chaff our footsteps stirred. But right at the back, a bit of roof had broken away, allowing a beam of light to filter down and illuminate the largest stall. Gem already leaned over the top rail, ignoring me in preference to watching whatever was in there. I crept up, Veve following just as quietly, and peered over the gate.

I gasped. Lying in the straw were two tiny foals, no bigger than Veve. They glittered like 24-carat gold, and if it hadn't been for the gentle rising and falling of their ribs as they slept, I'd have thought they were statues—an effect enhanced by the tiny, inch-long horns that spiralled out of their foreheads. They felt like peace and happiness, pure contentment and deep, dreamy sleep.

"Aren't they incredible?"

I nodded. I could watch them forever.

Veve snuggled up in the straw at my feet, and I leaned on the gate, staring at the foals. So beautiful.

I'd had a unicorn statue once. The unicorn had been white with a blue mane and tail, and golden hooves. It had been my favourite thing ever—until it had broken when my ex-best friend Grace had volunteered to help clean my room one day.

Quoise fluttered down the aisle and alighted on the railing next to me. Gem shot her a poisonous look and stalked outside.

I hesitated. Should I follow Gem, or stay here with Quoise?

"Lovely, aren't they?" said Quoise.

"Where's their mother?" Gem would be okay by herself for a minute, and maybe I could find out what Quoise had been talking about. That would probably make Gem happier.

Quoise perched on the gate. "We're not sure."

I glanced at her worried face. "That doesn't sound good."

"It's not. Usually you couldn't pry a unicorn mother away from her babies for all the love in the world." Quoise shrugged. "We haven't heard any bad news, though. Everyone's on the lookout," she added softly. "No news is good news, right?"

I nodded, wanting to reassure her, but inside I writhed. *No. Sometimes no news means that someone's too dead to call home.*

"Sanctuary's..." I adjusted my grip on the railing. "I mean, this is a good place, right? It's safe?"

"Of course it's safe," Quoise said firmly. "I told you that."

I nodded and cast around for a new topic. "So, are you good friends with the red fairy?"

"Ruby?" Quoise's eyebrows lifted in surprise. "I suppose so. Why?"

I shrugged. "You two come here a lot, is all. I was wondering if you came together or separately."

Quoise furrowed her brow. "How do you know we come here at all?"

I shrugged again. "I'm good at guessing things like that. Like, I can sometimes tell who's at the door before it opens, or if anyone's been in my room, things like that."

Quoise stared intently at me. "Emma," she said. "I want you to close your eyes."

I did.

"Tell me what you see."

"Noth—" The word was half out of my mouth by habit before I realised it was a lie. "Trails," I said, standing taller. "Maybe. They're faint, sort of hovering in the air." I moved my head. "Oh, there are some on the ground, too."

"What do they look like?"

"Um..." I scrunched my eyes tighter, trying to figure out how to describe the strange sensation. I'd felt this before, I thought, though I couldn't place where.

Then it struck me. "Wait, Sanctuary is magical, right?"

"Yes, but—"

I waved a hand to silence her. Of course. Sanctuary was magical. I *had* felt this before—it was how I knew who was at the door or if someone had been in my room at home. It was just that with Sanctuary's magic, suddenly I could *see* these trails that previously I'd only ever *felt*.

"Ruby's," I began cautiously, "is kind of red, like her wings. Only... it smells like steel?" I ventured, not quite sure how to describe the cold, sharp smell. "Yours is bl—"

"No, no, stop, I don't want to know what mine looks like," Quoise said, and I opened my eyes to see her hands pressed over her ears.

"Did I do something wrong?" I asked, stomach dropping.

Quoise flung her arms wide and zoomed up into the air, looping-the-loop and beaming. "No! I can't believe I didn't notice it before!"

"Notice what?" I said, excited and confused.

"Emma," she said, grinning. "You're a Road Master!"

Instinctively I grinned back. "I have no idea what that means. But yay, right?"

Quoise laughed. "You can read the psychic footprints left behind by others. It's a rare talent, especially combined with the ability to Travel."

I blinked again. All those years of pretending I had special talents so I could stand out from my sparkly sister. Ha. Which reminded me... "Oh, it's Edge, by the way."

"Edge what?"

I grinned. "My name. Call me Edge, not Emma."

Quoise nodded. "Right you are, Road Master Edge." She nodded down at Veve, curled up asleep in the straw. "Well, Ye Of Many Talents, wake the guard-mutt and let's continue."

Grin plastered to my face, I nudged Veve with my foot and followed Quoise out of the stables. But Gem, stony-faced and arms crossed over her chest, stood firmly in Quoise's way. "You'll have to tell us sooner or later," she said.

Quoise stared at her. "I have absolutely no idea what you mean."

"Of course you do," Gem shot back. "But fine. We have to go anyway."

I blinked. "Already?"

"*Yes.*" Gem took my arm again and shepherded me away.

"Wait!" Quoise zoomed around in front of us. For a moment, I thought she might have decided to break down and tell Gemma whatever it was that was happening. But all she said was, "Do you want me to do the crossing for you?"

Gem, lips pursed, nodded curtly. "I have to be home at quarter past five."

Quoise smiled as though nothing had happened—like she hadn't been having secret conversations with another fairy about ominous shadows, and Gem hadn't tried to call her on it. "We'll have to hurry then. It's already quarter to."

Frowning, I glanced from one to the other. "I feel like I'm missing something here. Why does Quoise need to help us get back?" I might have misread the situation entirely, but I'd been under the pretty firm impression that I'd be able to cross back and forth to Sanctuary myself, at least at some stage.

"Sanctuary is a refuge," Quoise said, slipping into what I now knew was her lecture voice. "A refuge from all types of trouble, from all conflict. That includes time."

"You said that before. Wait." My eyebrows shot up. "Sanctuary has no time?"

Quoise nodded.

"So I could, like, stay here forever and no time would pass back home?"

Quoise laughed. "If only. No. Usually, the time skips happen completely at random. You might find you've returned right after you left, or hours later. But fairies can get you back at the right point in your personal timeline."

I ran my hand over one of the white-flowering bushes as we neared the garden alcove. "My personal timeline?"

"You've spent about half an Earth hour here. So we can get you back half an hour after you left. For anything else, you need a Time Master."

"Is that like a Road Master?" I stared at Gemma's back as she entered the alcove ahead of us, shoulders tense and hands fisted.

"I suppose so, in a way. Time Masters can control what time the travelling takes them to, so they can even go back before they left if they wanted to, and were strong enough. They're much more common than Road Masters. About one in six Travellers, actually. Here we are, then."

Before I had time to ask any more about Time Masters, Quoise had planted her seed and we stood back in the glade by the stream. Quoise said goodbye and disappeared.

I turned to Gem. "Okay, what's going on?"

She shook her head tightly, hands still curling and uncurling by her sides as we tromped through the bush toward the path. "I have to get home. It'll take too long to explain now. Look, get to school early tomorrow and I'll explain it first thing, okay?"

I nodded, bewildered. We reached the path and heading up to the stairs in the boulders.

"I have to go this way," Gem said, pointing further down the path. "I'll see you first thing." She gave me a quick hug and jogged away.

It wasn't until she'd rounded the corner out of sight that I realised I hadn't told her about my Road Mastery. "Never mind," I told Veve. "At least we had a good walk, right?"

Veve whuffed happily.

Some days, being a dog sounded really, really tempting.

7

FRIDAY MORNING SUCKED. Anna was allowed to drive us to school on Fridays, and I'd used everything I had to convince her to get in as early as possible (not easy, considering she hated mornings as much as I loved them).

I'd half expected Gemma to be waiting by the front gates for me, but she wasn't there, or by our lockers, or outside our roll call room—and she never arrived. Although I'd obviously been looking forward to discussing Sanctuary with her, it was having to sit by myself again that sucked most of all. I'd kind of gotten used to having a friend.

In science I slumped into a seat at the back, for once not feeling up to the scrutiny of the front row. And at least the seats on either side of me were taken, which meant the only spare seat for Scott— Mr King of Lateness—was down the front. Tragic.

Speak of the devil.

I rolled my eyes as he posed in the doorway and turned back to my desk, pointedly opening my textbook and reviewing the chapter we'd been set for homework. I could feel his disappointment radiating from here.

I allowed myself a smug smile—something I immediately regretted.

"Something funny?" he asked, crouching beside me. "'Cause I did the reading too, and I have to say, I didn't find it that amusing."

Frogging elephants, I could smell his deodorant. It wasn't *bad*, but I didn't want a reason to have to smell him *ever*, even if he smelled like rainbows.

He poked my shoulder. "Hey, I asked you a question. Or do you think you're so special you don't need to be polite?"

I exhaled and gave him my 'Are you serious?' look. Because, you know, he was *so* polite to me. "Scott, you wouldn't let the Queen ignore you."

"Oh, so you're even better than she is are you, Princess?"

I clenched my jaw and carefully turned a page in my textbook.

To my great relief, Scott stood. Sadly, the relief was short-lived: he tapped the girl next to me on the shoulder and gave her his 'charming' grin—I could see it blinding her out of the corner of my eye. "Can we switch seats?" he asked.

Confusion surfaced through her adoration. "Where's your seat?"

He shrugged, still beaming. "Any seat that isn't this one."

She stared at him, open mouthed, struggling to convince her brain to function in the face of his blinding magnificent.

I struggled to contain my snickering.

Scott leaned over her desk and lowered his voice. "I'd consider it a... special favour." He let the words hang, rich and full of promise.

I nearly choked. No thirteen-year-old should be able to use his voice like that. Life was so unfair.

The girl giggled, snatched up her things, and departed.

I bashed my forehead gently on my desk. When were these girls going to learn?

Up the front, Mrs Johnston tapped a marker on the desk. "If you're *quite* finished, Mr Harden." She raised an eyebrow and for a fleeting instant I thought maybe she knew what he was up to. Would she make him move for me?

No such luck. He slid into the now-empty seat beside me with polished grace and beamed back. "Sorry, Miss."

Frogging elephants, he practically glowed. And now he was glowing right next to me. I could have stabbed something.

Him, for preference.

The rest of the lesson proceeded with surprising and merciful monotony, and as Mrs Johnston signalled to us to pack up our things and head off to the final class of the day, I thought that maybe Scott's motivation for his little seat-switching act might have innocent after all. He *had* told me not to judge him.

I stacked my books and shoved my stationery back into my pencil case, eager for the day to be over so I could investigate Gem's mysterious absence.

As I zipped up my pencil case, I saw that my favourite pen was missing. I hunted around on the desk, even though my books sat neatly stacked and I could see plainly that it wasn't there. I checked the floor, the lab desk behind me... Nothing.

"Looking for something?"

I jumped. "What are you still doing here?" I snapped, pre-occupied. It was only the first week of school, for crying out loud. I couldn't be losing stationery *already.*

Scott shrugged, shifting his books to one arm. "I thought I could help."

I glared at him. "Unless you can make pens appear out of thin air—no, wait," I said, tilting my head, "even if you can: *go away.*" I resumed my search, scrabbling under the desks.

"Last chance, Emma," Scott said in an oddly calm tone of voice.

I snapped upright, bashing my head on the edge of a desk. "And what *precisely* is that supposed to mean?" I rubbed my head and stood, pain pulsing in time with my heartbeat.

"I lost my favourite pen. I told you I don't need your help, and now you're *threatening* me? What, because humiliating me in the corridors yesterday wasn't enough for you? Because you get off on making life miserable for me? Besides," I said, giving up on the pen and swiping my things off my desk. "It isn't here."

Scott's lips twitched as though he was struggling through some inner conflict. Like I cared. I hope he conflicted himself to death. "What if I could tell you where it is?"

I stopped dead. At first it wasn't so much the words as his tone, quiet and intense. And the look he was giving me was *weird.* I mean, hi, it was a pen. But then what he'd actually said hit me, and I narrowed my eyes. "You pig."

He blinked. "What?"

I strode toward him, furious. "Give it back."

He rocked away. "What?! No, I—"

"Give. It. Back!"

"I don't have! That's not what—"

Oh, that Mr Innocent act. "My *pen,*" I yelled, dropping my books on the ground and launching myself at him. If he thought he could bully *me* and get away with it, he had another thing coming.

"Emma, calm down!" He stepped backwards, one hand up in surrender. "I don't have your pen! Honest!"

I punched him in the arm, not hard enough to really hurt him, but *boy* it felt good. "I've already lost my home, my friends, my *life*," I shouted. "And it was my *favourite pen*." I punctuated that last with solid pokes in the ribcage.

"Save me from the crazy-lady," he mock-yelled, fending me off with his free arm. "You're insane, Emma! I didn't take a thing."

I cried out in frustration and snatched his books from him, tossing them on the floor.

Scott scrabbled at them as they fell. "Hey, ow!" He jerked back, nursing his fingers. Blood seeped across them—a deep paper cut. "You *cut* me." He blinked in disbelief. "You actually cut me."

I stared in horror, heart hammering. "I didn't. You grabbed after your own books." But the anger was dying down, and guilt was more than happy to take its place. Despite my outburst, I hadn't meant to hurt him. I just wanted him to leave me alone.

Scott straightened coldly. "That was your last chance, Emma. I was going to tell you everything, and I could have told you where your stupid pen was. But you're a vicious, unstable, crazy-lady, and I'm so glad I found that out before it was too late."

He grabbed his books and stalked away. I stared, mouth open, my own books scattered on the floor like the aftermath of a very localised tornado. "Way to overreact," I muttered, but I wasn't sure if I meant him or me. Glumly, I began picking up my books.

At home that afternoon, I stripped off my uniform, pulled on some jeans, and hunted around for a clean shirt. As I did, a flash of orange under the bed caught my eye.

I stooped. My photo album.

I sank to the floor, cradling it in my lap. Grace, my best friend from Melbourne. I traced the cover picture with my fingers. We looked so happy. The picture had been taken after Year 7 camp last year. We'd had no idea that less than a year later we'd be torn apart; we'd planned to be friends forever.

The door opened and Mum stuck her head in. "Can you come help in the kitchen?"

I nodded, avoiding eye contact as tears breached my eyelashes.

"Are you okay?"

Sanctuary was wonderful, but... I shrugged, not knowing how to verbalise the ache inside me. "I miss home."

Mum came in and closed the door behind her. "I do too," she said as she knelt beside me.

I glanced up and my stomach dropped as I saw tears in her eyes too. I felt sick. "Why can't we just go home?" I asked, miserable. "They arrested someone. Doesn't that mean it's over?" I knew it wasn't that simple, but I had to ask, had to say it.

Mum smiled, but it was strained around the edges. "Even if they arrested the entire gang, your father doesn't have a job to go back to, Em. And I had to fight tooth and nail to get the position I'm in. If I told my bosses that I wanted to transfer back to Melbourne again..."

I nodded. "They wouldn't be happy." I knew it, but it didn't make things any better. "I miss home," I said again.

Mum scooped me into her arms. "You are home," she said. "You are home."

And as she rocked me like I was five years old again, patting my hair and humming, I could almost believe that I was.

8

I SAT AT the kitchen table on Sunday morning, contemplating a day's worth of homework, when the doorbell rang. Anna was shut in her room with music blaring and Mum and Dad were out in the yard, arguing over the awful prickly bushes around the side of the house, so I scraped my chair back with a tortured sound that pretty accurately described my feelings, and headed to the door.

My mood lifted considerably when I discovered Gem on the other side, beaming ear to ear.

"Hi," she said, a little breathless. That and her pinked cheeks suggested she'd walked over. She knew my house from riding the bus home with me, but all I knew was that she lived a little further down the line than I did. I'd have to get her address; if I'd had it, I'd have hunted her down yesterday to talk about Sanctuary.

"Sorry about Friday. I had to duck back into Sanctuary for something, and I messed up the timing getting back out. Mum nearly had a heart attack. She's a Time Master and she's been teaching me, but yeah. Anyway. Ready to go?"

I blinked, nonplussed by her casual dismissal of what sounded like a reasonably serious absence. "You... What?"

She grinned. "Oh, I kind of got stuck in transit or something. Mum went to Sanctuary to track me down, but I wasn't there, so she came back, but I wasn't here either, and I didn't get back to Earth until a couple of hours later. She was mental over it. It's never happened before. Crazy."

"Wait," I said. Somewhere in there the conversation had gotten away from me. "Your mum was in Sanctuary?"

"Oh, yeah, she's a Traveller too. Didn't Quoise tell you it can run in families? Mum's a Time Master, too, which is pretty handy, except when we cross paths, like Friday." She wrinkled her nose and screwed one eye shut. "But anyway!" Her blindingly bright smile returned. "Are you coming?"

"You know we have homework, right?" I raised an eyebrow at her. Wow. Family who were Travellers as well? Someone else's life had never sounded so appealing.

Her smile faded. "You're right. We could totally work on that right now. Or…" She grabbed my arm, utterly failing at keeping the excitement from her eyes. "We could go to Sanctuary and I could tell you what I know about what's going on."

It should have been a harder decision than it was, but really I only had a couple of maths problems to work through and a novel to start reading for English. It would take me a couple of hours, max. And after Gem's non-appearance on Friday, I was burning to know more about the shadows.

I slipped on some shoes, told Mum and Dad where I was going, and followed Gemma down to the glade. She headed off my questions, refusing to answer on the grounds that it would 'make more sense if I saw it', whatever 'it' was.

Once we'd crossed to Sanctuary, Gem led me up the hill to the stable.

One of the foals whinnied as we entered. "Poor baby," I crooned as I approached and hung my arm into the stall. "It's okay."

He snorted and flicked his tail before resting his chin back on the ground.

"Do you think their mother's disappearance has anything to do with the shadows?" I asked, sobering.

Gem nodded, also serious. "Absolutely I do. I've known Aphros—their mother—for years and there's no way she'd leave these little fellas alone for so long."

Finally, some answers. "So, any idea *how* her disappearance is related?"

"None at all."

"Do you know what the shadows are?"

"Nope."

"What's causing them?"

"No clue."

"So basically," I said, turning around and leaning my elbows on the door. "You have no idea what's going on."

Gem grinned. "Yup. Pretty much."

I rolled my eyes. "And that was so hard to tell me before."

Gem straightened, glancing furtively around. "Well, that's not all, of course. I'm not supposed to know this," she whispered. "But you know how Quoise and Ruby were talking about shadows in Sanctuary?"

I nodded.

"I know where they are. They're at the border crossing. That's what I wanted to show you."

She motioned me out of the stables and we headed farther up the hill. Close to the stables but hidden by a fringe of lacy-leafed trees, another larger building sat covered by rambling vines and fruit trees.

"The Lodge," Gem said with a wave. "It's pretty. We'll visit the main hall later. For now..." She gestured to a small doorway in what looked like the back of the building. We had to break a few vines to get the stiff door open. It creaked, protesting the whole way, but eventually I stuck my head in and saw a low hallway floored with some sort of glowing, polished material.

"Have you been here before?" I asked Gem as she shut the door behind us, only a little nervous.

"Not here-in-the-passageway here," Gem confessed as she squeezed past to lead the way. "This is an old emergency entrance. I only just discovered it. But I know where it leads, and I've been *there* loads of times."

I followed Gem down the passage for about twenty minutes until my skin began to crawl. I wasn't at all surprised when Gem halted.

In front of us stood another door, this one heavy looking and difficult to distinguish from the surrounding stone. "We have to be quiet," Gem breathed. "If the fairies see us..."

She trailed off, but I got the picture: this was one of those things that the fairies weren't keen on telling people. I wasn't sure how I felt about sneaking around and maybe—probably—breaking the rules, but before I could protest, Gem had eased the door open, checked for onlookers, and ushered me across this new hall and into another doorway. Light flashed as we passed through and I shivered. Then I saw the row of trees in front of us, and the shiver turned to a full-blown shudder.

"Well, this is the border," Gem said. "I'm sure you can see why."

I nodded. No wonder the fairies didn't want people here. Trees proceeded away from us in an orderly promenade before spreading out to form general bush some fifty paces away. But where the bush began, the scenery changed. On the near side, the trees stood tall and bore soft, delicate leaves. Lush grass carpeted the ground, and the scattered undergrowth was thick and healthy.

On the far side... Goosebumps prickled my arms. It *looked* like the kind of place the shadows would come from. The trees hunched and twisted, their leaves tinged in sickly yellow. The grass was mostly brown and crunchy, and the undergrowth, while definitely thick, was scrawny and full of thorns. To complete the picture, under every branch and bush and leaf, the shadows lurked, blacker than night.

"What is this place?" I asked.

"The Valley," Gem said softly. "It didn't always look so sick; it's gotten a lot worse in the last couple of months or so. Don't get too close," she added as I moved toward the promenade. "It's..." She rubbed her arms.

"Not right." I nodded. "I won't." I crouched a few paces away from Gem and stared. These shadows weren't as threatening as the ones that had bulged near the creek, but they still didn't feel right, and I studied them, trying to figure out why.

"The Valley," Gem said, sitting next to me. "It's... it's evil." Even though we sat cross-legged on the path almost as far from the border as we could get, she still shot it nervous glances, as though she expected it to come to life and pursue us.

"Yes," I said, impatient, because that much was blindingly obvious, "but what is it? Why is it there? Who lives there?"

Gem leaned back onto her hands and considered me. "You know about travelling, right? How it's powered?"

"A sacrifice of life," I said, nodding.

"Yes. Only it doesn't always have to be life."

I steeled myself against the images of stone altars and old, stained knives that flooded my mind. Still. Better than bloodied tiles. "The alternative isn't really an option, though, is it?"

Gem pursed her lips. "You'd think not."

My stomach twisted and I lowered my voice. "What, people do actually make death sacrifices to travel? But surely not of animals, or anything," I hurried on. "I mean, we use seeds. So they could use, I don't know, a plant or something, right?"

Gem met my gaze levelly. "Not seeds, Edge."

"And not plants?" I said, knowing the answer but not wanting to hear it.

"Not plants. The death of a plant is too cyclic. Its power is limited. You can travel using it, but not comfortably. I've heard... rumours, and they say it's like getting your brain squished out your nose. With a poker."

I winced. "Charming."

"Yeah, well, death magic is charming, what can I say." She shrugged. "And unlike life magic, it's a little hard to offer just a *bit* of death. Kind of an all-or-nothing type of magic."

I worked my tongue in my suddenly-dry mouth. "So... what do they use, then?"

"Animals, mostly. Small ones. Mice, rats, sometimes rabbits. Mostly."

I let the 'mostly' hang; some things I really didn't want to know. "So, fascinating though death magic is, didn't Quoise say you can't get to Sanctuary with it? What does this have to do with the border?"

Gem nodded. "You *can't* get to Sanctuary using death magic. That's why there's the border. That side isn't Sanctuary, Edge. It's the Valley of Death."

Ice trickled down my limbs. "You mean... the Valley is death?"

"Not literally," she added. "At least, I think not. I've never been there myself, seeing you have to use death magic to get there." She pulled a face.

"You can't just walk across?" I asked, surprised.

Gem shook her head. "Not without protection, or using death magic."

I rubbed away the goosebumps on my arms. "How is a place like that even allowed?" I muttered. "A whole place you have to murder to get to?"

Gem sighed and scratched at her wrist. "Well, I've heard the argument that death is a part of life. Mostly from people Mum suspected of *using* death magic, and as I like to remind them when

I can, death isn't so much a *part* of life as the *end* of it, but hey." She grinned.

I rolled my eyes. "Lame, Gemma."

Her grin widened. "I know."

"So," I said, rolling a blade of grass between my fingers. "Do you think that's why it exists? Because death does?"

Gem shook her head. "I... I heard a rumour once that it used to be a part of Sanctuary. Mum says she's never heard that though, and of course the fairies won't talk about it. I'm not sure if they don't know or if they're hiding something, but anyway."

"What about death magic?"

"As far as I know, that's always been around. It's nasty stuff, though," she said in hushed tones. "I've heard it contaminates you forever, corrupting you and making you evil, and if it goes too far you can't get into Sanctuary anymore."

"So what's across the border, then?" I asked, tossing the grass away.

"Nothing."

"Yeah, all those trees and mountains sure look like nothing to me." I raised a sceptical eyebrow.

"Well *I* don't know, do I? Do I look like the kind of person who murders small animals for fun?"

I raised the other eyebrow. "What about all those people that travel using death magic? No one's ever reported what's over there?"

Gem folded her arms. "Look, I don't know, okay? Stop harping on about it. It's the Valley, home to death and murder and everything nice and wonderful like that. I don't see why you're so obsessed with it."

"I'm not obsessed, I'm trying to figure out what's going on," I said, leaning over my knees.

We fell silent, me staring at the border and Gemma aimlessly plucking grass.

If you only glanced across the border, the trees didn't look much different from some I'd seen up in the Snowy Mountains, stunted and twisted from wind and snow. But even without using my Road Mastery, a longer look was enough to show that something about the Valley's trees was off. The twist of limb suggested torture, the yellow of the leaves illness and decay. It was impossible to forget, once you knew, that you were looking at the land of death.

I shivered and looked back at Gem. "I thought you said nothing could live there."

She glanced toward the Valley. "Nothing does. The fairies say the trees aren't really alive; they're just pretending to be, like a mask on a corpse."

"Lovely." I scrunched up my nose.

"Their comparison, not mine." Gem shrugged.

I hugged my knees to my chest. "And the shadows are concentrated here?"

"I think so. I mean, the fairies won't say anything, but I've poked around all over, and these are the thickest I've found anywhere. Why? Did you think of something?"

"Not yet." I shook my head. "Just... thinking."

"Sure. Think away."

I tilted my head. I was missing something here. Something right in front of me was a big clue, I knew it, but I couldn't figure out what.

Sighing, I rested my head on my knees and closed my eyes. We shouldn't be here, and no doubt the fairies had their reasons. If they hadn't told us about this place, probably there was nothing we could do anyway.

Images of bloodstained tiles flashed past my thoughts again, but I shoved them away, concentrating instead on a dim smudge in the dark that I couldn't quite catch—Gemma's presence—and... I bolted upright, eyes still closed.

"What, what it is?" Gem asked, scrambling to her feet beside me.

"Shh." It was hard to tell, but in places the darkness behind my closed eyelids seemed blacker than the rest. I opened my eyes. Right where the shadows were.

"They're darker," I muttered. I stared at them, teased by the knowledge that they were different from regular shadows but unable to figure out why. My gaze roved over them, back and forth, and then—ah ha. "Gemma, look at the shadows."

"I *have* been."

I shook my head. "Look closer. They're going the wrong way."

She stiffened next to me. "Oh my gosh, they are too!" She glanced up at the dusky sky above us. "Not that there's a sun here anyway. Which,"—she frowned—"the light issue here has always puzzled me. How are there shadows in the first place? How is there light?"

I glanced around. "That's another point. Those shadows are more like normal Earth shadows." Everywhere else the shadows were soft and indistinct, blurry and gentle. "So something in the Valley has to be causing them?" I asked, calculating the angles of the shadows again. It definitely looked like the light source was behind them, somewhere out there in front of us in the Valley.

"Looks like." Gem rubbed her arms again, probably to shift goosebumps like I had on my arms. "I knew they were no good," she muttered.

A flash of gold and pale green caught my eye through the trees. "What was that?" I pointed.

Gem jumped. "What?" She stared into the trees, breath held and ready to flee.

"I saw something," I said, lowering my arm. "I promise. A flash of light maybe, or something pale."

Gem shook her head and backed away. "Nothing lives in the Valley."

"How do you know?" I said, peering into the trees, hoping to catch another glimpse.

"Because I've been here forever and I know what I'm talking about, and no one lives there, okay?"

I glanced back at her. "Wow, okay then. Maybe it was a trick of the light, or something." It hadn't been and I knew it. I got up and moved closer to the border, heart hammering. *I shouldn't be here. I shouldn't be here!* But the mystery of the shadows and now the flash bound me fast.

"Emma, can we just go now please?" Gem said, shifting. "You've seen everything, you know everything I know. Let's go. This place is creepy."

"Exactly," I said, still staring into the trees. "But the shadows are clearly coming from here, so it's worth investigating, right?" And whatever it was that had flashed was somehow related. I stepped closer again. This was Sanctuary. Really serious bad stuff didn't happen here. If it had been that dangerous, surely the fairies would have blocked off the path. Well, with more than a couple of unlocked doors, anyway, I added guiltily.

"Emma, there's nothing over there. We need to go." Gem's voice had risen several tones and when I glanced back at her, she just about jittered.

My lips quirked; usually she couldn't *wait* to bend the rules to suit herself, and I...

I stared back at the awful trees and swallowed. I wouldn't be caught dead doing something this stupid. I sighed. Gemma was right. Time to go.

I turned, and another flash caught the corner of my eye. I whirled back to face it. "There!" I said, pointing. "I saw it again, right there!"

"It was probably just light on a leaf," Gemma snapped. "I'm going."

I regarded her carefully. "Do those look like the kind of leaves that reflect light?"

She glared at them out of the corner of her eye, unwilling to let her gaze linger on the place. "Maybe. It's the Valley. It doesn't operate by normal rules. Who knows what it might do?"

I peered through the trees. Was that a clearing in there? Maybe a clearing. I moved left, trying to see around a particularly large, scrubby bush.

"Edge, you're making me nervous. I'm serious."

Blah, moving left just meant a fallen tree was in the way instead. I stepped closer to the border, almost toe-to-toe with it.

"Edge, come back here, right now!"

I looked back at Gem—and as I did, gold and pale green flashed a third time in the corner of my eye. I whipped around.

I overbalanced. My foot came down on the border—and something wrapped around my ankle and jerked me into the Valley.

9

GEM SCREAMED.

I may have squeaked a little bit.

Okay, I may have squeaked a lot.

"Edge! Edge, come back!" Gem shrieked.

Sounded like a fantastic idea to me—but how? The grip around my ankle had tightened, dragging me deeper and deeper into the land of death.

My feet skimmed the ground, trees blurring past, and I only just had time to note that I'd been right about the clearing before I was dragged through it and back into the trees. Frogging elephants, this was *exactly* what that happened when you broke the rules! I should never have let Gem drag me to the border like that in the first place. Argh!

Gradually the pace slowed—though my pulse didn't—and I could see the trees more clearly. Their twisted trunks had split in places, revealing oozing red sap that looked scarily like old, bubbled blood. I swallowed hard and wished I could speed up again.

Just don't look. I told myself. I closed my eyes, but motion sickness threatened to empty my stomach, so instead I stared upwards, concentrating on the glimpses of sky and trying to watch where I was being taken so I'd know the way back.

Ahead, the ground sloped upwards, and through a sudden gap in the trees I saw a mountain rising to each side. I was headed straight for the pass in between. The Valley proper.

I squeaked and struggled against the force around my ankle. "Let me go!" I clawed at it, but there was nothing to grab, nothing to struggle *against* except constant, inexorable pressure.

My heart hammered in my ears. "Let me go!"

The force swerved me to the left; I headed now toward the mountain instead of the pass. I wasn't sure if that was better or worse—and before I could decide, the force around my ankle disappeared.

I stopped dead and stumbled to the ground. Clutching my ribs, I gasped, trying to work the air back into my lungs. It tasted fetid and ripe, and I choked, tears springing up.

My coughing sounded out of place in the oppressive silence and I stopped abruptly. The only sound was blood rushing past my eardrums.

"Where are you?" I spun in a slow circle, trying to find my captor. "Show yourself!"

Nothing appeared.

Shadows lurked under the trees and my breath hitched in my throat. "Show yourself!"

The hair on the back of my neck prickled and I whirled around, sure that someone was watching me. But there was nothing there except the awful trees with their oozing bark and strange, yellowed leaves that didn't move.

A sharp crack rang out and I squeaked. I whirled right around again before realising it was the sound of a dead branch falling. I gasped, pulse trilling and adrenalin lifting me up on my toes.

The trees loomed and the thick air pressed down, stifling. It was hot here, much hotter than in Sanctuary—and brighter. The sky was the blue-green of dusk, rather than Sanctuary's pearly grey dawn, though there was still no sun to be seen.

I shivered. Time to get out of here. I turned again, looking for something to orient myself. I recognised a fallen log and stepped toward it.

The invisible force clamped down on my ankle, rooting me to the spot. I clawed at my ankle, but there was nothing to see, nothing to grab. I panted, fighting panic. What *was* this thing?

And then I felt it: the slightest breath of wind in a heavy, dead land—and I couldn't tell if I sensed it physically or with my Road Mastery.

I stared at the edges of the clearing and there, toward the mountain—the flash of gold.

Help me. The words weren't spoken but I heard them clearly nonetheless, a soft suggestion like the faintest bells on a clear, crisp morning, or silver glimmering through fog.

I stilled, heart pounding, but for the moment in control of the panic. "Who are you?"

Please, the voice begged. *You must set me free.*

"Who are you?" I repeated, palms growing sweaty. "*Where* are you?"

Help.

I threw my hands up. "I can't help you if I don't know who you are!" Especially in the Valley, where the only residents were those who'd used death magic to get here. Those kind of people I didn't *want* to help. I struggled, pulling on my leg, but the grip tightened.

You can help me.

"How?"

Please. Your Road Mastery. Please! Desperation filled the speaker's voice and their grip on my ankle tightened.

I was losing feeling in my toes. What could I do? I couldn't just agree to help someone when I didn't know who they were or what they were asking—especially in the Valley.

A gasp echoed in my mind, accompanied by a breath of not-wind that felt green and gold, and smelled clean, like mint. Mint wasn't a death smell; it was too fresh, too green and alive.

I seriously couldn't feel my toes, and the gasps had turns to sobs, coming in raggedy breaths. I had no doubt that the being, whoever it was, could keep me here until my foot dropped off, or I agreed—or they died, I added as a scream, shrill and hoarse, cut across the sobs.

I took a deep breath and hoped that this wasn't about to be the last stupid thing I ever did. "Okay," I said. "Okay. I'll help you. What do I do?"

Your Road Mastery. Help me, please!

I closed my eyes and searched. There, toward the centre of the Valley—green and gold light flashed and pulsed in time with the screams in my head. I reached out toward it, and it grabbed at me like a drowning person. "Stay still!" I shouted as it choked me. "I'm trying to help! Just stay still!"

The flailing paused for an instant and in the calm I sensed something else: a deep darkness behind the green, building like a storm cloud. I snatched at the green-and-gold and pulled, gasping for air even though I wasn't actually moving. The green tore away from the black, and the sense of connection I had with it snapped.

The pressure on my ankle disappeared, and my Road Mastery blacked out. I gasped as the blood flowed back into my numb foot and my toes tingled with pins and needles.

"Hello?" I called, shaking my foot. "Hello, where are you?" I had no idea who I'd just helped, but if it got them away from the blackness, that had to be good, right? Shudders ran up and down my body. "Are you okay?" I shouted. "Please be okay..."

The mint-fresh breeze swept over me. *Flee.*

The urgency in the voice hammered my senses and terror froze me, mouth open wide.

It will sense you. Flee!

My heart pounded so hard I clutched my chest to hold it in. I backed away, staring wide-eyed at nothing, and licked at my lips.

Run! the voice said faintly, just on the edge of hearing.

I turned and ran.

My heart pounded as I dodged branches and jumped logs, running faster than I'd ever run in my life. The air suffocated me and my lungs burned with the effort of breathing.

Adrenaline shot through my chest; something had grabbed at my shoulder. I whirled around, nearly tripping, but all I could see was the trees. I bit back panic and ran again.

Something grabbed my other shoulder, tangling in my shirt. I didn't have breath left to scream. I reached up to swat it away— and my fingers met rough bark.

For one long moment I froze, eyes wide as I stared at the tree looming over me. Its twig-fingers snatched at my shirt. I shrieked, batting at it while my skin crawled all over.

I wrenched free and ran.

The trees grabbed at me. "*Come to us,*" their leaves shushed in the still, heavy air. "*Come, let us hold you, let us touch you. Give us your light, your soul, so sweet, so sweet your blood.*"

Tears streamed down my cheeks. Wet strands of hair tangled over my face, blinding me, choking me. My lungs burned. I gasped. I sobbed. Fear caught in my throat as I pushed through branches that whispered of devoured souls and death. Something caught my ankle. I stumbled, fell.

My fingers grazed the ground as I caught my balance. A shadow leapt up, tangling itself around my wrist. It dragged me down and smothered me in a cold so heavy it could only be death. *"So sweet, so sweet your soul. Let me live."*

I screamed, flailing. "Let me go! Let me go!"

Darkness closed out my vision, shadows multiplying faster than rats as they surged over me.

"Help!" I screamed as I lashed out at shadows and found nothing to hit. "Somebody, help!"

The shadows flattened me on the ground. My heart thundered in my ears. I fought for breath, trying to surface through their icy weight. What had I done to deserve this? I'd helped! I'd *helped*!

Dread flooded over me as I realised that that was exactly what I'd done. How could I have been so stupid? Everyone *knew* you didn't help random magical strangers!

The weight of my stupidity settled like a knot in my stomach, burning copper and hot. The shadows sprawled over me completely, but through the fire of anger and shame in my belly I could feel the dirt beneath my fingers, under my chest and against my knees. I would *not* die because of stupidity. That was the kind of thing Anna would do.

I forced myself to quit struggling, letting the avalanche of shadows pin me. I concentrated on breathing. The shadows pressed down too hard for me to fill my lungs deeply, but at least I could stop hyperventilating. I would not die here like this. I would *not*.

"Hold you, touch you... So warm and light, alive, we want your life."

You can't have it. "Three. Two. One." I heaved up off the ground, exploding forward like a runner out of the blocks. I had one chance to escape. The shadows wouldn't let me slip away again.

"Come back, come home to us." Pain seared my calves as branches raked them, but I clenched my jaw and ran. I felt the shadows snap behind me, leaving icy burns in their wake. Leaves fell like acid rain, stinging my skin, smoking my clothes. Sweat clouded my eyes, and fire raged in my throat.

I wouldn't make it. I didn't have anything left to keep going.

A beam of light shot through the trees and I pushed toward it. Green, and the smell of mint. Through streaming eyes I saw more green, proper green, the green of healthy leaves and grass. The border. *Sanctuary.*

I shrieked for all I was worth and lunged, one last, giant surge of effort to get me across the line. Branches grabbed my hair. I jerked my head away, screaming as my hair tore. I stumbled, fell—and the world slowed, brightened, and I reached out to steady myself against a tree, a tree with smooth, unsplit bark and healthy leaves. I stared at my hand on the trunk and the world stilled.

My chest heaved. My whole body was alight, but I was touching a tree, and it wasn't trying to devour me. I sobbed, crumbling to the ground. I'd made it.

And then Gem was there, shouting and kneeling beside me, cradling me in her lap. Bright gems flashed around her head, and I convulsed with laughter that hurt like a mule kick, because Gem and her gems. The gem-like fairies fluttered against me and soothed away some of the pain, and darkness edged my vision again—only this time it was a quiet dark, soft and warm and gentle, and I was so happy to surrender.

The last thing I heard was Gem: "I'd better get her home."

10

I CAME TO as Gem dragged me to my feet in the clearing by the stream, and blinked blearily at the long shadows that stretched across the ground. They filtered through the fog in my head and I jolted upright, screaming.

"Hey! Hey, it's okay," Gem soothed, holding me tight. "We're home. It's okay."

I collapsed against her and sobbed. My muscles ached and my skin stung where the burning leaves had fallen and the trees had scratched.

"Shh, it's okay." Gem stroked my hair. "What happened? What was it?"

I shook my head, burying my face against her shoulder. How could I possibly explain? Shudders wracked my body as I remembered the trees, their twig-fingers snatching and grabbing, their whispers of death and destruction. I sobbed harder.

"It's okay," she said. "You don't have to tell me. It's okay."

I hugged her back as the sobs gradually ebbed, relieved beyond words that she wasn't going to make me talk about it. Images raced across my mind, black shadows, grabbing trees, blood on white tiles, staring eyes, twigs snatching and snapping...

"Let's get you home." Gem pushed me back to arm's length. "Yes?"

I nodded and took in a deep, shuddery breath, forcing the flow of images away, washing them down a mental drain. "Yes."

She wrapped her arm around my waist, and guided me toward the path. I tried to keep my gaze from wandering, tried not to see the shadows that dappled the clearing, but they drew my eye like corpses. As we reached the beginning of the path, my gaze strayed across the creek. I gasped and whipped my eyes shut, stumbling against Gemma. The shadows there were the same as the ones from the Valley.

"Come hooome..."

By the time we reached the main track, the sun had disappeared behind mounting thunderheads. Gem glanced at the sky, biting her lip, and herded me along faster. I couldn't bring myself to care about something as mundane as a storm. The shadows, the same ones that had just tried to kill me, were here, in the real world, by the creek. Once I got home, I was never going outside again.

The rain broke as we headed toward my back gate and it was almost a relief. It took the pressure out of the air and seemed to melt the darkness away; as Gem eased me into the yard I saw that the shadows near the prickly bushes had shrunk.

Veve whuffed, curled tight and warm in her kennel, tail thump-thumping against it. Gem ignored her and steered me to the back door, where she stopped and removed our shoes. She eased me into the laundry, rummaged around for something to get the worst of the rain off, then stuck her head out into the hall.

"Gemma?" Anna joined us in the laundry. I had no doubt that I looked a complete mess, but my stomach was rolling and my vision blurring too much for me to care, and I just wanted to crawl into bed and die.

"What happened?"

"She fell," Gemma said, staring evenly at Anna.

Anna stared back, eyebrow raised—but then she sighed and opened the door to the hall. "Mum and Dad have gone down to the shops. You need a hot shower and bed."

I nodded. That sounded heavenly.

"I'll take her from here," Anna said curtly, glancing at Gemma.

My chest tightened. *No,* I wanted to say. *Don't be angry at Gemma. She saved me. She tried to stop it. It isn't her fault. She brought me home.* But all I could do was follow as Anna swept me into the hallway, sending one last grateful glance to Gemma over my shoulder.

Gemma nodded and let herself out.

"Come on," Anna said. "Let's get you warm."

Covered in scrapes and bruises and aching from head to toe, it didn't take too much effort to convince Mum that school on Monday was a bad idea, though thankfully I'd been able to convince her I'd only fallen down the stairs by the creek and didn't need to see a doctor.

And when nightmares kept me from sleeping again on Monday night and I woke on Tuesday pale and shaky, Mum herself suggested that I spend another day in bed. If it meant avoiding Gemma's questions and the outdoors for another day, I was all over it.

The rain continued through to Tuesday afternoon, cascading over the house and washing away the heat and dust. When it finally stopped, the world seemed bright and clean—shadow-free.

So Wednesday morning I rose and dressed for school— stiffly—and by the time I climbed on board the bus, the whole incident in the Valley could have been only another one of the bad dreams it had inspired.

A freaky, horribly realistic dream that left me spooking at shadows and avoiding close proximity with trees, but a dream nonetheless. *See me convince myself,* I thought wryly.

The only thing I couldn't dismiss, the part that seemed to grow more and more real instead of fading, was the voice. Even now I could close my eyes and tune out the noises of the bus, hearing the soft, urgent call. The stink of oil and petrol, musty seats and sweat-stained children could easily fade to mint with a streak of gold, and the waft of air caused by the passing of other passengers could be the breeze of the voice on my cheek.

The bus grumbled to a halt outside the school. I waited for the first rush to disembark before slinging my bag over my shoulder and following. As I jumped down the final step, I jammed my hat firmly on my head so I wouldn't get into trouble for arriving in 'inappropriate uniform'. The hat wouldn't stay on with my hair in a ponytail, so I marched onto the grounds with the brim pulled low and my chin up in the air so I could see, refusing to acknowledge the fact that this particular hat style also shut down my peripheral vision and helped me ignore the trees.

I jumped when a leaf skittered across my path.

I headed toward my locker, and with my hat down and chin up I nearly didn't see Scott lurking in a corner. I wondered if I could pretend I hadn't, but it was too late: he'd seen me and was heading over. Sigh.

"Feeling high and mighty this morning, Princess?" he sneered.

A certain coldness in his voice brought back memories of the shadows. "Thank you, Scott," I said brightly. "I had a lovely long weekend. I had over a hundred Scott-free hours. Too bad you can't have any."

I cringed internally. Maybe that was a little harsh. *Not* that I was going to take it back. I plastered on the fakest smile I could manage, and pushed past him to get to my locker.

He moved his shoulder to block me. "Oh, we're in a hurry are we, Princess?"

I tried to move him and my heart fluttered in momentary panic as I realised how strong he was. "Yes." I kept my voice level. "Considering the *bell* is about to go."

Scott lounged back against my locker. "True. But since I'm here, and your *Scott-free* hours seem to have ended, I have something to tell you."

"I don't want to hear it." I removed my hat and crammed it into my school bag. "I want to get to my locker. Move. Please." I glared at him.

"Or what, Princess?" Scott donned a lazy smile that said he had all the time in the world. "Besides, don't you want to hear my news?"

"Tsh." I threw my hands up in the air, frustration and anger burning away my fear. "Was Friday not clear enough for you, Scott? *I don't like you.* I will *never* like you, so please do us all a favour and *quit trying.*" I swung my bag at him, gently enough not to damage my lunch but firmly enough that he knew I was serious.

"Edge!"

I glanced down the hall to see Gem striding toward us, brow wrinkled in concern. "What's going on here?" she asked as she arrived and stood with hands on hips.

"*Scott* is going on here," I said, rolling my eyes. "I can't get to my locker." The first bell rang. "And now we're late."

Gem turned to Scott. "You leave Edge alone," she said sternly, and I felt a rush of warmth.

Scott snickered. "Edge? Do you call her that because no one wants her, so she has to hang out on the *edge*?"

Gem widened her eyes. "Wow, Scott! Did you think of that all by yourself? Oh my gosh, you're *so* clever." She fluttered her eyelashes at him and I snickered behind my hand. "Besides," she said, shrugging. "Last I heard, *some people* were pretty keen on our Emma here." She slung an arm casually around my shoulders and raised her eyebrow pointedly at Scott.

The outrage on his face was priceless. I wriggled my fingers at him, grinning.

But Gem wasn't finished. "So," she said. "Why don't you just move out of the way and let *Edge* into her locker? We're late."

"Oh yeah?" He squared his shoulders, posturing. A moment ago it might have been intimidating, but with Gem by my side I felt stronger, more sure of myself. "What are you going to do?" Scott continued. "*Tell a teacher?*"

"Tell a teacher what?"

All three of us jumped as Mrs Johnston appeared.

"Um, nothing," Scott said hastily, cheeks colouring as he edged away from my locker.

Gem shoved me at my locker, muttering, "Get your stuff." She turned to Mrs Johnston, eyes wide in practiced innocence. "I was going to *tell* you, Mrs Johnston," she said, "that Scott here wouldn't let Emma into her locker, and now"—the second bell punctuated her sentence perfectly—"we're late."

Mrs Johnston peered at Scott. "Is this true?"

His blush deepened. "Er, no, Miss. I was, um, offering to help Emma with her books."

I snickered behind the locker door as I shoved my bag in and grabbed my books out. Slamming the door shut, I turned just in time to see Mrs Johnston give him the Look.

"Get. To class."

He stared at the floor. "Yes, Miss. I don't..." He gazed up at her through his lashes. "I mean, can I have a late slip?"

"*No*, Scott. Class. *Now*."

He disappeared down the hallway.

"Thanks, Mrs Johnston," I said, avoiding eye contact.

"Miss Caro," she said, ignoring me. "Are you wearing makeup?" She arched an eyebrow and I snuck a glance at Gem.

Again, with the practiced, wide-eyed innocence. "No, Mrs Johnston," Gem said, shaking her head and looking horrified. "Why would I do something like that? I'm a your star student!" Her eye contact didn't waver. I restrained my own eyes from rolling.

"Hmm." Mrs Johnston scrutinised her face once more, then nodded. "Here." She drew two late passes out from her pocket and scrawled her signature on them. "Get to class."

We snatched up the passes and scattered like mice. I shot Gem a look as we hurried down the hall. "You are so wearing makeup," I murmured.

She shrugged, and the movement drew my attention to her fingers, clutching her books.

"You're wearing *nail polish* too?"

"It's pale pink!" she protested as she slowed outside our roll call room. "You can barely see it!"

"I think," I muttered as we slipped into the classroom, "we need to talk."

She snorted. "We do. But not about that. About the Valley."

My stomach dropped as we handed our passes to the teacher and took the only remaining seats, one on each side of the room.

Oh yes. We needed to talk.

11

MY ART CLASS was kept in over recess because one of the boys decided to be a moron and fling paint around the room, so I didn't get a chance to talk with Gemma until lunchtime. By then, I'd had all morning to remember that my nightmares were actually well founded, and I really didn't *want* to talk. I couldn't go home to Melbourne because it still wasn't safe, and I didn't want to go to Sanctuary because *it* might not be safe, so I might as well start facing the fact that I was stuck here in Nowra, nowhere to go except home and school.

Gem plonked herself on the bitumen opposite me and raised expectant eyebrows. "Well?"

"Well what?" I said, unwrapping my sandwich with complete and absolute focus.

"Well *what happened*?" She leaned toward me, eyes alight.

"I don't want to talk about it." I took a bite of my PBJ sandwich.

"Edge!" She flung her hands in the air, sandwich lettuce flying. "You can't go around having death-defying adventures and doing things that aren't even supposed to be *possible*, and then not *tell* me about them!"

"Watch me," I muttered. Diversion time. "So what's with the makeup?"

"Oh, I've been wearing it forever," she said breezily, unwrapping her own lunch. "You just haven't noticed."

I snorted. "Yeah, because we all know how unobservant I am."

She grinned and took a bite out of her salad roll.

"And the nail polish? I know for sure you haven't been wearing *that* 'for ages'."

Gem shrugged. "A present from my cousin on the weekend. I had to try it out." She wriggled the fingers on her left hand at me. "It's subtle. No one will even notice."

"Except me."

"Right, except you, but you're my bestie. You're supposed to notice stuff like that." She took another bite of sandwich, chewed thoughtfully, and swallowed. "So, is the whole Valley episode the reason we're eating in the middle of the overtly treeless car park today?"

I stuck out my tongue. "It's warm here."

"Unlike the freezing twenty-seven C it is everywhere else, you mean."

I stared at her, stomach churning. "Are you really going to make me talk about it?"

"Yup." She beamed at me.

I shook my head. "Don't look like that. It's not... I mean..." I sighed. "It wasn't exciting, okay?"

Her face grew serious, and I felt the words well up. I wasn't ready to confess my family's past to her, but this bit, this slice... She deserved that much. "I haven't slept properly since Sunday. I'm twitching at shadows, I can't go near trees without flinching, and the wind rustling through leaves sends nerves through my stomach every time. I'm jumpier than a grasshopper on crack and I'm sick of it." I pressed my face into my knees. "And I think I did something really stupid." I'd almost managed to forget that bit.

I felt Gem's hand on my shoulder. "Hey, it's okay, Edge. I'm sorry. I didn't realise."

I nodded without lifting my head off my legs. "I know. It's fine."

"So..." Gem hesitated. "What's this stupid thing you did?"

I sighed. If I was never going back to Sanctuary again, I should at least give her a reason. "So you know how in, like, every story in existence, you're warned not to agree to help someone magical when you don't know who they are?"

Gem nodded.

"Especially in somewhere like the Valley, right?"

"Edge," she said carefully. "What are you saying?"

"There was a voice," I said picking at my lunch. "It was the one who dragged me in there. I told you I'd seen a flash of gold," I said, raising my eyes to meet Gem's. "It... it asked for my help. Asked me to come to it." I stared at my sandwich again, fiddling with the crust. "I said I would, because it had me by the ankle, and my foot was going numb."

Did I dare tell her about ripping the green trace from the shadows? My pulse skipped. "But then I agreed, and it disappeared, and told me to flee."

I looked up at Gem again, anchoring myself, fighting back the panic. "So I did."

I held up my arms, still covered in scabbed scratches. "The trees fought back. The shadows nearly got me."

Tears prickled my eyes as Gem reached over and squeezed my hand. "Edge, that's awful. I'm so sorry."

I shrugged, sucking in air and forcing the memories away. "I'll live."

She shook her head. "I don't know, though. I don't think the voice can have been that bad, can it? I mean, it told you to run."

I shrugged. "It was scared of the shadows too, I think." Echoes of the green voice's fear skittered down my spine.

"Well, there you go, then." Gem shrugged. "I think it'll be all right."

The back of my neck prickled. "Let's go," I muttered, gathering my things. "Scott's listening."

Gem's eyes widened. "I was about to say that. How did you know?"

"He's standing right behind me." *Duh*. I wrinkled my brow.

"I know," Gem said. "I see him. But he's *behind* you. How did you know it was him?"

My stomach flipped as I realised I'd been using my Road Mastery. I sighed again and stood with my lunch in hand. "Come on," I said. "I'll tell you on the way."

We headed past the playground and through the walkway that led to the main lawn.

"I'm a Road Master," I said without preamble as we found an empty patch of grass.

Gem stopped short. "You're kidding."

I shrugged and flopped down.

I crammed the last of my sandwich into my mouth in an effort to still the nerves. If Gem laughed at me, I might just die on the spot.

Gem shook her head and plonked down beside me, face splitting into a beaming grin. "Edge! Why didn't you *tell* me! That is *so cool!*" She crushed me with a hug. "You're awesome!"

I swallowed and grinned back. "Thanks." At least that was one good thing I wouldn't have to give up.

"So." Gem guzzled down the last of her own sandwich. "Tell me, oh great and mighty one. How good are you?"

I laughed, pleased by the distraction. "Gem, I only found out less than a week ago. I haven't exactly had much chance to practice."

She rolled her eyes at me. "You might not have had much practice, but I'll bet you can still tell how good you are. Go on." She motioned with the last half of her sandwich. "Close your eyes and tell me who's behind you."

"Don't be ridiculous," I said.

Gem's lips twitched. "Just do it."

I closed my eyes. "We're not in Sanctuary, Gemma. I'm telling you, this is point—"

I gasped. They were faint, the visual equivalent of a slightly off-station radio, but all around me colours wove and tangled—and the harder I concentrated, the more focused they became, until I could see clearly the traces of people sitting within about ten meters of me, and could sense with varying degrees of clarity people all the way back to the playground.

I'd sensed people before of course, but that had been faint, or people I knew. But now that I knew what I was looking for—now I'd been exposed to Sanctuary's magic a few times—my brain seemed to have grasped the idea with enthusiasm.

"Oh. My. Gosh!" I said, grinning. "I rock!"

Gem exploded in laughter, throwing her head back and flapping her hands in delight. "Yes, dear Edgey, you do." She flopped sideways with her head resting on my leg and sighed happily. "So *that's* how you could tell where the shadows were coming from."

I nodded.

"Now we'll be able to get to the bottom of them for sure!"

I tensed, and the memories crowded back in. "Maybe," I murmured noncommittally. I'd told Gem enough for one day. I couldn't bear telling her that I wasn't going back to Sanctuary as well.

"I'm still worried about Aphros being missing," Gem said as we headed down the locker corridor after school.

I nodded as my stomach knotted. I'd forgotten about the motherless unicorn twins. "Yeah. I'll bet anything it's related to the stupid shadows."

Gem nodded back. "Absolutely. Hang on," she said as we neared the bathrooms. "Two seconds." She dumped her bag at my feet and disappeared.

I leaned against the wall and closed my eyes, glad hump day was over for another week.

"There you are, Princess."

I groaned. Why did the world hate me so much?

"Aww, Princess. Still too high and mighty to talk to me?"

I heaved a sigh and dragged my eyes open. "What do you want, Scott?"

"I just wanted to tell you that your little *friend*"—he pulled a face—"is safe with me."

I blinked. "Am I supposed to have *any* clue what you're talking about?"

Predictably, he ignored me. "Oh, and here." He thrust something green at me and I reached out reflexively. He stalked away.

I looked down. My pen.

Gem reappeared. "What's up?" she said. "You look like a stunned mullet."

I searched for something coherent to say, failed spectacularly, and held up my pen. "What world are we in?"

Gem grabbed up her bag and took me by the hand, patting it comfortingly as she led me down the hallway. "Now, I want you to concentrate, Emma. This is very serious. We are on this lovely little planet called *Earth*," she soothed. "It has trees that stay where they're planted and shadows that don't try to eat you, and this weird little species called humans who are supposed to be really smart but, if you ask me, are actually spectacularly dumb."

I laughed and shook her away, wriggling the pen at her. "My pen. Scott had it all along."

Gem shook her head. "Little wretch. We ought to feed him to the shadows."

I flinched to a halt. "No one deserves the shadows."

Meekly, Gem took my arm again. "I'm sorry, Edgey. You're right of course."

I nodded, and headed out toward the bus stop.

"We'll figure this out," Gem continued. "In fact, why not figure it out tonight?" She pulled out her phone, dialled, and held it to her ear.

I waited patiently to see what she had in mind.

"Mum? Hi, yeah, good. Look, can I stay at Edge's tonight? Yes? Awesome! Thanks! Bye!" She hung up and raised an eyebrow at me. "Think your parents will go for it? Your house is closer to the creek is all, otherwise I'd invite you to mine."

Nerves tingled through me. It didn't matter what Gem said, I was not going near that place ever again. But a sleepover might be fun—and it might keep the nightmares at bay. I shrugged. "Let's see."

A few minutes later, everything was settled: Gem would come and stay the night, ostensibly to help me catch up on the work I'd missed, and with any luck the company would calm me enough so I could actually sleep.

We approached the bus stop and a shadow flicked over me. I jumped.

"Hey, it's okay," Gem said. "It was only a bird. The shadows can't get you here."

I stopped again, searching out her eyes. I had to tell her that I wasn't going back. "What about in Sanctuary, though?"

She held my arms from behind, steering me into line. "Hey, that was the Valley," she said. "They can't get you in Sanctuary, either."

"Yeah. Unless, you know, I get *grabbed by some invisible force and dragged over the border.*" I gave her the Look.

Gem shrugged. "We won't go near the border."

"Gem, I'm not going back to Sanctuary."

"Sure you are!" She shooed me forward as the line moved. "You're a Traveller. You won't be able to live without it."

"I'm serious! I can't go back there! I practically signed my soul away to something that's probably evil, and *I nearly died.* I'm not going back!" I detached myself from her and turned away.

Gemma ducked around to meet me. "Edge, dear, I'm quite serious." Her tone was light, but she stared into my eyes like she was searching out a sickness. "You won't be able to stay away from Sanctuary. You almost literally do not have a choice in the matter."

I froze. "What do you mean, I don't have a choice?"

Gem shrugged. "You're a Traveller. It gets in your blood. You think you don't want to go back now, but the crossing is addictive—*Sanctuary* is addictive. You'll go back. You might not want to, but you will."

My mind whirled in circles as I tried to digest the weight of what she'd said. Addictive? I was scared, and more than a little annoyed at Quoise for not warning me before teaching me to cross.

"Hey, you okay?" Gem asked, bumping me with her hip.

"What? Oh, yeah." I stretched a thin smile into place. "I'm fine."

She nodded decisively. "Good. I'd hate to have to murder Scott or something just to make you smile again." She grinned wickedly, eyes sparkling.

"You're incorrigible, you know that?"

"Thanks. I've never been so complimented in my entire life."

I shook my head, darkness still heavy in my chest. But as we clambered onto the bus and Gem slid into the seat next to me, my tension eased a tiny bit. Having Gem as an ally made the shadows a little less dark after all.

12

A COUPLE OF hours later, I lay stretched out on my bed, watching Gem hunch in the middle of the floor. She'd decided that her toenails needed immediate attention, and after bemoaning my complete lack of supplies, had found a kindred spirit in Anna, who'd let Gem help herself to whatever she wanted—something she'd die before letting me do, as I'd noted to both of them.

I closed my eyes and rested on my folded arms, but I couldn't get comfortable. Something niggled in the back of my mind, something I'd been meaning to say, but hadn't. Scrunching my lips to one side, I surveyed the room. My wardrobe door stood ajar, blocked by my schoolbag. My pencil case poked out the top.

I propped myself up. That was it. "Gem, there's something weird about my pen."

"Mm hmm."

I twisted around to snag the pencil case and dug out the pen. I stared at the pen's translucent emerald casing. It wasn't anything I could immediately spot, but there was definitely something off about it.

"Bummer." Gem screwed up her nose. "Tissue? I smudged."

I plucked a tissue from the bedside table and threw it at her. She caught it as it floated down and glanced at my pen. "Looks fine to me."

I frowned, turning it over in my hands. "No," I said. "There's definitely something different about it. It feels..." I trailed off, unable to find the words.

Gem shrugged. "Scott had it. Of course it's going to feel weird. It's probably covered in his mutant DNA. Oh, urgh." She shuddered.

I giggled. "I thought you didn't mind him."

"What, Scott?" She stared up at me, shocked. "The hideous cretin who keeps tormenting my best friend? No way. I mean, he's gorgeous, and charming, and I suspect much smarter than he lets on, and did I mention gorgeous? But no. Just, no. Not after how he's harassed you."

I grinned, somehow relieved to know that Gem had my back on that one.

"Actually," Gem said, straightening. "It might be mutant DNA. Close your eyes."

"What?" I wrinkled my brow at her.

"The pen! Close your eyes."

I did.

"What can you see?"

My heart leapt. "Black."

Gem huffed. "Well duh, your eyes are closed. I mean with your Road Mastery."

I shook my head. "No, that's what I mean. The pen's black, it has a print, or is covered in one, or something, and it's all black."

Gem was silent, and I opened my eyes to find her staring at me, lips twisted. "Don't... take this the wrong way or anything," she said after a moment. "It's not like I know how Road Mastery works or anything. But are you sure? I mean, black on black? Definitely?"

I shook my head. "It's a different black. Promise."

Gem shrugged again. "Sure. So, what's it mean?"

I flopped back on my bed. "*I* have no idea, how am I supposed to know?"

"You're the Road Master."

"And you're the one who's been visiting Sanctuary since you were born." I stuck my tongue out at her. "Gem, seriously: I found out about this *last week*. One weekend does not an expert make."

I closed my eyes again, and colours swirled in the darkness.

"It's so weird," I said eventually. "It's like all of a sudden I'm a different person. I can do all this stuff and I didn't even know it existed a week ago. What will I find out *next* week?"

"Pigs fly?"

I rolled over and pulled a face at Gem. "Ah ha. Funny. I'm so glad you're taking me seriously. It's not like I'm having an identity crisis over here or anything. Thanks."

Gem sighed and recapped the nail polish. "Em, I know you think you're being serious when you say you're not going back to Sanctuary, but please trust me on this: you won't be able to not go. You know how calm everything is when you're there. Sooner or later you're going to get stressed out by school or Scott or the end of the world, and you'll know: the best way to destress is Sanctuary. You won't be able to help yourself."

I opened my mouth to protest but she waved me quiet.

"I'm serious. It's just the way it works. Once you know you can travel, you can't *not* travel, just like with your Road Mastery. Now you know you have it, you can't not see it."

I buried my face in my pillow. "I hate you."

"What?" she chirped. "I can't hear your insults clearly."

I sat up and threw the pillow at her. She squeaked, waving her feet in the air. "Wet! Polish!"

"I hate you," I said, ignoring her theatrics. "Because you're right. And I don't *want* you to be right, and I hate that you're right, and maybe someday I will go back to Sanctuary, but not yet, okay? Not soon."

Gem nodded. "Sure. I know. The shadow thing was horrific."

I flopped backwards on the bed, miserable. It wasn't just the shadows and the fact that they'd tried to eat me. What Gem had said earlier in the day was right: the shadows were hardly likely to get me in Sanctuary unless I strayed too close to the border, and there was exactly zero chance of *that* happening again. I grabbed my other pillow and smooshed it over my face.

"It's not just that," I mumbled. I didn't want to tell Gemma what had happened, didn't want to repeat and relive, but I knew that until I told *someone* here in Nowra what had happened, why I'd come here in the first place, it could never be my home. And I wanted to go back to Melbourne, of course I did... But Gemma was pretty cool. Maybe she deserved the whole truth after all.

I peeked out from under the pillow and saw Gem staring intently at me, hugging one leg to her chest with her chin resting on her knee.

I sighed and let the pillow flop back over my face. "There's more," I told it, staring at the pattern of light and dark where the stuffing filled it unevenly. "It's not just the thing with the shadows. That... Well, to be honest, it kind of feels like a dream now. A bad, scary, stupid dream, but a dream. It was too farfetched, too unreal, and it's like my brain's just stuck it in the 'imaginary' box and is trying to move on." I blinked a few times, feeling my eyelashes drag against the pillow cover and wondering how to say what needed to be said.

"November," I said after a moment. "My life ended in November." To Gem's credit, she neither laughed, nor made zombie comments.

My insides writhed and I squirmed. I gave up and flipped over, hanging my head and one arm off the edge of the bed.

"Dad had to go to court," I mumbled into the blanket. "He saw some drug lord doing a deal, or something. I don't know exactly. He wouldn't tell us. But the police called him, they wanted him to help them."

The momentum built, and all of a sudden the story was rushing out, uncontrollable.

"He didn't want to, said he knew it would get us all into trouble, but the police kept asking and asking and then there was this murder, someone from Anna's school. She didn't really know the girl but it freaked her out because the girl... Well, she *looked* like Anna. I know. I found her. In the bathroom at the train station, with one side of her face smashed in."

I took a deep, shaky breath. "So. Anna told Dad that if the morons were going to come after us anyway, he should definitely testify against them and get them locked up. So, he did. And the guy was found guilty of a whole bunch of stuff, though they never managed to pin the murder on anyone, and then we thought everything was okay, but then we started getting letters in the post. That *really* freaked us out, because one girl had already died, and if they knew where we lived..."

I shrugged, the old fear itching at my neck. "So we reported it to the police, of course, and all of a sudden..."

I gasped against a sudden sob that threatened to surface. "Then all of a sudden, we were leaving Melbourne, and on Friday I told my friends we were going, but I couldn't tell them where or why, and then Monday I was here in Nowra, with no friends, and no home, and no life."

I pressed my face against the blanket, trying to stifle the tears. I missed my old home so much my chest ached and my eyes burned. I wanted to crawl into the pile of cushions I'd had in my bedroom back in Melbourne, snuggle up in the sun, and go to sleep so I could wake up and realise this had all been a horrible, horrible dream.

Gem worked a wad of tissues between my damp, snotty face and the blanket. "Wow," she said softly.

I pressed the tissues against my eyes and breathed deeply before rolling over and staring at the roof. "Yeah. Wow, right?"

She crawled onto the bed next to me and pulled me onto her lap. "No wonder you're jumpy," she said, stroking my hair.

I scowled. "Yeah, well, you would be too if evil shadows had just tried to devour you, drug lords and criminals aside."

Gem was silent as her fingers worked through my hair, braiding and plaiting and then twisting it all together. I closed my eyes and let the rhythmic motion soothe me.

When she was done, she shifted under my shoulders. "We have to figure this out."

My stomach jolted. "Why?"

"Because you're not going to settle until we do."

I scrunched up my face. "I'm fine."

"You're not fine. You're tense and jumpy and I want you to come back to Sanctuary with me. I've wanted a friend to share it with as long as I can remember. Besides," she said, wriggling out from under me. "You promised to help."

I groaned, shrugging my shoulders up around my ears. "Can't we wait? Like, maybe just for a week or something?"

Gem considered me. "Will waiting help?"

I opened my mouth to tell her that of course it would—and stopped. I sighed as visions of bulging shadows filled my mind. "Probably not."

"So let's go then."

"What, *now*?" I sat up.

"The sooner we go, the sooner we can figure out what's going on, and the sooner you'll feel better," Gem said.

I stared at her, incredulous. "It's nine o'clock at night! And we're thirteen! What if we *can't* figure it out, did that occur to you?"

Gemma grinned. "No."

"Argh!" I threw another pillow at her. "Incorrigible!"

Gem put a finger to her chin in mock thought. "Hmm, you know, I think you've said that before."

My heart hammered in my chest. How was I going to convince Gem not to go? "But... it's dark!"

"It's just dark," she said. "This is Earth, not Sanctuary."

I shook my head. "No, I didn't mean that. I mean... It's late." Quite besides anything else, the parentals would have a fit if I decided I wanted to go wandering around at this hour.

"And?"

Frogging elephants, she sounded genuinely puzzled. "I have parents, Gemma," I said with exaggerated slowness. "They take care of me. This means they do things like make *rules*."

She wrinkled her brow, perplexed. "You're not allowed out after dark?"

I nodded.

She nearly had a kitten right there on the rug, gasping with silent laughter and holding her ribs.

I rolled my eyes. "Yes, Gem. I'm not allowed out after dark, by myself, in the wild."

"It's the clearing!" Gem gasped. "And you're not alone, you're with me."

"Yes, but there might be thugs," I explained patiently, ignoring the way my chest clenched when she mentioned the clearing. "Or child molesters. Or people doing drug deals they didn't want anyone to witness and if we saw them they might, you know, hunt us down and murder us. That kind of thing."

"Indeed," she said, twitching her eyebrows.

I rolled my eyes again and took her hand. "I know this is a confusing topic," I said, patting the back of her hand. "I'm trying to make it easy for you. My parents are the kind that believe in all the scary stuff that can happen to Children Our Age. There's no way they'll let me go down to the clearing at this time of night."

And of course, it was not totally, utterly, one-hundred percent convenient to blame my reluctance on them. Not at all.

"My parents *know* the kind of stuff that can happen to 'Children Our Age'," Gemma said, taking her hand back. "And they let me out."

"Your parents are special."

"Well, you're not going to sleep until we figure this out."

"I'm not going to sleep if I get abducted by shadows again, either." I tried the Look again.

Unmoved, Gem waved her hand dismissively. "Highly unlikely."

She was worse than Veve with a ball. Maybe we could find a compromise. "Well..." I said, not sure how Gem would receive my idea. "There is *one* thing we could do..."

Gem raised an eyebrow. "Seriously?"

My mouth went dry. I swallowed until my tongue remembered how to work, then stood, rubbing at my arms. "Why do you want to go to the clearing, precisely?"

Gem shrugged. "To see these creepy shadows of yours, I guess."

I scowled. "They're not my shadows."

"Sorry, I know—"

I dismissed her apology with a wave. "We don't have to go to the clearing to see the shadows," I said. "There are some in the yard."

Gem bolted upright. "What, your yard?"

I nodded.

"Really?"

I nodded again.

"Golly. No wonder you're jumpy. *Really.*" She shook her head. "Well then." She scrambled off the bed and headed to my wardrobe, where she scuffled around in the mess for a moment. "Shoes," she said, holding out my sneakers.

Obediently, I slipped them on, watching as she laced up her own.

"Jacket?"

I giggled.

"What?" Gem put her hands on her hips. "It's cool out there!"

"You sound like Mum."

She made an exasperated noise and helped herself to my wardrobe again, pulling out my denim jacket for herself and the cotton trench coat for me. "Come on," she said, buttoning herself up. "Let's skedaddle."

I giggled again, full of nerves. For crying out loud, we were only going to the backyard. I forced myself to sober. "Okay. Ready."

Gem eased the door open and peered out into the hallway. The TV blared in the living room, and I could hear the thump-thump bass of what passed for music in Anna's room. "All clear."

I stuffed my pen into my pocket. "Let's go."

We tiptoed down the hall to the laundry and opened the door, jumping when it creaked louder than Dad's deepest snores. We darted through, closed the door, and fell against it not-giggling—the silent, uncontrollable shaking that happens when you're trying so hard not to laugh that it makes whatever you're not laughing at fifty times funnier.

Yeah. Us. Very sensible girls.

A creak in the hallway snapped us back to sanity and in a frantic flurry we tumbled out into the yard. We clung to each other, breathing quickly.

"Do you think they heard us?" I managed.

Gem shook her head, lips pressed tightly together.

Something crashed into the back of us and we screamed. My heart pounded as I twisted around and caught Veve by the collar. She barked, just once. We gasped and took a moment to regain our breath—and our normal heart rates.

"Veve you beast, you nearly killed us!" I said. "Are you *trying* to get us caught?"

"We're only in the yard," Gem pointed out. "It's not like you're sneaking out or anything."

I nodded, but the unease had returned, clinging to my shoulders like a too-tight shirt. "C'mon," I muttered. "This way." I led Gem around to where the horrible spiky bushes lurked against the side fence. They were about half my height again, all gnarled branches and inch-long thorns, with long, serrated leaves. Mum had been on at Dad to get rid of them since we'd arrived, but for whatever reason, he kept delaying.

I shuddered at the blackness oozing out of them. "They're awful."

"Hmm," Gem said, twisted her lips and tapping a finger against her chin. "I see what you mean."

I turned away, marvelling at how cool and collected Gem appeared. I could barely stand to look at the horrible shadows; the sense of *wrong* emanating from them was almost tangible.

"Well," Gem said. "That's interesting."

"That's one way of putting it," I muttered. "So, why do you think they're here?"

Gem screwed up her nose. "I think... Eh, really, I can't remember a hundred percent. I need to ask Quoise."

"Well, what can you remember?"

She sighed. "It's to do with the way the dimensions are folded," she said. "Did the fairies tell you about that?"

I shook my head. "Kind of."

"It's like..." Gem waved her hands in the dim light. "Imagine crumpling some sheets of paper."

"How many?"

"I don't know, as many as you like!" Gem flapped her hands. "One for every dimension."

"I don't own that much paper." I was being persnickety and I knew it, but it was better than letting the darkness get to me.

"Edge! Stop it." She peered at me to make sure that I had. "So, you crumple up some sheets of paper, then smooth them out again and stack them on top of each other. Because they're crumpled still, they don't touch each other perfectly, right? They only touch in places."

"And that's our world touching Sanctuary and all the other dimensions?"

"Well, our world only touches Sanctuary. All of the worlds do, Sanctuary is the... I don't know, the central train station. But yes, you can get to all of Sanctuary's different dimensions."

I stared at the blacker-than-black under the bushes. "So that's..." I swallowed. "You're telling me I have a portal to the Valley in my backyard."

Gem nodded. "I think so."

My hands tightened to fists. I forced myself to unclench my fingers one by one. "Great. Just when I thought I was safe." I shook my head. "But why here? The Valley is..." I did some quick calculations in my head. "The Valley is east of Sanctuary, and we're west of the clearing right now."

"Crumpled paper. Only more twisted. It doesn't match up one for one, and distances between them are skewed. The clearing's what, ten minutes from here? But if we travelled over here"—she gestured at the bushes—"we might come out half an hour away, or an hour, or right next to it."

I ran my hands over my face. "I think my brain is leaking out my ears."

Veve bumped into my leg and I squatted beside her, running her tail through my fingers. "Are you done?" I asked. "Can we go inside now?"

"Edge!" She huffed in exasperation. "We haven't figured anything out yet!"

I burrowed my fingers through Veve's ruff. "Well we're hardly going to, standing in the yard staring at shadows and bushes. It's not like we're going to travel through them."

Gem tapped her chin again. "The question is, though, why can we see them at all? Your brain isn't the only thing that's leaking, methinks."

"That's lovely," I said, pressing my cheek against Veve's shoulder, which stank like dog but was at least warm and alive.

Gem began pacing. "I need to ask Quoise. Not that she'll tell me anything, although if any fairy was going to, she would. The Valley is definitely leaking, or expanding, or something."

"The clearing's still fine, though," I said.

Gem shook her head. "For now. But then again, maybe not. How do we know if the clearing is shadow-free all the time? These shadows aren't here all the time, are they?"

I shook my head, stomach dropping as I recalled the first time I'd been to the clearing, when I'd seen horrible shadows lurking in the trees on the Sanctuary side of the creek.

I'd thought the glade was safe, but apparently nowhere was.

"We should go and look."

"What?" I jerked my head up.

"We have to go to the clearing."

"I thought we established that I'm not allowed."

"I didn't say we should ask permission."

My pulse skipped at her serious expression. "You..." I stopped and cleared my throat. "You want me to sneak out?"

Gem shrugged, trying—and failing—to hide a grin. "You want to sleep tonight or not?"

I gaped some more. I never broke the rules or pushed the boundaries. That was something Anna did, not me. Anna was headstrong and independent; I was guilty. Even if I hadn't done anything wrong, my parents only had to quirk an eyebrow at me and I felt weighed down by guilt. "I won't sleep if I get snatched into the Valley!"

"I promise, we won't go near the other side. We'll just stand right near the tunnel and look." She grinned beatifically.

"No," I said flatly. "I'm not going." Veve wriggled, knocking me over, and I sat on the grass and pulled her into my lap.

"But Edge—"

Gem bent to sit.

Without warning, Veve exploded into snarls and shot toward the prickly bushes.

I may or may not have squeaked. Gem definitely did, landing butt-first, sprawled on the ground. "Veve! I'm going to wring your hairy neck!"

Just as suddenly, Veve's barking stopped. The silence pressed down, too loud, too full.

"Gem," I whispered. "Are you all right?"

"Yes," she whispered back. "Are you?"

"Yes. Can you see Veve?" Because all of a sudden, my heart was pounding. Not only was the silence too loud, but the darkness was too complete, and although I should easily have been able to make out Veve's silhouette with the residual light from the house, I couldn't see a thing.

I sensed more than saw Gem roll over and crawl toward the bushes. My Road Master sense prickled. "Gem, I think we should go back inside."

"Just a second." She crawled forward. "I want to find that dog and pluck the hairs off her tail. I'm covered in mud and filth."

The darkness shifted. I grabbed at her foot and missed. "The shadows," I hissed as blacker-than-black shadows bulged in the darkness. My heart pounded. "Gemma, we have to go. The shadows are wrong."

Silence.

"Gem?"

The darkness bore down on me.

"Gemma? Veve?"

Silence, heavy and thick.

My skin crawled and I breathed quickly, my chest tight with dread. "Gemma? Gem, this isn't funny! Answer me!"

I flailed forward in the darkness, waving my arms where Gemma had been crouching.

Nothing.

I froze as images of what I might run into instead multiplied in my mind. Panic wrapped a tight band around my chest and I thought the skin over my spine might writhe off my back.

"Veve!" I called hoarsely. "Here, puppy!"

More silence. No bark, friendly or otherwise, no brush of fur against my leg.

Something tickled my neck and I screamed, then realised it was a moth.

Gone. Gem and Veve, both gone.

Frantically, I scrabbled back from the bushes.

Shadows, in my own yard. That wasn't fair. I hadn't gone anywhere, I hadn't done anything. This was my *own yard*. I was *supposed* to be here.

Wind gusted across the yard and the hair on the back of my neck prickled. The Valley. Streaming out from the horrible bushes and not-right shadows, the cloying, sickly-sweet smell of the Valley.

I needed Quoise. She'd know what to do, and I couldn't just abandon Gem and Veve. I needed help.

The creek. Frog it all, I was going to have to go down to the clearing and travel across to Sanctuary.

Biting back tears, I headed back to the house. Thank heavens I'd taken to storing my seed packet in the laundry.

My heart hammered. Why had the shadows snatched them like that? They hadn't done any magic at all, let alone death magic. Could a dog even offer a death sacrifice? Morbidly, I imagined Veve stepping on a bug at a crucial moment.

Stupid. It didn't work like that. At the back door, I gritted my teeth. Gemma owed me big time for this. If she hadn't been so stupidly interested in 'solving the mystery', we'd still be inside painting toenails and discussing green pens. I blinked back my tears, snuck into the laundry, grabbed my seeds from the cupboard, and jumped out of my skin. "Anna," I gasped at the head poking into the room.

She raised an eyebrow. "It's twenty past nine. What on earth are you doing?"

"Um, playing with Veve?" My pulse screamed in my ears. *Please, you have to let me go. The Valley has them. I have to get help.*

"And you need seeds because...?" Anna stared pointedly at the packet in my hand.

"Um, we're playing a game?" *Please, Anna. Please!*

Anna rolled her eyes. "Let me guess. It's a game in the clearing by the creek?"

I shuffled. "Maybe?"

Anna sighed. "You and your guerrilla gardening. At least tell me you're taking the dog."

I hesitated before nodding. I mean, technically I wasn't going anywhere Veve wasn't, right? So I was sort of taking the dog...

Anna nodded. "Good. Though why you had to decide to revel in our almost-freedom at this time of night I'll never know."

I shrugged and tried to smile.

"Have you got your phone?"

I patted my pocket. "Yup."

"Be home by midnight, okay?" Anna said. "If you're caught, we never had this conversation, or I swear I'll get you in so much trouble you'll never go anywhere but school until you're fifty."

"Fifty-year-olds don't go to school."

"Try me," she said darkly, and disappeared.

Relief flooded through me. Anna was good to her word; she wouldn't rat me out.

I headed down the street to the gravel path through the boulders. The moon hadn't risen and the sky seemed darker than usual. I checked quickly with my Road Mastery and couldn't sense anything amiss, but it still sent a shiver down my spine.

At the bottom of the path, panic fluttered around the edges of my consciousness. Down here, even the stars seemed faint, and even though my Road Mastery told me nothing unusual was around, the shadows everywhere seemed too dark, too deep, too sharp to be quite real. Nerves thrilled through my stomach as I ducked under an overgrown eucalypt branch that hung over the path. "It's fine," I muttered. "It's just a perfectly normal tree."

But out of the corner of my eyes, I kept watch: if a tree tried to grab me, I'd be ready for it. Impulsively I picked up a long stick from the side of the path. *Take that, trees*, I thought. *Wood against wood.* If only I had something to use against the shadows.

I reached the scrappy tunnel all my travels through to the clearing had made, and hesitated. *Frogging elephants*, I thought, wanting so badly to press my eyes closed but terrified of what might happen if I did. I swallowed, scrubbing my sweaty palms against my jeans. Frogging elephants.

Trees, shadows...

I exhaled firmly and set my shoulders. This was not negotiable. My best-and-only friend was in danger, and so was my dog. This wasn't about the rules, or even being scared. This was about not letting the shadows win.

I marched into the tunnel, definitely not holding my breath and certainly not flicking nervous glances all around at the shadowy darkness. I would cross to Sanctuary, find Quoise, and she would have a plan to rescue them.

Everything was going to be just fine.

The shadows across the creek weren't at all darker than normal, tendrils of blackness drifting toward me, reaching, whispering things just beyond hearing. Of course not.

I crossed to Sanctuary, faster than I'd ever crossed before. Quoise had better have a plan.

13

I TUMBLED INTO Sanctuary already sprinting. "Quoise!" I shouted as I ran up the slope. "Quoise!" My breath caught in my throat and I slowed. "Quoise!" I called again.

Throat burning, I stumbled to a halt outside the stables, steadying myself against the wall and leaning over my knees. I gasped and swallowed, gasped and swallowed, and my heart rate began to settle. I seriously needed to be fitter if I was going to have to run for my life this often.

I straightened and looked around, chest still heaving but no longer on fire. The soft glow of Sanctuary enveloped me and a gentle breeze brought with it the scent of jasmine and salt water.

I'd never realised before how overtly calming Sanctuary was. Gemma was right; it was totally infectious. But I shook my head and started up the slope toward the Lodge. I needed my adrenaline. Much as might hate it, I had the strong suspicion that tonight would include another trip into the Valley. Nerves fluttered in my stomach as I entered the Lodge's main entrance for the first time.

I stared. There was a whole lot of fluttering going on in here, but none of it was due to my stomach. Scores of fairies, maybe even hundreds, flittered around the vast room, some darting quickly, some wafting gently, all a riot of shimmer and glimmer and colour.

A gold-winged fairy noticed me and darted over, hovering at eye level. "Can I help you?"

"I'm looking for Quoise, please," I said. "It's urgent."

She smiled. "Just a moment."

She left and I jittered, shifting from foot to foot and wondering if Gem and Veve were okay, if they'd been devoured by the shadows, and how on earth the shadows had reached across to grab them. Only the power of a death sacrifice was supposed to allow a person to travel into the Valley.

Yet I'd been drawn across by a mysterious green-and-gold stranger, and now Gem and Veve had been taken. I scrunched up my face, trying to remember if there had been any trace of green or gold, any smell of mint in the air when they'd disappeared.

I couldn't remember a thing. One second they'd been there, and then they hadn't.

I clenched my fists in frustration. Shadows behaving strangely, both here in Sanctuary and on Earth. People getting sucked into the Valley for no apparent reason. After I'd pointed out where the shadows were coming from, Gem had said it was like the Valley was leaking, darkness oozing out everywhere it touched.

And, I thought, sticking my hands into my pockets and rediscovering my pen, traces of darkness all over stationary Scott had stolen.

I let my subconscious ponder over that for a while, and was startled when it handed me a memory of a task we'd done in geography at the end of last year. We'd had to do mapping work showing the suburbs where we lived. I hadn't known the area well enough to it to register at the time, but Scott's had been just a little way down from the school—right across the creek from the clearing.

Of course, it might not mean anything, but what were the chances of that? I snorted, realised I was chewing my thumbnail, and shook my hand.

Somehow, this was all connected, and I was beginning to suspect that a certain irritating boy might be the link. If Gem and Veve didn't escape this whole episode intact, I might just have to wring his neck.

"Hello?" The gold-winged fairy had returned and was smiling apologetically. "I'm sorry, but you just missed her. She's gone down to check on the foals."

I screamed internally. How had I missed her? I'd just *come* from there. My best friend was missing, dragged into the valley of death sacrifices and all things evil, and I was stuck playing the physical equivalent of phone tag. Doing my best not to glare, I nodded my thanks and left the hall.

This time as I stalked back down the slope I was in no danger of losing my adrenaline rush to Sanctuary's calming effects. I was certain: Scott was involved in all this, and when I found out how, he was going to pay.

I ducked inside the stables, calling out as I did. "Quoise?" Relief flooded over me as I sensed her inside.

"Edge, is that you?"

Quoise would know what to do. "Yes, it's me."

Wings fluttered in the dimness, then light flared and Quoise balanced on the rail near me, hand glowing brightly. "Come to see the foals?" she asked. "They're doing so well considering." She shook her head.

"Yes, it's very sad," I said quickly. "But I'm here about Gemma. She's missing."

Concern flitted across Quoise's face. "Oh well," she said, brushing it away. "There are lots of places she could be. I'm sure everything's fine."

I shook my head. "No. We were in the backyard together—it was dark, it's nearly ten at home—and she just... disappeared. Veve too."

Quoise relaxed into a smile. "Oh, well, maybe a new portal has opened in your yard. That happens sometimes. She probably just travelled over and is hiding here somewhere."

I met Quoise's gaze willing her to understand how serious this was. "She... she did travel. But she didn't travel into Sanctuary. The creepy shadows are in my yard."

Quoise paled. "Gemma offered death?" she said hoarsely.

"No." I shook my head quickly. "No. Something dragged her across." Goosebumps rose on my arms as I remembered stumbling in the darkness, arms reaching for a person that suddenly wasn't there.

"You have to look for her, send out a search party or something," I said, tripping over my words. "You have to go, someone has to find her, you have to, please..."

I squeezed my eyes shut against the tears. *I don't want to go back there.*

"Oh, Edge," Quoise said softly. "We can't."

My stomach lurched. "What do you mean? You're a fairy! You're magical! You have to help!"

She shook her head. "We can't travel into the Valley. Fairies are creatures of Sanctuary, we're born of its magic. Fairies are life, Edge, and we can only exist where there is life magic."

"But things live in the Valley. There are trees, and there's grass, and..." I strangled a sob.

She landed gently on my shoulder and hugged my neck. "You know they're not really alive," she whispered. "I'm sorry. I can't go."

I took a second to collect myself. I'd suspected all along that I'd have to go in and look for Gem. This didn't change anything. "Okay," I said, taking a steadying breath. "Okay. So I'm going in alone."

Quoise spiralled into the air. "What? Edge, you can't cross the border! You'll die!"

Guilt tugged at me. "I survived last time." *Barely.*

"Only just!" Quoise said, echoing my thoughts.

"Do you have a better alternative?" I raised my voice. "She's my best friend, Quoise! Veve is my dog! I *have* to save them."

Quoise shook her head. "Edge, that's all very admirable, but you can't cross over. I can't honestly believe you got out of there *once,* let alone tempting fate a second time. And even if you can somehow survive, you've no idea where they might be, if it's not already too late. This is the Valley we're talking about here, not some fairground or a picnic."

"I *know* that!" I said, scrubbing my hands through my hair. "But I survived last time, so why can't I try again?"

"Because you can't!" Quoise shouted. Instantly she recoiled, as though shocked by her own volume. "I'm sorry. But you just can't."

Anna's voice rang in my head. *Don't you ever get sick of 'just because'?* I took a deep breath, focusing on calming myself. "I survived last time," I said, quieter. "Please. They're my friends. I have to try." Anna was right: this time, 'just because' wasn't good enough.

Quoise stared at me for a long moment, then sighed and fluttered away.

I held my breath, wondering if that was the best I could expect, but she returned and landed on the rail again, holding a wiry, cream rope.

"Take this, then," she said, offering it to me.

"What is it?" I asked, reaching out to accept.

"Unicorn hair. They're the only creatures who can cross the border safely; they belong equally to life and death. I'm not sure what it can do for you once you're in the Valley, but at least it'll get you across. Despite what happened last time, you can't actually waltz across the border like it's not there.

"And if the other fairies hear about this and you get banned from Sanctuary, don't come crying to me. Rules exist *for a reason*."

"I didn't waltz across," I snapped as I took the unicorn hair. "Something dragged me. And I know all about the reasons why rules exist," I added, stomach heaving. Georgia's blood plastered across tiles in a train station bathroom were all well and good, but this time, if I *didn't* break the rules, it could be Gemma's blood plastered all over the ground. It was slowly starting to dawn on me that maybe, just maybe, the way to defeat evil wasn't to play nicely by the rules and ignore it. Some things you had to stand up for. After all, wasn't that what Dad had done in the first place, testifying against that mob boss?

Hmm. That probably bore further examination, later, when Gem and Veve were safe. Somewhat distractedly, I lifted the unicorn hair to my face and sniffed, not really sure what I was doing or why. Mint. My stomach fluttered.

"What is it?" Quoise peered at me in concern.

Mint. To my Road Mastery, the unicorn smelled like mint, and mint had dragged me across. But she'd been missing for a week. "Unicorns should be able to cross, you say?"

Quoise nodded, concern shifting to confusion.

My subconscious dredged up another memory: Scott, outside the bathrooms as he'd handed me my pen. He'd told me my friend was okay. He couldn't have meant the unicorn, could he?

But at least it seemed that the one who'd dragged me into the Valley was benevolent, and not after my skin. I hadn't sold my soul to an insubstantial devil after all. I laughed. "I think," I said, shaking my head and stooping to tie the unicorn hair to my ankle, "that I might just be very all right. All things considered, anyway."

Quoise nodded. "Well then. Good luck, Emma Tanning. Come back again. If anyone can do it, it's probably going to be you."

I straightened and saluted. "Aye-aye, Quoise," I said. "I will."

Quoise took me to another little door behind vines like the one Gem had shown me. "We're boarding this up tomorrow," she said. "So don't think about sneaking through again."

I nodded, wondering how many of these there were, and if Gem's would be boarded up too. I couldn't voice exactly how much I never wanted to see the Valley again, or I'd turn and run—and she probably wouldn't have believed me anyway.

"Now," she said as I ducked into the passage, "I'll make sure that the other corridor is clear. You just... hurry. And be safe." She hesitated, then threw herself at me, hugging my neck. "Be careful."

"I will," I said, detaching her gently.

This passageway felt longer than Gemma's one, but eventually I crossed through the magical screen—the hallway had been empty, as Quoise had promised—and stood before the border.

I shuddered. The last time I'd been here, I'd nearly been lost to the Valley forever. This place was ridiculously dangerous, and forbidden for good reason. But Gem was my friend and Veve was my dog. I had to get them back.

And now, I thought, glancing down to where the unicorn hair hid under my jeans, there was more: the mysterious connection between the missing unicorn and my sudden abduction into the Valley intrigued me. Could it really be that she was trapped in the Valley too? What had I done when I'd pulled her away from the blackness?

And of course, how did Scott fit into everything?

I steeled myself and stepped into the shadows. There'd be time for questions later.

Nothing happened. I'd half expected to be dragged like last time, or to feel at least a tug, or a rush in my stomach—something to indicate I'd crossed into the land of death. Instead, I felt... nothing. And that creeped me out more than anything, because when I blinked, I got the sinking feeling that the reason the border was letting me through so easily was because the power of the Valley was focused elsewhere.

I shuddered. I had to hurry.

I gave Sanctuary one last wistful glance and walked farther into the Valley, trembling so hard I thought I might fall. The trees at least seemed to have forgotten our last meeting—or perhaps they'd only objected to my departure, not my presence. Well, I wasn't planning on leaving this time until I found Gem and Veve. One problem at a time.

I stepped forward and something stabbed me in the thigh. I jumped, but it was only my pen shifting. I pulled it out and frowned. On this side of the border I didn't have to close my eyes to sense the darkness all over it. It was like being in the Valley amplified my Road Mastery even more than Sanctuary did— which was weird because everyone kept telling me that life magic was stronger.

I could definitely use it to my advantage, though. I hadn't really had a chance to test the limits of my Road Mastery yet, and anything that boosted it could only help me find Gem and Veve faster.

I closed my eyes, preparing to shut out all noise—and the horrible, abnormal silence of the Valley pressed in on me. I shuddered, feeling terribly exposed standing in the middle of dormant zombie trees with my eyes closed. I couldn't sense anything anyway, so I did the most logical thing—I followed the shadows. They weren't trying to devour me this time, but they still stretched oddly, streaming out from the heart of the Valley.

Every so often I closed my eyes to check in with my Road Mastery, but nothing appeared. My pace slowed and I sank into a tired daze. It was late back home after all. Must be getting close to midnight. What would Anna do if I wasn't back on time?

I stumbled. My pulse spiked for a moment, but the log I'd tripped on lay there, not reaching for me. I stared at it for half a minute before I realised I wasn't moving. I blinked and shook my head, but I was spent. I'd been walking for at least an hour.

Surely I could take a little break...

I sank to the ground and leaned against the log, staring vaguely into the distance. What had I been doing? The feeling that I'd forgotten something nagged in the back of my mind, but I was so tired, and I just needed to rest my eyes for a second.

A strange noise, just out of hearing, floated across the black behind my eyes. My name. It sounded like someone calling my name in smoky tones that promised the fulfilment of all my desires. I reached toward it, and the emptiness surrounded me, emptier than nothing, all wrapped up in the smell of overripe fruit and cold stone and fetid, rotting marshes.

"Sweet, so sweet... Come home... You are home... Sleep now, rest. So sweet..."

I closed my eyes, yawning.

"Yes, sleep so sweet, you are home, you are free. Do anything here, so sweet, you are free. Welcome home..."

Soft darkness fluttered along my limbs, imbuing them with power. Idly, I wondered if I could make the dead log at my feet turn green. I touched it. Darkness rippled along, leaving behind saturated green and budding leaves. I smiled sleepily. And people said the magic of life was stronger. I could do anything with death magic.

I cradled my head on my arm and a whisper drifted through the tendrils of darkness around me. *"Welcome,"* it crooned. *"Welcome home."*

14

I STRETCHED AWAKE, stiff and sore but feeling lazy and warm nonetheless. I opened my eyes and blinked at the trees around me. Since when did my room have trees in it?

I clambered to my feet and groaned as pain rang out on the inside of my skull. Wasn't I supposed to be doing something? I stared mindlessly at a landscape that probably wasn't my bedroom, but I couldn't remember what I'd been doing. Why had I decided to spend the night outside with weird trees that seemed to be frozen in the act of reaching for me?

Bizarre.

I should probably find someone, tell them I was here. A fragment of memory swam through my mental fog. Someone. I'd been looking for someone. That was right.

I screwed up my face, concentrating, trying to extract more from my memory.

Fear, panic. A bad place. Hmm. I strained for more, but a soft voice whispered to me. I couldn't catch the words, but it felt soothing, a dark, peaceful fog of nothingness, and my tension ebbed away again.

My ankle itched. I blinked as I lifted my jeans, surprised to discover some sort of strange rope tied around my ankle. I fumbled at it, wondering if I should remove it.

A breath of wind whispered against my face and I caught a faint trace of something minty. My frown deepened. None of the plants here looked anything like mint. It smelled nice, though, so I shrugged and smoothed my jeans down again.

Lacking anything better to do, I began to wander in the direction the wind had come from. The air dripped with humidity and I shrugged out of my jacket. It seemed like a heavy, clumsy thing to carry, so I left it lying on the ground.

Idly, I wondered what the time was. Out of habit I reached for my phone in my pocket. I wrinkled my nose. Flat battery. I shoved it back, wincing as something stabbed into my thigh.

I got a fleeting sense of déjà vu as I pulled out a green pen, but it was like trying to squeeze water. I growled in frustration and, for lack of anything better to do, kept walking.

The trees went on and on and on, one apparently-endless backdrop of sameness, and I'd just about given up hope of finding *anything* in this stupid wilderness when I stopped short. Was that a hoof print, there, in the mud?

I squatted. It was. I tilted my head. No wonder it had caught my eye; on certain angles it seemed to glow, a faint, pale green that gave the impression that fog had settled in it.

And, I realised, twitching my nose, something nearby smelled like mint.

"Right," I told the world at large. "That's it. What is going on?"

The same soft wind breathed against my face and connections whirled in my mind. A hoof print that smelled of mint, a disembodied voice, a strange rope around my ankle that might, I thought glancing at it, be made of horsehair. Was this who I was looking for?

"You! What are you *doing* here?"

I jumped at the first cry, and again as I swung around and saw who it was. "Scott!" Immediately I frowned. How had I known his name was Scott?

He looked as surprised as I felt. "I can't *believe* you! You ruin everything!"

"Yeah, I'm good at that," I said automatically, then frowned again. Why had I said that?

An image formed in my mind of this blond-haired boy called Scott surrounded by shadows, laughing on a cold mountaintop beneath the stars. Only, as I watched, the stars began to go out.

"But how did you even get here?" His question interrupted my vision and I blinked. "I don't see *you* having the guts to make the crossing."

My head sloshed. I had the distinct impression I'd just been about to remember something important—but it was gone. I shook my head again, then realised Scott was staring at me expectantly. "Sorry, what?"

He rolled his eyes. "Maybe you got dragged through. This place is leaking left, right and centre," he added under his breath.

Dragging. That rang a bell. Someone had been dragged somewhere, and I was supposed to be looking for someone. I sized Scott up. Was he the kind of person I would look for? The cold mountain flickered at the edges of my vision. Probably not.

I shoved my hands in my jeans pockets, thinking, and remembered that my pen was still there. I pulled it out and stared at it. It was connected to all this, somehow.

Scott made a strangled sort of noise. "Odd thing to carry around."

I shrugged. "Your fingerprints are on it." I blinked. My response had been instinctive again, but this time it had jarred some other thoughts loose too. I examined them. The pen had weird blackness all over it, but it wasn't black like the shadows I could sense following me, lurking just out of sight. Instead, it was black like Scott. Or at least, part of it was. Possibly it was black like both of them. I shook my head, brain-pretzelled.

Scott made an exasperated noise. "Ten points to the Princess. I was the one who gave it back to you and it has my fingerprints on it? Shocking, that."

I nodded absently. Fingerprints. I didn't think he meant the same thing by that as I did, but I couldn't quite grasp what I did mean.

Another fragment of memory filtered through. "Hang on. You did! You gave it back to me, and it was missing." I shook the pen at him, quizzical. "Did you steal it?"

Scott threw his hands up in the air. "I did not take your stupid pen! I found it for you, you stupid cow! I was trying to be nice to you, and you attacked me!" He turned and stomped away.

I wrinkled up my nose, trying to remember what he was talking about—and realised he had just called me a stupid cow. I marched after him. "Excuse me!" I said, poking him in the shoulder. "I am *not* a stupid cow. Although," I conceded as another wave of peaceful confusion rolled over me, "I may be stupid."

His face worked, trying on five different emotions at once, and at length he sighed. "Did you fall asleep?"

"Maybe."

He rolled his eyes. "You fell asleep. It's this place. It lulls you in. Unless it knows you're already on its side, it'll attack you if you try to leave and put you to sleep if you stay." He ran a hand over his head, tense. "You really do know how to ruin everything, don't you? If you'd just *listened* the first time I tried to tell you..."

"Tell me?!" I interrupted, mouth on autopilot again. "You never did anything but be a big, fat, stupid ass to me!" Not that I could remember a single thing about it, but apparently my subconscious knew how to hold a grudge well.

Scott cut me a filthy look. "Well nothing else was getting your attention, was it, McFrosty."

I shook my head. I had no details to fuel my case, but I knew he was wrong.

He stared at me for a moment longer, and when he spoke his voice was level and controlled. "Follow me." He stalked away.

"Where?" I said, crossing my arms.

"I'm getting you out," he said without turning. "And then I never want to see you here again."

Getting you out of here. The words echoed in my head, and more memory fragments slotted into place. I was here to get someone out. But who? I shrugged uncomfortably and followed Scott through the undergrowth.

At last Scott held up his hand to signal a halt, and I stopped gladly behind him. Humidity cloyed the air and although I'd become accustomed to the smell, I was dying for some water. My shirt was soaked through and sweat dripped down my legs inside the heavy denim of my jeans.

Scott glanced at me. "Ready then?"

I shrugged. "Sure." On top of the horrible humidity and my complete inability to remember why I was here, the place was deadly boring. The trees didn't move, the air didn't move, and besides the hoof print I'd seen earlier, we seemed to be the only things alive in the whole world.

"Okay," he said. "I'll have to travel with you, there's no way you can do it alone. You don't have the ability—or the guts." He glared briefly, daring me to challenge.

I shrugged, not really sure what he meant and abruptly too tired to argue.

"Stay behind me," he said, gesturing ahead to a small, greyish-white platform a couple of steps across. "When I say the word, put one hand on me." He tensed as though dreading the moment.

I couldn't say I blamed him; it wouldn't exactly be the highlight of my life, either.

"Whatever you do," he continued, "don't break contact with me."

I rolled my eyes at his melodrama but followed him as he headed toward the platform. My stomach skipped as I realised the greyish-white was bone. "Charming," I muttered.

"Okay," said Scott, ignoring me. "You stand there. And *don't move.*"

I nodded and climbed into position.

Scott stepped up in front of me. He plunged his hands into his pocket and for an instant I thought that had been the signal, that I'd missed it and was going to be stuck in this horrible place alone.

I was so relieved when he pulled his hands out again that I almost didn't register the fact that he held a limp, white mouse in one hand and a pocketknife in the other.

Dread rippled over me and I gasped. *Death magic.* I couldn't remember what it was, didn't know how I knew what he was going to do—but I knew that it was bad. Blood drained from my face. "No."

"Put your hand on my back," Scott said quietly.

I did, pressing firmly to still my trembling. This was the only way out. I had to trust him.

"Close your eyes," he said softly.

I did.

His arms shifted.

The bottom dropped out of the world, and I screamed.

15

I SCREAMED AND I screamed, and still we fell, hurtling downwards so fast the air tore at my hair, my clothes, my skin. It hurt, frogging *elephants* it hurt, and it *would not stop*.

Then mercifully—finally—it did, leaving us sprawled on the ground under dark, shadowy trees, panting and gasping and wishing we could die.

Well, *I* wished I could die. Scott just scrambled to his feet and gave me contemptuous eyebrows. "Wuss," he said.

I may or may not have growled. "Why the frogging elephants did you not *warn* me that that was going to happen?"

"Would you have come if I had?"

"No!" I said, getting up and steadying myself against a tree trunk.

"Well, there you are then."

I stared about, trying to orient myself. "Where are we?"

Scott rolled his eyes. "You'll figure it out soon enough. That way, I think." He pointed to my left and I realised I could hear water trickling.

"Where are you going?"

Scott, heading the opposite way, paused. He opened his mouth, then stopped and shook his head. "Just go home," he said. "And don't come this way again, okay?" He disappeared through the trees, footsteps crackling in the dim light.

I sighed and headed toward the water. I broke out of the trees and reeled as memories slammed into place.

The creek. The clearing. *Veve. Gemma.*

My legs gave way and I crashed down into the water, crying out as rocks grazed my palms and memories battered my mind. What had I done?

Frogging elephants, I'd taken a *nap*. I buried my face in my hands, but I couldn't even cry. The failure was so incomprehensible, I couldn't do more than stumble around the edges of it.

Then fear stabbed through from another angle: Mum and Dad. What were they going to say? If they'd noticed I was missing they'd be going spare right now. I had to get home.

I struggled out of the stream, pulling my phone from my pocket. I glanced at it and winced. The cover was waterlogged, and even if the battery hadn't already run flat, I doubted I would have been able to turn it on. I shoved it back and hurried through the tunnel, relieved when I emerged on the other side to see that the sun was only just beginning to gild the treetops.

I forced myself to a jog, concentrating on my breathing—it helped block everything else out, and it was the only way to keep myself moving. I struggled against panic as I approached the house. What would my parents say? What would *Anna* say? Part of me wanted to turn around and march straight back to Sanctuary. I could look for Gem and Veve again and this time I'd find them, and we could hide in Sanctuary forever and be together and happy and not grounded for the rest of our lives. I didn't want to go to school till I was fifty.

I sighed. Even conveniently ignoring the fact that both of Gem's parents were Travellers, I didn't really mean it. I slipped through the back gate and constructed a cover story in my head.

By the time I reached the sliding door that led into the lounge room, I had it down pat. But as soon as I walked through the door, all excuses evaporated. Gem and Veve were gone.

Mum was in the kitchen, kneading bread dough. She raised an enquiring eyebrow at me as I entered. "You're up early. And you're soaking wet."

I nodded, dripping on the tiles and fighting the desire to run.

"Where's Gemma?"

I cringed, only half acting. "She went home."

"Home?" Mum's hands paused in the dough.

"She remembered that she needed some stuff for her history assignment today. But..." I tore my gaze from the floor and looked

Mum in the eyes, my own prickling with tears I didn't need to fake. "But Mum, Veve's missing."

Concern flooded Mum's face and she paused with her hands in the dough. "Are you sure?"

I nodded. "We looked everywhere. I think... I think she must have got out the gate." I squeezed my eyes shut. *Please believe me...*

A rustle of cloth, soft footsteps. Mum hurried to the door and slid it open. "Veve!"

I shook my head. "She's not there, Mum." The tears spilled over. She might never be there again, and it was all my fault. I should have told Gemma no. "I even checked down at the creek. I can't find her anywhere."

Mum re-entered the house and scooped me into her arms, soggy clothes and all. "Don't worry," she said, squeezing me tight. "We'll find her. I'll print out some posters at work and ring all the local vets. Don't worry. She'll be okay."

I locked myself in my bedroom, turned on some music to muffle my voice, and sat on the floor, cradling the home phone. Anna had stuck my phone in a bowl of rice in an attempt to dry it out, hissing under her breath to me, "Don't think I don't know what time you didn't make it home last night."

That had made my stomach drop, but it was nothing to the call I now had to make. Mrs Caro needed to know what had happened. My chest tightened and I gripped the phone. I couldn't do it.

I *had* to do it. A sob strangled my throat and in a rush I dialled Gemma's number. She had to know.

The phone rang and rang. Mrs Caro had probably already left for work. I moved the phone away to hang up.

"Hello?"

I froze.

"Hello, who is it?"

I inched the phone back to my ear, a movement that took hours. "Hello," I rasped. I swallowed and tried again. "Hello. It's Emma here."

"Oh, Emma! Hello! What can I do for you? You can't be wanting to speak to Gemma, she's with you, isn't she?"

Tears leaked from my tightly closed eyes. *Just say it, Emma*, I told myself. *Now. Do it.* "No, Mrs Caro. No, she's not."

"I'm sorry?" Mrs Caro said. "Yes, just a minute dear, I'm speaking with Emma."

"Oh, if you need to go…" I said hurriedly, praying that she would.

"No, no, it's quite all right. Gemma's *not* with you, did you say?"

My stomach flip-flopped. "No. That's what I rang about. Gemma… She's… I mean, last night…"

I gasped back the tears, trying to keep myself under control. "Mrs Caro, she's in the Valley," I blurted. "I'm sorry," I choked. "I'm so sorry, I tried to find her but I couldn't, and I fell asleep and then Scott found me and took me home and I didn't even know what was happening, and she's missing and I couldn't find her and I forgot! I'm so, so sorry!"

"Emma, calm down," Mrs Caro said firmly. "The Valley? Why on earth would Gemma be in the Valley?"

"She was dragged there. Last night, in the—"

"Don't say anything more," Mrs Caro interrupted. "You're on your way to school?"

I nodded, wiping away tears. "I will be soon. Mum's going to drive me."

"Does she know?" Mrs Caro's voice sharpened.

"No," I replied. "Just that Veve is missing."

"Veve?"

"My dog. She's with Gemma."

"Oh. I'm sorry," Mrs Caro said softly. "Really, I am. But… Well, at least Gemma has someone with her, right?"

My voice came out as a hoarse whisper. "Right."

Mrs Caro resumed her business-like tone. "I'll come and get you as soon as I can. Does anyone else know Gemma is missing?"

"Quoise," I said. "She let me into the Valley."

"Quoise? Oh, well, I suppose that's good." She took a deep breath and exhaled slowly. "Okay. Emma, it's going to be okay, you hear me?"

"I'm sorry," I whispered.

"It's not your fault," she said. "Whatever happened, it's not your fault. Hang in there. I'll meet you as soon as I can." She hung up.

I stared at the phone as I scrubbed away a fresh wave of tears. I had to get ready for school. And then Mrs Caro would arrive and have some perfect solution, and everything would be fine.

I pulled my uniform on, pointedly ignoring the little voice in my head that told me I was thinking wishfully. Of course Mrs Caro would have a solution. Of course she would. I just had to wait and see what it was.

16

I ARRIVED AT school alternating between depression and electric tension, wondering when Mrs Caro would arrive. I hurried off to roll call, hoping she'd be there before first period. In the meantime, I sat at the back of the room, doodling in my school diary, mind racing as I brainstormed ways to rescue Gem.

I'd gotten exactly nowhere when the bell rang. Mrs Caro still hadn't appeared, so I gritted my teeth and headed to Maths, determined not to spend too long there.

I took my usual seat front and centre, and did my best to look as unwell as possible. It worked. Five minutes into class, I called Mr Morris over and told him I wasn't well. He took one look at me and sent me to sickbay. Turns out being stressed out of my mind had its uses.

I lay on the sickbay bed trying to rest, but my mind buzzed. When the nurse came in and told me Mrs Caro was here to pick me up, I nearly melted in relief—and then snapped tight as a bowstring, because if I was Mrs Caro and knew what had happened, I'd probably want to kill me right now.

I headed out to reception. Mrs Caro nodded and shepherded me out to the car without comment.

The heavy clouds broke as we buckled up, rain pattering down on the roof. I let it fill the silence until we pulled out of the car park and onto the main road.

"Mrs Caro," I said, twisting toward her, "I know you're probably mad as anything right now, but I have to go back to the Valley. I have to find her."

She nodded. "I know."

"You do?" I frowned. I'd expected her to try to talk me out of it, not agree straight up.

"Yes. But I have some questions for you first."

"Of course, anything." I stared at her, wondering how she could appear so calm. Her only daughter was trapped in the Valley, and here she was coolly indicating and sliding in and out of traffic like it was any ordinary day. There was only one logical explanation: underneath her normal, composed exterior, Mrs Caro was a superhero.

We drove out to the subdivision where the Caros lived and stopped right next to a vacant lot that provided easy access to the creek path.

"Your house is closer, but I don't want to risk you being seen by someone who knows you," Mrs Caro said, twisting around. "So. You went into the Valley to find her, is that right?"

I nodded, watching the rain spatter on the windscreen.

"The first and most important question then is, how did you get there?"

I peeled down my school sock to expose my ankle. "Quoise gave me unicorn hair." I hadn't been able to bear the thought of taking it off this morning, even if it did itch like mad sometimes.

Mrs Caro's face softened. "That was kind of her, especially considering their standard policy toward anyone who enters the Valley. Then my next question is, did you leave the Valley of your own volition, or did someone force you out?"

"Neither, exactly. Scott brought me out." Briefly, I wondered why I hadn't seen his gloating face at school this morning.

"Who?"

"Scott, we go to school with him. I'm surprised Gem never mentioned him, half the year's in love with him. Anyway, he was in the Valley, and he found me, or I found him, I can't remember exactly. It's all a bit confusing." I frowned again and rubbed my forehead, cursing my fragmented memory. "He said the Valley had lulled me to sleep, and then... he used death magic to bring me home." I hesitated for a second, then my fears came tumbling out. "That's okay, isn't it? I mean, that *I* didn't use it. I did *want* to leave, but I didn't use the magic myself. So I won't be corrupted by the Valley, will I?"

Mrs Caro sighed and leaned back against the seat, eyes closed. "I don't think so."

"Can... can I rescue Gem now?" I ventured after a moment.

Mrs Caro laughed hollowly. "You'll have to."

My fingers twisted in my school skirt. "What do you mean?"

"Edge—do you mind me calling you that? It's how Gemma refers to you."

I nodded.

"Edge, the Valley is a dangerous place." She rubbed her cheek. "You already know that it's the land of death, while Sanctuary is the land of life, and to travel to either you need to use the power of death or life respectively."

I nodded again, wondering where she was going.

"What they don't tell you is this: life and death exist in a precarious balance in the middle worlds. But wait, before I get to that, you know about them being multidimensional, yes?"

"There can be thousands of people there at once but we can never see them," I said, reciting what Quoise had told me. How was this relevant? I crinkled my brow. "And they're all connected like crinkled paper?"

"You've been talking to Gem." Mrs Caro smiled tightly. "But yes, that's right. You can't see them."

I inhaled as I realised what that meant. "I can't find Gemma."

Mrs Caro softened. "You can see people who entered at the same point that you did. If you travelled over at the same place, your chances of seeing her would be vastly improved. But we don't want you to use death magic, and it doesn't matter anyway, because you have another advantage. You're a Road Master. And because you're a Road Master, it doesn't matter if you entered at a different point, on a different dimension; you can use your magic to find her."

"I tried that last time." I bit my lip and stared out the window. The rain made the green of the grass and leaves bright and it reminded me of the unreal colours of the Valley. "I fell asleep."

"Death magic is powerful," Mrs Caro said. "It's not like life magic, quick and spontaneous and creative; it's slower, more ponderous, erosive. Because of that, people underestimate it—but slow doesn't mean less powerful."

"Like water," I murmured, watching as rivulets formed on the roadside, washing through the dirt.

"Yes, like water. And the Valley is the accumulation of death magic; the land is slow and quiet, but strong. Convincing. And it recognises power—as does Sanctuary."

"What do you mean?" I asked, turning back to her. "How can land recognise anything?"

"Not the land." She shook her head. "The power feeding it. It senses power in the visitor and responds accordingly. Sanctuary, for example, will be more real, more beautiful, depending on your personal ability. For the weakest, it's nothing but a hazy, shimmering dream that leaves a lingering feeling of satisfaction."

I thought of Gem and I, running through Sanctuary with the wind in our hair, patting the foals, listening to the shush of the ocean. "You mean... I'm powerful?" A thrill ran through me, and for the first time in days, it wasn't a bad one.

Mrs Caro smiled. "Yes, Edge. You and Gemma are quite powerful. But right now, the important thing is that you are the right *amount* of powerful."

"What do you mean?"

"The last thing I need to tell you is the most important. I said before that life and death exist in a precarious balance in the worlds between worlds."

I swallowed, not knowing where she was going, but knowing from her tone that I wasn't going to like what she had to say.

"Both Sanctuary and the Valley feed off the power of their visitors, Edge. Usually, it doesn't matter who comes and goes. But something in the Valley isn't right. Gemma told me that you discovered that's where the shadows are spawning."

Fear curled up in my chest, cold and heavy. "It's leaking," I whispered, remembering first Gemma's words, then Scott's. "The shadows are spreading."

Mrs Caro nodded. "They're leaking. At all the entry points to the Valley, across all the worlds, the shadows are oozing out, and things are getting sucked across." Her voice trembled and she took a deep breath. "I did some poking around. Gemma is the first *person* to be taken. It's only been things until now."

My hands fisted as I thought of my pen with its lingering sense of the Valley all over it. Had Scott been telling the truth? "I still don't see how this relates to me," I said, throat dry.

Mrs Caro sighed. "I know. It's a lot to explain. I'm sorry. Basically, Mr Caro and I and a couple of others we know—who are very smart, but not very powerful—anyway, with the Valley leaking all over the place we suspect that there's a power imbalance there somehow. It's too strong, stronger than it should be, so we can't risk sending anyone too powerful over there in case they succumb and the Valley gains *their* power.

"But I can't just ask anyone to go into the Valley either," she continued. "Because you have to be powerful enough to see the Valley fully formed to have a chance of finding her. The Road Mastery counts for a lot, of course," she added. "How strong *is* your Road Mastery?"

I leaned over, head in hands. "Strong." *Frogs*, I thought. *Froggity, froggity, frogs*. This was Not Good, with a capital Not, and a capital Good. "I have the right amount of power," I mumbled into my palms.

"You have the right amount of power. You can actually see and feel and interact with the Valley, but you're not so strong that your presence there will immediately tip the balance in its favour. And with your Road Mastery, you have a chance of actually tracking Gemma down."

I can't go.

I have to go.

I don't want to go.

I have to rescue Gemma.

And Veve.

I twitched my fingers, imagining Veve's soft fur. I sat up. "I have to go."

"No. You don't have to," Mrs Caro said quietly.

I looked at her. Her eyes were wide and shining, her lips pressed tightly together and her hands gripping her thighs. "If I don't go?"

Mrs Caro swallowed. "Then I'll go. And we'll hope and pray that I can somehow track her down before the shadows find me, and if not that I can find a way to die if the shadows get me, because that would be better than the alternative."

I laughed hollowly, shook my head and popped the door. "I'll go," I said. I climbed out into the rain and stood there as it plastered my hair to my face.

Mrs Caro came around and stood beside me, her arm around my shoulders. "The Valley isn't fussy, Edge. It'll take any power it can get. It will try to seduce you, cloud your mind, make you think it's a wonderful place. It wants all the power it can get."

I fought back a scream, remembering my brain fog, the way I'd slowed in my search and eventually stopped, forgetting completely what I'd been there for. And those words it had whispered, like a caress as I'd fallen asleep: Welcome home.

A home was what I wanted more than anything in the world, a home where I belonged and was safe. What if it happened again? What if I wasn't strong enough to resist the Valley this time? And what if I *was* strong enough to give it enough power to tip the balance?

"What will happen if the Valley gets too powerful?" Rain dripped from the tip of my nose.

"The shadows will leak out everywhere, I expect," Mrs Caro said. "After that, I've no idea."

I weighed up my options. On the left, try to save Gem and Veve and risk the entire universe, because no one actually *knew* that I wasn't powerful enough to tip the balance, or that I *was* powerful enough to find them while resisting the Valley. On the right, stay here, be safe (at least until the shadows devoured the world), but risk the lives of my best friend and the puppy I'd helped raise.

Search for Gem, maybe fail, destroy the world.

Sit back, do nothing, fail my friend, and probably watch the shadows devour the earth.

Such. Great. Options.

"You do have one advantage," Mrs Caro said.

"What's that?"

"You have the unicorn ward."

I glanced down at the bump under my sock. "It's a ward?"

Mrs Caro nodded. "Unicorns are the only creatures who belong equally to life and death, as I'm sure the fairies told you—though maybe not. I'm still surprised Quoise gave you the ward at all," she said, frowning.

Guilt plucked at my stomach. "Well, Quoise did say not to tell anyone."

"Mm. Still. Anyway." Mrs Caro refocused. "At least you can walk freely into the Valley."

"At least?" I snorted, thinking I'd much rather the ward did something truly fantastic, like rescue Gem so I didn't have to go into the Valley at all.

"Yes." Mrs Caro held me at arm's length and searched my face. "Because otherwise, the only way into the Valley would be death magic. Thank heavens for small mercies," she added as she drew me into a wet, crushing hug.

I hugged her so hard my arms hurt. I loved Gem and Veve—but the thought of using death magic filled me with dread. "Thank heavens for small mercies," I whispered, and cried.

17

I STOOD IN the clearing, glaringly aware of my skin. Never before had it seemed so fragile—too fragile to protect against the rain dribbling down through the trees, let alone the power of the Valley and its shadows.

Mrs Caro laid a hand on my shoulder. "You can do this, Emma. I believe in you. And I know Gemma does too."

I'm sure it was fantastic to have so many people believing in me, but right then the person I needed to believe in me most was *me*, and I was having a hard time doing it.

Mrs Caro took a deep, focused breath. "Just remember to focus on the ward. And don't accept anything anyone offers. Even..." Her grip tightened. "Even Gemma, until we get her out of there and make sure."

I nodded, squeezing my forehead and hoping that all my new-found knowledge wouldn't leak out my ears.

"Off you go then." Mrs Caro released me and stepped back.

I dug around in my pocket for a seed and crouched. In some ways, it would have been a lot simpler if I'd just been able to travel straight into the Valley—but no way was I going to use death magic to get there. So, Sanctuary it was. I'd have to walk the long way—and convince the fairies to let me through again.

"Here goes nothing," I muttered as I thrust the seed into the soil. Nerves thrummed like electricity.

"Remember, I'll meet you at the Lodge at four," Mrs Caro said. "Find her, Edge."

Fear rippled through me as I slid toward Sanctuary, but just as suddenly warmth overtook it and I was there.

Sanctuary. A place of safety. I remembered asking Quoise if it was safe the first day I'd visited. It felt like a lifetime ago, though it was barely over a week. It hurt that it hadn't turned out to be a refuge after all.

Not that it was Sanctuary's fault, I thought as I left the alcove. Stupid Valley. Stupid shadows. I rubbed the goosebumps from my arms and set off. The breeze brought with it the smell of salt water, and I wondered if I wished hard enough whether I could just turn into a dolphin and swim away. Sanctuary was magic, right? Surely it could turn me into a dolphin if I wanted, and then I'd never have to worry about anything ever again.

Unless shadows liked water too. Ha.

I neared the stables and something hissed. Pushing wet hair back off my face, I peered around and realised it was—for reasons best known only to her—Quoise, beckoning me behind the building.

I followed, impatient. "What is it?"

She trembled in mid-air. "You're back. Are you... Are you okay?"

"I'm fine," I said, biting off the words. "What do you want?"

"You... You couldn't find Gemma?"

I shook my head. "But I'm going back again and this time I will find her, and you can't stop me."

Quoise bit her lip. "Edge, it's been over twelve hours. The chances of finding her—"

"Aren't great, I know. Mrs Caro brought me." I lifted my hand to Quoise and she landed. "Why are the shadows moving?"

Quoise shook her head. "We don't know."

"So guess."

"It could be any number of things."

"So name a few." I stared her down.

Quoise hung her head. "The balance is out. We don't know how, or why, but there's..." She waved her hands. "A hole, a sinkhole, near the middle of the Valley that's sucking in power." She peeked up at me. "Please don't tell anyone I told you."

"I thought you couldn't travel into the Valley."

"We can't."

"Then how do you know about the sinkhole?"

"All fairies are Road Masters, Edge," she said softly. "Strong ones."

"You can sense the sinkhole from here?" I asked, surprised.

She nodded. "You'll feel it as you get closer, I'm sure of it. You're... you're really serious, aren't you? You're going back in." It wasn't really a question.

"Gemma and Veve are in there," I said, not really answering.

Quoise glanced down and nodded. "At least you're still wearing the ward."

Irritating bloomed. "Quoise, why didn't you tell me about the sinkhole last time? That seems like a useful piece of information to have known. Not to mention the fact that the Valley would try to put me to sleep!"

"I..." She shook her head. "Things have changed since yesterday. The shadows... One of us, one of the fairies..." She hung her head. "Ambergris is gone. *Someone* needs to do something."

She buried her face in her hands. "I'm sorry," she whispered after a long moment. "I didn't want you to get hurt. But no one goes in and out of the Valley, Edge. Not without death."

I wished Quoise was large enough to hug. Instead, I sank to the ground and patted for Quoise to join me. She fluttered down and snuggled by my side. I cupped her with my hand. "I'll be okay," I said to her at last. "Mrs Caro explained to me how to slip between dimensions so I can use my Road Mastery to track Gem down."

Quoise perked up. "Yes, that will make it easier, if you can do it. Do you know what her soulprint looks like?"

Soulprint. So that's what they were called. I shook my head, stomach sinking. "You'd think I would, since I spend all day with her. But I don't know, I guess I haven't figured out how to use my Road Mastery properly yet."

Quoise smiled. "That's something I *can* help you with. I mean, I shouldn't, and *please* don't tell anyone I'm helping you. But if you're certain about going back in again, I have to at least *try* to make sure you survive." She flew into the air. "Come on. Follow me."

She led me up to the Lodge, past the cavernous entry hall with its bustling flocks of fairies, down a glimmering corridor, around a few corners, and into a room whose walls were plated glass. Behind the glass stood row upon row and stack upon stack of tiny, wooden drawers.

Quoise fished out a charm from a chain on her neck, flew midway up the left wall two-thirds of the way along, and pressed the charm against the glass. A portion of it vanished, just enough to allow Quoise to open one of the drawers. "We keep a record of everyone who comes through Sanctuary," she said, extracting a glass vial as long as her leg and bringing it down to me. "Just in case."

I took the vial. "What do I do with it?"

She smiled. "Open the stopper and dip your finger in. Then just use your Road Mastery."

I pulled the cork out of the vial, biting my lip and wondering what to expect. I dipped in a finger; a flash of light consumed my senses. I winced.

"It's all right," Quoise said. "That's just its power activating. You'll see it in a second."

And sure enough, I did. The tube glowed golden through my closed eyelids and I focused on it, opening myself up to my Road Mastery. Quoise sparkled over to my right, a deep iridescent blue the colour of her wings, accompanied by the smell of rain and the soft sound of tinkling bells.

The tube brightened, sucking me into it. A deep, dark blue surrounded me, velvety and soft to the touch, studded with gems that might have been diamonds if they hadn't been twinkling so brightly. Something soft sounded just out of hearing, making the back of my neck itch in irritation—like trying to remember something important I'd just forgotten.

"It's the night sky," I murmured. "Only it's velvet. She's the night sky as a fabric."

Quoise chuckled. "Indeed."

I opened my eyes in wonder. "No wonder she loves glamour." And no wonder she'd irritated me when I'd first met her, I added to myself. That high-pitched noise was fine now I knew what it was, but the constant sensation of being about to remember something would have been a big turn off.

Quoise's chuckle deepened to a laugh as she took the re-stoppered vial and put it away.

"I'd better get going," I said as she returned.

"Wait." She drew a second, smaller vial out from behind her back. She considered it for a long moment, tiny fingertips white with the strength of her grip, then handed it over. "The sinkhole," she whispered.

I took it, heart hammering in my chest, and dipped my pinkie in. Another surge of light, then blackness blacker than black, and the smell of overripe fruit, stagnant water, and fetid carcasses. I gagged.

Quoise took the vial from me and restoppered it. "It shouldn't even *have* a soulprint," she murmured, avoiding eye contact. "I don't know what's wrong."

I wiped my mouth with the back of my hand then rubbed my forehead. "It's awful."

"I know." She returned it to its drawer. "Do you want me to come with you to the border?"

I considered it for a moment, but heading back into the Valley was something I had to do alone, and there was no point pretending otherwise. I shook my head. "I'll be okay. Thank you, though."

She hovered in the air near my face. "I'll keep the other fairies out of the passage again." She placed a hand on my cheek. "Good luck, Emma Tanning. May you do what no one else can."

I bowed my head. "Thank you."

I exited Quoise's passageway and stopped. Goosebumps rose on my arms as I surveyed the border. The shadows had engulfed a tree I was positive had been in Sanctuary the other day. Add that to my list of things to do in the Valley. One: save Gem and Veve. Two: save the world.

Ah ha. Didn't lists make everything look so nice and simple?

Okay, I told myself. *Enough stalling. Butt into gear; let's do this.* I reached down and brushed my fingers against the unicorn ward, making sure it was secure.

I backed up, squared my shoulders, and ran. I jumped over the border, yelling, "Yaaaah! Take that, stupid Valley!"

I landed heavily, rolling my ankle. "Oh joy." I bent down to massage it. "The perfect start to my adventures." I prodded it, trying to determine the extent of the damage. The smell of mint rose up and the ward began to glow, a soft, pale green shot through with gold glitter. Heat seeped downwards toward my damaged ligaments. The light and warmth flared, and the pain was gone.

Heh. Turned out unicorn wards were useful for more than just crossing the border. Nice to have a pleasant surprise for a change. I glanced around me and wondered how many *un*pleasant surprises the Valley held. That put a damper on things.

Better get moving. But which way? I closed my eyes and concentrated on Gem's soulprint, but the woods around me stayed empty. Was I going to have to search every dimension to find her? How long would that take? Mrs Caro had said there was one dimension in the Valley for every entry point, and they knew of at least a hundred of those.

My heart sank as I realised just how impossible finding Gem and Veve was going to be. I closed my eyes again, searching for anything that might give me a starting point.

There, what was that? A patch of darkness darker than the rest, and the smell of rotting fruit. I cracked an eye open to check out my chosen direction. Great. Just perfect. I'd managed to choose the only corridor of swampland in this entire life-forsaken place.

"Oh well," I told myself as I headed off. "It can't be worse than Scott."

18

I TRUDGED THROUGH the swampy muck, reminded of the one and only time Dad had convinced me to go hiking with him. Sure, I had fond memories of the bonding time and all, but I could have lived without a repeat of the mud- in-my-boots, hair, eyes, nostrils, everywhere-else-possible experience.

I tripped and landed face-first. *Eww.* As I pushed myself up, mud dripping off me, I wondered if this was a good time to quit. Home had never seemed so appealing—or so clean.

I ground my teeth. I couldn't turn back now. Gem needed me. I shook off the worst of the mud—and froze.

A hoarse whisper, full of darkness and power, wrapped around me. *"Home. Come to me. So sweet, alive, come home."*

The Valley. Concentrating, I realised that I could sense the whispers with my Road Mastery. I had to wonder if that wasn't the whole reason the Valley seemed to amplify my senses—just so it could hijack them and seduce me. Well. It was *not* going to beat me again. I shut down my Road Mastery to a mere trickle, forcing the whispers from my mind.

I walked. At last I left the swamp behind and headed into more trees, though these ones were mercifully free of yellowed leaves and oozing red sap. Then, just for a change of pace, I walked some more, the ambient heat drying the mud so it caked and chafed.

I still had no clue where I was going, and I had nothing for reference other than the vague sense of shadowy darkness ahead that I checked periodically. My hips ached and sweat was loosening the mud so now it squelched as well as chafed. The air pressure seemed to increase and heat rippled off the ground, the whole world stifling.

Just as I thought I couldn't walk any more, the trees opened up and I saw a shallow valley in front of me—and a dark, shadowy area in the tree line opposite. I sighed, cracked off as much mud as I could, and headed toward it, hoping that this was the right way to find Gem.

Close up, I surveyed the shadows, absently rubbing more dried mud from my arms. Although the shadows seemed scary enough, the power sink still felt distant. I closed my eyes. I was definitely in the right spot; the sinkhole gaped in front of me, a yawning black hole. But somehow, it also *wasn't* there. I needed my Road Mastery to see what was going on, but did I dare risk the whispers?

I cast about, but no other options presented themselves. I sighed and opened my Road Mastery up fully. Hopefully I could find what I needed before the whispers returned.

I frowned. Tiny slices of the sinkhole were less black than the rest—it was layered across the dimensions. I cast up and in, and found what I was looking for: the centre of the power. It was there in front of me, all right—but on a different dimension. If I wanted to get to it, I'd have to figure out how to slip between them.

I opened my eyes and stared. There was no guarantee that this strange power sink had anything to do with Gem and Veve, and they were my first priority. But on the other hand, I didn't have any better clues about their location, and tracking this hole across the dimensions would allow me to figure out how that worked. Mrs Caro had said that Gem was in a different dimension, after all.

I stared at the sinkhole, worrying at my lower lip with my teeth, unable to shake the knowledge that the blackness in front of me contained one heck of a lot of power—enough to allow shadows to spawn and leak through the gaps between worlds.

Gem had been snatched by leaking shadows. The Valley had a soulprint, and it shouldn't. The two facts had to be related.

I sighed, and ran my hand over my head. I'd have to try dimension hopping. Mrs Caro had told me it was a little like travelling to Sanctuary; I had to imagine where I wanted to go and then sort of twist sideways to get there, only instead of just imagining what the new place looked like, I had to use the Road Mastery.

Sometimes physically twisting helped, she'd said, although she'd obviously never done it herself. She couldn't help me any further, saying that I'd just have to use my Road Mastery and hope for the best. I was getting good at hoping for the best.

Using the sinkhole as a focal point seemed to help; where the rest of the landscape around me blurred indistinguishably, I could at least sense the layers of the hole. Maybe that would be enough.

I backed up a few paces and drew up an image of another dimension. The world would look exactly the same as it did now, with all the trees and branches and leaves and even the blades of grass in exactly the same position—but the shadows would be larger, deeper.

When I was confident that the image felt real, I twisted, spinning myself in a tight circle. I felt a flash of nausea, then nothing. Tentatively, I opened my eyes.

The shadows were darker. I grinned. Mrs Caro had warned me that it might not work the first few times I tried it, but I'd done it first go. "Take that, Valley," I said. I closed my eyes briefly to check my position: about halfway closer to the centre of the sinkhole. That was good.

A wave of nausea crashed over me and I groaned. Mrs Caro had also warned that there might be side effects. I wrapped my arms around my stomach and hugged tight, holding my breath against the pain. Who was I kidding? What did it matter if I could skip between the dimensions as fast as blinking? There were still hundreds of them, all as large as the Valley itself, and unless I got some clue about where Gem might be, I'd have to search them all.

Eyes closed against fading nausea, my breath hitched. A flicker of blue in the dimness; a sparkle of diamond and the brush of velvet against my fingertips. Without thinking, I strained toward it and slipped sideways, crossing the dimensions as easily as breathing.

Insubstantial claws shredded against my skin. My eyes flew open and I screamed from the very centre of the Valley's black hole.

19

BLACKNESS RUSHED INWARDS, crushing my mind, my senses, everything. How could I have forgotten how dangerous the Valley was? I cursed myself even as I turned to mush. This was the *last time* the Valley would get the better of me.

Wind rushed and whirled and my head roared. My stomach cramped, nausea rising in waves until I gulped, choked, and threw up. Acid burned my throat and I coughed and gagged, struggling for air.

The shadows pressed against me, cloying my skin, my nostrils, and I couldn't breathe, couldn't see, couldn't think. I whirled, throwing my hands out for something, anything to steady me, but I found only air.

Where were the trees? Had the shadows eaten everything? I thudded to my knees, cradling my head in my hands.

Black. Darkness. Everywhere, in every direction, as far as I could sense—nothing but darkness and thick shadows.

I couldn't even feel the ground; I wasn't falling, but there didn't seem to be anything solid holding me up, either. I caught my breath, heart hammering as I slipped and landed on my butt.

Mrs Caro hadn't mentioned anything like this.

Mrs Caro. Gem. Veve.

Thirty seconds, I told myself. That was how long I had to be scared, and after that, I had to put the fear aside and move. I wrapped my arms around my legs and gasped, fear eating at my chest, hollowing my stomach, and slicking my hands with sweat.

My thirty seconds were up. I inhaled as deeply as I could, sucking in the air and holding it to assure myself that at least, no matter what else happened, I wasn't dead yet. I could still find Gem.

Oh. Gem. Her dark blue soulprint; a patch of shadows lighter than the rest. My heart pounded and hope bubbled up. Gemma had been here. I didn't know Veve's soulprint—I didn't even know if animals *had* soulprints—but hopefully where Gemma had been, Veve had been too. I closed my eyes, squeezing my clammy hands tight, and flung out my Road Mastery.

Nothing.

I sighed and stood up, nausea washing over me for the third time. I froze, unable to convince myself I wouldn't fall if I tried to move. *Gem*, I reminded myself. *Veve.*

I reached out with my foot and tested the not-ground in front of me. Solid. I could walk. I groaned at the thought of yet another indeterminate hike.

With no landmarks and not even the sense of air on my skin, I had no idea how long I walked, but my legs began to feel heavy and my lower back ached. My left foot had blisters, and its blisters were beginning to get blisters—school shoes are supposed to be sturdy and supportive and all, but they're definitely not designed for hiking. Thankfully, the unicorn ward was more than earning its keep, healing the blisters on my right foot almost as they appeared.

My brain powered down and I drifted into semi-consciousness. It wasn't until I rubbed an itch on my eyelid and saw a faint flicker of light ahead that realised I'd been walking with my eyes closed.

Lacking any better option—I still hadn't seen anything more of Gemma's soulprint—I swung toward the light. It grew brighter, and as I got closer I saw that it was a pillar of charcoal grey and black light, spiralling upwards into nothingness. Despite how bright it seemed, it wasn't strong enough to illuminate anything— that, or there really was nothing here for it to illuminate.

I stumbled to a halt in front of it, shoulders sagging and head pounding.

You are well met, Emma Tanning.

I stared vaguely, sure the voice was a by-product of my exhaustion-addled brain.

Will you speak?

I blinked. "Um, hi?"

The pillar of light sparkled. *Hello.*

"You're... the light, talking?" Well, I was smack in the middle of the Valley, surrounded by unfathomable darkness. I don't know why I hadn't expected weird things.

I am light, and I am power. I am the sum of everything, and what everything might be.

I snorted, fighting the urge to mouth off. I was too tired for this. I had friends to find.

You doubt my nature?

"No," I said. Best not to anger whatever the light actually was. This was the Valley, after all. I bit the inside of my lip. "It's kind of a mouthful, though. Do you have a shorter name?"

Lucky for me, glowing pillars of light didn't seem to understand sarcasm.

Many have called me Master, Emma Tanning.

I raised an eyebrow. "Seriously?" There was no way I was calling anything dead in the heart of the Valley 'Master'. Learned that lesson last time, even if it *had* turned out all right in the end.

I am always serious. The pillar flickered again, showing off. *I am force, I am power, I am inevitable. I am great and vast and wide, and all come to me in the end.*

Yeah, yeah, blah-blah-blah. I twisted around, trying to decide which direction I'd investigate next.

I would that you would come to me, Emma Tanning.

Shivers prickled down my spine. How did the thing know my name, anyway? I shrugged, feigning nonchalance. "I'm here, aren't I?"

It is not quite the same, the light said. *But since you are here, will you come?*

The light sparkled and twinkled, ribbons of black and grey twining and dancing, and I couldn't look away. My thoughts slowed, and I knew I'd been about to say no, but I couldn't quite figure out why. The light was beautiful, and I wanted to go to it, to step into it and embrace it, to let it fill me so I could dance with it too. I stretched out my hand.

Will you come?

"I... don't know." I'd meant to say no, really I had... But something about the voice seemed familiar, and it half seemed to me that this voice had spoken to me once of home, of freedom.

The light flared. *Yes*, it said. *Home. This is my offer to you, if you will come: all the power of the universe at your command. The power over life and death, the power to keep any creature from dying. The power to create something out of nothing, to live forever and ever, to rule the world as you see fit and to sculpt it into something better and more perfect, something truly yours.*

But more than that, Emma Tanning: think what you could do with such power.

Images flashed into the air in front of me, breathtaking in their clarity. Me, laughing with Gemma and Grace, surrounded by all my old friends. My old room, comfy pillows softer and more inviting than ever. Anna, smiling and laughing, arms wrapped around Kade's waist. Mum and Dad, happy and peaceful, not even a hint of danger in the air.

My breath hitched in my throat and an intense homesickness hit me right in the gut. Why couldn't I ever seem to stop running? Why couldn't I just find a home that would be safe? First Melbourne had been stripped away from us, and now Sanctuary was being taken too.

Safe. With all the power in the world, I could make a new home, and this time I make sure that no one would ever take it from me again. My family, my friends—we'd all be safe, forever.

Do you accept my offer? the light said, reaching out to caress me.

I stiffened, closing my eyes. It was evil. It had to be. This was the Valley.

But I wanted the safety the vision had offered me so much. It wasn't wrong to want to be safe, was it?

"Ye—" My ankle itched and I frowned at it. The ward. I scratched and as I did the smell of mint filled the air. Another light appeared, this one pale green, much fainter than the grey-and-black pillar and far less impressive.

Edge, said the new light in a voice that tickled my subconscious. I'd heard this voice before too, though I couldn't place where. My frown deepened. Had it once led me to safety?

Edge, can you hear me?

"I can."

The pillar of light flashed and I cringed away, shielding my eyes. *Speak not to others in my presence!* the light cried. *I am your master now!*

I inhaled deeply, mint filling my awareness and driving away the fog that I hadn't noticed clouding my thoughts. "No," I said, squaring my shoulders. "You're not my master."

You said yes. That is enough.

My stomach clenched. "No, I only said 'ye'. That's not yes."

She is right, the mint voice chimed in. *You have no claim on her.*

That is for her to decide, the pillar snapped. *Emma Tanning, do you accept my offer or do you not?*

Images flared to life around me again, bigger and brighter and stronger. I cried out as their reality overwhelmed me. My path was suddenly so clear: let go, just release my fears and worries and I could step right in to this heaven and it would be real, and true, and mine forever and ever.

I stepped forward.

Green light flickered in my parents' eyes.

My chest tightened and I reached out to them. "No," I whispered. "Please."

Cracks rippled over their skin and a minty breeze breathed in my face. *It is not real.*

I grabbed at the fragments of the images, trying desperately to hold them together, but the hairline fractures became chipped edges became chasms and the false people exploded outwards, shards of skin vanishing into the dark. "No," I sobbed. "No, please! Let it be real!"

It can never be real. It is a lie.

My chest ached, but even as I clutched at the shattered fragments of my dream life, I recognised the truth the minty voice spoke. This *wasn't* my life, it wasn't real—and any power that could make it real could only ever create an illusion. A mask on a corpse.

With tears streaming down my cheeks, I opened my hands and watched as the last of the ragged pieces fluttered away.

The pillar of light flared. *No! You will be mine!*

I screamed as fingers of light stabbed at me. "No!" I shouted. "I won't, I won't!"

The green light flared also. *Leave her be,* it said, and the black-and-grey pillar froze, shrieking. The green light inched toward it and as they met, light exploded. Screeches battered my ears and I clapped my hands over my ears.

20

WHEN THE NOISE stopped, I lifted my head to see—nothing. I was alone again, and there was nothing to do but walk.

The blackness weighed me down. Maybe I'd just been imagining things like trees, and grass, and light. Maybe I'd always been stuck in this soul-sucking darkness, and I'd simply invented other worlds for entertainment. I stopped. Was there any point continuing? Even if I *was* looking for someone called Gemma, even if she *did* exist, how was trawling through this indeterminate nothingness going to help?

A smudge of light ahead and to the right interrupted my thoughts. I swung around toward it. Someone was standing in the middle of the light, a boy with blond hair and—I looked down at my own clothes. They were hard to recognise through the dirt caked over them, but I thought perhaps that the boy's uniform matched mine.

He turned toward me and I had a flash of recognition. "Scott!"

Good. I hadn't imagined my other world after all.

"What are *you* doing here?" he said, shocked. He furrowed his brow and scowled at me. "I thought I made myself clear: *Stay. Away!* Or are you just going to haunt me forever?"

"I'm not haunting anything," I snapped. "I'm trying to find..." I hesitated, wondering if I should tell him about Gemma. "Something," I said instead.

He raised an eyebrow and looked pointedly at the darkness. "Here?"

I balled my hands into fists by my sides and lifted my chin. "This is where I saw it last." Close enough to true; I'd seen Gemma's soulprint at the edge of the shadows.

Scott's eyebrows shot up. "In the heart of the Valley?"

I squirmed. I knew this was the sinkhole, the part of the Valley that was sucking power in, but hearing Scott say it made it uncomfortably real.

Scott laughed. "You didn't realise? You walked right on in here and you didn't even realise what it was? Princess, you're so stupid you don't even know how much you don't know."

"Oh yeah?" I said, temper flaring beyond rational thought. I stepped forward. I'd had enough of all this. I ached, my head pounded, I was bone-tired and I just wanted to find Gemma and go home. "Well what are *you* doing here? Enjoying a little casual murder, Scott?"

"What did you say?" His voice was eerily calm as he matched me step for step.

"You think you're so big and powerful," I said, squeezing my nails into my palms so I wouldn't hit him. "But you're using the power of *death*, Scott. *Death.* At least what I know, I know about life."

"Sanctuary?" he sneered. "That's what you're comparing this to?" He laughed. "Sanctuary doesn't have *half* the power of the Valley, Princess. You can do things here that you couldn't even *imagine* in Sanctuary."

My stomach twisted as I realised he was probably right. "But what will you have in the end, Scott?" I said quietly, glimpsing a future devoured by the shadows. "What will be left when the Valley has it all?"

"Left? Left?" Scott laughed again. "Princess, what's *left* won't matter. Because what I will have in the end is everything." A wistful expression crossed his face, and I wondered what images the pillar of light had offered him. "Death comes for us all," he said, also quiet now. "You can't win by avoiding it."

Tears prickled my eyes. "Oh, Scott. Is that what you really believe?" I asked, overcome by pity now I saw what his exterior hid: a desperate little boy.

His face hardened. "I don't *believe*, Princess," he spat. "It's true. Embrace the power of death, and live forever." He drew something out of his pocket.

I tensed, expecting perhaps another nearly-dead mouse—and my breath caught in wonder. Sitting on his outstretched palm was a fairy, a perfect sepia replica of Quoise or Ruby or any of the others. But instead of eyes, lifeless glass gave her a glazed appearance, and as she shifted I noted a tiny key sticking out of her back. "Clockwork," I breathed.

Scott stared at her. "No," he said. "So much more." He tossed his hand upwards and I tensed, ready for the fairy to fall and smash. But instead, she shot up into the air, wings fluttering frantically until she righted herself and hovered over Scott's shoulder. He smiled—and I shied away. Hunger lit up his eyes and touched his lips; his smile was mirthless and cruel.

All of a sudden I noticed what I'd been seeing with my Road Mastery all along. Scott's soulprint was black, I'd known that, but standing here in the darkness I realised something else: his soulprint wasn't just a smudge of black in the dark. It *was* the dark. His soulprint blended seamlessly with the heart of the Valley, and I couldn't find where one ended and the other began.

The Valley didn't need me. It had Scott, and he had darkness enough to feed the Valley until it grew to consume the entire world. I stepped backwards.

Scott's lips stretched wider. "You see, then," he said. "It's not really death magic. It's just... rearranging life." Abruptly he raised his fist in the air and the fairy launched toward me on a wave of Scott's power. She pulled her lips back in a snarl, revealing vicious, pointed teeth.

I shouted and scrambled backwards, losing my footing. The fairy tucked her wings back and dove. The invisible floor sagged beneath me. My heart lurched and something snapped, cracked, and I fell.

Twist! I screamed at myself as I plummeted through a world made of ink, pursued by Scott's awful parody of life. *Twist!*

I threw myself sideways in the air, but I couldn't clear my mind enough to imagine another place. *Any place*, I told myself. *Anywhere!* But the only thing I could think of was a stretch of velvet night, studded with diamond stars. The fairy scratched at my arm, tiny slices that stung like acid.

Frantic, I twisted again—and the buzz of the fairy stopped. A heartbeat later, I slammed into the ground. My breath left me in a whoosh and I lay gasping and gaping, not even enough air to cry.

21

GRADUALLY MY HEART rate slowed and I found enough oxygen to breathe. The realisation that Scott was fuelling the shadows kept my head reeling, though. What could I do about it? I had to do *something* about it; I couldn't just leave Scott to his own devices in there with his mad, reanimated fairies and overwhelming shadow-soulprint, not if I wanted a chance of getting rid of the shadows. But Gem and Veve needed me more. I pushed myself upright, groaning at my host of new bruises. First things first. Save Gem and Veve, then worry about the fate of the world.

I stood up, dusted myself off stiffly, and stared around. Shadows licked at nearby tree trunks. I was already backing away before I realised that they washed up against the bright edge of my clearing as though there was a physical barrier.

I sagged in relief, thinking that for now, I couldn't possibly get any luckier.

Then I heard the barking.

Spinning around, I stood stunned for a moment as Veve and Gem made their way across the clearing toward me, Veve leaping forward in great bounds before realising Gem had fallen behind and racing back to round her up. Something tickled my cheek, and I realised it was tears.

Then, gasping, I was running toward them, my eyes blurry, my chest tight, but my shoulders suddenly lighter than they'd been in weeks. Veve bounced up against me, toenails scraping my legs, but I didn't care, because she was there, and so was Gem. I drew Gem into the tightest hug in the world, and she squished me back, and just for a second, everything was right.

I held her at arm's length and scrutinised every inch of her, and my stomach sank. "Are you okay?" I said, and she nodded, but wouldn't meet my eye. "What... What happened?"

She gave a half-hearted smile and shrugged. "It doesn't matter, does it? You found us." She gave me the barest flicker of a glance. "How?"

"Your soulprint," I said. "I found it right when I needed to."

No response. I bit my lip.

But before I could question her further, white and gold flashed in the light, and it smelled like I'd crushed an entire potful of mint under my feet. For the first time in weeks, maybe months, my chest wasn't tight.

"Look," I whispered, spinning Gem around.

"I know," she whispered back. "She's been looking after me."

I stood transfixed as the unicorn made her way over to us, and as she walked, my entire world was caught up in white so pale it made paper dark, gold so bright it dimmed the sun, and the faintest traces of pale green in her mane and tail that reminded me of sea foam.

At last, she stopped in front of us and dipped her head. I bobbed the most awkward curtsey in existence. "Hello," I offered.

"Well met," the unicorn replied. "You have come to take them home?"

I opened my mouth, then changed what I was going to say. "Are *you* coming home?"

Something in the unicorn's face changed—her eyes a little tighter, perhaps—as she answered, "I am bound to this place a little while longer. The balance must be kept. I thank you for pulling me out of the darkness of the Valley, but if I leave now, night will fall. You must restore the balance. But first you must take Gemma home." She turned her head to the side, gaze boring into me.

I swallowed, not sure what she was asking. It was Scott and his stupid experimenting that had put the balance out, not me. How was *I* supposed to restore it if even she couldn't?

"Alas," the unicorn continued, "I cannot come with you, but I can take you some of the way. Will you ride?"

My eyes widened. "Ride?" I breathed.

The unicorn tossed her mane. "I am more than capable of carrying you both," she said haughtily.

Gem giggled and I cut her a sharp look. "Of course you are," I said. "I just..." I floundered for a moment before regaining myself. "We would be honoured." This time I made a slight bow, and although it was hardly the most natural thing I'd ever done, it was a whole lot less awkward than the curtsey. Either way, the unicorn seemed happy with it, and turned broadside on so we could mount up.

"Um," I said, pausing with one fist wound in her mane and the other hand atop her back. "What... What should I call you?" It felt weird to be simply climbing on board a unicorn, and outright rude to do so without at least introducing myself.

"Sorry," Gem said, wincing and seeming for a moment more like her usual self. "Edge, this is Aphros, Sanctuary's unicorn. Aphros, Edge."

"Hi, Aphros," I said as Gem gave me a boost up.

"Hold tight now," Aphros said, and I just had time to wrap both hands in her mane and feel Gem's arms grip around me when she launched away like a rocket.

Before we knew it, we'd come to the base of the immense mountain and Aphros halted. "I am sorry," she said, flicking her tail. "This is as far as I may go."

We dismounted, Veve gambolling around at our feet. As Gem stepped away, I hesitated. "Please," I said. "What do you mean that the balance is out? Can I fix it?"

Aphros bumped her nose into my hand, and the darkness behind my eyes exploded into light.

Well, not all of it was light; it was a great, seething mass, bright golden light intertwined with darkness, shifting—alive. But one thing was clear: the darkness was winning.

"This is the balance," she said softly.

I nodded, lip between my teeth.

"That is why I cannot leave," she said, so soft it was hard to hear her over the crush of leaves as Veve and Gem moved. "Were I to leave this place, darkness would be free to rule. And from here, it could touch all the worlds."

I shuddered, thinking of the horrible bushes back home. "What can I do?"

"Restore the balance."

"But *how*?"

"The boy has given the Valley's power life. You must stop him. If you do not, the Valley will extract all of his life force for its own—it will be free to roam the worlds, and the boy will be dead."

I shuddered. Great. All I had to do to save the world was stop Scott. Good thing it wasn't anything too difficult.

Sweat beaded on my forehead and ran down my temples. My shirt clung to me, and I thought I might finally understand how it felt to be a fish, constantly breathing water.

Ahead, Gem slumped against a tree and groaned. "Why does it have to be so *hot*?"

I wiped the sweat from my upper lip and nodded, leaning over and resting on my knees. Beside me, Veve panted heavily, sides heaving, her tongue slopping thick, gooey saliva all over the ground. "Poor beast," I said, half-heartedly ruffling her ear.

In response, she flopped to the ground in the shade. I was so tempted to join her.

Gem bolted upright.

"What? What is it?"

Her face had gone deathly pale, and her hands fisted in the hem of her shirt. "The shadows," she said. "The shadows moved."

My stomach dropped and I stared wildly. "Where? Which ones?"

She pointed ahead, directly between us and Sanctuary. I concentrated on them, willing them to stay still just long enough for us to get home.

Nothing moved. I shook my head. "Gem, I think you're imagining things. The shadows before didn't stop and start, they just came after me. And they whispered. These shadows are quiet." I took her by the arm. "Come on. It'll be okay."

Gem yanked her arm back. "I am not going into the shadows."

I frowned at her. "Gem, these are just normal shadows, I promise. They're not going to hurt you. I should know."

"No!" Her voice was tight with barely-submerged panic. "You can't make me!"

"Gem, this is the way home. There are shadows everywhere right now," I said, gesturing to the forest around us, "and it's getting late. Which means soon there will be more shadows, and we won't be able to tell the real ones from the dangerous ones."

As if on cue, Veve leapt to her feet and barked, tail straight and stiff, the corners of her mouth and ears drawn forward.

"I can't go in there," Gem said, backing away. "I won't."

I shoved aside my own rising panic. I had to focus on getting Gem home. "Gem," I said, taking her arm gently. "The shadows in front of us are normal ones, I promise. This is the way home. It's going to be fine."

Her eyes showed far too much white and her breath came in ragged jerks, but she allowed me to pull her forward a step.

Veve growled. I turned my head just slightly, not wanting to panic Gem any further. My heart leapt. Shadows, Valley ones this time, moving slowly through the trees behind us.

"Gemma," I said in my best no-nonsense voice, "it's time to go. You mother is waiting for you, and for me, and I am taking you back there alive and unharmed. *Let's go.*"

She took another step, breath hitching, then another, until she stopped on the fringe of the shade under the trees.

"Come on," I said, ignoring Veve growling behind us and the flickering of black in the edges of my vision. "In we go." I stepped forward, expecting Gem to come with me, but instead she jerked back on my arm, her breaths getting faster and faster.

"I can't do it Edge, I can't, I'm sorry, I can't," she babbled. "He'll see me, he'll find me, he'll get me for sure. I can't go in there. I can't."

"Who?" I frowned. "Scott?"

"No, *not* Scott!" she said, voice high pitched and squeaky. "*Him!* Because he was there, in the dark, and I was lost and alone and I had no idea what had happened or where I was, and he said he'd help me, he did." Tears spilled down her cheeks and her fingers knotted in the hem of her shirt. "And the light, it was so beautiful." She gulped, and nerves zinged down my limbs and into my fingers and toes.

"Gemma," I said, very quietly, with absolute control, watching as the shadows crept into the light behind us. "Did you agree to his bargain?"

She sobbed.

"Gemma," I said more forcefully. "*Did you agree?*"

"Yes."

I reeled like I'd been punched into the ocean, and there were no words I could find to drag me back to the surface. A bubble of anger rose, and I clung to it like a life raft until I could see Gemma sobbing in front of me again. "How could you?" I whispered—but I knew how. I'd so very nearly done the same thing, and I wasn't really angry at Gem, but at myself for nearly being caught by the shadows.

Shadows.

Veve wasn't barking.

I turned slowly, fear a molten ball in my stomach. Veve stood frozen, ringed by shadows that shifted and melted a foot away from her. Her eyes rolled as she tried to keep them in sight, but she seemed to know that she shouldn't move. "You'll have to jump," I said quietly. "Come on, girl. Jump over this way."

Gem turned beside me and inhaled sharply. "Veve!"

If she hadn't stopped to panic, Veve might not be trapped right now; but on the other hand it was nice to know that she cared about my dog. And seeing Veve stuck seemed to galvanise her; she straightened her shoulders and frowned in her classic thinking face. "We have to distract them so Veve can jump out," she said.

My heart pounded. Distract them. I knew what she meant, of course: one of us needed to touch the shadows, draw them away. And Gemma had said yes to the Valley.

"I'll go," she said, jaw set. "The Valley's already got me anyway, so it shouldn't want to hurt me."

"Don't be ridiculous." I pushed her gently out of the way. "I've beaten them before, I can do it again. Also," I said, indicating the unicorn hair ward. I gave a stretched smile. "I'll be fine."

I edged toward the shadows. "As soon as I touch them, reach over and grab Veve's collar," I said. "Then run like the blazes. Sanctuary's that way."

"I know where Sanctuary is," Gemma said, and her eyes sparkled with unshed tears. "Thank you."

"Heh," I said. "Don't thank me. There are still the zombie trees to fight through."

Half a smile. "It's going to be okay."

She *had* to say that. My control slipped a little, and I took a deep breath. "Sure. Ready?"

She nodded.

I stepped to the edge of the shadows and fighting against all my instincts, dipped my toes in. Cold dread washed over me.

"So sweet, so sweet your life."

I pulled back, but the shadows followed, swirling and massing. Out of the corner of my eye I saw Gemma snatch at Veve and dash back.

"We're clear!" she said. "Veve's okay."

The shadows wound around my ankle. *"Hold you, touch you, so warm, so alive."*

I tried to kick free, but they clung tighter, inching their way toward my knee. I fought down the panic that threatened to suffocate me. "I'm stuck," I shouted. "Just take Veve and go!"

"No! I'm not leaving you here!"

"Want your life, so sweet."

I twisted around and glared as Gem set Veve down and ran toward me. "Go away! I'll be fine!"

Veve barked ferociously.

"...sweet, welcome home..."

"No." Gem caught my arm and pulled.

I slipped and fell. Shadows leapt up to my waist and spread down my other leg.

"Home, coming home, coming to us, touching us, life, we want your life."

Gem heaved again, but the shadows stretched with me, only a few strands snapping back like over-taxed rubber bands.

"Come, come home."

Cold.

Everything from my waist down was cold, and it was slowly rising, like stepping into a pool in the middle of summer—only this time I knew there'd be no resurfacing.

"...want your life, life so sweet..."

"Emma, your ankle!" Gem shouted.

I looked down. The unicorn ward! Around it, my ankle was free of shadows. Tears sprang up. "I don't know what to do!"

"*I* don't know!" Gem said, still holding me tightly under my arms. "But if you could get the ward to cover all of you..." She pressed her forehead against mine, upside-down, and it was sweaty and cool. "Please don't die."

The shadows climbed. *"Liiiife. So sweet... Come home, sweet home, sweet life."*

The cold made it hard to breathe; I took short, shallow gasps. How on earth was I supposed to extend the ward? I closed my eyes, fighting to clear my mind—and saw the minty-green wreath around my ankle. The unicorn's soulprint. That's how it protected against the shadows.

Instinctively I reached out to the ward's glow, both with my mind and my fingers.

"What are you doing?" Gemma shrieked, but even as the shadows closed around my hand, I shook my head. This was the only way.

"Home! Come home, come life!"

The shadows, sensing victory, leapt up my arm.

Gem sprang away. Good. I couldn't rescue both of us.

I touched the ward, and in my mind's eye I saw a flash of silver. I got a strange sense of being outside my own body and caught glimpses of silver and lace, and the soft smell of old, faded roses. Nausea welled in my gut, like I'd just seen my own insides plastered on the ground.

I forced myself to concentrate. With my fingers as the bridge, I trickled some of my own soulprint out to meet the greenness of the ward. Another flash of silver lit up the space behind my eyes and the greenness billowed and blossomed.

The shadows screeched, a noise almost too high to be heard that made all my hair stand on end. I fed a little more of my soulprint into the unicorn ward, and the green bloomed out around me. The shadows shrieked and jerked back as though stung.

I lay still for a moment, panting and wide-eyed as I waited for the writhing shadows to grab me again.

Gem snatched at me from behind and dragged me to my feet. "Come on!" she said. "Run!"

We took off through the trees. I stumbled and slid, but Gem hauled me upright. Veve bounded along in front. The trees roared as we ran under them. They grabbed at us, branches tangling in our hair, our clothes. Scratches stung my skin and my chest burned from the cold of the shadows; panic chased us like a sheepdog, nipping at our heels.

Veve yelped and fell. Gem jerked away and back again in an instant, Veve's collar firmly in her grip.

Trees whipped and slashed. Blood ran into my eye from a cut on my forehead; soon I'd have no skin left. I'd fall to the ground any second and not be able to get up, and the shadows would find me there and devour me.

Veve yipped and rocketed out of Gemma's grip. Gasping, I lifted my head and saw green.

The border.

I stumbled; Gem righted me. She tripped; I caught her. Together, lungs burning and hearts exploding, we pounded toward the greenery.

Clean air fizzled over us. Branches no longer reached for us; twigs didn't catch in our skin and clothes. We looked at each other, gasping. Something burned my ankle and I jumped. The ward. I reached to touch it and it crumbled to ash, leaving behind the acrid smell of burning mint. "We made it," I said and sank to the ground.

Gemma collapsed beside me. "We made it."

22

UNLIKE THE LAST time I fell out of the Valley and back into Sanctuary, no one was waiting to soothe our hurts. Probably, I told myself as we limped toward the passageway, that was a good thing; it certainly seemed like the fairies would be mad if they found out we'd been into the Valley again. Maybe even mad enough to ban us from Sanctuary. But that didn't stop me wishing for something to ease the hundred million pains that had taken up residence in my body.

"I'm sorry," Gem said as we squeezed into the passage, Veve limping along behind.

I hugged her with one arm. "Rubbish. We got out, didn't we? Oops," I added as we half collided. The floor of the passage slopped gently, but it was enough to make us both unsteady.

"Yeah," Gem breathed. "I guess."

I didn't have the energy to reassure her any further. I knew she was probably thinking about that pillar of light—it seemed to lurk in the edges of my vision, reminding me of the life I could have had—but there was nothing we could do about what had happened. I just wished we knew what would happen now that Gem technically belonged to the Valley.

We emerged into the main hall of the lodge, and almost immediately Quoise appeared in front of us.

"You're alive," she whispered, glancing furtively behind her. "Come on, follow me. Quickly."

Gem and I exchanged glances and followed.

Veve whined.

"Aw, come on, girl," I said, summoning up the energy to ruffle her ears. "We're nearly there, I promise."

Quoise led us to a small room with nothing but a couple of couches and another door. "Stay here as long as you need," she said, and began to leave.

"Wait," I said. "The unicorn. Aphros."

Quoise stiffened to attention. "What about her?"

"She's in the Valley," I said. "She helped Gem and Veve."

"Is she trapped?" The sharp concern in Quoise's voice could have sliced steel.

"No." I shook my head. "At least, I don't think so. Not anymore." Visions of tearing green-and-gold away from black during my first visit to the Valley flashed through my head. "But she said that she can't leave, because if she does, the balance will be out, and the Valley will devour Scott and take over the world."

Quoise nodded curtly. "Thank you. Now." She wagged a finger at me. "I don't want you getting it into your head that you need to go running over to deal with that, okay? The fairies can handle it just fine. Just let us do our jobs."

"I promise," I said, not bothering to add that the Valley was the very last place I ever planned on going again.

Quoise left, closing the door behind her, and Gem flopped on the nearest couch. "Scott's involved?" she mumbled into a pillow.

"Yes," I said, heading to the other door. "I'll tell you later. Bathroom!" I exclaimed with delight as I opened the door. "*Shower!*"

"You first," Gem said, arm over her eyes, free hand resting on Veve's head. "I'm just going to lie here for a couple of years."

I flashed a smile and closed myself in the bathroom. I stripped off, turned the water on as hard as it would go, and sighed. It was over.

Well, Captain Moron, Chief Officer of All Things Stupid, Destroyer of My Life *Scott* was still roaming around creating chaos, but still. For *now* it was over. And really, I was done being responsible. For all that Quoise thought she needed to warn us away, I was more than happy to let someone else deal with Scott. I'd only just turned thirteen, for crying out loud. Adults had to be good for *something*.

At first the hot water stung my cuts like acid, but I ground my teeth and the pain eased away. I leaned my head against the cool glass and rested.

The water was going cold and my fingers wrinkly by the time I turned the shower off. Voices murmured through the bathroom door—probably Gem and Quoise. I towelled off, then snagged a dry towel from the large stack and wrapped it around me. Hopefully Gem wouldn't kill me for running the water out.

I opened the door, wondering if Quoise would be able to rustle up some clean clothes, and froze. There was a plate half-full of grapes and orange wedges and bread on the table, and Veve was curled up in a tight ball in an arm chair next to a gleamingly-empty silver bowl—but the most startling change to the room was that Mrs Caro sat on one of the couches, Gem snuggled against her side, tear-tracks down both of their faces.

"Um. I'm sorry," I said, and began shutting myself back in the bathroom.

"Edge!" Gem called, right as her mother said, "Emma! Thank you!"

I paused with the door half-closed and leaned against it, not sure if I wanted to go out or stay hidden where I was.

"Em?" Gemma called. "Come on, it's just Mum."

I sighed explosively and went out to perch on the edge of the other couch, clutching my towel. "My clothes are gross," I said by way of explanation.

"It's fine." Mrs Caro gave Gem another squeeze, filthy attire and all.

"Maybe," I agreed. "But only if Mum doesn't kill me for ruining my school uniform." Gem's gaze met mine, and without warning we laughed.

Mrs Caro stared at us for a moment, then joined in. "Oh girls," she said, wiping tears away. "I'm so sorry. And I'm so, so grateful that you made it back alive." She squeezed Gem to her with one arm, and my stomach flip-flopped. When I got home, there would be no celebrations. Well, I'm sure Mum would be pleased Veve was back, but it sucked that I'd just about been to hell and back and couldn't even get a 'well done' from my parents, because they couldn't know about it.

Mrs Caro stood. "Well. I may be a Time Master and all, but if we don't head off very soon, I won't be able to get you back on time, Edge. Gemma," she said, helping Gem up off the couch, "I know you must be desperate to get clean, but can you hold on just until we get home?"

Gem nodded and leaned her head against her mum's shoulder.

"I ran the water out anyway," I confessed.

Gem gave me a mock glare. "Thanks."

Mrs Caro clapped her hands together decisively. "Right then. Edge, there are clean clothes over there. Get dressed and we'll all head home."

Bed, I thought longingly as I scooped up the clothing and headed back into the bathroom. Home.

Mrs Caro dropped me off at half past four, and I went straight to bed. Mum woke me up when she got home and asked if I was okay. I told her I'd gone to sickbay and Mrs Caro had brought me home, since she'd been in at the school anyway.

"Why didn't you call me?" Mum asked.

"Because Mrs Caro was right there," I said. "I promise I'll call you next time, okay?" I squeezed her hand and she squeezed back.

"Okay," she said. "Make sure you do." She fussed, plumping my pillows and smoothing my hair. "Are you going to stay home tomorrow?"

I closed my eyes, imagining how lovely it would be to spend the entire day asleep. I sighed, and shook my head. "No. I have to hand in my art homework."

Mum smiled. "That's very responsible of you."

"You have no idea," I might have said, but she was leaving already and my eyes were closed anyway, and within three seconds I was asleep.

23

I TRUDGED INTO school with two minutes to spare the next morning. Thankfully Mum had offered to give me a lift so I didn't have to get up early for the bus, so I'd managed an even twelve hours of sleep. Shame I still didn't feel much better.

I wondered if Mrs Caro had given Gem a lift this morning, or if battling shadows in fairyland was just par for the course when you were a family of Travellers. I could just imagine the conversation: You fought off soul-sucking shadows? How lovely. Make sure you wash the blood out of your shirt, and don't expect to take a day off school! I snickered as I walked into the building.

"What's so funny, Princess?"

I jumped. For a fraction of a second I hesitated with my lip in my teeth. Then I narrowed my eyes at Scott. "What? No backup this time?"

He lounged against the lockers like he owned the whole freaking world—which, judging by the shadows pooling around his feet, he soon might—and smiled like the cat who got the proverbial cream. "Why? Do I need some?" He quirked an eyebrow at me in a manner that might have been flirty on anyone else.

I ignored him and tried to move past.

Of course, he stepped into my way with his arms folded over his chest. "So. What's so funny?"

I sidestepped him and stalked through the swelling sea of kids, but he trailed behind.

"Finally figured out how pathetic that little play land of yours is?" he jeered. "That what you're laughing at?"

I stopped short and Scott ran into me. Ha. Take that, Mr Smarty Pants. I swivelled to face him. "Number one," I said, counting off on my fingers. "What I find funny is none of your business. Number two, I will never, *ever* stop for you again, understand? And number three, my name is Emma. Not 'the Princess', not 'hey there'; *Emma*. And number four?" I stepped nose to nose with him, grateful not for the first time that I was a little tall for my age. "Never bring your stinking, filthy death magic near me again."

"Oh yeah?" Scott yelled as I spun away. "Well number five: I hate you! I've always hated you, and anyone who says different is a liar!"

I gave him sarcastic jazz hands over my shoulder, then glanced left as Gemma bumped into place. "Hey."

"Hey. What's up?"

"Scott's up. As usual."

She glanced back to where he still stood watching us, and her eyes widened. "Whoa," she said. "He's *hot*."

I raised my eyebrows in the most sceptical face I'd ever had reason to pull. "You're joking, right?"

"No! He totally is!"

I rolled my eyes and dragged her onwards. "I think the Valley addled your brains. Come on." My stomach lurched, but I managed to keep my face blank. If Gem guessed what I was thinking, she'd panic, because what I was thinking was this: She'd agreed to the light's bargain. What if it really *had* messed with her head?

"But seriously!" she said, resisting my efforts to herd her down the hall. "Something about him is different. I... I don't know." She shrugged.

I stopped and took a good long look at Scott, who had finally given up on staring at us and was heading off in the opposite direction. Gemma was right. Something *was* different. Without my Road Mastery, seeing what Gemma would see, he exuded cool confidence. No, not just confidence. Power, raw and effortless. I could see how that might be attractive, especially on someone like Scott, who was admittedly easy on the eyes. But with my Road Mastery open, I could see the truth: the power wasn't his. It was the Valley's. Scott himself was almost gone.

I shook my head. "That's not the kind of gorgeous you want, trust me." This time, Gem let me lead her away.

Roll call passed uneventfully. Science was first up after that, and the class milled around outside, waiting for our pre-test. Most people whispered furiously about possible questions, or muttered parts of the periodic table under their breaths. Even if I hadn't been wound up from spending yesterday in the Valley, the nerves jangling around the hallway would have had me jittering.

I felt like shouting at the class. It was only a pre-test, for crying out loud. It counted for nothing!

By the time Mrs Johnston opened the door, I felt sick. We filtered into the room in silence and took up our usual seats. For me, that meant Gemma on one side and Scott on the other—but for the first time ever, Death-boy didn't even glance at me as he sat down. I was glad, but it still felt weird.

Mrs Johnston told us to open our tests, and I shoved aside thoughts of Scott and Sanctuary and the Valley, and concentrated on the questions in front of me.

As I skimmed the first page, I was immensely grateful that Anna had used me as a revision partner (ha, more like a revision *wall*) for the last few years. This stuff was easy.

Twenty minutes in, Scott raised his hand. Mrs Johnston walked over, and a few seconds later he was scraping his chair back and leaving the room.

I bit my lip. I mean sure, he *might* just have needed the bathroom, but this was Scott we were talking about—and to be honest, right now I wasn't even sure that it *was* Scott. His soulprint was so damaged it could easily be the Valley acting through him instead.

Finish the test, not follow Scott to the Valley, and hope that the fairies caught him before it was too late... Or ditch the test and head back into my worst nightmare on the off chance I could save Scott from the Valley, and the world from Scott?

I heaved a sigh and stuck my hand in the air. Mrs Johnston acknowledged me disapprovingly, but came over. "Yes?"

"May I go to the bathroom?" I whispered in my best 'I'm-so-innocent voice'. "I'm nearly finished."

She glanced at the paper and her eyebrows lifted. "Looks good. Yes, okay, you can go. But be quick. And quiet!"

I snuck out of the classroom and paused in the hallway, closing my eyes to fix on Scott's dark soulprint. Sure enough, he was nowhere near the bathrooms, heading instead to the strip of bush at the back of the school.

I sprinted down the stairs and along the side of the buildings. Whatever else happened, I had to try to stop him crossing; with so much of the Valley's power in him, even that might be enough to drag him under forever. Much as he was an unbearable git, I'd meant what I'd said to Gemma on Monday: no one deserved the shadows. And if Aphros was right, we couldn't afford for the Valley to have him.

Leaving the school buildings behind, I hurried across dry grass to the scruffy gum trees at the back of the school block. White shirt flashed through the trees and I headed toward it.

Scott was concentrating so hard, he didn't even hear me approach; he sat cross-legged in the dirt with his eyes closed, darkness swirling around him. It billowed and spiralled—the Valley was calling to him, or he to it. Either way, the crossing would be over in an instant, and if his soulprint was anything to go by, so would his life.

This was it. I had to stop him.

24

I LAUNCHED INTO a sprint, adrenalin surging. He raised his hands, still oblivious. I slammed into him, wrapping my arms around him and knocking him flat. Sitting on his chest, I did my best to pin his arms the way I'd seen in movies.

Scott lay dazed for a moment, then blinked up at me, slow grin spreading over his face. "Well. This is nice, then."

My impulse was to jerk away, but if I did that he'd be free again. Urgh. I shoved aside my disgust and squeezed his arms tighter. "I thought you hated me now, Mr Smarty Pants."

He sighed, and all of a sudden seemed old. "Emma, let me go."

"No."

He shifted underneath me, ribs rubbing against the insides of my thighs, which catapulted the moment straight to the top of my most awkward moments of my entire life. "You can't stop me, you know," he said, interrupting my conniptions. "Not with this much of the Valley running through me."

I gasped. "You know!"

He frowned. "Of course I know. How would I not know?"

I didn't answer. It was stupid, of course, but a tiny part of me had hoped that maybe it hadn't been his fault, that maybe the Valley had seduced him and taken up residence without his permission. But I'd been into the heart of the Valley, and I'd seen the pillar of light. There couldn't be any doubt: Scott had made a deal with the darkness.

A shout. I swung around to see Gem bursting through the trees. The world pitched sideways, my face slammed into the dirt, and the fetid stink of the Valley overtook my senses.

"Edge!" Gem hauled me to my feet and dusted me off.

"Where's Scott?" I looked around.

"Gone." Gem bit her lip. "Are... are you okay?"

I ground my teeth and bit back a retort. She was only trying to help. "I'm fine. Let me go, I can stand. I'm fine!" I pushed her away and bent double, running my fingers through the grass. Of all the times to have not had my seeds in my pocket.

"Have you got any seeds?" I asked Gem. I froze. No. Seeds would be too slow.

Her face fell. "No. They're in my bag."

I exhaled, straightening casually. "Yeah, mine too. Can you go grab some?"

Gem stiffened, hands fisting at her sides as she scrutinised me. "No," she said at length.

I tried not to let my irritation show. "Please?" With Scott that full of the Valley's power, every split second counted. There was no way I had time to go into Sanctuary and run all the way into the Valley, and I'd be frogged if I'd let Gemma see what I was planning to do next.

After all, it was just death, right? Like the life magic, I guessed there was no minimum threshold for *how much* death. Gemma had said once that you couldn't offer just a little death, but what if you could? I needed her out of the way so I could test out my theory. If it didn't work and we had to go the long way around, we really might as well give up now.

"No." Gem crossed her arms. "Because as soon as I'm out of sight, you're going to try something, and I'm not having you go without me."

"Gemma, just go away," I snapped. Death magic. The very thought of it made me shudder. I *couldn't* let my best friend see me use it.

"Edge." Her voice trembled, though she tried to hide it, and out of the corner of my eye I saw her swipe at her cheeks. "If you tell me again that you don't want me to come with you, then I won't. But I thought we were friends. And friends don't tell each other to get out when they need help most."

My chest ached. She had no idea what she was asking. I shook my head and raised the other thing worrying me instead. "You agreed to the Valley's bargain, Gemma. Have you stopped to think that maybe, just maybe, that's how Scott got into this whole mess in the first place? That maybe, now that the Valley has him, it will want you too?"

She grabbed me by the shoulders. "But don't you see? That's *why* I have to come. It will think I'm coming back to it, and it will *help me.* Otherwise how would it ever be able to get ahold of me, if it killed me as soon as I went back? It... It would be like a virus that was too strong and killed its host before it could infect a new one and then died too." She looked proud and defiant at that.

I hesitated. Surely Scott hadn't been corrupted in just two short visits to the Valley. Maybe there was something to Gem's logic. But there was still the matter of the death magic. "Gem," I said softly, all too aware of the time slipping away. "We can't cross to Sanctuary. By the time we did that and then got to Scott in the Valley, it would be too late."

She paled. "What..." Her tongue darted out to moisten her lips. "What are you saying?"

Hands clenched, I looked her in the eye. "I'm saying I need to use death magic to put me straight over to where Scott is."

Gem squeaked and her hand flew to her mouth.

"Please don't stay," I said, lowering my gaze to the ground. "I don't want you to think less of me than you already do." I turned around and waited for the sound of footsteps in the grass.

Two steps, three, four... Then a hand on my shoulder. "Edge," she whispered, then again louder, "Edge. I don't think less of you. I think you're awfully brave. I wish I was half as brave as you."

My throat constricted, but I still didn't turn.

"And I think that you'll have to try a lot harder than that if you don't want me to come with you."

I gave up and turned, searching her eyes for any hint of loathing or falseness. "Really?"

She wound her arm through mine. "Of course."

I could have said more. I could have told her that I didn't *want* her to come with me; that it would be all right; that I didn't need help and I knew what I was doing. All of that could have kept her safe, but it would have been lies. So I said nothing. I just wrapped my arms around her and hugged.

25

"SO, HOW IS this going to work then?" Gem asked, and to her credit she barely sounded nervous at all.

I, on the other hand, had to clear my throat twice before I could get words out. "Um, well, the theory is that you need to offer a sacrifice, right?" Despite the time pressing down on us, I didn't want to rush the explanation. Gem might just spot a flaw I hadn't thought of that could kill us.

She nodded.

"And it's life or death, and usually seeds or small animals."

"Yes." She nodded again.

"So I thought..." I cleared my throat. "I thought that I could probably use myself."

Gem squeaked, but I held up a hand to stop her. "Look, we're in a huge hurry here, okay. Either this is going to work and we have a shot at stopping Scott, who is by now at least"—I checked the watch I was wearing while my phone was still in its rice bath—"six minutes ahead of us. Six minutes is an awfully long time when you're as close to going under as he is. He might be gone already. But either this works, and we can try to stop him, or it doesn't work, and I promise you, I will go to Sanctuary the proper way and let the fairies deal with the fallout." I drew an X over my chest. "Cross my heart."

"Or it doesn't work and we die."

I rolled my eyes. "Thank you. I totally hadn't considered that possibility."

Gem sighed reluctantly. "Okay, fine. But... sacrifice yourself? You're not... you're not planning to kill yourself, are you?"

I started. "What? No! Why would you...?" I gave my head a shake to purge the thought. "Never mind. No. Look, the way I see it, it doesn't need to be a complete death in order to work. After all, we're making the seeds grow, but not to full height instantly. There's an initial spurt of growth that provides the power. So it's probably the same with death. There's an initial power surge in the process, and then the power ratio tapers away. Right?"

Gem gave me dubious puppy eyes. "How do you start to die and yet not?"

"Blood," I said simply. I took her hand. "Are you ready?"

She nodded, keeping her distance.

"Good. Hold onto my arm." I drew her close and tucked her hand into the crook of my elbow.

Positioning the sharp rock I'd found in the dirt over the back of one hand, I glanced at her. She stared at the rock, transfixed and pale-faced. "Probably best if you close your eyes," I said. "And if this is anything like the time Scott transported me, it will hurt."

Her jaw tensed, but she closed her eyes.

"Good." I closed mine too and imagined where I wanted to be: in the Valley, right near the sinkhole. Jumping straight into it was an experience I didn't care to repeat, but I'd bet anything in the world that that was where Scott had gone.

I held my breath and tore the rock across my skin. *Ow.* Blood welled, then dripped. I shook my hand gently and blood fell to the ground. I concentrated on the Valley.

For a heartbeat I thought it hadn't worked, then, once again, the world disappeared in mind-bending agony as fire ran through my veins.

Gem stood over me and brushed off her school skirt, the movement making her swirl in a field of bright, swooping lights.

"Well," she said as I clutched at my temples and groaned. "That wasn't as bad as I expected. I'd like to be mad at you for even *thinking* about trying it, but," she looked around, "we're here. So I suppose it's okay." She held out three hands.

I blinked. Two hands. Three. Four. One. Seven? "How many hands do you have?" My voice came out groggy.

Gem knelt in front of me and peered into my eyes. "Oh my gosh. I *knew* it was too good to be true. Are you okay?"

I blinked rapidly, trying to clear the doubles and triples from my vision. "Maybe?" I slurred. "Feel... funny." Without warning I toppled over backwards. I lay still, staring up at the sky, trying to orient myself. Surely the ground wasn't supposed to be whirling underneath me.

Gem exhaled in frustration. "We can't go on like this, Emma. I *knew* this was too dangerous." She tugged on her hair.

"No," I said from my position flat on the ground. "I'm fine. Gimme a second."

Gem's face clouded. She reached out and squeezed my hand. "Hurry."

Nerves squeezed my insides. Scott was probably gone by now, if not completely then at least irreparably. The fairies wouldn't be able to do anything but damage control, and considering they hadn't even been able to stop the shadows from spawning in the first place, I doubted there was much they could do to stop them spreading over Sanctuary, Earth, and wherever else it was that Sanctuary could take them.

I sat unsteadily. "Look, see. Sitting. Ta da!"

Gem snorted. "Hilarious. Are you sure you're okay? We don't have to go, you know."

I crouched awkwardly, head hanging. "Yeah, we kind of do."

Gem nodded and helped me up. "I know. I was just trying to make you feel better."

"I'm good," I said. I wobbled a little as I gained uprightness, but I ignored my whirling head and gave Gem the cheesiest grin I could manage. "See?"

She sighed. "I'm going to ignore the fact that you're about to fall over and just agree, because I know you won't stay here even if I tell you to. So let's go." She began walking, heading straight for the Valley's sinkhole.

"Wait," I said, skipping a couple of steps to catch up and nearly falling onto her shoulder. "How did you know which way to go?"

She did sarcastic jazz hands around her head. "Valley girl, remember?"

I snorted. "Funny."

"I try."

I bumped her hip—or tried to; it turned into more of a stumble. "It's going to be okay," I said. "I mean, maybe not the Scott thing. He could be..." I stopped, unable to voice it aloud. "But anyway, I mean you. The Valley. After this, we'll never have to come here again, and you'll be just fine."

"Assuming the shadows don't take over Earth too, you mean." She shot me a tight smile. "Thanks for trying."

"It's true, Gem," I said. "You're my best friend. I won't let anything happen to you. I promise."

26

MY HEAD CLEARED as we walked, and a minute later we stopped in a fringe of trees, staring down at the sinkhole. It was definitely bigger than before, taking up most of the treeless valley, a swirling mass of dense darkness.

Gemma rubbed at her arms. "That's it?"

I glanced at her. "Yes. Didn't you see it the last time?"

She shook her head. "I don't remember. I don't remember anything except the light, and then I was with Aphros."

I wrinkled my brow. "Yeah, how did she do that, by the way? Did you ever ask her?"

Gem shuddered. "It was..." She licked her lips. "It was because I approached the light. It's the Valley itself, its thoughts and mind, whatever, and because she's both life and death, she can talk to people when they're right in the heart of either Sanctuary or the Valley—or when she is, I guess." She glanced sideways at me. "She must have been in the sinkhole when she grabbed you and dragged you over that first time."

I nodded, remembering how I'd torn her out of it without knowing what I was doing. I shivered as I remembered her voice cutting off, and her frantic command to flee.

"Anyway," Gem continued. "She told me to come with her, but I didn't listen. The light... It showed me things, Edge." She turned to me, eyes wide and pleading. "I saw... what it would be like if..." She swallowed, and I could tell she was fighting a break down.

I hugged her. "Hey, it's okay. I don't need to know what you saw. It showed me things too." I cleared my throat as I recalled the perfect life it had offered. "I just wanted to know what Aphros did."

She drew back and wiped her tears, drawing in a great, shuddery breath. "After I'd said yes to the light, it tried to"—she waved her hands in front of her—"I don't know, absorb me, or something. But Aphros's pillar of light got there first, and it covered me, and I felt like, like, I don't know, like cold was burning through me, but it was refreshing, not painful. And then it stopped, and I was with her."

"Okay," I said. "Let me think a minute before we go in." I chewed on my lip, trying to puzzle it out.

Point one, the pillars of light were soulprints, I was sure of that. I'd seen them too when I'd been in the sinkhole, and they'd set my Road Mastery blaring. And for Gemma to be able to see them without Road Mastery, they had to be strong, really, really strong.

Point two, the unicorn's soulprint could manifest like that in the heart of the Valley, and presumably in the heart of Sanctuary too, if Sanctuary had one, because she was made from life and death magic. So non-magical beings wouldn't have their soulprint show up like that, probably. Interesting.

Point three, Gem had agreed to the light's bargain, and it tried to consume her. Scott had agreed to the bargain too, I was assuming, and now his soulprint was tainted by the Valley's. Had the light tried to swallow him up as well? Was that how he'd been entangled? If so, it meant that while Gem belonged to the Valley (because she'd agreed to its bargain), she also belonged to the unicorn, because Aphros had absorbed Gem into her own soulprint. That definitely bore thinking about. It also meant that her soulprint might become tainted by the Valley's, but that was a problem for later.

I stared at her with my Road Mastery and caught a tiny whiff of mint. "Gem, where's Aphros?" I asked casually.

"Over there," she replied immediately, pointing. "Why's that?"

I shook my head. Interesting. So Gemma was bonded to the Valley, *and* to the unicorn. All we needed to do was bind her to Sanctuary as well, and she'd have the complete set. Ha.

I rubbed my face. My brain was about to start leaking out my ears. So Gemma could sense the unicorn. The unicorn had to stay in the Valley because if she left, there'd be nothing to keep the darkness in check. Which meant the unicorn had some way of keeping it in check. But she needed me—or someone else, anyway—to deal with Scott, because if the Valley got Scott, she wouldn't be able to help.

I really needed to find Scott.

"So what are you thinking?" Gem said at last.

I laid it out for her, including the bit about her being somehow bound to the unicorn, just as Scott was to the Valley.

She blinked at that. "So, what? Aphros will gradually start taking over my body?"

I shook my head. "No. I think the Valley is only doing that to Scott because it doesn't have a body of its own, and it wants one. Aphros... I have no idea. You can tell me where she is without thinking, so there's that, and when I look closely at you I can see traces of her on you. They're faint, not like with the Valley on Scott. He must have been coming here for quite a while to get that entangled. Or maybe it's because the Valley wants his body. I don't know," I concluded. "I'm not sure what it will do. But..." I hesitated, knowing she wasn't going to like this bit.

"What?"

"I don't think it's safe for you to come into the sinkhole," I said in a rush. "I know you said it might be fine, and the Valley might not hurt you because it has some kind of connection with you, but that's part of the point; the longer you spend in there, the stronger that connection will get." I searched her face. "I don't want to lose the best friend I ever had now I've found her again."

Gem crushed me in a hug. "You idiot. You're my best friend too." She took a deep breath. "Okay."

I blinked. "Okay? Okay as in you won't come in with me?"

She rubbed her arms. "I won't pretend I don't want to. I don't think it will hurt me, like I said before. But for one, I trust you and your Road Mastery. And for two..." Her eyes became haunted, and when she continued her voice was hoarse. "I *want* to come in with you. Badly." She hugged herself and goosebumps broke out on her skin. "And if I want this badly to head into the middle of an evil sinkhole of power... Edge, I don't think it's me doing the wanting."

I wrapped my arms around her. "Oh Gem," I whispered into her hair.

We broke apart, both with tears in our eyes, but this time her voice was steady. "And anyway. Someone has to stick around to tell Sanctuary what happened if it all... You know."

I nodded. "You're the best, Gem."
She tried a smile. "You too. Be careful."
"Promise," I said. "I'll be right back."

27

INSIDE THE SINKHOLE, I looked around, both with my eyes and my Road Mastery. Black everywhere. Sighing, I picked a random direction and walked. Forever later, the scenery changed: a tiny, fleeting flicker of darkness emptier than the rest, howling like wind over bare hilltops. Scott. I altered my course a little to the right and crept toward him. Nerves jangled in my stomach and I eased my feet down. I doubted very much that he was a Road Master, and there was no way he could see me in this darkness, but a stray rustle of my uniform could easily give me away.

I smoothed my hands down my skirt. Frogging elephants. In my school uniform *again*? That was just asking for a grounding, since the one I'd been wearing last time didn't even make it back home—the fairies had burned it as contaminated.

I inched closer—and there was Scott. Around him the darkness had lifted a little, but where it had gone from the air, it had gathered in his eyes, pupils dilating to fill his entire eye space—or else the iris and the whites had turned black. Either way, the effect was horrific. I shuddered.

He turned to me, jet-black orbs piercing and terrifying. "You found me."

I forced my hands to unclench. "Yes."

"Please," he said, smile lean and hungry. "Take a seat." A stool appeared at his gesture, metallic and glimmering, slightly too perfect to be real.

"No thanks." I folded my arms over my chest to stop them trembling.

"Oh, come now, Emma Tanning. You are visiting my home. At least allow me to be hospitable."

Chills ran down my neck. Scott didn't talk like that, and he didn't call me by my full name. I sat, unwilling to anger the Valley's sentient power as it spoke through a boy I'd once known.

My heart pounded. I was too late.

Scott was gone, and now I'd have to fight the power of the Valley itself if I ever wanted to get out of here alive. I closed my eyes—and the wind swept toward me over mountaintops.

It was faint, but there was no mistaking Scott's soulprint. Surely he had to be in there somewhere if I could still sense that.

"There. Isn't that better?"

I nodded.

"Lovely." Scott sat on a matching stool that appeared under him right as he landed on it. "So. I'd like to have a talk with you, if I may."

If I may? Seriously? And it didn't think I'd notice that it wasn't Scott talking? Then again, maybe it didn't care. My fingers twitched. "Sure."

He leaned back, crossing his ankles. "What do you know about the shadows?"

My eyebrows lifted. "The shadows?" Not the first thing I thought it would ask, that's for sure. "Um, they're a product of death magic, something to do with the Valley's power. They're leaking over at the crossing points between worlds, and things are being snatched into them." Including Gemma. And Veve. More chills chased down my spine.

"Half right," Scott's body replied. "They are indeed a product of 'death magic', as you so belittlingly call it, and I see how you might call it leaking. Things are not, however, being snatched. They were called, by me as I tested the limits of my newfound power and sought to expand them."

I stiffened and my hands fisted. "Called? How about stolen? Kidnapped, even. I'm pretty sure Gemma didn't hear your voice and come running."

The Valley-Scott laughed. "Ah, my ignorant Princess."

Ice spiked through my veins. How dare it use that name? How *dare* it!

"All you know about death magic, you have been told from liars. Tell me, what do you think of death magic, Emma Tanning?

Tell me truly, now that you have felt its power yourself."

My throat went dry. "I haven't…" I stammered. "I mean I…" I scrubbed my hands on my skirt, leaving trails of sweat.

Valley-Scott laughed again. "You see? I know everything. I even know where your friends are—the annoying green one, who I will soon be able to destroy once and for all, and the one like the night sky who forsook you."

I half stood before I remembered that attacking the heart of the Valley outright might not be such a good plan. "*She did not forsake me.*" My fingernails bit into my palms. "You *tricked* her."

He scoffed. "I tricked no one. I made the terms of my bargain clear."

"Oh? Like you made them clear for me? Here, Emma, have all this power and you can protect your family; here, Emma, create a perfect life for yourself using death; oh, but Emma, I won't tell you that I'll *devour your soul* if you do." I glared at him. "Seriously?"

Valley-Scott narrowed his eyes at me. "You tread close to danger, girl."

"Really? And here I thought this was a picnic."

"Enough!" Valley-Scott stood up, black eyes gleaming. "You have been told my magic is filth, that it corrupts your soul and destroys the balance. But it was the fairies that told you this, and they are creatures of Sanctuary. Not one of them has ever set foot in the Valley, because if they did, they would cease to exist." He loomed over me. "And yet you would trust their opinion on the sacrifice?"

I opened my mouth to retort that yes, actually, I did—only he had a point. The fairies were suspiciously close-mouthed about a lot of things, come to think of it, and Quoise had even admitted that helping me could get her into huge trouble. But all I'd been doing was rescuing people from the shadows, from the Valley— the death magic they were supposed to be against.

Valley-Scott looked smug. "You see? Even you, with your charmingly inflexible opinions on morals, find them untrust- worthy."

My head was whirling. This was too much. It was *all* too much. I'd used death magic to make a crossing, and while I'd felt sick afterwards, there didn't seem to be any lasting damage done.

Either the fairies were lying, or it was a cumulative thing, something that built up the more you used the magic, like, like plaque—or like Scott and Gemma slowly falling under the influence of the Valley.

That shook me free of my spinning doubts. "No," I said, standing up. "You are not going to get to me like this."

Darkness flared around us. "Why, whatever do you mean?" His voice snaked around me as he crooned. "I'm just trying to show you the truth."

I shut my eyes. "No, you're not. Even if the fairies are hiding things, or are biased, or whatever, it doesn't mean you're telling the truth. I don't believe you, I don't accept anything you have to offer, and I deny your power over me!" I'd started out talking normally but by the end of my speech I was shouting. "Keep away from me!"

Valley-Scott raised his hand, ready to strike. I felt him tense for the blow, saw his hand approaching.

I caught it. "No. You will not use that body against me anymore."

I laid my free hand against Scott's cheek and, heedless of the dark that boiled around us, leaned my forehead against his.

"Scott," I said desperately. "I know you're still in there somewhere, I can sense you. I don't know if you can hear me, but if you can, please listen. I don't like you. I think you're a jerk, actually. But I'm willing to concede that at least a little bit of that might be the Valley's power acting through you, and although I still think you're a stupid idiot for getting yourself tangled up in all this, I'll make you a deal: resist him now, and we can start over.

"I'm not promising you anything, not even the tiniest bit of anything—all I'm saying is, if you help me now, just this once, to beat the darkness, then you'll have a clean slate with me, okay? From there, it's up to you."

Come on, I thought desperately. I closed my eyes against the warmth of his forehead and strained with all the Road Mastery I had.

Come on, Scott. I know you're in there. Listen to me! I grasped at the faint breeze, the sense of wide-open spaces. *Come on!*

My hand was slipping from around his wrist. Any moment now I'd lose my grip and he'd punch me, and that would be the beginning of the end.

"Come on, Scott," I murmured. "Come on."

His cheek twitched under my palm. The wind gusted once and vanished. He strained against me harder, and I could barely keep his fist from grazing my chin. My fingers ached.

Please! Scott! Come on!

I couldn't hold him. His wrist slipped from my grip and I cried out, bracing for the blow. "Scott! Please!"

The sense of wind across a night time hilltop strengthened and at the last moment, Scott's body crumbled. He collapsed to the ground, almost dragging me down.

I fought to catch him, snatching after the last whisper of his soulprint with my Road Mastery. *Oh no you don't.* I wrenched after his soulprint, feeling like I was split in two as I tried to hold onto both it and him. Slowly, slowly, I hauled the soulprint back toward us and stuffed it into his body.

He gasped. "Emma." He clung to me, unable to bear his own weight, head against my stomach.

My heart just about stopped. He'd done it. I'd done it. We'd broken the Valley's hold on him and for just a moment, the darkness retreated.

I drew Scott upright and he hung around my neck, burying his face into my shoulder and sobbing. I stood stunned for a moment, arms awkward, then sighed. I hugged him, patting his back with one hand. He was a complete cretin, and I didn't like him one iota more than I'd ever done, but I'd promised him a clean slate. Right now, he was just a terrified kid having a break down.

Something pointy poked me in the hip. I shifted, and the pointy thing fell out of Scott's pocket and clunked on the ground. I twisted down and snagged it, holding it up over Scott's shoulder so I could examine it.

I nearly dropped it again when I saw it was the clockwork fairy he'd set on me last time. I turned it over. It might have been an instrument of evil, but it sure was well made. Not a blemish on her.

...Except a small mark on her shoulder. I brought it closer and squinted.

The fairy clattered to the ground a second time.

I swallowed hard and forced myself to breathe. Her shoulder had read, *For the Princess.*

28

MY HEART POUNDED, but the clatter of the fairy barely had time to die away before something crackled and fizzled over my shoulder. Scott jerked upright and stared open-mouthed, fingers digging into my back. I pried him loose and turned, stomach heavy with dread.

The pillar of light. It snapped and popped like electricity, and before I could react, lightning shot out of it. Scott crumpled to the ground. I screamed.

I crouched over him and felt for a pulse in his neck, my own pounding. He was *not* going to die now, not right after I'd given him a clean slate. He was going to have a chance to be a decent human being, he *was*.

A pulse fluttered under my fingertips, weak and erratic, but there.

I drew myself up and faced the light, shielding him behind me. "What was that for?"

"He is no use to me any longer," the light said. "If he will not submit, he will die."

"And you're trying to convince me that you're the *good* side?" I threw my hands up. "You're disgusting!" *Not to mention cold, calculating, ruthless, and evil, but hey, let's not get carried away here.*

The light flashed within arm's reach. "My offer to you still stands," it crooned. "The power to change the world, Emma Tanning. It needn't all be bad. You could do whatever you wanted.

All I ask is a body to share, that I might walk the worlds and see for myself the things that I have heard."

Anger bubbled in my chest. "First of all, I'm not agreeing to *anything* you have to offer. I wouldn't have *any* power, because you're stronger than me, and the only thing you want me for is my body. Second of all, why do you even *want* a body? I mean, not why," I corrected myself as things clicked into place. "How. *How* can you want a body. Because you're..." I waved my hands. "You're a place. A thing. You shouldn't want anything at all."

The light licked around me, closer and closer. "Because I live." Intense hunger filled its voice. "And I desire only what all living things desire: life. More life. More, always more."

I stiffened as a tendril of blackness swept across my arm. The touch was feather-light on my skin, but weighed heavier than the world on my Road Mastery. Fear thrilled through me. It was true. The Valley was stronger than me, so terribly, fearfully strong. I wasn't going to make it out of here alive. Aphros had said that I had to separate Scott from the Valley; she hadn't mentioned anything about having to fight the Valley afterwards.

Maybe she hadn't meant me to. Maybe she'd known I would die here, and didn't care. She was part death, after all.

"Do not judge me for desiring only what we all desire, Emma Tanning. Especially when I know that you too desire life."

Images forced their way into my mind, images of greatness and adoration. I shoved them down.

Aphros had saved Gem. She stayed in the Valley because she was holding it in check. And she could manifest her own life force here in the heart of the Valley. She couldn't be evil.

Aphros? I thought it as loudly as I could, reaching out with my Road Mastery. *Are you there? Can you hear me? I need your help.*

A breath of wind touched my face—mint.

Please, I said quickly. *You have to come. I've got Scott and he's okay, except he's unconscious, and the light, the Valley is here, and I can't fight it, it's too big, too strong. I don't know what to do.*

The light crackled louder. "What are you doing? To whom are you speaking?"

"None of your business," I snapped. "And besides, you still didn't answer my question. You're a place. A thing. *How are you alive?*"

Aphros's answer came. *It is too strong. Too alive. It has taken on too much of the boy and I cannot stop it.*

I covered my face. I'd been too slow. I'd saved Scott, but it had been too late after all. *Please, Aphros. Please, you have to try!*

The light popped and crackled. "The boy gave me life," it said. "Together, we were stronger than we could ever be alone."

It continued, but I'd frozen in place. Stronger together than alone.

Aphros, I sent urgently. *You can manifest your soulprint here, can't you?*

Yes.

"Answer me!" The light darted around me, touching bare skin at my knees, elbows, neck.

I gasped as deathly cold stole air from my lungs. Gulping, I scrunched my eyes closed. *If I were to step into your soulprint, what would happen?*

The same as for the girl, Gem. Her thoughts sharpened. *We would become one for an instant. I could draw you to me, if you wanted.*

My heart pounded. *Only an instant?*

I am not like the Valley. I have no need for a body that is not mine. Her thoughts dripped with loathing.

"Emma Tanning, I command you now: speak! Answer me, or you shall die!"

Air squeezed from my lungs. I gasped again. It hurt, burning like ice. I had no breath to answer, even if I'd heard the light's question.

I shoved the pain aside, locking it away in the edges of my mind. *So what would happen?*

A connection would form. A bond.

Any second now, my heart would break out of my chest. *Could we beat the Valley together?*

Silence, in which my senses numbed as my body began to fail. But then, *Yes.*

Green light flared, a twisting, spiralling pillar almost as large as the Valley's. I heaved with everything I had, lights of exertion popping in my eyes, and threw myself sideways. Cold like an icy shower in midsummer gripped me and was gone, and with it went the pain. I sucked in air and stood.

The Valley light howled in anger. "You will not take another from me! You will not!" It lashed toward me.

I ducked, but the light grazed against my head. It hurt, a blinding agony that stole all thought for just an instant.

Scott's body began to rise slowly from the ground.

I threw myself at him. "Leave! Him! Alone!"

Darkness snaked up out of his body and wrapped around me. I fought and struggled, but it wound tighter until it engulfed me, binding me to Scott's body, and I saw the part of it that had come from him, the part of it that was alive—hatred and anger and fear so human I reeled.

We can separate them, Aphros said. *Pull it out as you pulled me. But you must destroy the human part; I cannot touch it.*

Wind roared in my ears I called up my Road Mastery more deeply than I ever had before and threw it wide. The unicorn's power amplified it, stretching and moulding it to a knife's edge. I swung it down and cleaved the darkness in two, and as the lighter side fell away I drew myself up to face the remainder.

"No!" it shrieked. "I will not go! I will not be reduced!"

I stretched out through the storm that raged around us and took the darkness in my fist. I squeezed. It writhed and shrieked. My hand burned, fire and agony white hot against the black, and I screamed as I crushed the darkness into nothing.

It gave one last anguished howl, and vanished.

My hand and chest burned. I staggered, Scott's full weight suddenly in my arms, and we dropped to the ground. The darkness had shredded; light shot through the gaps, illuminating the area like sunrise after rain, and the last of the black mist began to evaporate.

You have done well, Aphros sent on a sunbeam. *It is over.* The weight of her presence lifted from my chest, and gaspingly, I could breathe.

29

THE REMAINING SHADOWS drained slowly away, taking with them the rancid smell that would forever be linked to the Valley in my mind. All around, the trees began to lift, branches righting themselves, leaves regaining their colour. Even the grass seemed less downtrodden.

And there, up in the tree line, a glimmer of midnight blue and diamonds; the smell of mint and gold. Grinning madly, chest lighter than air, I ran over to them. Gemma untangled her fingers from Aphros's mane and flung herself at me. "I knew you'd come."

"Are you okay?" I asked, crushing her in return with my burned hand held awkwardly to one side.

"I'm fine!"

I laughed, the sound of relief bursting up through fear. "Then come on! Let's go home."

Together we loaded Scott onto Aphros's back and climbed aboard ourselves. Of course, Gemma made me sit in front, so I had an unconscious Scott draped over my thighs. But I was still sky high from crushing the darkness; a little thing like Scott on my lap wasn't going to ruin it for me. And *he* never needed to know what had happened.

I laughed at that. It was over. We'd won.

Gem hugged me from behind. "I'm so glad you're my friend."

I tilted my head toward her. "Me too."

"I don't know about you, but I plan to get home and sleep for forty-eight hours." She grinned.

"Forty-eight?" I joked. "I'm sleeping for a week."

Gem laughed. "Maybe a month. A month could be good." A second later she piped up again. "What about May?"

"What about it?"

"All the assessment in the world is due in May. Can we sleep past that, do you think?"

I smothered a giggle. "Sure. Why not?"

At full speed, it only took Aphros twenty minutes to reach the border of Sanctuary. She leapt over the boundary at a canter, continuing up through the promenade of trees and on to the main entrance hall via the wide, airy passage Quoise had showed me. Fairies scattered left and right as she cantered through, all of them shouting excitedly as they realised it was Aphros.

We continued straight out of the lodge and down to the stables. Of course. The unicorn twins.

Aphros paused outside the stables to let us off, but before she could enter, Quoise burst from the doorway, followed by Mrs Caro and—

"*Mum?*"

"Emma!"

Our respective mothers swept us up into hugs before I could even process the fact that my mother was in Sanctuary. There were frantic explanations on both sides—the school had called them in a frenzy because we'd gone missing, and Mrs Caro had guessed what had happened. She'd called Mum, told her she knew where we were and that we were in danger, and asked her to come to the clearing. She'd given a quick explanation and before Mum could protest disbelief, Mrs Caro had brought her over to Sanctuary.

On our side, we explained why we'd ditched school and gone back to the Valley despite our promises not to—and why we had an unconscious schoolboy on a unicorn with us.

Quoise took one look at Scott and flew straight up toward the Lodge, no doubt seeking medical assistance.

Aphros reappeared at the stable door. I ran to her, beaming. The fingers of my good hand tangled through her mane and she hooked me closer with her nose. "Are they okay?" I asked.

"Never better."

I hugged her tight. "I... I just have one quick question."

"Ask."

I bit my lip, then tumbled the question out in a rush. "Am I going to become evil because I used death magic?"

She snorted, a sound that echoed with laughter in my head. "I am made of so-called death magic, as I am made of life. Am I evil?"

"Of course not." *Of course not!* I squeezed her tight. "Thank you, Aphros," I murmured into her neck. "Thank you."

"Thank *you.*" She stepped away. I straightened and watched as she went to Gem. I'd nearly forgotten that Gem was bound to Aphros too. They talked quietly for a moment, then one of the unicorn foals whinnied. Aphros untangled herself from Gem's hug and hurried back inside.

Mum swept me up from behind in a bone-crushing hug. I fought for air, but I wasn't going to tell her to stop. Instead, I let her usher me to the alcove, with her proclaiming that I'd have dinner when I got home, whatever I wanted to eat, and a hot bath with the fancy bath salts, and I could sleep for the rest of the week if I wanted to.

Mm. Bed. I gave Sanctuary a last look: its lush, emerald grass and perfect dusk sky, the only shadows normal and harmless. Safe. *Home.*

"What's wrong?" Mum asked, because I'd stopped, and I shook my head and kept walking.

"Nothing," I said. "Nothing's wrong at all." Because then we crossed back to Earth and we came out in the clearing, and as I looked around and saw that the shadows there were normal too, it also felt like home.

And I had two of them.

And they were both safe.

And no one would take them away.

"I love you, Mum," I said.

"I love you too, Em." She squeezed my hand as we climbed the steps through the granite boulders that led up to our street. She opened the back gate for me, pushing a bouncing Veve aside. "I'm proud of you, Emma," she said. "Welcome home."

SANCTUARY - BOOK 2
THROUGH ROADS BETWEEN
AMY LAURENS

1

SOMEONE TAPPED LIGHTLY on my bedroom door. Groggy with sleep, I felt about in the dark for my phone. The lock screen told me it was nearly 2am. My pulse kicked. It had to be about Gemma, my best friend. My *sick* best friend. "Come in," I said hoarsely.

Mum crept in, house phone in hand.

"Is Gemma okay?" I asked before she spoke.

"I understand," she said, and it took me a second to realise that she was talking to the phone. She hung up and sat on my bed.

I shifted my legs out of the way and waited, barely breathing. The darkness pressed in around us, heavy, full of secrets and fears.

"Is it really something only you can fix?" she asked me. In the shadows, I watched as she twisted the phone in her hands.

I wriggled over and lay my head against her hip, revelling in the comfort of her choc chip cookies and steel soulprint—the unique sensory aura that all people had, and that I could sense and sometimes manipulate because I was a Road Master. "I don't know if I can fix it," I said truthfully. "But I know the doctors can't. She'll die no matter what they do." My pulse stuttered again. Gemma wasn't going to die. I wouldn't let her. "I need to get her to Sanctuary, I think," I said, referring to the home of the fairies that Gemma and I had the ability to travel to.

Unfortunately, Sanctuary wasn't the only other world in existence. The Valley, known more properly as the Valley of Death, was Sanctuary's opposite; where Sanctuary was based on life magic, the Valley ran on death.

And now it had its shadowy tendrils wrapped firmly around my best friend.

In the waiting night, I pressed my eyes shut, trying to remember exactly what the Valley's connection to Gem had looked like. More or less like Scott? Less. Definitely less.

"And Gemma can't just go there by herself?"

"Mum." I shook my head. "She's sick. Like, really sick. Keep her in the hospital overnight sick, remember?"

Mum shot me a sideways glance that I could read more from the slight shift of her head than any ability to see her eyes in this darkness. "No need to sass me, Emma Tanning. You have to understand how absurd this all is from the outside. If it wasn't for Mrs Caro, or…"

I wondered if she was remembering her brief visit to Sanctuary a couple of weeks ago. I shifted awkwardly. "But you've seen it. You know it's real."

She sighed. "You're sure it's something… magical? That's wrong with her?"

I sniffed. "Of course I'm sure. What did Mrs Caro say?"

"That the doctors can't find anything."

"Exactly. 'Soul being drained by Valley of Death' isn't exactly in the medical textbooks, is it?"

Mum hugged me tight. I squirmed until I could breathe. "Be careful, Edge," Mum told me, giving me one last squeeze.

"Always."

The house creaked in the darkness around us, finally cooling after another hot, summery day.

"Liv?" The door protested briefly as Dad nudged it open.

Cool air from the lounge room's aircon unit followed him in, chilling my arms.

"What's wrong?" he murmured.

"It's Gemma," Mum said softly. "She's getting worse. Maria says they need Emma. To… help."

Help. I had to help her. I'd fixed Scott; surely I could save my best friend too.

"I'm going to drive Emma down now," Mum said as I wriggled out from the covers and crossed the night-still bedroom to find clothes.

"Do you want me to come?" Dad asked.

"It's fine," Mum said. "You have meetings tomorrow. I can stay home if I need to."

I couldn't, though, I thought as I pulled on my jeans. No matter what happened tonight, there was no way I was missing school tomorrow. A certain teenage boy held answers to some very important questions, and I'd get those answers or die trying. He wouldn't even know what hit him.

"I'm ready," I said, interrupting Dad as I straightened out my shirt.

Mum stood, the bed pinging and creaking as she did. "Let me get dressed too."

I waited in the front hallway. Tree shadows rippled through the narrow windows on either side of the door, reaching across the floor tiles, rustling, straining. I stood right where they ended and watched as my toes dipped in and out of darkness.

In and out, in and out. Dark and light, dark and light.

One step in either direction and I could be safe, or drown forever.

"Ready?" Mum said behind me, keys clinking too loudly in the night.

I stepped to the front door, into the shadows. "Ready." *I'm coming, Gemma,* I told her. *I'm coming.*

2

THE MORNING HAD started out uneventfully enough. I'd been away at school camp the whole previous week, and Gemma hadn't. She'd messaged me while I'd been away to say she was sick, but hadn't offered any details.

Seeing her slumped against my laminated blue locker at quarter past eight on a Monday morning, it *looked* like she'd been sick: dark circles under her eyes, brown skin sallow, dark hair uncharacteristically limp, school uniform rumpled. "Should you be here?" I asked.

She shrugged.

I let it drop, and squeezed her tightly, inhaling the summery warmth of her soulprint. Camp had been a long week without my best friend.

A whiff of darkness crossed my road mastery sense. I furrowed my eyebrows, twisting around.

"What's up?" Gem asked, releasing me.

"Nothing." I scanned the crowds around us, but Scott was nowhere to be seen. "I thought I felt something is all."

Gem smiled tiredly, hugging her books.

"How's Sanctuary?" I continued, shoving my bag in my locker and pulling out the books I needed for the first two lessons. "Have the twins grown much?" Sanctuary was the home of the fairies, a world outside our own, and a secret we shared as Travellers, who could harness seed magic to cross between worlds.

"I haven't been over much," she confessed.

Worry twanged in my chest. Gem and I practically lived in Sanctuary, when we didn't have to be at school or doing mundane things like eating dinner and sleeping.

But she continued before I could say anything. "Filibere"—one of the baby unicorn twins—"discovered fire geckoes. It was pretty funny."

I laughed, hoping it would encourage her to describe the incident in more detail as we headed down the hall to roll call.

Gem smiled some more, but didn't elaborate.

I ushered her into the classroom ahead of me and frowned at her back. This lack of her usually-abundant enthusiasm was concerning.

More concerning, however, was the fact that Scott had already arrived and was sitting front and centre in the classroom, displacing Gem and me from our usual seats. There was an empty desk to either side, but everywhere else was full. We exchanged glances and sat next to him, me relieved that at least Gem had thought it was weird too. Whatever was wrong with her, at least she could still recognise Scott Behaving Oddly.

I stared at Scott as I sat, avoiding outright suspicion but still an awful long way from friendly as I scrutinised his blond hair—lacking its usual gel spikes—was everyone sick today?—and the knock-off designer glasses he only wore when he really had to.

Scott and I... I shook my head as the teacher came in, and refocused on the front of the classroom.

Scott still hadn't so much as glanced at me. It had been like this for the last three weeks, which was entirely preferable to the uncomfortable attentions he'd bestowed on me before that, but seriously. I'd saved the guy's life. You'd think he could do more than point-blank ignore me.

And yet. After nearly a month of pretending neither Gem nor I existed, here he was, sitting down the front, where he knew we always sat.

Out of the corner of my eye, I saw Gem trying half-heartedly to get my attention. I leaned back in my chair and raised my eyebrows. She tilted her head pointedly at Scott's back.

I shook my head slightly, glancing at the teacher and trying to look like I was still paying attention.

"Say something," she mouthed.

I rolled my eyes, but nodded. Resettling in my seat, I considered my options.

Mrs Johnston, our roll call teacher (and, coincidentally, our science teacher), was handing around some paperwork. Perfect. I grabbed three copies from her and, gritting my teeth, leaned over, placing two of them on Scott's desk. "Pass one to Gem, will you."

Scott took the papers wordlessly and handed one to Gem. His own copy he lay carefully on the desk in front of him, staring down at it without reading.

I chewed on the inside of my lip. Not what I had been expecting. A cutting remark, a line about doing my work for me, something. Not... nothing. Emptiness. What had happened to his spark? Scott had been pretty quiet around us since the whole Valley-shadows saga, but he'd also tried pretty hard to avoid us. And he'd been his usual attention-seeking self around everyone else, as far as I could tell. This... I had to be honest, it felt like he had something to say but couldn't work up the nerve to do so.

I sighed heavily and leaned toward him. "What's up?"

He shrugged, eyes still on his paperwork.

"No but seriously. I almost thought we had the plague, the way you've been avoiding us. What do you want?"

He cut an angry glance at me, a flickering flame of a thing that lasted a bare instant. "Who says I want anything?"

I leaned back in my seat and tapped the short end of my pages against the plastic desk. It made a pleasing sound, like the papers were far heavier than they looked. "Me. And I've been in your head, so I should know." Oh, that came out *totally* wrong. This time I was the one who avoided eye contact.

It did the trick, though: his stare now bored through the side of my skull instead of his papers. I ignored it as long as I could, then gave in and turned—and winced at the intensity of his gaze. The full weight of his soulprint knocked into me, a sense of vastness—an open mountaintop under glittering stars, a cool night wind, and *distance*—that set my teeth on edge.

"I can't—"

"Can't what?" I asked.

He closed his eyes suddenly, a blink that became a pause that became a struggle as his jaw clenched and twitched.

Just tell me. Whatever it is, just tell me and get it over with. I shrugged away nervous tension.

Visiting Sanctuary was supposed to be mildly addictive; the feelings of peace and calm it induced released hormones in the brain, causing visitors to want to seek out the experience again and again and again. Probably, the Valley had some way of enticing its followers to return too—and knowing the Valley, which utilised the power of death instead of the power of life, it wouldn't be as kind as Sanctuary. I'd have to keep a watch on Scott.

Eyes still closed, Scott raised his hand.

"Yes, Mister Harden?"

"Bathroom?" he said, gruffer than usual but also less arrogant, and therefore somehow nicer.

Mrs Johnson nodded from the side of the room where she crouched, discussing something with another student. "Hurry up."

His chair scraped backward, the floor screeching in protest, and Scott left.

It was only then that I noticed Gem was slumped forward, one cheek pressed against the cool desk, staring vacantly out the window. Leaning over Scott's empty chair, I put my hand on her shoulder, bizarrely relieved that it still felt warm. "Gem?"

She didn't move.

"Hello? Gemma?" I said, ducking down to peer closely at her face. She stared some more, utterly ignoring me.

I poked her. Still nothing.

Panicked adrenalin flooded my stomach. "Come on, Gemma," I said. "Come back to me." I closed my eyes and let my road mastery senses take over; the world became overlaid with the multi-sensory soulprints of everyone within fifty metres. I narrowed my focus toward Gem—and abruptly, she fell out of her seat.

The girl next to her screamed and Mrs Johnston appeared as if by magic. "Move back," she commanded as students crowded in to see what had happened.

I stayed in my seat. There'd been something, just as she'd fallen, something in her soulprint...

Ah. There. That was what I'd sensed just now—and this morning when I'd first seen her. I swallowed hard, pushing down nauseated fear, and opened my eyes.

Mrs Johnston performed quick checks for breathing and a pulse before rocking back on her heels, some of the tension in her face and shoulders draining away. "Rahim." She pointed at one of the boys at the back of the crowd. "Go to the office right away. Tell them we need an ambulance. Go!"

Ambulance? *Please let Gem be okay. Please.*

The boy disappeared out of the classroom door. Moments later, Gem groaned, shifting on the floor.

My heart skittered and I remembered how to breathe. Slowly, I released my white-knuckled grip on the desk.

Her eyes rolled open. "Wha..." She squeezed her eyes tight then blinked rapidly.

"Hush," Mrs Johnston soothed. "Just stay where you are. I think it's best if you don't move for now."

Students at the back of the room shuffled aside as the school nurse bustled into the room. "Is she breathing? Is she conscious yet?" she shot at Mrs Johnston, who promptly filled her in on what had happened. The nurse nodded emphatically. "Good. Tracey's calling the ambulance. They should be here shortly, but it looks like it was just an absence seizure."

On the floor, Gemma rolled to one side.

"Should she be doing that?" Mrs Johnston asked.

I leaned forward, perching right on the edge of my seat. *Let her be okay.*

The nurse crouched near Gemma. "Do you hurt anywhere? Can you feel your toes and fingers?"

Gemma scowled. "I'm fine," she said. "I must have fallen asleep or something. My shoulder hurts where I landed on it, but I'm fine."

Gem's sassy attitude dispelled a little of my tension—but not all of it. Not with her soulprint... like *that*.

The nurse allowed her to sit before checking her eyes carefully with her pen torch. "I don't *think* you have a concussion," she said, "but I'd rather you stayed down on the floor until the paramedics get here." Gemma opened her mouth to protest, but the nurse cut her off. "Hush now. You just sit tight. They'll be here soon. How much longer till the first lesson?" That was to Mrs Johnston.

"A minute," Mrs Johnston replied, glancing at the classroom clock.

Around us, students began to pack up their belongings surreptitiously. I clutched mine to my chest, hoping Mrs Johnston wasn't planning on kicking me out. I wasn't budging from this room.

"And I suppose there's a class in here next?" the nurse continued.

Mrs Johnston nodded. "But they can wait in the hallway for a bit."

"Good. The ambulance won't be long."

The rest of the students filed out as the bell went, eyeing Gem as they passed. I waited until they'd all gone, then sat down on the floor.

"Don't you have class?" Mrs Johnston said, raising an eyebrow.

"Please." I hugged my books tighter. "Just for a minute."

Mrs Johnston sighed. She turned and dug through her own things on the teacher's desk, then handed me a signed late slip. "I've got to go," she told the nurse.

The nurse nodded. "I'll stay. It's fine."

Mrs Johnston left, locking the door behind her.

"Maybe you'd better lie back down," the nurse told Gemma. "Just in case."

I patted my knee, and Gemma lay down with her head in my lap. I waited until the nurse settled herself by the doorway, ready to tell the next teacher that their class would have to wait for a bit, then leaned over Gemma.

"I know what's wrong," I whispered.

She stared up at me, eyes glassy with tears. "Edge," she whispered back. "I'm so sorry."

I hugged her awkwardly. "I'll keep you safe," I promised. "It's going to be okay."

3

VOICES MURMURED OUTSIDE in the hall, but in the class-room it was dim and quiet. Satisfied that Gemma wasn't going to lose consciousness again in the next three seconds, I closed my eyes.

Her soulprint (twinkling diamonds in a sky of midnight velvet, plus a high-pitched, barely-audible whirring that made me feel like I was on the edge of remembering something important) shone in the darkness behind my eyes. But there, right at one corner, a black thread grew, stretching away into the distance—and it stank of fetid water and overripe fruit.

"I can feel it," she said quietly. "The Valley. All the time, I can feel it, clawing away at me, tempting me. All the time. It's driving me mad. I thought it would get better after a while, but it's not. It's getting stronger."

I chewed the inside of my lip, weighing our options. "Does your mum know?"

She half shrugged. "I don't want to worry her."

"Oh, you're right: worrying that her daughter feels like the shadow-spawning home of all death and destruction is getting stronger would be *totally* overreacting!" I cut my gaze over to the nurse by the door and lowered my voice. "Yeah. No one needs to worry about *that*."

Gemma's face stilled completely. "I didn't mean it like that."

I let my breath out in a rush of sound. "I know. But you should still probably tell someone."

"I am," she muttered against her hands. "I'm telling you."

"Someone responsible."

She ignored me, and I sighed. The nurse cracked the door open, letting in the chatter of the students. I closed my eyes and let it wash over me, white noise to drown out my thoughts. Everything was going to be fine. I'd saved Scott, and I'd save Gemma too. She'd be just fine.

"The Valley's getting stronger again," Gem said softly.

I scowled. Scott had definitely seemed like he'd wanted to tell me something. "If he's been messing around in the Valley again, I swear, I'll create some more shadows just for him."

Gem stared wide-eyed up at me. "Scott?"

The nurse's soft shadow crossed my lap right at that moment and I flinched. "Okay. Sorry," I told whatever power-of-the-world might be listening. "I didn't mean it and I won't feed anyone to the shadows, including Scott." It had been nearly three weeks, but sudden shadows still made me jumpy, and occasionally I had nightmares of being chased and devoured by darkness.

Of course, it beat nightmares about a dead and bloodied girl called Georgia, who looked uncannily like my sister Anna—the reason we'd moved to Nowra in the first place. Dad had testified against a prominent crime lord and—shockingly enough—the gang hadn't taken it so well. The girl, Georgia, caught the same train home as Anna and, if you didn't know the school uniforms well, you could easily mistake Georgia for Anna. Someone had, and Georgia was found dead in the bathroom at the train station.

Minor correction: *I* found her dead.

And yet, my experience with the shadows in the Valley had terrified me enough that they'd replaced finding a dead body in my nightmares. What more needed to be said?

It occurred to me that Gemma hadn't responded. I glanced down, and stiffened. She was staring sightlessly again.

"Um, excuse me?" My heart pounded as I tried to get the nurse's attention.

But she had her head outside the classroom, talking rapidly to someone.

"Excuse me?" I said, louder.

The nurse pulled the door open all the way, and two paramedics strode in.

"I think she's unconscious again," I said, willing my voice to stay level.

They crouched beside me immediately. "Thanks. We'll take it from here."

And before I could do more than blink, I'd been moved gently aside. The paramedics loaded Gem onto a stretcher, popped it up to full height, and wheeled her from the room.

I clutched my books over the nausea in my stomach, willing myself to forget the stench of the Valley as it left the room with my best friend. I tried to pretend my eyes weren't shining with tears.

"Haven't you got class now?" the nurse said, not unkindly.

I inhaled deeply, nodding, not quite ready to trust my voice again.

I forced myself to loosen my shoulders and exhaled firmly. If the Valley was getting stronger, I'd talk to Aphros—Sanctuary's unicorn—and we'd send it back where it came from. We'd done it before. If we needed to, we could do it again.

I stood up. Everything would be just fine.

I'd caught the bus to the hospital as soon as school had finished, texting Mum to let her know what had happened, and Anna to let her know I wouldn't be on the normal school bus home.

I cleared my throat outside the hospital curtains before peering inside. Mrs Caro smiled at me over a worn magazine, though her eyes remained tight. She tilted her head toward the bed where Gem lay.

I slumped. Black circles smudged Gem's eyes, her dark hair fanning across the pillows like a frame for her too-pale face.

"Sleeping," Mrs Caro said unnecessarily.

I hesitated, half in, half out. "Should I go?" I needed to tell her about the Valley, but if she needed me to go, if she'd had enough trauma for one day...

My hands fisted involuntarily, responding to the cloud of shadows I could sense hovering over Gem's bed.

"Don't be silly," Mrs Caro said. She gave another tight smile. "Did you know the doctors can't find anything wrong with her?"

I shifted uneasily. "They won't."

Mrs Caro's gaze sharpened. "Why not?"

I gripped the straps of my school bag with white knuckles. "It's the Valley." Adrenalin spiked as I remembered being alone in the soundless, sightless dark of the Valley's sinkhole—and then the glowing pillar of light that was the Valley's magic made conscious appearing ahead of me.

It had offered me the world, too, the power to make everything right and keep all my loved ones safe forever and ever. I'd only escaped because Aphros, Sanctuary's unicorn, had sent her soulprint to interrupt the conversation.

Gemma hadn't been so lucky. She'd agreed to the light's bargain—and even though she'd renounced it later, it looked like the Valley was here to collect its payment regardless.

She nodded once, decisively. "Unsurprising."

"It's..." I flicked a nervous glance at Gem. "It's getting stronger. Fast."

"Do you know why?"

I shook my head.

Mrs Caro closed her eyes and leaned back against the wall.

Somewhere beyond the blue curtains, heart rate monitors bipped and nurses chattered, rustling their paperwork and shuffling their footsteps.

"I'm sorry," I whispered.

Mrs Caro's eyes blinked open, wide with sur-prise. "Sorry? Oh, Emma. You have nothing to be sorry for. Thank you for letting me know what the problem really is. Who knows how long Gemma might have tried to hide it."

She reached out and I let her hug me. "It's going to be okay, isn't it?" I said when she let me go.

She held me by the shoulders. "I don't know. But Aphros will."

I nodded. "But she'll probably have to see Gemma in person," I said. That wasn't a bad thing, though; exposing Gemma to the calming magic of Sanctuary might actually be helpful. "What's the earliest we could get Gemma there?"

"The doctors want to look into the seizures. They have her booked in for an MRI, but I'm not sure they'll find anything, because if you're right, there's nothing for modern medicine to find. I suppose it'll have to be tomorrow afternoon. I can't imagine being able to sneak her out before that—although if it's very desperate I could take her out against medical orders. What do you think? Will that be necessary?"

I bit my lip and tried to compare the strength of the Valley's bond with Gemma now compared to this morning, trying to calculate how fast it might be growing. "Tomorrow morning would be better," I said. The connection lurked at the edge of my awareness constantly, like a hungry predator that kept my teeth on edge.

Mrs Caro sighed. "And tonight would be even more preferable. Still." She picked up the magazine again. "Keep your phone on you. I'll let you know when we're out and heading to Sanctuary."

I nodded. "Call me anytime," I said. "I'll sneak out if I have to."

Mrs Caro peered sternly at me over the magazine. "Edge, dear, there may be no one else on the planet who can help me save my daughter right now, but I'm not going to drag you away from bed in the middle of the night without your parents' permission. You go home now and rest," she continued over my protests. "I'll call the house if it's really urgent. I think," she said, glancing at Gemma, "that it will not be necessary."

I gave her a half smile. "I hope so too, Mrs Caro. I hope so too."

4

WHICH LED TO the here and now, sitting in a car, staring out the window as dark houses flashed past, normal people curled up asleep, warm and safe and oblivious to the shadows. A few weeks ago, I'd been just like them, oblivious to the horrors of the night.

Well. Not strictly true. I'd been under witness protection and infinitely aware of the *human* horrors of the night, but that was different.

I snorted softly. Very different. Back then, I'd been helpless. The shadows might be scarier than any mobster, but I'd beaten them once, and I'd do it again. My hands clenched in my lap as we turned over the bridge. This time, I wasn't helpless. This time, I could fight back.

The red and green lights of the channel winked at me in the darkness, the dim night lights of the town reflecting off the river. In the dark, there was no way of telling how fast the river flowed, or where the treacherous currents were—except the lights, red and green, steadfast sentinels in the night. There was a way through this nightmare. I just had to find it.

We pulled off the main road toward the hospital and my stomach clenched.

"Okay?" Mum asked.

I nodded curtly.

A moment later, we pulled into the hospital's carpark, gravel crunching under the tyres. I sat still for a moment, staring at the fluorescent lights of the entrance.

"You coming?" Mum asked from outside the car, peering back in at me.

"Yeah." I couldn't feel the Valley from here, not really—neither my road mastery nor the Valley's connection with Gemma were that strong—but I knew what I'd feel as soon as I walked in: queasy, oily stagnant-water stench, rotten fruit, fear.

I unbuckled my belt. Worse, Mrs Caro had said. How much worse? How much worse did it have to be before she'd call me in the middle of the night?

I set my shoulders, clenched my hands at my sides, and strode toward the hospital.

Inside, I stopped dead as Mum pushed the curtains of Gemma's bed area aside; the sight of the dark shadows wreathing Gemma's soulprint felt like a physical punch to the gut.

"What do you think?" Mrs Caro asked me, face pinched and tight.

I shook my arms briskly and exhaled, forcing my road mastery down to a mere trickle so the shadows felt less overwhelming. "You were right to call me," I said. "The connection's a lot stronger. We need to get her to Sanctuary right away."

She nodded, lips pursed. "I thought so. Thank you for coming. Thank you for bringing her," she added, turning to Mum.

I caught a brief glimpse of Mum's face, odd expression twisting her features. I ignored it, and took Gemma's hand as she lay barely conscious.

"It's fine," Mum replied. "This is really something only Emma can fix?"

Mrs Caro's lips stretched into a sad smile. "If anyone can."

"How are we going to do this?" I said, aware that I might be interrupting and not really caring. "She doesn't look like she can walk far."

"She can't," Mrs Caro agreed, joining me at the bedside. "But I can probably find a wheelchair to get her to the car."

I nodded. "Do it."

Mrs Caro left. I felt Mum's eyes on me again, and realised the reason for the odd expression: nowhere else in my life was I permitted to treat an adult as an equal like this. "I'm not being rude," I noted, without looking at her.

"I know," she replied. "It's just... unusual. You're barely thirteen, and Maria treats you like you're in charge."

That's because I am, I didn't say. "Road mastery isn't common," I said instead. "According to the fairies, there are only a handful of people with it. And most of them can't do what I can."

"Like what?"

I glanced at Mum. We'd had plenty of opportunities to discuss this in the last couple of weeks, and she wanted to discuss it here, now?

She met my eye levelly. Oh. A distraction, perhaps?

I gave her a brittle smile and leaned my butt on the edge of Gemma's bed so I could face her. "I can sense people's soulprints," I said. "Like... a multi-sensory trail unique to each person. It's strongest right where they are at the time, of course, but I can see where people have been recently, or if there's somewhere they go a lot, I can usually pick that up as well."

"But why call it *road* mastery then? It doesn't seem to have much to do with roads."

"I..." I closed my mouth and bunched my lips to one side. "I don't know. I can see the paths people travel, I guess? That's like roads, right?"

She shrugged, pouting her bottom lip in a 'beats me' expression. "Doesn't seem like the most obvious name."

"I guess not," I said, eyes on Gemma. She hadn't moved since we'd arrived, although she was breathing the deep breaths of sleep now rather than seeming to fight for air. I really hoped she was going to be okay.

"You said you can sense where someone's been, but only for a little while. How long?"

"Depends."

"On what?"

"A lot of things. How many other people are around. How many other people have crossed over the trail. How often the person uses that route. Those are the main things." I thought of our house, layered with months and months of usage. "The house, I can sense all of you as soon as I open the door. Before, even. Our Melbourne house?"

We'd lived there for ten years. Mum nodded.

"I could sense you all turning into the street. Not that I knew that's what I was sensing."

I remembered visiting Sanctuary for the first time with Gemma and the fairy Quoise, and learning that I was a Road Master. In

Sanctuary, my talents were a lot stronger, helped by Sanctuary's magic, but there had been some sort of crystallising effect that had transferred over to this world: previously, I'd had a bunch of vague sensations attached to people I knew well or dealt with regularly, but nothing I could consciously pick out. I could tell when someone I was close to approached before I saw them, and sometimes people would irritate me or give me the creeps for no apparent reason.

After visiting Sanctuary, everything became sharper: instead of just vague sensations, I could describe people's soulprints—although admittedly in terms that often made no sense to other people. I could pick out individual soulprints and follow trails, much like I imagined scent hounds could do. "About fifty metres or so," I said.

Mum wrinkled her eyebrows.

"Your next question was going to be, 'How far away can you sense someone?' The answer is, about fifty metres or so. Unless, like I said, it's a place the person visits a lot and there's a sort of residual sense of their soulprint there."

Mum glanced at the luridly-lit hospital ward. "Must be a lot of soulprints flying around here."

Innocent enough words, but something in the way she said it made me narrow my eyes. "Yes. Lots. Why do you say that?"

She shrugged, still peering around. "I just... It feels crowded in here. Noisy. There are lots of people, so I assume you can see lots of soulprints, right?"

Noisy? Apart from the hum of machinery and the beeps of monitors, the place was almost silent. I shifted forward, squinting one eye at her more than the other. "Mum, are you a Road Master?"

She laughed and rubbed at her arms.

"No, I'm serious," I said. "It often runs in families. Gemma's family has time mastery. Mrs Caro's pretty good, she can get us back up to a couple of hours before we even left. Gemma's mastery is weaker, but it's good enough to make sure we always get back on time."

Mum frowned. "How would I know? I can't do anything like you say you can, with seeing soulprints and things like that."

"I couldn't before I went to Sanctuary, not properly."

"I've been to Sanctuary, and nothing changed." She stared at her hands, suddenly motionless in her lap, and for the first time I realised that maybe she *wanted* to be able to join the magic of Sanctuary.

I guess it made sense. It seemed like most people wanted to believe that magic was real, and Mum *knew* it was real, but couldn't join in. That... had to suck, actually.

"Are you *sure* nothing changed?" I asked, watching her carefully. She shifted as she thought; there was definitely something she wasn't telling me. "Nothing at all?"

She shifted her weight again, staring at her hands a moment longer before meeting my eye. "Sometimes... I think I hear something when your dad comes into the room. And Anna. And when you're around..."

"Stop!" I said, holding my hands up. She looked startled; I smiled to soften my tone. "We're not supposed to know what our own soulprints look like."

She blinked. "Why not? It would make sense that you couldn't *sense* your own, but why can't you even know what it is?"

"...I don't actually know," I said. "Quoise told me it's one of the fairies' rules." Like ignoring the shadows. Hmm. "But seriously, you hear something around Dad and Anna?" I grinned.

She squirmed, looking totally out of character. "I'm not a hundred per cent sure," she said. "I can't hear it all the time. Just... I don't know. Would I be more certain if it was actually something like what you can do?"

I shrugged. "Not necessarily. I didn't know until Sanctuary, remember. Does Anna sound like a faint clacking? Like keyboard keys or something?"

Mum's face lit up. "Yes! That's exactly it! I would never have been able to tell you that, but you're right. It's exactly like keys clacking, only very faint, like they're several rooms away and I can only catch them when the conditions are just right." She tilted her head like she was listening. "I can hear you now," she said softly. "It's a pity you can't."

My stomach jolted. What would I hear if I could hear my own soulprint? What did it even mean that part of my soulprint was a sound? Soulprints were an unpredictable combination of the senses, and usually only two or three of them. Gemma was an image—twinkling stars—a sound—a high-pitched, mildly irritating whirr—and a texture—dark velvet. Mum was two smells—fresh-baked chocolate chip cookies and steel—and the feeling of a smooth, polished steel rod.

I always took that to mean that Gemma was a little annoying but super nice once you got to know her, and a bit obsessed with glamour. Mum was homey and the basic personification of comfort, with a backbone of steel determination.

"I guess that's conclusive then," I said. "You're a Road Master, Mum. Congratulations." I smiled warmly.

She smiled back before wrinkling her brow. "Then why can't I cross to Sanctuary too?"

"The two things don't go together. Separate talents. But," I frowned too, "travelling also tends to run in families. I don't know. I'll have to ask Quoise."

Mum shrugged. "Maybe you get the travelling from your dad."

Now there was a thought: Dad in Sanctuary.

Before I could meditate on it further, a rolling, wheeling, tick-tick-tick drew nearer. Mrs Caro pushed back the curtain and snuck inside, pushing a worn grey wheelchair. "Are we ready?" she said furtively. "They might notice this missing soon."

I looked at Gem, lying in the bed, and opened my road mastery out a fraction wider again. I recoiled. "Yeah," I said, stifling the need to brush the filthy magic off me. "We need to go."

5

WE MADE IT to the cars without a fuss, and from there it was less than ten minutes back to our house—the closest place to the glade by the creek where we could cross to Sanctuary. Mum had pointed out that technically, Lynburn Avenue was closer, but Mrs Caro and I had quickly shut that idea down.

"The Valley crossing is on that side of the creek," I'd explained. "And trust me, we don't want Gemma any closer to the Valley than we can help right now." I'd side-eyed the growing cord of blackness attached to her soulprint, now as thick as three of my fingers.

So we'd parked outside our house, and now were contemplating how best to get Gemma to the glade.

She'd roused when we'd moved her to the wheelchair, and as Mum and I headed to the Caro's car in the driveway behind us, I could hear Gem's voice. My pulse skipped with relief.

"You can't carry me the whole way there," she was saying to Mrs Caro.

"And you can't walk. You're barely able to sit."

True enough; we'd put the passenger seat back as far as we safely could, and despite her protestations, Gem couldn't even sit up by herself.

I popped her door open and leaned in to hug her gently. "How are you feeling?"

"Useless." She turned her face away, but not before I saw the tears spill over. "And stupid, and a complete waste of space."

I hugged her again, awkwardly, crouching and laying my head against her side. "You're not useless," I told her. "Or a waste of space. And you're not even stupid."

"I am," she whispered as Mrs Caro got out. "If I wasn't stupid, the Valley would never have tricked me in the first place."

"It's not your fault, Gem."

"Pretty sure it is, actually," she whispered, and despite everything, I smiled for a second, because just for that one sentence she sounded like herself.

"Okay," I allowed. "Maybe it is. But we all still love you a lot, Gem. We're not going to abandon you because you made one dumb choice."

She didn't answer, her whole body quivering. I hugged her tight.

Someone tapped me on the shoulder—Mum, motioning me aside.

I stretched upright, knees protesting as blood flowed back to my legs.

Mum and Mrs Caro had rigged a stretcher of sorts between them using some rakes and a tarp. They loaded Gemma on, locked the cars, and we set off down the street. I led the way, my phone's torch shining brightly.

After a tense few minutes navigating the stairs through the boulders, we reached the bottom. In daylight, I'd be able to see the creek in front of us, but at night there was only an inky blackness.

I tripped on Mum's foot as I tried to get in front of them again to light the way. "Sorry."

"Spooky, isn't it?" Mum said quietly.

"What? No. It's just dark." Spooky was the Valley shadows.

Crickets chirped and some other sort of insect whirred, and something rustled in the branches above us. We walked on in silence.

"Stop here," Mrs Caro said breathily as we neared the place where we had to turn off the path. She and Mum lay Gem's stretcher carefully on the ground. "Where's the easiest way in?"

I shone my torchlight into the trees, searching for the clearest way (we made a point of entering through a different place each time, trying to avoid making an obvious tunnel). "In there," I said after a moment, shining my light a little to the left.

Mrs Caro nodded. "Lead on."

I led the way into the bushes. They protested, scratching and scraping, reminding me of my first desperate run through the Valley when the trees had come to life and tried to stop me from leaving.

I took a deep breath. No Valley here.

The back of my neck prickled.

I opened up my road mastery and cringed. "We'd better hurry," I said. The shadows around Gemma's soulprint were massing; the entrance to the Valley just across the creek must be calling to them.

"Is she getting worse?" Mrs Caro asked, breathless and sharp.

"No," I said, snapping a branch and ducking into the little open space by the creek that we called the glade. "But the shadows are."

"Shadows?" Mum asked.

"Again?" said Mrs Caro.

I shook my head. "No. They aren't..." I struggled for the right words. "Last time," I said, turning to Mum, "the Valley sent out shadows that tried to lure people in for it. Food, kind of."

Kind of? Exactly. Chills ran down my back as I remembered the shadows' words: *Eat, eat your soul, give us your life, life so sweet, so sweet your blood.*

"These aren't like last time," I told Mrs Caro. "They're not as *real*. They're just..." I eyed Gemma uneasily. "Testing."

Mrs Caro's lips still looked concerned.

"Let's just get started," I said. I felt Mum giving me the same odd look she'd given me at the hospital—but I couldn't help it: this time, I really was in charge.

Thankfully, Mrs Caro nodded. "Do you want to do the crossing, or should I?"

"Can I?" I asked, reaching into my pocket for my packet of seeds. I never went anywhere without them these days. "I'm not sure I can carry the stretcher."

Mrs Caro nodded. "Of course."

"Are we ready?" I asked as we clustered around, making sure everyone could touch my free hand. "Gem?" I flicked the torchlight over her to check she was still with us.

She stared past me, and for a moment I thought she was about to seize again. Then I realised: she wasn't staring blankly. She was staring into the trees on the other side of the creek—at the main entrance to the Valley. I rubbed away the goosebumps that rose on my arms. I didn't want to know what was going through her head right now.

"Gem," I said gently. "I need your hand."

She didn't move.

Mouth pressed firmly in a thin line, Mrs Caro took one of Gemma's hands in her own, then sandwiched it between hers and mine. Mum laid her hand on top, and it was time.

I closed my eyes, shoved my seed-finger as deep into the dirt as it would go, and waited for the tiny spark of magic that happened when a seed took root.

Normally it took a couple of days for a seed to germinate and release its power. Travellers like me and Gem and Mrs Caro, though, could speed things up, making the seed germinate immediately and harnessing its power to cross between worlds. With my eyes still closed, I pictured the Sanctuary alcove in as much detail as I could manage: silvery-green grass tickling beneath my knees, soft ground with a little spring and give, the fresh, clean smell of the breeze, the perpetual pearly twilight of the sky above...

Within a second, the scenery around us shifted and we opened our eyes in Sanctuary.

I smiled as the sense of peace that accompanied the transition flooded over me. If anywhere could make Gemma better, Sanctuary could.

Gem, however, didn't seem peaceful at all. She twisted and writhed on the stretcher, moaning under her breath.

I leaned closer.

"Can't stand it..." she mumbled. "Hurts..."

I looked up and met Mrs Caro's eye. "The Lodge?"

She nodded. "The fairies will know what to do."

Mum and Mrs Caro lifted the stretcher once more, and we headed up the grassy slope, past the unicorns' stables, and to the fairies' Lodge, stopping once or twice to give the stretcher-bearers a breather. I offered to switch for a bit, but they both shook their heads determinedly until I gave up asking and led them up the slope in silence.

We headed straight to the front doors of the Lodge. I swung them open, standing awkwardly to the side while Mum and Mrs Caro brought Gemma in.

The cavernous room shimmered and flittered with movement as fairies of all colours and hues made their way through it. Their butterfly wings flashed, some flying in or out of connecting doorways, some hovering by bookshelves that lined the far walls, and some congregating around a lovely hanging garden that served as their reception.

I let the doors fall closed and turned toward the reception desk—and something small and blue zipped in front of my face, forcing me to stop with the stretcher right behind me.

It was Quoise, the fairy assigned to watch over Gemma and me while we were in Sanctuary, and our first point of contact.

I opened my mouth to greet her, but she interrupted me, cheeks pale and eyes strained. "You can't be here," she said tightly. "Quick, quick, get outside. Hurry!"

I frowned.

"Quoise," said Mrs Caro firmly, not at all diminished by being still a little out of breath, "Gemma needs help."

"Doesn't matter, doesn't matter!" Quoise muttered, herding us back to the door.

A shout echoed out behind us. "Stop!"

"Pretend you haven't heard," said Quoise. "Don't stop, don't stop!"

Quoise pushed at Mum's shoulder, trying to get her moving again.

Too late. A fairy I hadn't seen before with emerald-green wings and a tiny gold coronet interposed herself between us and the door. She drew herself up to her full height in mid-air—which, although not tall, was still a good palm's width taller than Quoise—and glared at us, white-lipped with outrage. "How *dare* you trespass here!"

We stared.

"I think there's been a mistake," I said. "Gemma's here—"

"Exactly!" the fairy snapped. "*That* is the mistake."

"...for help," I finished lamely.

"Get out," the fairy told Gemma. "If I see you here again, or hear word of you here again, I will personally see to it that your future life, such as it is, will be a misery. I will not allow you to destroy what we have made." The emerald-winged fairy folded her arms over her chest and inclined her head toward the door.

Utterly confused, we left, Quoise hovering anxiously behind.

"Quoise."

The emerald fairy's tone made me flinch.

"Where are you going?"

"Just... down... Aphros," Quoise stammered. "I'm going to see Aphros, Your Grace."

"See that you do," the emerald fairy commanded. "I don't have to remind you of our rules, do I?"

"N-no, Your Grace," Quoise said.

We exited as fast as we could with the unwieldy stretcher and headed down the slope.

"Your Grace?" I said as we moved out of earshot.

Quoise shrugged, discomfort twisting her features. "She is the Keeper. Sanctuary's leader. Everything we do is done according to her word."

"I didn't realise Sanctuary was a dictatorship."

"It's not like that!" Quoise said, voice strained.

"Quoise," Mrs Caro said in a 'Really?' tone of voice. She seemed less puzzled by the situation, now that I thought about it, and I wondered if she'd run into the Keeper before.

"The Keeper," I said slowly as we walked. "Did she... Did she just ban Gemma from Sanctuary?"

Beside me, Quoise nodded.

"But... why?"

Quoise fluttered along silently.

"It's the Valley, isn't it?" Mum said, looking from Quoise to me and back again.

At the front of the stretcher, Mrs Caro stared resolutely ahead.

Quoise nodded, lip between her teeth. "I'm sorry," she whispered. "There's nothing we can do."

"No." I shook my head. "There has to be something. I can do something." *Surely.*

Quoise shook her own head in response. "Edge, there's nothing. She accepted the Valley's offer, and even though you contained the shadows and destroyed the Valley's avatar, Gem is still bound to it." Quoise touched my cheek. She looked over at Mrs Caro. "I'm so sorry. There's nothing we can do."

6

"WAIT," I SAID as Mrs Caro and Mum began walking again, Gemma moaning as the stretcher shifted and bumped.

"Why?" Mrs Caro said. "You heard Quoise. They won't do anything."

"It isn't 'won't', Maria," Quoise said in equally snappy tones.

"Wait," I said again as my heart raced. The implications of the Keeper's ban echoed around my thoughts. Gemma could never come back to Sanctuary again. "We can't just leave."

Mrs Caro gave me a weary look. "Edge, you heard the Keeper. Gemma's banned. There's nothing else we can do."

Gem twisted, muttering incomprehensibly.

I can do something. I have to try something. Quoise went still in the corner of my vision, and I turned to her abruptly. "What is it?" I demanded. "What aren't you telling us?"

Quoise's wings quivered as she perched on the edge of the stretcher, staring at Gem. We walked onward, nearing the alcove, our feet shushing in the grass.

"Please don't tell them I'm talking to you about this," Quoise said softly.

Shh, shh, shh went our feet.

"The Valley and Sanctuary exist in opposition; just as we fairies can't cross over to the Valley because its magic will destroy us, so too the magic of Sanctuary will eventually destroy Gem. And that's assuming that the Valley doesn't consume her first and use her as a way to destroy Sanctuary. She's dangerous, Edge." She wrapped her arms around her tiny body. "That's why the Keeper banned her. It's for the best."

Mrs Caro shot her a sharp glance.

"But that's rubbish!" I said. "You can't just kick her out of Sanctuary and leave her be! The Valley will consume her, and then she'll come after Sanctuary anyway! This is just like last time, when the fairies wanted to ignore the shadows and pretend they'd go away."

Quoise cut me off with a shake of her head, wings flapping in agitation. "Not all of us were ignoring them."

Mum turned to me. "Can you do anything?"

My chest ached. I *had* told Mum that I could fix Gemma—that's why she'd driven me to the hospital in the middle of the night. But last time, there had been a literal personification of the Valley to fight. I could *see* the Valley's connection to Gemma's soulprint, but I wasn't sure how to detach it. "I don't know what to do. I was hoping the fairies would help me figure it out."

"If anyone can do something, you can," Quoise said softly.

I tossed my head. My eyes were getting scratchy and a head-ache was threatening; it had to be getting close to four in the morning back home. "I got rid of them last time because I had help from Aphros, and the Valley's power was embodied. A body I could fight against. I didn't actually do anything to the shadows, if you recall."

Still. Maybe Aphros would have an idea. And I wasn't leaving Sanctuary without at least *trying*. I set my jaw. "I need to talk to Aphros."

The mothers exchanged glances. "With or without Gemma?" Mrs Caro asked.

I bit my lip. "With. She'll need to help me manipulate Gemma's soulprint."

Mrs Caro gave her head a brisk jerk. "So we'll have to cause a diversion, then."

"I'll do it," Quoise said, fluttering into the air.

Mrs Caro gestured with her head and Mum helped her put the stretcher down a little way from the crossing point, where a neat little rockery filled one side of the alcove. "Thank you, Quoise," she said, stretching with her hands on her lower back, "but I've got this one. I'm sure you're more than capable of holding the Keeper's attention when necessary, but we all know your principle personality feature is general niceness."

Quoise flapped her wings, cheeks pinking.

"I, on the other hand," Mrs Caro continued, "can be very annoying when I want to be." The smile she gave was all tooth, like a shark.

Mum turned to me. "Would you rather I stayed or went?"

I shrugged. "It doesn't matter."

She grinned, and I caught a glimpse of the steel rod that was an integral part of her soulprint. "In that case, I'll go with Maria. It's been a while since I got to be really annoying."

They left together, hurrying back up the slope like they hadn't just carried a nearly full-grown girl on a stretcher up the same slope and back down it.

"That was revealing," Quoise murmured.

I blinked. "You're telling me," I said, shaking my head a little.

"I'll go get Aphros," Quoise said, stirring herself.

"I can just call her," I said.

When we'd banished the shadows last time, I'd stepped into Aphros's soulprint so we could fight together. Since then, we'd maintained a strange sort of connection between us; I could tell where she was, no matter how far away—and if we concentrated, we could talk to each other too.

"If I stay here," Quoise said, "it'll draw attention to your presence. I'll go hang out with the babies," she finished, referring to Aphros's twins, Filibere and Lily.

I nodded, not sad to have a few moments alone to process everything that had happened.

"Back soon." Quoise took off at full pace, a blur in the air. I'd never seen her hurry like that before; I was impressed.

My eyes lost her in Sanctuary's dim twilight and I turned back to Gem, pulse stuttering as I realised her eyes were open. "Hey," I said softly as I perched on a dark grey rock next to the stretcher.

A flame-coloured bush crept from the crevice between my rock and the next, and a trail of white pebbles swirled away to my right. The little rockery was pretty, calming. I wondered if there was something in its design that amplified Sanctuary's calming magic. Maybe not. Pretty things could be soothing too.

Gem blinked up at me.

"How are you feeling?" I asked.

She worked her jaw. "I heard it all," she rasped.

My chest constricted. "I'm sorry."

A pale smile hovered over her features. "You'll fix it," she said simply.

I squeezed her hand. "Yeah."

So much for not making promises I couldn't keep. I didn't have to close my eyes to feel her connection to the Valley, thick as my wrist now, and greasy. I hoped desperately that it was just Sanctuary amplifying my road mastery, and not that the connection had actually strengthened that much since the hospital.

Footsteps rustled in the grass outside the alcove and a white horsey head appeared. "I am sorry," Aphros said as she entered the alcove. "The fairies were following me. I took the roundabout route."

Judging by the slivers of shadow clinging to her mane, the roundabout route involved travelling through the Valley—a smart move, since the fairies couldn't follow her there. She tossed her mane. "Show me."

I moved aside and gestured to Gem.

Aphros recoiled.

"That bad, huh?" I murmured.

She snorted and moved closer. "Help me."

I held my hands out helplessly, wondering exactly what it was I was supposed to do.

She moved parallel to the stretcher, then shifted further so my outstretched hand rested lightly on her flank, stomping a hind foot absently.

Right. That then.

With my hand touching her, she could interact with my road mastery, helping me to direct and control it. I closed my eyes and focused on Gemma's soulprint.

"Hmm."

"Hmm what?" I said, pulse fluttering. "Hmm good or hmm bad?"

She exhaled noisily and shifted her weight. "Just hmm. Quoise said the shadows were massing around her, but they've actually connected themselves with her soulprint."

No duh, I thought, examining the thick cable of darkness that stretched from Gemma's soulprint out toward the Valley.

"That is more serious than Quoise suggested, but I do not think it is insurmountable."

"Come again?"

"I think you can separate Gemma from the Valley."

Relief trilled through my body and I let my arm relax, disconnecting from Aphros's silky side with a feeling like pins and needles.

Aphros swung toward me. "Why did you let go?"

I blinked. "I thought we were done."

"I said you can separate Gemma from the Valley, not that you could do it without killing her."

All the tension that had melted away snapped back into place. "But... I thought..."

Aphros nuzzled my side. "I am not finished. Lend me your hands once more, and let us see what can be done," she said gently.

Apprehensive, I placed my hand on Aphros's neck and turned wide-eyed to look at Gemma.

"Please save her," I whispered to Aphros. I'd lost friends moving here from Melbourne, but it'd turned out they hadn't really been friends at all. Gemma was the first friend I'd had who hadn't tried to make me be someone I wasn't.

"I'm sorry," I told Gem. "I should have tried harder. I should have found you sooner." If only I'd gotten to her earlier when she'd disappeared into the Valley, maybe the shadows wouldn't have sunk their claws into her.

"Aphros," I breathed. Our connection meant I didn't have to speak aloud at all, especially when we were this close, but it felt too serious a thing to ask in silence.

"Mmm?"

"Why didn't you save her? You saved me," I continued, remembering a pillar of mint and gold appearing in the darkness right as I was about to sell my soul to the Valley.

Aphros twitched. "Road mastery," she said simply. "Your soulprint is easier to find, because it quests, always searching outward with your senses. You are easy to find," she repeated. "I did not find Gemma soon enough."

"Oh." My chest felt heavy and tight.

"There," she said, tone shifting toward certainty. "Right there. Can you see, Edge?"

I closed my eyes again and looked. In front of me, Gemma's soulprint stretched and grew; Aphros was directing my vision, zooming me in, something I couldn't do by myself. One day, I'd have to have a good long talk with Aphros about what my road mastery could and couldn't do.

We drew closer and closer to the stretched-out sky of Gemma's soulprint, and I realised as we did that instead of doming out evenly like a velvet blue-black sky, her soulprint seemed to buckle and pull. The cord, I realised: the connection to the Valley was pulling on her soulprint, distorting it. "I see it."

"Look closer," Aphros said, and directed my vision right to the very root of the Valley's fetid, black connection.

Tiny fibres stretched out from the cord, sinking themselves into the warp and weft of Gemma's print. I could see how we might be able to pick them out from her soulprint—but I could see too the wear it would cause. Gemma's soulprint would be permanently weakened there.

"What happens when our soulprints fray?" I asked Aphros quietly.

"It depends on how bad the wear is," she said, equally as quiet. "Sometimes the fray can heal. Sometimes it remains the same, a leak in the owner's energies; they would feel always exhausted, like they are battling against the current. Sometimes the fray gets worse."

I swallowed. The fibres from the Valley's cord stretched out a good way into Gemma's soulprint. "But Scott was okay. And we separated him from his connection with the Valley."

"The boy was as good as dead anyway. We tried in desperation. We are all lucky he was strong enough to heal."

Strong enough to heal. I hadn't thought of Scott like that before. "So what can we do?" *Please. Please let there be something we can do.*

"I think," she said carefully, and my vision suddenly blacked.

I blinked, disoriented, before realising Aphros had pulled away.

"I *think* that there is nothing we can do that would not end in irreparable harm."

My stomach sank.

"But..."

"But? But what?" *Don't torment me like this, Aphros,* I sent silently to her.

She snorted, tossing her mane vigorously. *I am not tormenting you. I am trying not to promise things I have no knowledge of.*

Ha. I could definitely identify with that, even if I was doing an abysmal job of avoiding it.

"I do not think we can fix her," she continued aloud. "But there might be something we could do to slow its progress."

"What?" I said. "What could we do?"

"The problem is not the connection, per se. The problem is that the connection is growing, yes?"

"It started as a tiny, thin thread," I said. "And now... Well, you can see how thick it is now. And she's gotten much worse since it has."

Aphros's soft hair rubbed against my fingertips as she nodded. "If we could constrict it somehow, and possibly stretch it out, it would thin."

My pulse sped up. "Like clay," I said. "Roll it out longer and it gets thinner. But how do we roll it?"

"I do not think we can roll it, as you say, but perhaps..." The darkness behind my eyes lit up as Aphros zoomed me off again, directing my road mastery first to the place where the Valley's cord interwove with Gemma's soulprint, and then a little way down the cord itself.

"Lend me your strength."

I didn't exactly understand what she meant, but I could sense her asking for something from my road mastery, like someone holding out their hand for a thing you were carrying. I struggled for a second, wondering how to give her what she seemed to want. Extra power? My road mastery itself? I tried reaching toward her with my road mastery sense, like concentrating hard on an object just out of reach.

A silvery fog extended toward her. Aphros tugged on it gently; I felt it deep inside my head, like she was pulling on my thoughts.

I watched, wondering what she would do with the power she'd taken from me—and then the space around the Valley's cord glimmered, gold and green and silver, and the scent of mint and old roses surrounded me.

The colourful glimmer solidified, and although I couldn't see her precisely, I sensed Aphros working, feeding more power into the glimmer, honing it, shaping it—until at last, a bright gold-and-silver pipe encased the Valley's cord, drawing it out as fine as wire.

"There," Aphros said at last. The vision faded away as she shifted from under my hand. "I think that will hold for at least a few days."

I blinked rapidly, my head reeling a little. Whatever she'd done, Aphros had just drawn a heck of a lot of power from me. I felt spacey and just a little bit unreal.

But beside me, Gem shifted in the stretcher. "Edge?"

I bent down to her, chest lightening. The dark circles under her eyes had faded a little, and her eyes were clear. "How are you feeling?"

"Better," she said. "Not great, but better."

I reached down and hugged her tight, and she half sat up to hug me back. "Thank you," I said over Gemma's back to Aphros.

She inclined her head, but before she could speak, Mum and Mrs Caro raced into the alcove.

"Out!" Mrs Caro said. "Quick, out! Out!"

I stared for a moment, unable to move.

"The fairies!" Mrs Caro said. She and Mum snatched up the stretcher, ignoring Gemma's protests, and hurried to the crossing point.

I joined them, barely touching Mrs Caro's hand before the world faded away. *Don't worry, Gem*, I thought as the world reformed around us. *Aphros and I will do that every week if that's what it takes. You're going to be just fine.*

7

THE BELL WENT for recess, and blearily I packed up my things and stood. Mum had offered to call me in sick for the day, but there was one certain person I needed to see; I had questions that needed answering.

Sadly, this Tuesday started with drama then health, neither of which I shared with Scott. Still, I'd survived them both and now I had recess to track him down—and find a way to make him talk.

We'd gone back to my house last night and before Mrs Caro had loaded Gemma in the car and taken her home, I'd explained to them all what Aphros and I had done.

Mum asked if Gem would be allowed back in Sanctuary now, but Mrs Caro had shaken her head sadly. "I've had dealings with the Keeper before," she'd said. "She never changes her mind."

"But what if Gemma is healed?" I'd asked.

Mrs Caro had shrugged. "Possibly. But we don't even know if that's possible, Edge. It's not like we've had the opportunity to really study the Valley or its connection to people before. We have no idea what's normal and what's not, and what of it might be reversible."

My stomach had twisted. Actually, we had a perfect way to figure out what was normal and what wasn't, and he would be showing up to school in only a few hours' time.

So here I was, half asleep and yawning my head off as I shoved my books into my locker and retrieved an apple, heading off to find the one person I wanted least in the world to speak to.

I found him on one of the school lawns, surrounded by his stupid mates, laughing with them at something.

I blushed awkwardly, even though I knew it wasn't likely they were laughing at me. "Scott?" I interrupted. "Can I talk to you for a sec?"

Valiantly, I ignored the ooo's and wolf whistling and headed to an empty corner of grass. I stood there with my arms folded protectively over my ribs and watched as Scott extricated himself from his circle of minions. The sly smile slipped off his face as soon as his back turned on them, deepening to something just shy of a frown, eyebrows deeply furrowed.

"Come on," he muttered as he stalked past.

I stayed where I was, not wanting to be seen following his orders—then sighed explosively. I wanted to talk in view of his mates even less.

I followed him around the corner and through a walkway to within sight of the front carpark.

"What?" he said, turning and halting abruptly.

I exhaled my frustration. "How much do you know about what's going on with Gemma?"

He shrugged. "What, you mean the weird fit thing in class yesterday? And the fact that she looks more zombie than human?"

"Yeah. That."

He shrugged again. "What about it?"

I chewed my tongue a little. No matter how I said it, he was going to ark up. "What was it like?" I said. "When you first connected to Valley?"

Immediately, he shot me a suspicious look. "I don't remember. Why?"

I plucked a leaf from a nearby tree, running it through my fingers over and over. "How much do you remember about Gemma's involvement when we... You know." Too many questions. But surely he must know, or have guessed.

His eyes narrowed. "What are you not saying? You think Gemma got contaminated when she tried to help you get me out of the Valley and you think I know how to fix it, is that it? Because I don't, and I had nothing to do with it."

I worked to keep my voice level. "I'm not blaming you for anything, Scott," I said, a hint of bite creeping in despite myself. "No one is."

"Then what do you want?"

I shredded the leaf into tiny pieces and scattered them on the ground like confetti. "Look, no one's accusing you of anything," I said, "because it has nothing to do with you. Gemma's connected to the Valley. Not because you contaminated her," I added firmly as he began to protest, "but because she met the pillar of light and accepted its offer."

Scott paled. His eyes widened for a fraction of a second before he re-exerted control.

I squinted at him. "What's going to happen to her, Scott?"

"I... I have no idea." He leaned away, suddenly transfixed by the traffic outside the school fence.

I closed my eyes, shoulders slumping. "Scott, please. Her connection to the Valley is getting stronger literally every hour. I can see it, and it's terrifying. Even you—" I swallowed, my throat abruptly dry. I stretched my fingers out by my sides. "Even you didn't progress that fast until nearly the end," I said roughly.

Out on the road, a car backfired. Scott jerked, staring at where it had been.

"Do you have any idea why the Valley's hold on Gemma is getting so much stronger so fast?" I asked. "Or why she's going practically catatonic?"

"No," he said curtly.

"Is there anything she can do? Any way to fight it?" *Please, let there be something.*

"No!" Scott faced me at last, hands fisted by his sides. "I told you, I don't know anything, okay? It's not my fault she got caught up with the stupid Valley and I don't know anything that will help! It's not my fault," he repeated. Before I could note that I'd already agreed to that, he continued. "I'm not even connected to the Valley anymore. Check. I know you can." His gaze pinned me, defiant.

I bit my lip. I could, though I had no idea how he knew it. He'd probably guessed I had some sort of funky powers going on, considering I'd literally saved him from darkness that ate your soul, but he didn't know that I was a Road Master—if he even knew what a Road Master was.

It was probably a good idea to make sure the Valley wasn't sinking its claws into Scott again. But even without the Valley, Scott's soulprint was... uncomfortable. It gave me the heebie jeebies every time I brushed against it.

But I needed his help, and if he wouldn't give that, I still needed all the information I could get. I exhaled. "Hold still."

His eyes widened briefly, but he obeyed.

Clenching my teeth, I forced myself to search for his soulprint. I scrunched my eyes shut harder: his soulprint wasn't there.

Eyes still closed, I reached out for him. I brushed his shoulder and the crisp cotton of his uniform shirt. I shifted upward, over his collar to where I could press the tips of my fingers lightly against the skin of his neck. Ah. There was his soulprint, just as usual: a dark night sky, a cold wind, a black hilltop under the stars with a clawing sense of space, vastness... Emptiness.

I pulled away hurriedly, choking down instinctual fear borne both from the actual physical sensations of Scott's soulprint, and the horrible, tangled memories it conjured: Scott, his soulprint ripped and torn, enmeshed in the Valley's grip; another girl, Georgia, face crusted with blood and eyes staring blankly at the roof of the bathroom where I'd found her. I breathed deeply through my nose and focussed on expelling the negative energy, just like the police psychologist had taught me.

I realised Scott was staring at me and turned toward him. "What?" I glanced to where his fingers touched his neck, right where my fingers had been, and a thrill of nerves ran through me. Before all the kerfuffle with the Valley, Scott had harboured a pretty intense crush on me; he'd tried to get my attention every way he'd known how. Pity that ninety-nine percent of them had involved humiliating me.

He'd pretty much ignored me since the Valley incident, so I'd sort of forgotten about it. But now...

I pulled my gaze back to his face, forcing myself to act nonchalant. Now I'd probably better not forget about it again.

"What did you do?"

I ignored his question and regathered my thoughts. "You're not connected to the Valley," I said. "But something is definitely wrong."

His soulprint had been faint, hard to find—but was that because of what was happening *now* in the Valley? Or was it because of his connection a couple of weeks ago? I hadn't exactly been seeking him out to check on his recovery, after all.

"Take me with you."

I blinked at him. "Sorry, what?"

"Take me with you." His gaze was unflinching as he clenched his hands.

"*Where?*"

"You know where."

"Actually, I—" I stopped.

There was really only one place he could be referring to, wasn't there? "*Sanctuary?*" I asked, voice pitched low.

He nodded, a short, jerky movement that looked like it cost him far more than it should have. "Sanctuary."

My eyebrows creased together. "But—can't you just go yourself?"

His jaw worked. "No. My mum—I only—I don't know how."

There was a whole lot of information to be mined in that broken whale of a sentence, if only I had the time and brainpower. But Scott, being almost literally the root of all evil for a time there—well, it had never occurred to me that he might not know how to get into the better parts of the other world.

"I'll... consider it?" Voluntarily taking Scott to Sanctuary? It seemed a little like inviting the fox into your chicken coop, and I wasn't quite sure how I felt about it.

Scott's jaw worked again, and I wasn't sure if he was preparing to argue with me or what. "I'll help you," he blurted.

The half-time bell rang. "What?"

"Take me with you. Show me how to get there, to... You know. Show me, and I'll tell you what I know about..." He swallowed. "About what's wrong with Gemma."

I stared as students streamed around us, laughing and chatting and shouting in the middle of their carefree lunchbreak. A quiet breeze lifted wisps of hair off my face. "Promise?"

Scott's hands clenched again as he nodded. "I'll tell you," he said. "I promise."

8

I ARRIVED IN the glade after school, half expecting Scott not to be there. But he was ready and waiting, pacing back and forth and trying just a little too hard not to look at the crossing to the Valley on the other side of the tea-coloured creek.

"You okay?" I said as I sat on a rock. At my feet, a host of out-of-place plants grew—feathery carrot tops, their roots nearly ready for picking; a small host of native paper daisies; and a little way behind, a neat row of sunflowers, merrily bobbing their heads in the hot afternoon sunshine.

Scott stopped short. "Yeah. Fine."

And my name was Googlymuffin, and Gemma was in perfect health. Yup. Just fine. I motioned him to a nearby rock. Once he'd perched gingerly on the edge of it, shoulders tight, I pulled a packet of seeds from my pocket and flashed it at him.

His eyebrows lifted. "Carrots?" he said. "I thought you were showing me how to get to Sanctuary, not... *gardening*." He waved dismissively at the plants.

Okay, now I did roll my eyes. "Less sass, more listening," I commanded. I shook a couple of tiny carrot seeds onto my palm and held them out. "Step one, seeds." I glanced up to see him concentrating on my hand. "You used death sacrifices to power your crossing to the Valley. We use life magic, contained in seeds."

His jaw worked. "You used shadow magic too."

I snatched my hand back, fingers closing protectively around the seeds. "Yeah, but I never killed anything to do it."

Scott frowned. "Then how did you do it?"

"I sacrificed part of myself, okay?" I snapped. Memories of my hand sliced open, blood dripping to the ground to power the crossing...

Nausea welled in my stomach, just as it had after using the death magic.

I hadn't turned into a monster as I'd feared, and it had been totally necessary at the time, given Scott had been almost completely possessed by the Valley and only a few minutes away from taking over the world—but it wasn't something I enjoyed thinking about. Not least because it had hurt like someone pulling my brain out my nose with a hot poker. "I thought you were here to learn about life magic."

Scott held his hands up with his palms facing me. "Whoa, I am. Sorry!"

I glared at him for a moment longer, then held out the seeds again. "Look, the principle's exactly the same," I said. "Visualise where you want to go, shove the seed in the soil, and use your travelling abilities to activate the life magic in the seed."

Scott tilted his head. "The life of the seed powers the crossing?"

"That is literally what I just said."

"So why doesn't the seed die? I mean, you're using its life to power your crossing, so how does it still have life left?"

I snapped my mouth closed and glared at him some more. "Because life creates more life." That seemed plausible, right? Mentally I added his question to a growing list of things to ask Quoise.

He shook his head. "That doesn't make sense. If—"

"Look, it just works, okay? Are we going to do this or not? Because I totally have other things I could be doing..." I licked the tip of one finger and stuck a carrot seed on it.

Scott held his hands up again. "I hope you're not going to be a teacher when you grow up."

I narrowed my eyes and stretched a deliberately fake smile into place, tucking the seed packet back into my pocket. "Give me your hand."

He blinked. "My hand? Why?"

I hissed through my teeth. "So I can transport you to Sanctuary, idiot. Hand?"

He stretched out hesitantly and took my free hand. His palm was warm and soft—but the skin contact heightened my road mastery. I tightened my grip so I wouldn't accidentally pull away in response to the cold, prickling emptiness of his soulprint.

Scott stared intently at our joined hands.

Quickly, I shoved my finger with the seed on it into the ground and made the crossing to Sanctuary.

The instant we arrived, I bounced to my feet, releasing Scott and dusting myself off.

I stalked to the far side of the entrance alcove, where the rockery tumbled and swirled, grey boulders the size of wombats spiralling across a field of white pebbles.

Scott followed. I tried not to watch him, but from the corner of my eye I could see him staring openly at his new surroundings, and part of me was deathly curious: what would he think of Sanctuary?

"It's so quiet," he said softly as he stopped next to me, still peering around. "It's…" He drew in a long, steadying breath.

"Yeah," I said. "Calming hormones. I have no clue how it does it, but being here increases your body's production of calming hormones. Here," I added. "Watch this."

Amidst the rockery, small, red-leafed bushes glimmered and flickered like fire. I plucked a leaf off one and crouched where two of the larger grey rocks met and formed a crevice—a cave for something small. It seemed a likely spot. I waggled the leaf enticingly. *Come on. Come out and play.*

Ah ha. Deep in the shadow, something moved. Behind me, Scott started to speak, but I waved at him urgently with my free hand, and he quietened.

Waggle waggle. *Heeeeere, little critter. Come get the leaf. Nice, tasty, flaming leaf…*

Pounce! One instant, just a leaf: the next, a fire-bright lizard-shaped creature hung from it, large, hinged jaws snapped tight on the leathery frond. I swung it around and dangled it at Scott.

He eyed it suspiciously. "What is it?"

"Fire salamander." I offered it to him. "Go on. Take it."

Cautiously, he reached out toward the foot-long lizard. An inch away, he stopped. "Will it bite?"

I smiled a gentle baby-panda of a smile. "Trust me."

For just a second he flicked his gaze toward me and his eyes met mine. "I do."

He took the lizard more carefully than I'd have expected, but his grip was sure and gentle, like he was used to handling animals. My stomach dropped as I remembered a tiny white mouse, near dead, right before Scott had wrung its neck.

Scott laughed—not at me, but a tiny, barely-heard sound of genuine delight. The salamander was licking his thumb while warm, happy flames radiated from its back.

Oh. That was... unexpected. Maybe he wasn't a complete monster after all. "Come on," I said. "I'll show you the unicorns."

He followed, still cradling the salamander as we left the entrance alcove.

Halfway to the stables, I realised that a small flock of fairies was making their way down from the Lodge, and that they would reach the stables at about the same time we would. I licked my lower lip, wondering how they would take to Scott.

Scott had noticed them too, casting nervous glances at them as we continued up the hillside.

Even though Sanctuary lived in perpetual twilight, it felt darker than usual this afternoon. Or maybe that was just the lack of Gemma; nearing the stables with Scott by my side instead felt a little surreal.

Aphros appeared in the doorway of the stables, and abruptly, some of Scott's tension melted.

I'd forgotten that they'd met while Aphros was trapped in the Valley. Though, had I remembered, I certainly wouldn't have expected a welcome this affectionate—from either of them.

I hesitated a few paces away. Maybe this was why Scott had wanted to visit Sanctuary so much? They seemed pretty darn friendly. Especially considering that I was the one who'd saved Aphros from the clutches of the Valley's evil soulprint—the evil soulprint Scott had brought to life.

A tiny, logical part of me that I didn't want to listen to right now pointed out that I could literally speak straight to Aphros's mind; Scott was hardly going to replace me.

And then I didn't have the chance to listen to any part of me, logical or not, because the fairies arrived, the Keeper at the front in her emerald-green tunic and tiny gold coronet.

"What are you doing?" she hissed—at Scott, at Aphros, or maybe both?

Aphros turned to her. "Welcoming a newcomer," she said mildly.

In the depths of the stables, the twin baby unicorns whinnied.

"*Newcomer*? Fraternising with the enemy, more like," the Keeper replied, planting her hands on her hips.

Aphros tossed her mane, the point of her horn scribing an arc dangerously close to a gold-winged fairy. "That is a matter of history," she said, stamping a hoof. "I make friends in the present."

"And I'm sure that works out very well for you," the Keeper said, "but it is my job to keep the traditions of Sanctuary, and I'm quite attached to history." She shifted her gaze to Scott, who caught her eye briefly before staring off toward the pines that separated the meadow from the beach.

"As for you," the Keeper continued, her voice heavy with distaste, "I cannot even understand why you would show your face here, after all you did, and nearly did. Are you that proud, that you must come in here to gloat?"

Scott didn't reply, though his fingers twitched by his sides.

"I brought him here," I said, stepping forward.

"Yes, I should have guessed as much," the Keeper replied with a similar level of disgust. "Queen Rule Breaker herself."

My stomach did a complicated flip-flop. "I only break rules," I said through clenched teeth, reminding myself of all the reasons I couldn't—shouldn't—shout at the ruler of the fairies, "when someone's life is at stake."

The Keeper's left eyebrow didn't believe me. "Oh? And whose life is at stake, that you would bring him"—she jabbed the word at Scott—"here?"

"I didn't know bringing him here was against the rules," I shot back. "It seems like they're changing daily." I inhaled sharply, hoping I hadn't just crossed an irreversible line.

The Keeper pursed her lips. "Well. I suppose you'll just have to learn to keep up, won't you." She gave me a saccharine smile and turned to Scott. "Scott Anthony Harden, you are herewith formally banned from Sanctuary. If I catch you here again, you can be sure it will end unpleasantly."

"Oh, because today's visit was such a picnic." I glared at her.

She glanced disinterestedly at me. "Be careful, Emma Jeanette Tanning. You are on your last warning yourself." With that parting blow, she led her posse of fairies back up the hill.

"Lovely creature," said Scott. "Is she always so friendly?"

Aphros snorted.

I shook my head. "Come on. We'd better go."

"Why?" Scott said, eyebrows lifting in mild surprise. "She's gone."

I shook my head again. "The fairies can sense it if we stay here. They're all... They can sense who's in Sanctuary," I added, not wanting to get into the fine details of road mastery right now.

He nodded, expressionless. "So let's go, I guess."

We farewelled Aphros and set off back toward the entrance alcove.

"What else have *you* done to piss her off?"

I cut him a sharp glance, but he seemed to be asking genuinely enough. "Apart from illegally entering the Valley to get rid of the shadows and save your life? Brought Gemma here for help."

His eyebrows were even more surprised this time, and he walked backward for a few steps, watching my face. "You're kidding."

"Nope. They kicked her out and told her never to come back, same as you."

Scott stuck his hands deep into his pockets. "Friendly bunch. I can see why this is supposed to be the land of all that's good and pure."

I glared at him—but a weightier thought intruded. "You'll still tell me, though?" I said. "What you know about Gem? Even though the Keeper kicked you out?" In my defence, I'd had no idea the Keeper would react like that, although I supposed a less-than-rosy greeting should have been expected. But... "It wasn't like it was Gem's fault," I added quietly.

He shrugged, hands still in his pockets, and tears of anger welled in my eyes. "Hey," he said sharply as they spilled over onto my cheeks. "None of that. Of course I'll still tell you."

I inhaled, swiping at my cheeks. "I'm not crying," I said. "I'm angry."

"Yeah, my eyes leak all the time when I'm mad, too."

"Shut up."

We entered the alcove and I exhaled noisily. "No. Don't shut up. Talk. Tell me what you know."

Scott nodded. "I will. Promise." He hesitated, side-eyeing me. "Tomorrow."

"Tomorrow? Gemma could be dead by then!"

He drew back, alarmed. "No way. It doesn't happen that fast."

I shrugged. "It pretty much is this time."

Scott puffed up his cheeks and released his breath slowly. "I guess it makes sense. You didn't actually damage the Valley at all, you know. You just... disconnected it from its current body."

"*Your* body." Oh, oops. Probably shouldn't have reminded him of that.

Reminded. Ha. As if he'd ever be able to forget.

"My body," he agreed carefully. "And whatever... *humanity* it had managed to absorb. But you didn't fundamentally change it, or distil any of its power, and now it has a new human connection—and this time it knows exactly what it's doing."

"Help me," I said levelly, trying to pin him with my gaze. "Help me fight it."

He shook his head, not a negative, just... overwhelmed, I realised. "You have no idea what you're asking."

"So tell me."

He met my gaze briefly. "I will," he said. "Tomorrow."

"I said, tomorrow she could—"

He cut me off with a wave. "There's something you need to see first, to understand. I'll bring it to school. Tomorrow." He said it firmly, and I knew this time there'd be no arguing.

Stubborn git-face. "Fine," I said, because what other choice did I have? "Tomorrow. First thing. I'll meet you at my locker. *First thing.*"

He nodded and stretched out a hand. "First thing."

I stared at his hand. Did he want me to shake it? Because he wasn't holding it right if he was.

Sensing my confusion, Scott gestured impatiently. "To go back?"

Oh. Right. Of course.

I took his hand. "It might be late when we get back," I warned. "The time slips happen at random without a fairy to help."

He bared his teeth, and if I didn't look too closely, it might have been a smile. "That's fine," he said. "No one at my house cares what I do."

I sat on the grass and closed my eyes. "Well, here's hoping it's not too wildly out," I said. "Because at my house, everyone cares what I do."

9

THE BELL WENT for lunch and I slammed my science textbook shut.

I'd waited by my locker until the last possible moment both before school and at recess—still no Scott. I'd sat through a double period of Maths, then a lesson of English, and now Science—all classes I shared with both Gemma and Scott—but there'd been no Scott. My chances of him showing up for the day now were slim to none.

I fought my way out of the classroom a little more vigorously than usual, and once I had finally reached my locker and shoved my books inside, I slammed the door shut viciously. This would teach me to trust evil, shadow-spawning, good-for-nothing morons with pretty hair.

Really, the pretty hair should have been the giveaway, I thought as I snatched my sandwich out of my bag. Showed he was really just a selfish idiot who only cared about appearances.

A sea of students ebbed and flowed around me, and I cast about for direction, oddly adrift. There was no Gemma to follow, no Scott to avoid.

I clenched my free hand—and then, just for the feel of it, pinched my sandwich until my thumb and forefinger met through the bread. Untrustworthy froghead.

I stomped across the lawns and found an unoccupied bit of garden edging to perch on. I could only hope that the block Aphros and I had done would hold.

If not, I'd sneak Gemma in again and we'd do another one. Again, and again, and again, until I figured out a way to fix this, if that's what it took.

Something thumped onto the paved path at my feet. I blinked, then craned up to see who'd dumped the book.

My heart practically clawed at my ribcage. Standing with his back to the sun so it glowed around him like a misplaced halo—was Scott.

"What the—"

He shifted, halo diminishing—and I could see how complicated his face looked, eyes sad and scared, lips tight to match the line of his shoulders. "Just read it," he said.

"But what is it?" I glanced back at the thick, worn book—journal?—lying on the ground.

"Nothing," he said. "Just read it." He twitched, fingers curling as though he wanted to reach down and grab it. A moment of pain and longing, then he stalked away.

"Hey!" I called, standing. He ignored me, and what else could I say? Come back? I need your help? Where have you been all morning? Why weren't you here when I needed you?

I swallowed hard and screwed my eyes shut against welling tears. None of that. I couldn't say any of it, not to Scott, not here.

A cloud crossed over the sun and the world dimmed to muted greys. I picked up the book, sat back down, and let it fall open on my lap.

It settled somewhere about three quarters of the way through, revealing page after page of careful, deliberate handwriting. Scott's?

January 12. Nothing new.

January 13. Nothing important.

January 14. Nothing that matters.

I turned to the front, wondering if there would be an explanation. Was this some kind of weird diary after all? Scott definitely didn't strike me as the kind of person who'd keep a diary, but then again, you never knew.

The front page was blank, but the second page... I frowned.

I am Scott Anthony Harden. My birthday is July 9. If I am in trouble, I should call 000 and ask for the police.

The next lines listed his address and a note that he lived with his Mum and Dad—but it had all been crossed out, with a line ruled neatly through it.

'With Mum' had an extra line—probably, I realised, squinting at it closely, because it had been crossed out first, before the rest of the sentence.

Below, written neatly, was 'I live with Aunt Sally', with a slightly more distant address.

I traced a finger over the ruled-out lines, chest constricting, brow knitting. He'd moved, no longer with his parents but an aunt—and his mum had somehow gone first.

I turned the page.

Mum is five foot six with dark hair and dark eyes. She gets angry easily, especially when she comes home late at night—avoid morning after. I frowned. Why would Scott want me to know this? How did it help? And why not just tell me, rather than writing it down?

Spare money usually in sock drawer—the top right one—socks are for feet (warmth). Pizza (good food) delivery is 120 000. Press those numbers into the spare phone Dad gave you—hidden under the loose floorboard at the foot of my bed (sleeping place). Do not call Dad.

Abruptly, I flicked the page over. These notes seemed far too personal; surely Scott hadn't intended for me to read that part.

I cleared my throat, letting the journal rest open on my lap as I scrubbed my sweaty palms against my thighs.

The next page wasn't any better, beginning, "Dad is usually out of town working." Hurriedly, I skipped to the end.

Blank. I flipped back until I found Scott's writing again, then turned back a small chunk of pages.

November 27. I forgot my name today. It's been months since I've forgotten anything—the gaps seem to actually be healing now, and I haven't forgotten anything since I... Since Mum left. But I forgot my name today, and I didn't have the book to remind me, and I panicked.

Then the new girl, Emma, asked me—Scott, right?—and all I could do was nod.

She didn't care, just sat down next to me, half ignoring me as she explained that the teacher had told her to work with me this lesson— and we did, we worked, and she never said much and I never had to worry about whether she'd ask me something I couldn't answer, and I didn't care if my name was Scott or Steve, because who I was didn't matter to her, and I could have been anyone.

A couple of blank lines, and then in a different coloured pen, an annotation:

I never want to be Someone again.

November 27. That would have been my first week at the school, at the end of last year when we'd moved up suddenly from Melbourne. I'd forgotten I'd ever worked with Scott on anything. That had been... in English, maybe?

I glanced back to where he'd written my name, and adrenalin spiked through my stomach. I remembered speculating at one point that all I'd done for Scott to be infatuated with me was ignore him, not falling over myself at him like everyone else. Scary how true my throwaway comment seemed to have been.

But how did this help me with Gem?

Wait, he'd said something about forgetting.

Lightning struck in my head, and I clenched the book.

Memories. Scott had been losing his memories, and this was where he'd recorded everything he'd need to know if he suddenly forgot something important.

The Valley. The Valley must have made him lose his memories—at least in the beginning, because he'd said in that entry about me (nerves ran through me again) that he hadn't forgotten anything for a while.

Gem didn't seem to be forgetting anything. Was that because it was all happening too fast? Surely that would have sped up the memory loss too—unless the Valley had all the memories it needed?

I flipped back to near the start of the book and began hunting for anything that sounded magical, anything that might be linked to the Valley—or death magic.

My stomach churned and despite the heat of the day, goosebumps rose on my arms; what if memory loss was the result of using death magic?

I couldn't *think* of anything I'd forgotten; there didn't *seem* to be any holes in my memories—but if I'd forgotten, if using death magic had stolen things from me, would I even know before it was too late? Suddenly, Scott's obsessive annotating—'socks are for feet (warmth)'—made sense.

But this line of thought wasn't helping Gem. I shook my head and resumed skimming the entries in the journal.

Gradually, over the next half hour, a picture formed: Scott (and possibly his mother?) had travelled on something he only called 'the roads' to find the heart of the Valley, a physical location that it seemed could only be reached on said roads—and there, something had happened. He avoided saying it outright, and I guessed it was one memory he wouldn't be sorry to lose. But whatever else had happened, the Valley had been woken there.

The warning bell for the end of lunch rang, and I stood, hugging the journal to my chest, lighter than I'd been in days. The power of the Valley had a physical location, and it could be woken—which meant it could be put back to sleep. If I could find this place, put the Valley back to sleep...

Surely then the connection between Gem and the Valley would disappear, and she would be okay. Surely that kind of disconnection wouldn't harm her, because I wouldn't be messing around with her soulprint; the connection would just... vanish.

I hugged the journal again and tucked it carefully into my locker—Scott seemed to have totally disappeared once more.

That was a pain—I had approximately a thousand million questions to ask him now—but at least—at *least*—I had a plan.

Find roads.

Find Valley's power.

Shut it down.

Save Gemma.

Lists. Lists really did make the world seem bright.

10

I DIDN'T MANAGE to find Scott again for the rest of the day, so as soon as I got home, I changed out of my uniform and ran down to the glade. If I couldn't ask Scott about the roads, at least I could brainstorm with Aphros.

I arrived in Sanctuary and sought out Aphros, not with my road mastery, but with our mysterious connection that had developed when Aphros had joined her soulprint with mine in our final battle against the Valley.

A hint of minty freshness drifted through the air and instinctively I breathed deeply. Aphros's soft green-and-gold soulprint blossomed against my senses, a trail of colour and scent winding through the grass at my feet.

Aphros's soulprint led me out of the alcove, up the meadow, past the Lodge, and to a small garden of trees and pale-coloured flowers. As I neared, the trail broadened, becoming brighter and clearer to my senses—and it was joined by another pair of trails, also pale green and gold, but one with a hint of cornflower blue and the other with twirls of bronze. My lips twitched upward. The unicorn babies always brought a smile.

"Hi, Aphros," I said as I approached her. She stood with her back to me, watching the two foals frolicking in the grass. Lily, the one with the blue in her soulprint, sniffed at a bush covered in the little white star flowers that were everywhere in Sanctuary, and sneezed. Filibere, the bronze twin, flared his nostrils at me warily. "It's just me," I told him, holding out my hand. He cautiously inched closer, propped about two paces away, and dashed around the clearing before coming to a halt behind his mother.

I gave him half a smile. "Yeah. I'd hide too if I thought it'd do any good."

"Wouldn't we all," a soft voice muttered—Quoise, appearing from behind a tree.

"Hi," I told her, and she greeted me back. "So, I have news," I said, plopping down on the ground beside Aphros.

Quoise fluttered down to perch nearby. "Oh? How's Gem?"

"Did the block hold?" Aphros added, nose twitching.

I nodded. "I think so. I haven't seen her today yet though. But Mrs Caro would have called if something had gone wrong, I'm sure of it." She'd helped me get out of school once before to save Gem; I knew she wouldn't hesitate to do it again if Gemma really needed me. "But I talked to Scott today."

Quoise leaned closer; Aphros's ears twitched.

"Well. Talked, not so much. He showed me a journal," I amended. My pulse jumped and I licked my lips. "Did you know he was losing his memories?" I said, turning to Aphros.

She shook her mane. "No. He showed no signs of this while I knew him."

I puffed my cheeks up and exhaled. "It had probably stopped by then. It seems," I said carefully, "like the memory loss was connected to something he called the roads. And on these roads is a physical location where we can access the power of the Valley."

Quoise stiffened immediately, and Aphros stomped her hint foot.

"What?" I said as Quoise looked back at Aphros, eyes wide like she was pleading. I looked back and forth between the two of them, then planted my fists on my hips. "Alright, what's going on? What are you two not saying?"

They held their gaze a while longer, and I opened my mouth, but Quoise sighed, shoulders slumping, and turned toward me. "A lot," she muttered, with a furious glance at Aphros. "There's a lot we're not saying."

Aphros snorted. "You can say that again."

"Wow, thank you. That's so helpful."

Quoise sighed. "You tell her," she said, nodding to Aphros.

Aphros shook out her mane. "It's your mess," she muttered, but she swung toward me. "I'm not sure where to start, exactly," she said. "As far as I know"—she shot a hard glare at Quoise—"Sanctuary and the Valley were both created in the same way."

Quoise shrugged. "That's what I've always been told."

"Wait," I interjected. "Sanctuary and the Valley were *created*? By who?"

Quoise shrugged again. "I'm not sure if the Keeper knows and isn't saying, or is just pretending she knows so she can lord it over the rest of us." She gasped, hands flying up to cover her mouth. "I can't believe I said that," she mumbled through her fingers, eyes wide.

Aphros snorted again. "This is your influence on her you know," she said to me.

I opened my mouth to protest but caught a glimmer in her eye. I grinned instead. "Okay, so the Valley and Sanctuary were created in the same way. How does that relate to Gem?"

"You are familiar with the balance," Aphros said, and I nodded.

"That was the representation of Sanctuary and the Valley's magics. It isn't real, it is a projection, but the *sources* of the magics? Those are real."

I frowned. "So Scott's right. Somewhere out there"—I gestured broadly—"is not only a magic box that powers the Valley, but also one that powers Sanctuary."

Aphros exchanged a glance with Quoise. "Essentially, yes. You got close to the Valley's power source when you entered the sinkhole to find Gemma—and Scott."

I nodded. "From what I can see, Scott's suggesting that we find the Valley's power source on these roads, then we might be able to shut it down. That wouldn't damage Gem like trying to actually remove the connection, would it?"

Aphros tilted her head. "I *think* not."

Quoise buzzed her wings in agitation. "For the record, I think this is a very bad idea. Going anywhere near the Valley is dangerous, let alone into the very source of power itself."

"I survived the sinkhole last time," I pointed out.

Aphros cleared her throat.

"Well, yes, with help."

Quoise shook her head. "Don't underestimate this, Edge. You made it out. But a fairy died last time, remember?"

My stomach flopped. "I remember."

"That's part of why the Keeper is so scared of Gem being here," Quoise continued. "Sanctuary's magic is literally all that keeps us alive. Earth has a little magic, enough that we can travel over for visits, but the Valley—the Valley has nothing to sustain us, so if we cross over there, we die. Instantly. And Gemma being here... It's like she's bringing the Valley's magic into Sanctuary. For us, that could literally be life threatening."

I folded my arms across my chest. "You didn't seem to be too threatened when the Valley's shadows were trying to *take over* Sanctuary earlier in the year."

"Don't assume you know everything that goes on in the Lodge," Quoise said evenly. "Just because we didn't project panic doesn't mean people weren't worried. Why do you think I helped you?"

I shook my head. This *did* explain why Quoise had seemed so reluctant to help me, and why she'd given me the unicorn-hair ward without really telling me what to do with it. "Okay," I said. "I acknowledge that this is a really dangerous thing to do. But do you have any better suggestions for how to fix Gemma? Any other secrets that might help?"

She sniffed softly. "Plenty of secrets. None that may help, other than your hair-brained scheme."

"*Scott's* hair-brained scheme," I pointed out.

"Strangely enough, that's not encouraging."

Aphros snorted. "Maybe you could take a walk down to the Lodge," she murmured.

I glanced sharply at her. "Why the Lodge? I thought we weren't talking to the fairies about this. Quoise excepted, obviously."

"Library?" Aphros said over my head at Quoise.

Quoise's wings snapped out and she shot a metre up into the air. "Yes. If we have any information on these roads, that's where it'll be." She grinned. "So, Edge, breaker of all the fairies' rules, how would you feel about a little trespassing?"

"Will it help Gemma?" I asked, standing up.

"Probably," Quoise said, "though I can't promise."

"I'm in," I said. "Like you even had to ask."

She led the way from the garden as the twin unicorns collapsed in an adorable heap by Aphros, exhausted from their exploring.

My heart hammered. We had a plan, and we were doing something about it. "Just a little bit longer," I murmured, thinking of Gem. "Hold on."

11

QUOISE HAD LED me through winding corridors in the Lodge until at last she'd stopped in front of a dark wooden door. She'd opened it with a flourish. "Ta da!"

I'd peeked through, and my jaw had dropped. Shelves rose far above my head, at least two storeys high—and where they ended the room kept going, a vast void at least another two storeys high, dotted with the same kinds of fairy furniture I'd seen in the main foyer: small tables and chairs sprouting from the walls, comfy couches, hammocks and cushions suspended from the roof at different heights, a few platforms rising out of the shelves themselves.

And all around, the walls were utterly filled with books, all the way to the magnificent roof, where intricate floral and leafy patterns twisted and wound, making the ceiling seem like a living garden. I could live in this cavernous room for the rest of my life.

"Pretty, isn't it?" Quoise had said as I'd stepped, awed, into the space.

"Uh huh."

"We don't generally let visitors in here, you know. Come on. Keep your head down and look innocent." She had let the wooden door fall shut behind us. "For this we need the restricted section."

And now we'd been in the restricted section for nearly an hour, hunkering down behind shelves every time someone came close. The tiny text of the book in my lap was blurring, and my stomach rumbled. I slammed the fairy-sized book closed—inasmuch as it was possible to slam a book the size of my phone—and leaned back against the shelves.

"Nothing?" said Quoise. Her voice sounded flat and tired.

"Not a thing," I said.

"I'm so sorry," Quoise said. "I was so sure there would be something here. We write *everything* down. I must not have the search terms right." She dragged a hand over her face.

"It's fine," I said, closing my eyes as I leaned against a shelf. "We'll find something eventually."

Quoise kicked the shelf she hovered next to, the movement jolting her in the air. "It's just so stupid," she said. "Before I met you, I never questioned any of this." She gestured broadly at the library around us. "But last month, with the shadows, and Aphros, and *you...*" She shook her head.

"What *about* me, though?" I said, propping one elbow on the shelf and leaning my head on my hand. "What can I do that you guys can't? You said that things were happening here in the Lodge to deal with the shadows, but it sure didn't look like it. You're all Road Masters," I pointed out. "So what did I do that you couldn't have done?"

Quoise sighed, a full-bodied exhale that left her sagging, defeated. "You're a Road Master, Edge," she said tiredly.

My brows crinkled. "I know that."

"But you don't know what it *means*," she said, staring at the books on the shelf. "Because I didn't tell you. I'm not supposed to."

I sat very still.

"You can do a lot more than you think," she said at last. "We can sense everyone's soulprints. But unlike you, we can't manipulate them. What you did, separating Scott's soulprint from the Valley? We can't do anything direct like that. We can see, but not touch."

"I can only do that with Aphros's help, though," I said.

"For now."

The room didn't move, but it might as well have. "So you're *not* Road Masters?"

Quoise shrugged. "To-may-to, to-mah-to."

"So what else can I do that you can't?"

She frowned. "Hold on, road mastery. That's it!" She shot up into the air and disappeared.

I sat, wondering if I was supposed to follow her.

I didn't have to wait long; she returned shortly, carrying a vivid green book, the exact colour of new spring grass. She dropped it on my lap. Embossed gold lettering curled across the cover, tendrils snaking to the edges and over the spine.

Through Roads Between: a field guide to road mastery.

"Road mastery!" Quoise explained, wings quivering with excitement. "There might not be anything on Scott's roads or the heart of the Valley specifically in the library, but everything there is to know about road mastery is here. Open it!" She gestured at the volume, almost as tall as she was and at least an inch thick.

"How did you even carry this?" I mused as I flipped it open. I skimmed down the contents until my fingers found Chapter Five: On The Roads. That sounded promising.

The chapter header was in the same curling, dangerous font as the cover. I skimmed through a couple of paragraphs, then settled into reading.

Thus far we have explored the various ways to use road mastery skills in the everyday world, the text read. *But the true purpose of road mastery—and indeed, the talent for which it is named—is to enable those equipped with such a skill to travel the Roads Between. These roads extend between the waypoints and the worlds and are usually by-passed by the skill of travelling, or moving instantaneously from one location to another. However, while the traveller is limited to visiting only places that they can clearly envisage in their mind, using the roads enables the road master to explore and discover organically.*

"This sounds promising," I said to Quoise, who perched on the shelf behind me so she could read over my shoulder.

"But does it say anything about what the roads *are?*"

"I dunno." I skimmed a finger further down the page. "This bit sounds right, though."

The Roads Between are dangerous and generally impassable, I read aloud. *Consisting of the chaotic soup from which the likes of the Valley of Sanctuary and Repose was carved. All dangers, all confusion, all chaos exist therein, and for a non-Road Master to step on them alone is death. Road Masters, however, may sense the thread of purpose that unites the roads together, and may follow it from one land to another.* I craned around to Quoise. "Sanctuary was *carved?* By who?" I added when she nodded.

She shrugged. "No idea. That's just what we've always been told. It could just be a story, a myth."

I read on. *There are two things to consider when contemplating the use of the roads: firstly, how to navigate them, and secondly, how to find them. Although this might seem a counter-intuitive order, to find the roads without knowing how to navigate them is as much a trap for the Road Master as for the ordinary person, for a Road Master can find the sensory input of the roads overwhelming unless they have been conditioned and are prepared for what they will experience.*

Indeed, it is a surfeit of sensory input that indicates the location of the roads; a whiff of scent where none should belong, a half-heard noise with no apparent origin; any sensory signs that are over and beyond expectations for that location; these are clear signs that the roads are near.

Quoise stiffened.

"What? What is it?"

Her eyes widened, bright and excited. "I know where the roads are."

"*What?*"

"The roads. Scott's right. There *is* a way to the power source of the Valley, and I know how to find it."

Adrenalin leapt through me and I leaned toward her. "You can get me there?"

She shook her head. "I can't travel on the roads—the book is right," she said, gesturing to where it lay in my lap. "You need a proper Road Master to travel these roads, like you. I can't travel with you," Quoise said, shaking her head, "but I can get you to the entrance. There's a place... You'll get wet. But there's a cave, down by the beach, I think it should be large enough for you to fit. Inside, the air is strange, and every now and then you can hear echoes, like stray soulprints hovering in the air. I've been there a few times, and..."

She shivered and met my eye intently. "Edge, if it's true, if where I'm thinking of is the start of the roads, you can't just wander onto them, not without training. There are massive power blocks in place that you'd have to break through—they're there to stop people wandering in accidentally, but they're strong, and..." She swallowed. "You could... get hurt. And then you'd have to know what you were doing once you were *on* the roads. If this book is right, if it's the place I'm thinking of, you could end up stranded over there, unable to move or think, completely overwhelmed."

"Slow eventual death?" I asked.

She nodded. "Slow eventual death. Please. Just... think about this, before you try it. You need training. Somehow." She rubbed her face, frustration wrinkling her brow.

I shook my head. "I'm doing it. You know I am." I held up a hand to forestall her protests. "But I don't have to do it alone, and I don't need to spend weeks training. If I took someone with me who'd been on the roads before, that would make it okay, right?"

"Maybe, but—"

"Scott," I said levelly, holding her gaze.

Quoise inhaled sharply. Doubt and fear crossed her face, but she drew herself together and they melted into simple concern. She nodded, a short, sharp jerk of acknowledgement. "Yes. That makes sense. If what you've told me about him is true, if he's been on the roads as a non-Road Master... Well, that would explain the memory loss. He's *not* a Road Master—goodness knows how he found the roads," she added, frowning—"so when he travelled the roads, they took some of his memories as payment."

That... made a lot of sense. Except for the bit about him getting onto the roads. Could he be a Road Master without anyone knowing, perhaps? Quoise had only realised I was because I'd told her about the trails I could see. Maybe he was hiding something else after all—maybe that's why he'd wanted me to read the journal, rather than telling me about it face-to-face—he didn't want to risk accidentally telling me too much.

"And provided he hasn't lost any of *those* memories," Quoise continued, "then yes. Yes, that would work."

I nodded decisively and stood, stretching out my neck. "Well then. I guess I'd better go convince him to help me."

"Edge," Quoise said, fluttering up and resting her fingertips on my cheek. "Oh, Edge. Be careful."

"Always," I said, smiling, and we both knew that while it wasn't exactly a lie, there was definitely a large helping of wishful thinking. "I promise."

One day, I'd learn not to make promises I wasn't sure I could keep.

But in the meantime, I had a Scott to convince, and I needed all the bluff I could get.

12

AS I HEADED back down the slope from the Lodge, the smell of salt drifted in from Sanctuary's beach. I peered over at the pine trees that separated meadow from sand. Somewhere over that way lay Gemma's only hope.

A niggling at my road mastery drew my attention to the entrance alcove. I pursed my lips. Scott. *My* only hope—at least if I wanted to stay sane while on the roads. But what on earth was he doing here?

He opened his mouth as I approached, but I shook my head in warning. I grabbed his arm and practically dragged him back to the alcove. "What are you *doing* here?" I said. "The Keeper banned you!"

Scott shrugged, extricating his arm from my grip. "So? I needed to talk to you. Where else was I supposed to find you?"

"Oh, I don't know, at *school*? What happened? I looked everywhere for you!"

He shifted awkwardly. "Sorry. Did you read it?"

Abruptly, I sagged. I had bigger things to worry about than fighting with Scott about—well, anything. And really, Scott had bigger things to worry about too. "Yeah. I read it. I... I'm sorry."

Scott shrugged again. "It happens."

Yeah, losing your memory from magical roads and being possessed by the Valley of Death; no big deal. Happens all the time. "So what did you want to talk to me about?" I stepped a few paces to the left to perch on one of the rockery's better-sized boulders. Better to chat here than back home; here, I had Sanctuary's calming atmosphere on my side, and if we hung out near the entry we could easily escape in time if the fairies noticed Scott's presence.

(How they could miss him at all was the real mystery; here in Sanctuary, his soulprint was back to full strength again, and the sense of vastness tugged constantly at the edge of my awareness. He wasn't connected to the Valley anymore, but there was *something* going on with his soulprint, that was certain.)

Scott said nothing.

I ground my teeth. I couldn't press him too hard; I really did need his help. But how could I convince him to talk?

Anna.

My sister was an expert at getting information out of people, whether they wanted to talk or not. What would she do in this situation?

Ha, right. Reverse psychology it was.

"It's okay," I said. "If you can't talk about it. I found some information in the library about the roads that might help."

He shot me a wary glance, full of suspicion. "What information?"

My turn to shrug. "I'm a Road Master. That's how I saved you, back... you know. Anyway, I'm a Road Master, which means I can sense people's, uh, soulprints. Auras, sort of. Quoise found a book in their library that explain how Road Masters can use the roads you mentioned."

He stared at me intently. "I know what the books say. The books are wrong."

I didn't hit him in the face, and I mentally awarded myself five million points for restraint. "Look," I said. "The heart of the Valley is on the roads. Gemma is connected to the Valley. If I go on these roads, I can get to the Valley, shut it back down again, and ta da!" I jazzed my hands. "Gemma will be saved."

"Travel the roads?" Scott said a couple of pitches higher than usual. "To the *Valley*?"

"Yes. That was your plan, right?"

"No! The roads are crazy dangerous! That's why I showed you the diary!"

I gave him sceptical eyebrows. "A note of explanation might have been useful, in that case. Or, you know, walking up to me and going, 'Hey, I got connected to the Valley because I found its massive power source on these things called the roads, but don't try it, because you'll *die*.'" I tilted my head at him emphatically. "Anyway," I said, leaning back and relaxing. "I'll be fine. You're not a Road Master. I am."

"You keep saying that like it matters," he said.

"Uh, it does?"

He turned his face away. "Not as much as you seem to think."

"What do you mean?" Was this what the book had meant about needing training?

"The roads," he said. He gave a sniffly inhale, dragged his arm over his face, and sat down next to me. He'd missed a spot: one damp tear-track was still visible near the far side of his chin. "You can't travel them alone." His voice sounded strangled.

I frowned. "But the book said—"

He cut me off with a wave. "I told you. The books are wrong." He twisted his mouth. "No, not wrong, just incomplete. Look, I don't care what the books say, you can't travel the roads alone. You need a Road Master to navigate the roads, but you need someone else to move the Road Master."

My frown deepened. "*Move* the Road Master?" I needed someone to carry me? What?

Scott sighed deeply and scrubbed his hands over his face, mumbling.

"What?"

"Nothing." He stared at me, one hand still twined through his hair, gripping it like he had to hold his head to keep it on. "I—" He stopped, the sudden sort of stop that meant his mind wanted to speak but his tongue was having none of it.

I drew my knees up to my chest. In the soft glow of Sanctuary, his eyes were partially hidden, and I could almost forget the haunted look they often held. This, I reminded myself, was a boy who had seen too much. "For Gemma?" I prompted softly.

"Gemma." He deflated, releasing his hair, as though Gemma's name was some sort of charm against the tension that had filled him.

The silence ticked away, the smell of salt water ebbing and flowing with the breeze.

"You can't go near the Valley," he said at length. "Please trust me on that. Even if you're a strong enough Road Master to travel the roads—which, given what you did with the Valley before, you probably are—you can't go near the source of the Valley's power." He shifted and met my eye, sad and a little desperate. "Please. You have to trust me on this. Promise you won't go near it."

"How do you know about road mastery?" I asked so I didn't have to make another promise I wasn't sure I could keep.

His whole body tensed, shoulders hunching, jaw and fists alike clenching and twitching.

Here it came. The *real* information I needed.

"My—" He scrubbed at his face. "My mother was a Road Master."

I gaped. "Your *mother*?"

Again, he nodded.

All the disconnected pieces of information I'd carried in my head the last few months clicked into place, a Rubik's cube finally solved. "Your mother was a Road Master. She took you on the roads when you were younger,"—frogging elephants, how young? How young was he when his mother decided that her son was old enough to join her quest for darkness? Anger coursed through me, and I fought to keep my voice level—"and she found the heart of the Valley."

Another nod, more miserable than ever. Scott stared at the ground as though he might sink into it at any moment.

"And then... What? She connected herself to it somehow and it became alive?"

"She connected herself to it so she could use it as a power source. Only it works both ways, and she wasn't prepared: the Valley was stronger than she was, and it started draining her life force in order to make itself alive. She..." His hands balled in his lap and my own chest ached in response. "She died."

I remembered the double line through his mother in the list of people he lived. How much had it cost him to rule that line, to know that she was never coming back?

Then I remembered her profile; maybe he'd had mixed feelings about her death.

"I'm sorry," I said in a small voice, because what else was there to say?

He raised and dropped one shoulder, a too-simple gesture for all it contained. "Anyway," he continued, "you can't go on the roads alone. If my mum's experience is typical, you'll be able to see the path, but you'll get overwhelmed by all the information you're getting and won't be able to move your body. You need someone with you to keep you grounded. But even then, you can't go near the Valley. It's too strong, too powerful. It'd suck you right in along with Gemma, and then it would use your power to take over the world. All the worlds."

Misery pooled in my chest. I inhaled deeply; the breeze had died, leaving the air thick and heavy.

No hope. That's what Scott was saying. There was no hope for Gemma. "Why did you show me the journal?" I said, arms wrapping around my stomach to keep the despair from spilling out.

He frowned at me.

"If there's nothing we can do, if the roads are too dangerous to travel, why tell me about them?" Why torment me with the possibility of success, only to snatch it immediately away? My throat ached. "Just tell me why."

His face softened as he realised what I meant. "No," he said, touching my knee more gently than I would've believed possible. "I didn't say there's nothing we can do. I came here to talk to you because I think there *is* something we can do. But I'm not familiar with the magic of Sanctuary," he said, withdrawing his hand to flick a leaf off the rock beside him. "So I don't know if it will work."

"Aphros will know," I said immediately.

Scott nodded. "Probably." He took a long inhale, and shed the last of his grief like an old skin. The Scott I was used to seeing at school reappeared, and I wondered how often he'd had to change his skins before. He leaned over his knees. "What I *think*," he said carefully, and I realised I was wrong: this wasn't school-Scott either, but something new, something different. "Is that going to the Valley's power source is too dangerous, and disconnecting her like you did with me must also be really dangerous, or you'd have done it already."

Perhaps, I reflected as he spoke, this was Real Scott, interested and animated and logical. Now there was a thought.

"But the Valley is supposed to be a sort of mirror of Sanctuary, a yang to its yin, or something. What if Sanctuary also has a power source?" he asked, eyes alight. "If we could find that, if we could link Gem to *that*..." He shrugged, hands splayed, palms to the sky. "It might be enough to balance the pull of the Valley on her life force."

"Her soulprint," I amended automatically, and he nodded.

Balance. When I'd first met Aphros, she'd told me that I needed to restore the balance between Sanctuary and the Valley.

I nodded again, lighter. "That could work."

Aphros? I pulled on the strange thread that connected us, and felt her turn her attention to me. *Scott thinks that if we anchor Gemma to Sanctuary permanently, it would balance out the connection with the Valley and make her okay. Do you think that would work?*

A long silence, then, *Yes. That would work. Well.*

I grinned as relief flooded over me. "Aphros thinks it will work," I told Scott.

He blinked. "Did you just use road mastery to ask her? I didn't know it could do that."

"Something like that," I replied, still grinning. "You're amazing. Thank you so much."

He scowled. "Don't thank me too much yet. We still have to survive the roads, and *find* Sanctuary's power. And Gemma will have to be with us; I don't see how she can forge the connection otherwise."

The buoyant feeling faded. I frowned. "Take Gemma on the roads?" Gemma was so fragile right now; how would we take her on the roads, especially if they were as dangerous as Scott seemed to think they were?

"Can't we just... I don't know, take her to meet the avatar of Sanctuary's heart, like the glowy light pillar in the Valley?"

Scott snorted. "The Valley only had a 'glowy light pillar' because it had already leached enough energy to make itself seem alive. Unless you're planning to donate your life to the cause..."

He tensed suddenly. "Don't. Don't do that, will you. Don't give your life force to the heart, no matter what it says, okay? Just..." He stared earnestly at me. "Please don't do that."

I rocked back a little. "Whoa, chill: no sacrificial life-giving for me, okay? I promise." I sighed heavily at yet another promise I wasn't sure I would—or could—keep. I'd save Gemma any way I could, and hopefully it wouldn't come down to anyone dying—but if I had to give my life energy to Sanctuary's heart so it could manifest enough to save Gem... Well, it was Sanctuary, not the Valley, right? Making a contract with Sanctuary seemed a lot less dangerous than making one with the Valley. I'd cross that magical bargain bridge when I got to it. *If* I got to it.

"Though really," I said, "How safe is it to take Gemma on the roads in the first place? Isn't that going to be both hard and dangerous?" I tilted my head, not really sure what I wanted him to say. Of course it was going to be hard and dangerous. I still had to do it.

His gaze bored holes through me. "That's why I'm coming with you."

Right, I thought. *Okay then.* But I couldn't pretend I wasn't just a tiny bit relieved that he'd suggested it before I had to ask. Scott had done this before, and he'd survived. We could do this. We really, actually could. The smile I offered was a fragile, newborn thing, but that was how he knew that it was real. "Thank you," I said, and I meant it.

13

"I STILL DON'T see why we can't just get Gemma and go," Scott muttered to me.

"Shh," I told him as I texted Mum an apology for missing dinner. Frogging time skips. Still, arriving back forty minutes late was better than the one time I'd run into myself and fainted, or the time I'd spent the next thirty-six hours with an echo of myself haunting the corner of my eye, doing everything I did, just offset five inches to my left. Nothing more disconcerting than looking down and thinking you had twenty fingers and four arms.

Can I go check on Gemma? I texted.

"You said she's progressing fast," Scott continued as we crunched down the gravel path. The creek slunk along to our right, dark and sleepy in the dusk that was only a little bit brighter than Sanctuary's usual dim glow.

Fine, Mum replied. *Be home by 8.*

I assured Mum that I would be, tucked my phone in my pocket, and shook my head at Scott. "It's late, I'm exhausted, and from what you've said, we'll all be better off if we get a good night's sleep before we try this."

"Oh, sure, we're all gonna to sleep real well tonight."

"Hilarious," I said drily. "Look, I'm going to head over to Gemma's to see her and let them know what the plan is. I'd really appreciate it if you'd come too, since you know a lot more about the roads than I do, but I totally understand if you don't want to." My footsteps crunched onward as I waited for his response.

Scott shrugged. "I guess."

I exhaled. "Thanks."

We walked on, and by the time we got to Gemma's house fifteen minutes later, the last sliver of sun had disappeared behind the treed horizon.

I tapped lightly on the door, then cracked it open. "Hello? It's just me. Can I check on Gem?"

Mrs Caro appeared in the hallway. "Edge! And Scott!" she added, making an admirable attempt at hiding her surprise. "Please, come in."

We did, and she shepherded us to the kitchen.

"How's Gem?" I asked.

"She's okay," Mrs Caro said, her smile stretched as she slid a fancy-looking pie out of the fridge and set it on the bench. Moments later, two bowls and two spoons joined it. "Here."

"You don't have to," I protested weakly as my stomach rumbled.

Scott didn't say anything, but the way he was eyeing up the pie spoke volumes.

"Nonsense," said Mrs Caro. "When's the last time you two ate anything? How long did you spend in Sanctuary today?"

"A while," I confessed as she slid gleaming slices of lemon meringue into each bowl and pushed them toward us. I sat on one of the stools, its feet scraping eagerly over the tiled floor, and picked up the spoon.

Scott hesitated.

"Come on," I said. "Don't be shy." I shoved a giant spoonful of pie into my mouth and with the now-gooey spoon, gestured at him to sit.

Reluctantly, he did, jaw twitching, glancing over his shoulder like shadows might appear at any moment. He picked up the spoon and ran his fingertips down the length of it, feeling the weight of it in his hand. Only once he'd positioned, and repositioned, and positioned his grip again did he scoop up a gleaming mound of lemon curd, white frothy meringue perched on top like clouds.

I watched, fascinated, as he closed his mouth over the spoon like it might be fragile. He slurped the pie off, and rolled it around in his mouth.

"This," he said after he'd swallowed and was refilling his spoon, "is magic."

My lips twisted sideways in a barely-concealed grin. "Never had it before?"

Eyes still closed, he shovelled in another mouthful and spoke around it. "We don't do dessert much at my house."

Belatedly, I remembered his mum. I looked down at my own pie, appetite diminished.

A creak of wood rescued me from the melancholy direction of my thoughts: Gemma, coming down the stairs. I brightened at the thought of her walking under her own steam; the block was holding better than I'd hoped.

But my mood sank again as she entered the room: her skin was sallow, her eyes dull, her hair limp and tangled, and her whole posture defeated.

I hurried over and guided her to one of the armchairs. She sank into it and I curled up at her feet, knees against my chest.

Scott brought me the rest of my pie and sat in the other armchair—an unexpected kindness.

Even more unexpected was the fact that he leaned forward, concern furrowing his brow, and took Gemma's hand. Deftly flipping it over, he found the pulse in her wrist and stilled. "How do you feel?" he asked her.

I bit my lip. He seemed to have an end in mind, so I was happy to let him take the lead, but I didn't want to hear Gemma's answer. Either it would be a lie, and that would be terrible, or it would be the truth, and that would be worse.

"I'm... I'm fine," Gemma said breathily, clearly opting for the lie.

I laid my cheek against her knee. It felt cold and knobbly, unalive, like coats on a coat rack or a lumpy mattress. "Mrs Caro, do you have a blanket?"

"You're not fine," Scott snapped. "Stop being stupid."

Gemma sank further into the chair.

"Hey," I snapped back at Scott. "Be nice."

He cut me a glance full of razors. "She looks just like Mum did, right before... before... You know. Just before." He nodded sharply. "I need to know what she's feeling. I might be able to tell you how much time we have. But I can't do anything if she won't tell me the truth." He jerked his head at Gemma, frustrated.

I squeezed my eyes closed and pressed harder against Gemma's knee. "Gem?" I said softly. "Please tell him the truth."

Her breathing was ragged, like she'd just run the cross-country course, or... like she was dying.

Mrs Caro's footsteps drawing near made me open my eyes, and I leaned aside as she covered Gemma in a thick, fuzzy blanket, tucking it in all around her.

"I feel like garbage," Gemma said breathily.

"Any hallucinations? Voices?" Scott said sharply.

Gem shook her head.

Scott released her wrist and leaned back in his chair. "That's good then. How's she look to you?" he added to me.

"Aphros and I put a kind of block around the connection so it can't grow, and it seems to be holding so far." I'd tell him later about the tiny, hair-thin cracks I could sense on the block itself—later, when Gemma couldn't hear me.

"It won't hold forever though," he replied quietly.

Mrs Caro settled herself on the arm of Gem's chair. "Any thoughts on what else we can try?"

Gem said nothing, but followed the conversation intently with her eyes.

Briefly, I filled her in on what Scott had told me and what Quoise and I had found in the library, pleased when Scott actually interrupted to correct me at one point.

When I'd finished, Mrs Caro gave one sharp nod. "Be careful."

I smiled. "Always." Sort of. Ish. I was pretty sure my debt to the universe was racking up fast, with all these false promises I kept making.

Hopefully saving Gemma from the Valley—and thereby preventing the Valley from escaping to take over the world again—would balance the sums in my favour.

We stayed for a little while longer, talking about nothing in particular, and then it was time to go. "I have to get home," I said, standing.

Scott stood too, and Mrs Caro followed, nodding. Gemma had fallen asleep in the chair, long lashes curling against her brown skin, and I tucked the blanket in tighter, smiling a little. "Love you, Gem," I murmured to her.

"So you'll try getting on the roads tomorrow?" Mrs Caro asked as she walked us to the door.

I nodded. "First thing after school."

She caught my arm gently as I exited, let Scott draw a little way ahead, and bent close to my ear. Scott and I had downplayed the danger of the roads without even needing to discuss it, but Mrs Caro had never been slow.

"I know that your road mastery lets you... do *things*," she said. "You did really well, with Scott and the shadows and all. Really well. But..." Her fingers flexed as she released my arm. "Be careful. You're going to hate me for saying this, but you're only young, Emma. Gemma... I know she's your friend, but she isn't..." Mrs Caro drew in a shaky breath. "I appreciate your help more than you'll ever know. But Gemma isn't your responsibility, Edge. Don't put yourself in danger for her sake. I couldn't face your mother."

I smiled gently. "Mrs Caro," I said. "If last year taught me anything, it's that no one is ever safe. My Dad did the right thing when he testified. I couldn't do anything less. Mum and Dad would understand."

Mrs Caro shook her head sadly. "Be careful, Emma. Just... be careful."

I gave her a long look. "Of course, Mrs Caro. Of course."

Bah-bing. There went my debt to the universe again. But it didn't matter, because soon—very soon—Gemma would be well again. And then the rest of it wouldn't matter.

14

THE NEXT AFTERNOON, Scott and I met in the glade straight after school. Thick humidity cloyed the air, and crossing to the coolness of Sanctuary provided welcome relief.

No sooner had we arrived in the alcove than Quoise appeared from the corner of the rockery. "Psst," she said, beckoning us over.

Exchanging glances, Scott and I went.

"What's up?" I said as we neared.

"The Keeper's about to have our heads is what," Quoise replied, wringing her hands and fluttering fitfully back and forth. "What have I done?" she said, her usually high-pitched voice even higher than usual.

I shot another puzzled glance at Scott, which he returned without comment. "I don't know. What have you done?"

"Told you about the roads, that's what I've done!" She stopped in mid-air, arms flailing wildly. "And now the Keeper knows, and we are all in Very! Deep! Trouble!" This time, the look I exchanged with Scott was grim. "Do you have to be here for this?" I asked Scott. "If they sense your soulprint, there's no way they won't investigate."

"I'm not leaving." His mouth set in a determined line as he crossed his arms. "Let them come. I'll handle it."

"Mm." I pursed my lips. I had no doubt actually that he would, and even less doubt that I wouldn't like his methods. "Look," I said to Quoise. "You didn't tell me anything that Scott didn't also tell me. All we need is for you to show us where the roads begin, and then you're free to disappear."

But Quoise had passed the point of reason. She rocked back and forth in the air, arms wrapped around herself, muttering. "The Keeper suspects, of course. It would take only a nod from me, and you'd be banned from Sanctuary for life as well. Do you realise that? Do you know how serious this is?"

My stomach dropped. Quoise was supposed to be my *friend*. "What," I said sharply. "You mean as serious as my best friend being consumed by the Valley, and maybe, y'know, *dying*?" As serious as the fairies lying about whether or not I could help her, about them keeping the true purpose of my abilities from me?" I folded my own arms and narrowed my eyes. "You and Gem once told me that travelling to Sanctuary is like a beneficial addiction. The atmosphere of Sanctuary gets into your head, makes you calm and focused, and your brain likes the feeling so much it makes you a calmer, better person—and it makes you want to come to Sanctuary more. So what do you think happens when you ban people?"

Quoise shook her head. "That's not the point."

"It *is* the point. My best friend is dying, or as good as, and instead of helping her, you've tossed her out of the only place that provides—ha ha—*sanctuary* for her. And because I'm trying to help her, you're threatening to do the same to me. Seriously." I tossed my head. "Either you're going to go tell the Keeper or not, but I doubt it, because otherwise you would have just *done* it instead of warning me. So quit making threats you're not planning to keep."

Scott snorted softly, and out of the corner of my eye I caught a look of approval.

Why yes, Scott, I can stand up for myself, thanks for noticing. I was too focused on Quoise to spare him an eyeroll, but I angled myself slightly away from him.

Quoise opened her mouth, stopped, folded her arms, and scowled. "You don't understand what you're asking of me," she said. "How much trouble I could be in, even for just saying *this* much to you." She hugged herself again. "Edge," she whispered fearfully, eyes wide, "they could kick me out of Sanctuary."

I stretched forward and held my hand palm up in front of her. "I won't let them," I said.

She sighed and stepped onto my hand, peering up at me as I brought her close. "Edge, dear, you've done extraordinary things in the short time I've known you, and I appreciate the thought, but if the Keeper wants to kick me out, there really isn't anything you can do to stop her."

"What happens if you get kicked out?"

She shrugged and turned away a little, tugging at her hair and hunching her shoulders.

"Quoise. What happens?"

She heaved a sigh and glanced up. "I won't die, if that's what you're worried about. But my magic will diminish the longer I'm away from Sanctuary."

"Oh. That... isn't so bad, is it?" Other than crossing to Sanctuary, I hadn't really seen much evidence of what fairy magic could even do.

She stared mournfully at me. "Edge. Magic is, is... Magic is like being able to hear my heart beating to know I'm still alive. And Sanctuary is my home. Where else would I go?"

Magic aside, I knew a thing or two about having your home ripped away. "I won't let that happen," I said, and even though I didn't know what I could do if it came to that, I was also telling the truth.

Scott shifted next to me. I nudged him to keep quiet, but he leaned forward until his face was level with Quoise. "You have to help us," he said. "Not for Emma, not for Gemma. For yourself. Because if you don't help us, if you do nothing and Gemma dies, or if Emma dies trying to save her, a part of you will always wonder if it might have been your fault. If maybe you'd helped, then it would have turned out differently. And although you'd try to push the guilt aside and pretend like it didn't matter, like it was nothing, it would eat you alive from the inside out until one day you broke from the strain."

Part of me wanted to punch him, because tears were coursing down Quoise's cheeks, but the part of me in control told the rest of me to shut up. We *needed* Quoise on our side—and he was right.

"Help us," he said softly. "Or at least, help Emma. Don't choose to live with the guilt."

I shivered; his words sounded personal, like he was talking to himself. *I'm sorry, Scott,* I thought. *Whatever it is, I'm sorry.*

Quoise drooped, head dropping into her hands, face pressed against her palms. "I'll show you," she said, muffled through her hands. "I'll show you where the roads begin." She drew in a shaky breath, lowered her hands, and smiled a wobbly smile. "I can't come with you on the roads, but there isn't anything else I can do anyway. I'll show you."

I remembered how to breathe, and Scott strode away, face complicated and tight. "Thank you," I told Quoise. "Thank you so much."

"For the record," she said, flitting higher into the air, "I still think this is a horrible idea. Going anywhere near the Valley is asking for trouble."

I blinked. "Oh," I said, following as she led the way to the meadow. "I'm not. We're going to try to find Sanctuary's heart," I told her as Scott tagged along behind. Deliberately, I kept my eyes on Quoise so he could have a second to right himself. "We'll link Gem to that, and the two connections should balance out."

Quoise frowned. "Really? Well, that's less dangerous, but I don't think it will work. Creatures belong to either Sanctuary or the Valley. The powers of life and death shouldn't be mixed."

"Aphros manages it," I pointed out.

That was the entire reason Aphros had been able to help me last time: as a unicorn, she was bound equally to Sanctuary and the Valley, and as such was able to come and go across the border like no other creature.

(Except that one time the Valley's power had grown, fed by Scott, leaving Aphros trapped there until I'd managed to extricate Scott from his nightmare.)

Quoise snorted. "Oh, yes. Turn Gemma into a human unicorn, then. No problem."

I shrugged. "Better than hunting down the Valley, right?"

She snorted again and didn't reply.

Quoise led us across the meadow, through the little grove of pine trees, and on to the beach. The waves shushed in the background, incessant, questioning. Where? Where? Where?

I could only hope the entrance to the roads wasn't underwater or something.

But Quoise led us to an outcropping of rocks, casting furtive glances over her shoulder toward the Lodge every so often.

"How likely are they to notice us?" I asked the after fifth time.

"Hm? What? Oh, I don't know. It depends on how busy they all are, and on how many other people are here right now."

"Other people?" Scott asked, frowning.

"Dimensions," I said. "Sanctuary exists over multiple dimensions. You can only see the people who entered from the same point you did. Prevents the place from feeling crowded."

He blinked and looked around. "How many other people are here?"

I shrugged. "Most people can't interact with it like we do. We're in the—what, ten percent?"

Quoise nodded. "More or less. About one in ten thousand of you can travel, though it runs stronger in some old families. Of those, only about one in ten are strong enough to see Sanctuary as a fully developed world. For the rest, it's varyingly substantial."

"Wow," said Scott as we made our way over the rocks toward the surf.

I sincerely hoped the entrance wasn't underwater. Getting Gem here was going to be difficult enough. "The fairies record the soulprints of everyone who visits Sanctuary," I continued, happy for the distraction and somewhat gratified by Scott's interest in it all. "But because there can be hundreds—or even thousands, I guess—of people here at once, they won't necessarily pick out your soulprint right away."

"Which is the only reason you didn't have more of a welcoming party," Quoise muttered.

"How would they have known we were coming, though?" I asked her.

She rolled her neck irritably. "We can sense you mid-crossing, if we're concentrating hard enough. And if we can sense you travelling, we can be there in the alcove by the time you're here."

"You're that fast?" I didn't mean to sound so surprised, but this week had been the first time I'd seen Quoise move faster than my walking pace.

"Yes. The time slips help too," she added.

"Wow."

Quoise disappeared behind a craggy outcrop taller than me— and didn't reappear.

I hopped off the rocks onto a tiny patch of sand, scrambled around the side of the outcrop, and peered around before I realised that she'd disappeared into a little cave.

My heart sank. I'd have to get down on my belly to crawl in there; what would we do with Gem?

"Not claustrophobic, are you?" Scott grinned and threw himself onto the sand.

"Only with you," I shot back, elbowing him aside as I raced him into the cave.

Inside, there was just room to sit without out heads bashing the rocky roof, and I peered around in the dimness cast by a ball of light in Quoise's hands. One knee pressed against Scott's and the other dug firmly against the cold rock wall. Shivers traced my spine. "We'll never get Gem in here," I said, breathing shallowly and a little too fast.

"Yeah." Scott looked grim until he noticed my face. "Hey, it's okay," he said. "I was only kidding about the claustrophobia."

"I wasn't," I said, closing my eyes and thinking spacious thoughts. "You're too close."

Quiet.

I cracked an eyelid open to see him staring at me with downturned lips. "It's fine," I said, nudging him with my knee. "I'd rather you were here than not."

Quoise cleared her throat. "Okay, I found it."

We both turned our heads toward her.

"Hands?"

I hesitated. I'd seen far too much of Scott's soulprint to ever like-like him, but we seemed to be doing an awful lot of hand-holding lately, and I wasn't really sure how Scott felt. Obviously a lot less awkward than I did; he grabbed my hand and held it tightly, and the half-smile he shot me was as complicated as my stomach felt.

I took a deep, steadying breath. Problem for another day. "What next?"

Quoise did that jerky-rocking thing again, full of nervous energy. "If I make you try to find it on your own, it'll take you hours. We don't have hours. I'll have to take you over. But I can't come with you. And you don't have Gemma. I assume you're taking Gemma?"

I nodded.

"So you'll have to come back with her. But I can't risk taking you over again. So I'll show you now and you'll have to do it yourself again next time, okay?" She wrung her hands.

"It's okay, Quoise, it's fine. I'll manage," I said, accidentally squeezing Scott's hand tighter.

It was her turn to take a steadying breath. "Yes. Yes I know you will. Now, close your eyes."

We did.

"Edge, I'm going to touch your cheek, and when I do, you should be able to sense the roads, okay? Your road mastery would usually be able to sense the roads without me—that's what it's for, after all—but in Sanctuary there are blocks, hiding them. I'm acting as a conduit for you this time to get around the block, but I can only hold it open for an instant, and then it's all on you, okay?"

I nodded.

"I mean it, Edge: I can only hold you over on the roads for a split second this time; the fairies can't stay on them any longer than regular people. You'll have literally half a second before the weight of the blocks comes crashing down on you, and you have to hold it open, or best case scenario, they'll force you back here with the worst headache you've ever had in your life."

My stomach clenched. I really didn't want to know what the worst-case scenario was. "I'm ready," I told her. "Let's do it."

Now Scott gripped my hand tightly, palm sweaty and slick. I could only imagine what memories this was dredging up for him.

Quoise fluttered to my shoulder and laid a tiny, cool hand on my skin. For a long moment, nothing happened. I opened my mouth to question her, but she pressed against me, warning me to silence.

I could feel the tension thrumming through her, running down her arm, through her hand, and into my cheek—into my blood stream, pumping around my body with my life. The energy grew and built, billowing into life inside me.

My skin tingled, energy arcing and crackling between my fingertips and over the edges of my ears. Power built inside me, a lightning storm in my chest, clouds rolling, light sparking, thunder crackling. It built and built and grew and built until my ribs strained.

I couldn't hold it, not anymore; was Quoise still holding the block open? Was this it?

Panic shot through me, flooding my system with adrenalin that through the energy storm, felt like liquid fire.

Pain lanced my cheek and I realised it was Quoise, trying to get my attention. "I'm letting go now!" she shouted.

No! I wanted to scream. *I can't do this! I can't hold it!* But I nodded, and the pressure on my cheek disappeared.

The energy of the storm coursed through me. Now I did scream. My lungs burned, my blood was on fire.

Power. So much power, and it was trying to consume me. How could anyone survive this?

"Road... mastery!" I heard someone gasp.

Instinctively I flung open my road mastery and grabbed—at what, I had no idea; I had no plan, no clue—but somewhere deep in the roaring chaos of the storm, my road mastery found an anchor—something firm, like solid ground.

I snatched at it, pulled, pulled harder.

Please. Please let me in!

Lightning sparked through the air, cracking over me—and through me.

I pulled harder at the solidness.

Something snapped.

The world around us shifted.

I gasped as my feet hit solid ground in the midst of the storm.

I stumbled forward, raising my hands instinctively to my face.

Scott snatched at my fingers, wrenching my shoulder and crushing my hand.

Wind roared. My ears hurt. I clapped my free hand over one ear; it didn't help.

Power boomed away from me, rolling outward in an expanding shockwave that rang the world like a gong.

The storm died. I had a vague sense of something shattering, someone crying out in pain.

Then, suddenly, the darkness behind my eyes blazed to life: burning ribbons of colour leading in every direction, tangling, twisting, twining—paths, every one of them, paths that I could walk.

Wonder swelled in my chest, buoyed by the energy currents. I was bigger than the world; the Earth could fit inside my heart. On these paths, I could travel anywhere. Everywhere. Allwheres.

If only I could make myself move. I inhaled, and a thousand scents filled my lungs, sweet and spicy, old and new, dry and humid, cinnamon and steel, oil and decaying leaves, roses and seaweed and sweat, sunshine and chocolate, brine, mangoes, vanilla, lemongrass, orange blossoms and ink, jasmine, lavender, rosemary.

Another sharp snap.

The world died.

Panic gripped me, and I flung my arms forward, searching for the paths that had suddenly disappeared. My breaths tore raggedly at my throat. The colours, the smells—gone. Where had the world gone? What was wrong?

I was dead. I had to be dead. Everything was dull and lifeless and gone.

A soft touch on my cheek.

Gentle fingers probing my hand.

I remembered how to open my eyes.

Oh. Not dead. I was on the beach in Sanctuary, and the waves sparkled in the dusk light and shushed on the sand. Scott and Quoise fussed around me, Quoise's wings flashing like the sky, Scott's eyes shining like tears—and none of it felt real, none of it felt alive, because I'd been on the roads—and the roads? The roads were glorious.

A green-winged form rose up from the rocks. "There," the Keeper of the fairies said. "Quoise Allesandre, former fairy of Sanctuary, you have had your last request. The girl is alive and well. Now, all three of you leave before I change my mind."

She floated in the air, stately and immoveable. "And if I ever," she added as she turned away, "find any of you here again?" She raised her sceptre over her head and lightning sparked. She smiled, a terrible, hungry thing with teeth of its own. "You *may* live to regret it. Or," she concluded, as she flew away, "you may die if you prefer."

"Come on," I said, ignoring the way the world spun as I sat up. I scowled at the Keeper's diminishing back. "Let's go get Gem."

15

WE CROSSED BACK to Earth in silence, Scott and I holding a dejected Quoise between us.

"I'm so sorry," I said. The oppressive humidity of a building thunderstorm shrank the clearing and changed the colour of the light; Quoise's wings seemed lurid and out of place.

She didn't reply, but instead flew straight to a nearby gum tree and perched high in its branches, knees to her chest, arms hugging them tightly.

"What happened?" I murmured to Scott. "How did the Keeper find us?"

"Something about you breaking through the blocks," he said, equally quiet. He stood shoulder to shoulder with me, hands deep in his pockets as we stared up at Quoise. "The Keeper dragged you back off the roads. Nearly killed you in the process," he added softly.

I tried to find some part of me that cared, but it was like it had happened to someone else, or else to someone in a story. All I could remember was the bright glory of the roads, then dullness as I returned to the real world. "Do you think she'll be okay?" I asked instead.

In the distance, thunder rumbled. It wasn't half past five yet according to my phone, and already the night was closing in, dark and foreboding.

"I hope so."

I shot him a quick glance, surprised by the apparent genuineness of his emotions.

My phone buzzed.

I drew it out of my back pocket again, and my heart jolted all the way up to my teeth. Mrs Caro. "Hello?" My pulse raced.

"What just happened?"

"I found the roads," I said, watching Scott in the dim light as he continued watching Quoise. "How's Gem?"

"Not good. Whatever you did, I think it's broken the block you and Aphros put in place. I assume you're back in Nowra now?"

"I'm in the glade," I said through the buzzing ache in my chest. I'd broken her. We'd had her holding steady, and getting onto the roads had broken her. How would she survive if we actually took her onto them? I clenched the phone until my fingertips turned white.

"Right," said Mrs Caro. "Time to find out if your plan will work. I'll meet you there in fifteen minutes."

"But—"

Scott turned to me, quizzical expression lifting his eyebrows.

"What if it doesn't work?" I whispered as I met Scott's eye. "What if it makes her worse?"

"Oh, Edge," said Mrs Caro as Scott stepped forward to squeeze my shoulder a little awkwardly. "We're *all* just doing the best we can."

"It will work," Scott murmured in front of me. "We'll keep her safe."

Thunder rippled overhead.

Quoise fluttered down and perched on my shoulder. "Is that Maria?"

I nodded mutely.

Quoise nodded once, decisively. "Then let's do this. Let's get Gemma fixed."

I closed my eyes, because it was that or collapse in a heap, totally overwhelmed by everyone's support. I cleared my throat. "Okay. See you in fifteen."

"Call your mother!" Mrs Caro said sternly, then hung up.

I set an alarm for fifteen minutes and tucked my phone away. I looked from Scott to Quoise. "Thank you," I told them, exhaling heavily. "You both..." I shook my head. They both had so much to lose by helping me—but I couldn't do it without them.

"She's my friend too," Quoise said, leaning her tiny cheek against mine.

And, shockingly, Scott nodded. "Me too. I think. Probably." He inhaled, backing away. "I need to grab something. I'll be back before they get here."

Before I could protest, he'd vanished into the bushes. I could only hope he meant it, and that he'd be back—he was just as necessary now as I was.

"Are you going to call your parents?" Quoise said after Scott's crackling footsteps had faded.

"Right." I pulled my phone back out again.

Easier to lie by text, I decided. She wouldn't hear my heart pounding or my voice trembling then.

Mum, can I stay the night at Gemma's?

"You're a bad influence on me," I told Quoise.

"Me?" she squeaked.

I nodded. "I never broke rules before Sanctuary." Of course, that had been the way to stay safe, then. And now? I rubbed my free shoulder against my jaw. Now the only rules seemed to be 'do what it takes to keep your loved ones safe'. I wasn't thrilled by this way of living.

"Ha," said Quoise. "I never did either until I met you. Maybe," she added softly, "we'd just never come across rules that needed breaking."

Did some rules need breaking? Is that how life was? It made me itch, just thinking about it. But if so, how did you know which rules were which?

My phone buzzed. *Are you going to Sanctuary?*

Which rules needed breaking? Only the bad ones, I decided. However you figured that out. *Yes.*

Is Mrs Caro going with you?

Yes. At least that was a truthful answer she'd appreciate.

Can you fix Gemma this time?

...I hope so.

Be careful, Mum texted. *Stay with Maria. Stay safe.*

Always, I replied, because that was my line. *Love you.*

Wind gusted through the treetops, bringing with it the smell of rain. The light died away, dim as twilight. Beside us, the creek chattered in the dark, whispering and chuckling.

Thunder clapped again. Any minute now the rain would break and we'd be soaked. I stepped a little further from the creek, into the shelter of the trees.

Minutes ticked by, measured by the pounding of my heart and the moaning of the wind through the treetops. Their leaves rustled and swished; branches screed against each other, making lonely calls in the early night.

My alarm blared through the glade and I jumped. Still no sign of Mrs Caro and Gem—or Scott.

I shifted restlessly.

"Shh," said Quoise. "They'll be here."

"Yeah," I said. The air pressed down on us, thick and heavy, and I shifted again as sweat trickled down from the back of my neck. Usually small insect noises filled the glade instead of silence, but now the world crouched quietly, holding its breath and waiting.

Leaves and branches crackled. I swung toward the noise, relief washing over me as I recognised Mrs Caro and Gem in the light of Mrs Caro's phone.

I pressed my palm against the rough, dark bark of a tree to steady myself: Gem was walking. Our block on the Valley's connection had broken, Mrs Caro had said, but obviously not completely or Gem would be unconscious again.

"Gem," I said hoarsely, and hugged her gently.

She squeezed me back.

Quoise landed wordlessly on Gemma's shoulder. Gem inclined her head toward the half-foot tall fairy and Quoise patted her cheek.

Now all we needed was Scott.

Before the next roll of thunder could sound, he appeared, hands deep in his pockets again and collar upturned.

"Time to go?" Mrs Caro asked.

I nodded and led the way to the middle of the glade. The air zinged with the energy of the storm. I wrapped one arm around my best friend. Mrs Caro supported her from the other side, and Scott closed the gap in the circle, forgetting to be awkward.

Wind gusted over us, pricking goosebumps on our exposed skin. We pressed close together. Tonight was a night made for not being alone.

We travelled to Sanctuary, a four-headed beast linked by our hands and our mutual need for comfort. The twilight of Sanctuary seemed light in comparison to the dark we'd left behind, but even so I couldn't shake the oily, creeping sense of dread.

"Get out," a voice said levelly.

We turned.

My mouth opened and my eyes grew wide.

The archway that led out of the alcove was barred, entirely filled with glittering, jewel-winged fairies. But these were not Sanctuary's fairies as I had seen them before; in place of their usual light, gauzy dresses, these fairies were clad in something silver and shimmery that gave the sense of being both solid and liquid at once. Most of them had sceptres, smaller versions of the Keeper's one, or orbs that glimmered like gems.

The Keeper flew from the group, gold circlet glinting in her blonde hair, emerald-green dress setting her apart from the others. Her raised sceptre was almost as tall as she was, and as thick as two of my fingers. "You have one minute to leave," she said. "Or else you will suffer the consequences."

Quoise darted forward. "Viri! Why are you doing this?"

The Keeper gave her a long look. "Quoise, they, like you, have all been banned."

Gem stiffened beside me at that.

"You of all should understand what that means."

"Forty-five seconds," Scott murmured.

I glared at him. This was Sanctuary. These fairies had welcomed and supported me since I got here, and Gemma and Mrs Caro had known them practically since birth. Sure, we were technically trespassing now, but it was *Sanctuary*. What were they doing to do? Shout at us?

"This is your final warning," the Keeper said. "Leave, and you will be preserved."

Quoise stretched out her hand. "But we need—"

"What you need," the Keeper snapped, "is to obey the rules. You know the reasons why they were written. You know what the consequences will be." She softened, voice mellowing. "Quoise. Do not make this harder than it need be."

Anxiety clawed its way down my spine. "Quoise," I whispered, barely audible. "Please, we need you."

In front of us, Quoise folded her arms over her chest and tossed back her head. "I know the reasons why these rules were made," she said loudly, eyeing off the wall of fairies. "As do we all. For protection. For safety. But those rules were broken years ago, and not by any of us here."

The Keeper laughed cruelly. "You bring that creature here into Sanctuary and dare to suggest that all of you are innocent? By his hand was the Valley woken! Through his power was Ambergris killed—or had you forgotten that?"

"Get ready," Scott murmured, hands still in his pockets, at odds with the tension in his voice.

I didn't seriously think they would harm us, but his unease was contagious. I shrugged uncomfortably.

The Keeper turned her back on us.

The wall of fairies tensed.

Quoise turned to us, sad and defiant and lovely. "I'm sorry," she said as she returned.

"Get down!"

I stared at Scott for an instant.

Then I saw them. The wall of fairies had raised their orbs and sceptres. White light snapped and crackled around them; the air smelled like dirt and growing things.

"Down!" I echoed Scott's shout, lunging at Gemma. We hit the ground en masse as the blinding white light shot from the fairies toward us. I cringed, bracing.

Scott stood up, something small and brown in one hand.

The shadows around Gemma roared.

Scott lifted his hands in the instant the white light streaked at us. Darkness shredded the air, and the shadows left Gemma's soulprint to flank Scott. He tilted a hand and at the last possible moment, the shadows flattened into a shield.

The light hit them.

The world thundered; the ground boiled.

Gemma shrieked—I could see her mouth open, but I couldn't hear her over the gale of magic.

Life magic—and death magic.

Clashing.

Jaw locked in fury, I snatched at Scott's wrist. How dare he? How *dare* he!

Edge? A minty-green voice cut through the chaos.

Nearly choking on my rage at Scott, I locked one hand around his wrist, grabbed Gemma in the other, and twisted away.

16

"HOW *DARE* YOU?" I shouted, flinging Scott away from me as soon as we landed. Hot tears welled and I swiped at my eyes. "After everything that's happened, why would you do that?"

All that sob story about his mother taking him on the roads and him losing his mind... It was frogging garbage, all of it. He used death magic because he liked it, plain and simple.

Scott stood where he'd landed, eyes wide.

I stepped to him, fists clenching at my sides. I got up in his personal space and resisted the strong urge to slap him. "Don't you *ever* do that again."

His shock broke into a scowl. "I saved your butt and you know it. Those fairies might have been using life magic, but it wasn't going to tickle when it hit you," he said scathingly. He lifted his chin and held my gaze. "I saved you."

"Uh, Edge?"

I brushed Quoise gently aside. "You killed an innocent creature on my behalf," I snapped at Scott. "Don't expect me to thank you for it."

"Emma!"

"What?" I snapped some more, turning. My eyes widened.

Gemma hovered a foot or so off the ground, eyes completely black and shadows sleeking around her hands and ankles and shoulders.

I rounded on Scott. "This is all your fault! You used death magic and now the shadows have her!"

"I didn't do that! Shadow magic doesn't work like that! The only way for the Valley's power to strengthen like that is through its connection to her soulprint, or if..." He trailed off as he looked around.

"If *what*?" But instinctively, my gaze followed his and I looked properly at the trees around us for the first time.

Gnarled trees, bent and twisted.

Yellow-leafed trees, with black fungal spots and oozing, dark red sap.

I sucked in a sharp lungful of air and nearly choked as swamp smell and rotten fruit hit the back of my throat.

"Do you think it's safe to move her like this?" Mrs Caro murmured.

"How did we even get here?" said Scott.

"I..." My throat was too dry to talk. *I'd* done this. *I'd* brought us here—to the Valley. *Aphros? I send to her. Are you here somewhere?*

I'd caught hold of her soulprint and followed it, just as I'd done to find Gem when she'd been stuck in the Valley; I hadn't even thought about it—it was just an instinctual response to danger.

Hooves thundered on the ground and a moment later Aphros galloped into view. She caught sight of Gemma and propped to a halt, snorting and tossing her mane.

"Aphros," I said, running to her. "I tried to come to you. That was all, I just tried to follow your soulprint like last time. I'm sorry. I'm so sorry." I buried my face in her mane for a moment, breathing in the equine smell of her body while my road mastery absorbed the minty green-and-gold of her soulprint.

My babies, she said, nuzzling me. *They took my babies so I wouldn't help you.*

"No." I clenched my fists and stepped back. "No, they wouldn't."

She gazed mournfully at me.

I inhaled deeply. We were in the Valley. Gemma was just about taken by the shadows. All of us were banned from Sanctuary, and the unicorn babies were being held hostage. "No!" I swung out wildly, punching the air—then forced myself to stand rigidly still. There would be time to get angry later. Right now, I needed to save Gem, and much as I might hate it, I needed everyone—Scott included—to help.

"Right," I said, and my voice rang out through the trees. "Here is what we are going to do. Scott, am I right that there's an entrance to the roads here in the Valley?"

He nodded.

"Is it far?"

He shrugged. "I'm not sure. I'd need to figure out where we are first."

Aphros tossed her head again. "In the place where we first met," she said.

Scott nodded, his mouth a thin, pale line. "Not far, then. Fifteen minutes." He eyed Gem. "Maybe a little more if she won't come quietly."

I nodded back. "Right. Aphros, I'm so sorry about your babies, and I promise to help you, but do you think you could carry Gem to the roads for us first?"

She stomped her hint foot. "Of course."

"Babies?" said Mrs Caro.

"The fairies have them hostage," I said, turning to her. "Which is the next thing. After we've gotten Gemma onto the roads, there's no point in you guys waiting around, especially not here in the Valley. Mrs Caro, *technically* you're the only one of us not banned from Sanctuary, though after all this..." I gestured broadly around—and right on cue, the ground below us rumbled again. Death magic plus life magic colliding in Sanctuary had *really* been a bad idea.

Urgh. Problem for later.

"Would you be willing to go back to Sanctuary with Aphros, Mrs Caro, and try to free them?"

"Holding babies hostage?" she said, eyes glinting dangerously. "Try and stop me."

I nodded. Which left... "Where's Quoise?"

Silently, Scott pointed into the trees. Quoise huddled above a fallen log a little way away, hovering in the air in a tight fetal ball.

I exhaled heavily. "Scott, Mrs Caro, try to get Gem onto Aphros," I said over my shoulder as I went to Quoise.

"Quoise?" I called softly as I approached.

No response. This close, I could see her whole body quivering.

"Quoise, are you okay?" Stupid question, but I had no clue what else to say.

"Don't touch me!"

I crouched next to her. "Okay." I ground my teeth. I had to get Gemma to the roads, like, yesterday, but instead of getting the job done, I was stuck talking down a panicked fairy. "Are you hurt?"

Quoise drew herself into a tighter ball. "We're in the Valley. I'm not even alive right now. You're probably just an after-death hallucination."

I frowned. She might be being a little melodramatic, but on the other hand, she did have a point. "Quoise, you're not dead."

No response again.

"I don't think you understand," I said, bouncing a little. "Quoise, we're in the Valley, and you're *alive*."

Cautiously, Quoise lifted her head. "But Ambergris died. The shadows got her."

"No shadows here." I gestured absently, then frowned. For practically ever the fairies had treated the Valley and the shadows as though they were one and the same. But apparently, they were not.

Quoise bumped down onto the fallen log and startled. She stared at the log as though it might try to devour her. When it didn't, she reached a cautious hand out to test her luck further.

She looked up at me, eyes wide with wonder. "I'm alive."

I nodded.

"I'm in the Valley, and I'm *alive*."

I held my hand out to her. "Can we go save Gem now, please?"

Quoise gave herself a little shake, then shot into the air, spiralling as she flew up, up, up over the treetops. An instant later she was back, and businesslike. "Let's go."

We rejoined the others and set off, Scott in the lead, Gemma riding on Aphros with Mrs Caro on one side and Quoise on the other, and me bringing up the rear.

I'd felt a moment of joy as Quoise had celebrated not being dead in the Valley, but it was soon overtaken by other, less pleasant feelings. The shadows wreathed around Gemma, invisible to everyone else but heavy and foreboding against my road mastery.

I shut my senses down to a tiny trickle, but it didn't help; the way that Gem perched on Aphros, stiff and unblinking, her stare oddly bird-like as she turned her head this way and that...

Even without my road mastery, it was impossible to forget that the body in front of me very nearly belonged to the Valley.

Fifteen minutes had never seemed so long. One heavy, trudging step after the other, we walked, the skin on the back of my neck prickling constantly as though spiders crawled through my hair. How many hours was it now since I'd gotten up this morning? I had no idea, but my eyelids felt sandy and my limbs grew heavier by the moment. At the end of this all, I was going to sleep for a week.

Eventually, though, we stopped, and I went forward to join Scott.

"Just here," he murmured.

I nodded, still annoyed at him—even if I now had even more evidence that the fairies had never been telling the truth, he'd still killed a mouse or something on our behalf.

"I'm sorry you can't come," I said to Mrs Caro as she guided Gem over to us, and I was. It would have been nice to have an adult there. But Scott had convinced us earlier in too-graphic terms that the smaller the party the better: one Road Master to navigate the roads, one normal person to guide the Road Master, and Gemma, to be healed. Any more jeopardised the safety of us all.

Mrs Caro smiled, a thin, stretched thing. "It's okay," she said. "I trust you."

I'd known that for a while—she'd trusted me to get Gemma back last time, after all—but right now, standing literally on the borders between worlds, her trust rested like iron rod across my shoulders. It suddenly felt like a very weighty thing indeed to be a Road Master, and to be the only one who could save your best friend.

I allowed myself a precious instant to hate the universe, and then I took a deep breath: this was it. I laid a hand on Scott's shoulder because I had to, gently took Gem's hand with my other, and closed my eyes.

"Wait." Scott's voice trembled, sending adrenalin pumping through my veins.

"What?" It came out snappier than I'd intended, psyched up as I was for the most dangerous journey of my life.

"I... forgot to tell you something."

Nerves trilled through my stomach. "You *forgot to tell me something*?" This time the words were exactly as snappy as I intended. I glared at him.

He squirmed. "When we cross through, there might be... things there."

I fought the urge to dig my nails into his shoulder. "What kind of things?"

He mumbled.

"Pardon?"

"Guardians, I think. They protect the roads from intruders. We might have to get past them to use the roads."

"What. Kind. Of. Guardians?"

He whispered: "I don't know." A fleeting glance at my face, ghost-like before the winds tore it away. "You'll have to concentrate."

"On what?" This was like playing cryptic crosswords with Gemma's life at stake. How could he have 'forgotten' to tell me this earlier?

He avoided my eye, shifting while his clenched jaw twitched. "You don't understand," he said. "The roads... They're different for people who aren't Road Masters. They mess with your mind, your memory. You know that, you saw the journal. My memories of the roads are all patchy and strange, out of order, like a dream." He tilted his head. "You know when you wake up after a really intense dream and you're struck with the mood and a few images you know used to make sense, but nothing to tie it all together?"

I nodded. I'd had those kind of dreams a lot, usually with images like a dead girl's body in a train station bathroom, or dark shadows chasing me through the trees.

"It's like that."

I sighed and released his shoulder long enough to pinch at my forehead. So there would be things trying to keep us off the roads; so there would be people trying to stop us from doing what we needed to do. That was hardly unusual these days. "Okay," I said while exhaling. "We'll manage. We'll both keep an eye out and hopefully we'll..." Do what? Run away? Defeat them? Did we have to fight them? I sincerely hoped not.

Mrs Caro had been watching the exchange silently, pale cheeked and tense. She opened her mouth, then closed it, then opened it again, fingers twitching similarly at her sides. "You don't have to do this," she said. "If there's a danger, if there's a risk..." She shook her head in short, jerky shakes. "I can't tell your mother that something has happened to you too."

"We'll be fine," I said firmly. "Won't we, Scott." I directed him a significant look.

He shrugged. "Sure. You're much stronger than my mother was."

Adrenalin surged through me again. Hearing other people talk about my abilities still thrilled me in some strange way; it made them real, and to know that people thought I was strong, that I was good at what I did... I nodded. "We'll be fine."

"Emma," Mrs Caro began.

"Ready?" I muttered to Scott.

"Emma, I'm not going to let you do this. I don't know what I was thinking. This is far too dangerous, and you're thirteen, for heaven's sake. This is ridiculous. We're going—"

Her words cut off like a switch, because contrary to her advice, one hand on Scott and one on Gemma, I'd entered the Roads Between.

This time, I was prepared for the power storm that surged as we entered. I let it rush through me, filling me with light. It still hurt—but now that I knew what waited for me once the pain was over, I could bear it a lot more easily.

Sure enough, the power soon burst away in a circle of sound and light, like someone had rung the world—and we were on the roads.

17

COLOURS AND SMELLS and sounds swirled around me, mesmerising this time rather than overwhelming. The sensations seemed to ebb and flow: now the high, silver tinkling of bells and chimes, then raucous squawking like parrots or maybe someone dragging a saw over tortured metal.

Blues and greens flashed around as though we were under-water in a cool, clear pond; they gave way to the hot oranges and soft pinks of a sunset, before fading to deep blackness, studded with firework-flashes of green.

I smelled cut grass, dirt, hot concrete, baking cookies, melted chocolate, burnt chemicals, wet dog, something floral. I stood, frozen in place by the gloriousness of it all. As before, trails of colour led away in every direction: forward, backward, left, right, even up and down. I could stare forever.

Something prodded me in between my shoulder blades, and a sharp pain squeezed my fingers. It reminded me of the frustrated gesture of someone who'd been trying to get my attention for a long time—and sudden realisation percolated down through the sensory stimulus: Scott. Scott was here with me, and he wanted my attention.

I turned, light-blind, searching for him. Nothing. Not in any direction. Just constant, firm pressure on my hand, as though nothing short of death or dismemberment would induce him to let go.

I could feel him, but not see him. Why?

A glimmer of stars resolved in the current blackness, a localised patch of night sky and velvet. Next to it, the smell of vast hilltops at night, the feel of cold autumn winds, and a dark, starless sky. Scott. Gemma and Scott. I couldn't see them, but I could see their soulprints. Smiling, I squeezed back at Scott's invisible hand.

His grip relaxed a fraction: relief. I couldn't see him, but we could manage basic communication at least. I wondered if he could see me.

Right. So the next thing to do was choose a path, I supposed. But which one? I didn't even know what the heart of Sanctuary looked like, let alone where it might be. Scott had said to use my road mastery, just like when I was searching out a person, but I couldn't see anything that seemed like it might belong to Sanctuary.

The darkness brightened to tropical greens and yellows. Sounds like torrential waterfalls rose and fell around me, and the smell of charcoal drifted by. I closed my eyes and inhaled deeply. Ice crystals on the wind. Eucalypts breathing under a hot summer sun. Stagnant water. Lavender.

A tug at my hand brought me back to awareness. Urgh. I'd gotten lost in the roads again. "Focus, Emma," I muttered.

I gazed around, and suddenly adrenalin spiked through my veins. I retraced my metaphorical steps, combing the roads with all my senses, wondering what had prompted it.

There, again. A flash of darkness off to the right; a deep, booming pulse like a kettle drum; and underneath all the other sounds, a slowly building note, long, drawn out, and getting louder.

I swallowed.

There are things on the roads.

Scott's grip convulsed around my fingers; he'd seen it too. All I could see was its soulprint: dark, black, empty, with the glimmer and heat of fire inside. My hairs stood on end and my pulse raced. I couldn't decide whether it would be worse to see the creature itself—who knew what nightmares it would conjure?—or to see and feel this, because the creature's soulprint wasn't just sight and warmth; like all soulprints, it was a multidimensional thing, with elements from all my senses, and right now every one of them was screaming the same thing to me in a hundred different ways: *Run. Flee. Get away. Now.*

"How do I fight this, Scott?" I whispered through dry lips. "What do we do?" *I don't know what to do. I don't even know where I am.*

The booming note came again, and the building shriek in the background was nearly loud enough to drown out the chiming of the roads. Beside me, Gemma's soulprint shifted. My stomach dropped as I realised that it was dissipating, bleeding out into the air around us.

No, not the air around us; it was bleeding toward the presence, the thing, the menace that was trying to warn us off the roads and away.

No. I had not come this far for something to steal away Gemma's soul now, not when we were here, when we'd made it to the roads, and we were so darned close.

I grabbed tightly onto Scott's and Gemma's fingers and clenched my teeth. Then I did something that felt a lot braver than it really must have been: I closed my eyes.

It was habit, mostly—I could see the soulprint right in front of me with my eyes open, so I didn't actually expect closing them to help—but I did it anyway, and it felt like turning my back on a monster you knew was coming, with inch-long claws and jaws full of teeth, and you knew it was going to pounce any second but you didn't know when—and I did it anyway, ignoring the fact that my breaths were coming in ragged gasps, because I couldn't let my friends die, I couldn't, and I'd saved them before, and I was going to do it again.

I'm not afraid, I told myself. Or if I am, it doesn't matter.

Eyes still closed, I sent my road mastery senses questing toward the beast, or guardian, or creature, and the world around me sparkled silver. It felt like moving through curtains of cellophane, startling and beautiful and noisy and impossible to hide.

Hide.

Gemma's soulprint stopped dissolving. The creature swung toward my road mastery sense, or where I felt like it was, several paces out in front of me. My road mastery was noisy here; I couldn't examine anything without drawing attention.

And apparently here my road mastery was tangible, something I could separate from myself.

I could draw the guardian away.

We could hide.

I flexed my grip on Scott's hand and raised our knotted fist a little, bending my knees, ready to run.

Carefully, slowly, I let my sense of road mastery continue off to my right, away toward the creature, crackling and swimming and glittering through silver fog.

"One," I murmured. *Please let this work.*

"Two." Gemma's soulprint was still hazy, partially dissolved around the edges.

"Three!" I leapt into a dead run, heading along a shining green path of light that smelled like fire and felt like rain.

Scott and Gem followed.

For a heart-pounding moment I thought we'd done it, that we were free, the strange and horrible guardian left behind with my road mastery senses.

But then another fire-hearted darkness reared up at us from below. The air left my lungs; suddenly it felt like my body and brain weren't connected any more, and abandoned, my body had forgotten how to breathe, or pulse, or move.

My road mastery. I'd left it too far behind.

Blackness closed in over my vision, and silence crept into my ears. Something tugged at my hand (perhaps?) and fire flashed under my feet.

A scream. Was that a scream? Was I screaming, or someone else? Where was I? I felt wrapped in cellophane, but my hand hurt, and it was too hot, like I was sitting in a fire, and my insides were melting.

Something, out there in the darkness, something glittery and silver and wreathed in fog. It seemed familiar, like it had once been mine. I reached out, and it came.

The darkness took over.

At least it was quiet.

18

THE SOUND OF sobbing was the first thing I recognised. "I'm sorry," a voice said. "I'm sorry! Please just let her live!"

I touched my fingers to my eyelids and realised they were closed. My body felt soft and floaty, and I had the discomforting realisation that I wasn't actually lying *on* anything. To avoid thinking too hard about that, I opened my eyes. Two dark shapes leaned over me, one dark grey, the other dark blue.

Then I realised the dark blue one wasn't actually leaning over me so much as leaning against the dark grey one for support, and I remembered. "Is she okay?" Their actual faces resolved in front of me. I tried to reach for Gemma's cheek. Something held my fingers tight. I glanced down. Oh. Scott.

He followed my gaze and hurriedly let me go. "Are *you*?"

I brushed Gemma's cheek lightly. "I'm fine."

I should probably check if that's true or not, I thought. But surprisingly, I did seem fine. The disconcerting feeling of being torn in two was gone, and the panicked fear that the guardians of the roads had created was gone, leaving a nagging sense of anxiety and being watched, but nothing else.

"I actually am," I said, looking at Scott. "Are you?"

He swallowed before nodding. "She seems to be okay too," he said, tilting his head toward Gemma gently. "What... what happened?"

I frowned. "Didn't you see them?"

His jaw twitched. "Nightmares."

I pressed my eyes closed. "Don't tell me."

"You mean you *didn't* see them?"

"No. I couldn't even see you guys. Wait." I struggled to sit. "Why can I see you? Where are we? Why aren't we still on the roads?"

Scott glanced around nervously and licked his lips. "Actually, I was hoping you could tell us where we were. Last I knew, we were on the roads, and one of those... things... came at us, and you dragged us off running, but another one jumped up from below... And then nothing. This." He gestured to the uniform greyness around. "I thought you were dead," he added softly.

I forced a bright smile over my lips. "Never." But I pulled my knees up to my chest and hugged them anyway. "Did I..." I didn't know how to finish that. Did I seem all here? Had I been unconscious long?

None of that was quite right anyway, because what I really wanted to know was, had I actually separated myself from my road mastery ability, and if so, had it hurt me permanently? And, most importantly, was this something that could help me fix Gem?

I glanced at Gem. She stared back, silent and a little glassy-eyed, but more alert than she'd been in a couple of days and without the black-eyed stare of the Valley. "Are you with us?" I asked softly.

She gave a quiet, careful nod, and my heart trilled joyfully.

I gave her a tight, one-armed hug. "Love you," I murmured.

"You... too."

Gemma was going to be okay. I was okay, Scott was okay, we weren't in immediate danger, and Gemma was going to be okay, because I would succeed at this or die trying. I took a deep, stabilising breath and looked around. "Okay," I said. "Problem solving time. Clearly we aren't on the roads anymore, because a) I can see you both, and b) there are no monstrous guardian things, and c) I'm not overwhelmed by soulprints anymore. So question one: Where are we?"

Scott narrowed his eyes at me. "You have follow up questions to that, don't you?"

I blinked. "Of course I do. Question two: How did we get here? Question three: How do we get back? Question four: Do we *want* to get back? Et cetera. Want me to keep going?"

He shook his head in mild disgust. "I'm not saying it's not a good thing," he said, "keeping your head in a crisis. But really. You take it to the extreme."

I rolled my eyes. "Grey," I said, gesturing around. "Absence of sensory input. I'm guessing some sort of pocket existence off the roads?" I stood up and arched my back. "The roads connect different realities, right?"

Scott nodded.

"So we're in a different one. We've slipped off the roads. Yes?"

He shrugged. "Seems plausible."

I reached up to crack my shoulders—and my fingers brushed against something solid. I jerked my gaze up, but I could only see grey, grey and more grey. Carefully, I reached out my fingers again. Solid. "Hmm."

"Hmm what?" Scott said, scrutinising my hands.

"There's some sort of barrier here." I tested out a couple of steps, fingers trailing over the ceiling that wasn't cool or warm or soft or hard, just... solid.

Like the floor, I realised, and stooped to check. Sure enough, there was that same weird sensation of solid nothingness. "How big do you think this place is?" I said. It was the kind of infinite grey that could have gone on forever, or—I halted. Or there could be another wall just a meter or so away. And a corner. And another wall.

Quickly, I sketched out the bounds of our new world: about three and a half large paces square, and just tall enough for me to comfortably reach the roof. "Okay that's weird," I said, and told the others what I'd found. "What's the point of a world that's like, ten square meters?" I frowned.

"Experiment gone wrong?" Scott chirped.

I rolled my eyes again. "Genius. Thanks."

Gem inhaled. "It's... It's the only thing I could think of," she said. "Sorry."

I blinked. "You brought us here?"

She nodded carefully. "I... travelled."

"Gem, you genius!" I hugged her gently. "Well," I said, "that solves that mystery. But now how do we find the roads again?" I pressed my hand against the not-wall again, thinking, feeling. I frowned. "I think there's something through here." I reached out with my road mastery.

My stomach lurched, thick and queasy as my road mastery extended away. Quickly, I reeled it back in. I pressed my hand against my belly and grimaced. Okay. So, taking it easy then.

Carefully, I tried again, reaching out slower than I'd even thought possible. My road mastery bumped up against the wall of our new world, and for a moment I thought that would be it—but then they slipped through a shimmering net of resistance like a fish popping through jelly, and I gasped.

The roads were right on the other side.

And so was my road mastery.

I breathed deeply to still the panic and reeled my senses back in, panic easing as they reconnected with my body.

What would've happened if we had fallen off the roads, and my road mastery had stayed behind?

Nausea rolled through my stomach, and I opened my eyes, recollecting myself. "Roads are through here," I said, tapping the not-wall.

"Should we keep going?"

I raised an eyebrow at Scott. "Or what? Sit here for the rest of forever?"

It was his turn to roll his eyes. "Or do you need a break. You were just unconscious on the floor for five minutes, after all."

I shrugged. "I'm fine." My stomach was fine too. No nausea at all. Nope. Not even a bit. No siree. "Besides," I said with a significant glance at Gem.

With a sigh of longsuffering, Scott dragged himself to his feet, then helped Gemma up.

I gave her a tiny smile—it was so good to see her on her own two feet. "How are you feeling?"

She nodded carefully. "Better."

I squinted at her. The cord that connected her to the Valley hadn't changed, but at least she wasn't going wild on us again. "Good."

I squared my shoulders and inhaled. "Over here, you two." I offered them my hands, palms up.

Together, they reached out and laid their hands in mine. I stared for a moment at the tangled knots our fingers made together.

"Wait, shouldn't we have some kind of signal or something?" said Scott.

My eyebrows twitched upward. "Good idea. One squeeze for danger, two squeezes for run, that sort of thing?"

He nodded, a little grim. "Okay, one squeeze for danger, watch out. Two squeezes if any of us see something that's unusual but not dangerous. Three squeezes means run like the blazes."

"And we can twist our hands like this," I said, rotating our knot of fingers, "to indicate direction."

They both nodded.

"Are you sure you're going to be okay to walk?" I said to Gem. "I have no idea how long it could take. We pretty much just have to walk until I can sense something Sanctuary-ish." Her face wasn't quite so pale as it had been, but it was still several shades lighter than its usual mid-brown.

She shrugged.

Scott gave her a long, considering look. "I think I'd better carry you."

She squirmed and shook her head. "You can't... Too heavy... Not the whole way." She turned her gaze on me, desperate for my support.

I bit my lip. "I don't know, Gemma. Why don't you let him give you a piggyback for a bit or something?"

Her eyes shone wetly, and I sighed. "You know what? Just walk for a bit. We'll be okay. If we run into more of those guardian things, I know what to do to distract them now, and if that doesn't work I'm sure you can just travel us into another helpful world for a rest."

"I'm sorry," Gemma whispered, and I realised my tone had been more cutting than I'd intended.

"No," I said, pressing my forehead against her shoulder. "Don't be. It's okay." I breathed slowly in, then sharply out, trying to dispel the unease in my gut. "We'll be fine." Hopefully she didn't notice the rubberiness of my smile.

I inched forward until my toes touched the not-wall of our grey, misty world, and closed my eyes. "Hold tight, guys," I said, squeezing their hands. "Roads Between, round two."

The pain seemed to pass a little faster this time, the power build up and release more predictable, more bearable. I could see how someone might get used to this to the point where it felt like nothing.

The sensory overload was just as intense though, and like last time, I couldn't see my friends once we were back on the roads.

But I could see their soulprints, strong and contained beside me—no leaching out this time.

The black cord of the Valley's hold on Gemma stretched away into nothingness, and I stared at it until I felt a strange rippling pressure on my fingers.

I looked down. One for danger, two for interesting, three for run. Where did weird rippling rank on that scale?

Oh, right. Move. I had to start moving again.

I looked around, hoping for a clue as to which direction we should go. No strange, dark creatures this time, which was great, but there was nothing else to show the way either.

I ripple-squeezed Scott's hand back, and held my lip between my teeth to one side. Often when I'd been looking for things before, it had been my road mastery that had shown the way. When I'd been in the Valley's sinkhole a few weeks back, I'd navigated by following traces of Gemma's soulprint. But here there was nothing to distinguish one path from another, and no one we knew had been here before. Well. No one I knew.

Lights played all around me, magenta and candy pink and pale lemon and autumn red, ghost gum grey and ocean blue, pale, baby green and a flash of bright, glowing gold.

Sounds: The roar of the ocean, traffic horns, something metallic clinking softly, a violin melody, whispers against my face.

Smells: Burnt sugar. Tar. Mud. Roses. Laundry powder. Mint.

Sensations: Fire-warmth. Pins and needles. Cold steel. A soft, careful breeze on my cheeks.

I blinked, trying to detangle my thoughts. Somewhere in that litany of sensations was a thread of something familiar. Something, somewhere... I scanned the roads again. What was it? What had I recognised?

A flash of gold.

Mint-green freshness.

A breath of wind whispering against my face.

"Aphros?" I whispered. But surely she couldn't be here, hadn't been here; she'd been just as naive about the roads as we had.

Scott rippled his fingers against mine, more urgently this time.

Movement. I had to move, or the sensations of the road would crowd into my mind and paralyse me—a heavenly paralysis, but paralysis nonetheless.

Mint green and bright gold. Soft, gentle breezes.

Maybe Aphros had been here before, maybe she hadn't, but right now, it was all I had to go on, and it was as good as anything else, and a lot, lot better than nothing. "Okay," I told my friends, even though they couldn't hear me. "Let's go."

19

UNFORTUNATELY, THE WAY forward seemed largely in parallel with the Valley's cord, stretching away at Gemma's soulprint—and the longer we walked, the stronger it became. At one point, Scott tugged me to a stop, and there was a briefly confusing kerfuffle—until I realised that Gem had given in, and Scott was piggybacking her after all.

My right hand felt empty without her.

Several times—okay, maybe more like several times a minute—Scott had to tug on my hand to remind me to keep moving—the roads were utterly mesmerising, and glorious.

But eventually we reached a place where the trail that seemed like Aphros petered out and something warm and golden pulsed beneath my feet. I crouched, trailing my fingers over—whatever it was we were standing on. I didn't want to think too hard about that one, because while we'd been walking, the trail had some-times led directly up or twistingly down, and it seemed like directions here were somewhat... flexible. I didn't want to meditate on what was or wasn't holding us up, and whether it would or wouldn't continue to do so.

Scott jiggled at my hand again, and I squeezed back twice. *I see something, not dangerous. Give me a second.*

I tilted my head from side to side, trying to figure out what was different about this particular patch of road. Because apart from the fact that the trail that looked like Aphros had disappeared, and the pulsing warmth beneath us, something seemed... brighter, maybe. Sharper. I looked around and realised that in fact, everything *was* sharper—including Scott and Gemma's soulprints. Something was sharpening my road mastery here, making it even stronger than before. I closed my eyes, trying to focus, but it was hard with the sensory overload of the roads constantly tugging at my awareness.

The smell of steel. A glint of copper. Old paper rustling. The weight of books in your hand. Sunlight through green leaves. The smell of snow-sharp air.

Focus.

A heartbeat, subtle but persistent. Sparkling golden light. Vivid red. The texture of linen. Grey stone. Cinnamon and spice.

Focus!

Rushing water. Pipes rattling. Melted cheese. Thick, silky fur. Brilliant, blinding white. The persistent heartbeat.

FOCUS!

The heartbeat. Golden light.

I'd helped Aphros restore the balance earlier in the year when Scott's association with the heart of the Valley had nearly torn the worlds to shreds, and I'd seen the balance as a giant, writhing ball of gold and black light.

Gold light. Golden in exactly the way of the warm, pulsing glow beneath our feet.

Was this the heart of Sanctuary, then?

I knelt down and peered at it, one hand still firmly anchored in Scott's. It seemed likely that this *was* the heart of Sanctuary, but if so, how did I get to it? The heart of the Valley had been much easier to access; I'd just walked into the giant black cloud of nothingness, then walked until I'd found the pillar of dark light.

Of course, the Valley had already been embodied in Scott by that point.

Hmm. Scott. How had *he* gotten to the heart of the Valley? If only I could talk to him properly and ask him. If only I'd thought to ask before. That's if he remembered, which he probably didn't. I clenched my jaw in frustration and drummed my fingers on the not-ground.

Warmth from the heart radiated up to me, suffusing me with peace and happiness. Definitely Sanctuary. I'd figure this out yet.

Maybe I didn't have to get to the actual heart; maybe I could reach it from here somehow, and convince it to attach to Gemma.

I shook my head. I couldn't see any other option right now, so I might as well give it a go. I put steady pressure on Scott's hand, trying to encourage him to sit. After a confused moment or two, he got the idea and I watched as his soulprint sank down next to me. Gemma seemed to disentangle herself from him, and after another moment I felt the pressure on my hand change. I smiled, and squeezed Gemma's hand gently. She squeezed back, and a little bit of relief loosened the tension across my shoulders.

Well, I thought, taking a deep breath, here goes nothing. Closing my eyes, I stretched out for Gemma's soulprint and the thick black cord woven into it. Bile rose in the back of my throat as I brushed against the Valley's cord, the smell of rotten fruit cloying my senses. Swallowing hard, I contemplated the fabric of Gemma's soulprint, wondering how I was going to connect it to the golden heart below me.

I wish Aphros was here.

Carefully, holding Gemma's soulprint as though in one hand, I extended the other part of my road mastery down to the warmth below. It bumped against something solid, clear and see-through but preventing me from getting to the heart nonetheless.

But there, just ahead, swirling in the heart, the fresh scent of mint.

Last time, I'd gotten to Gemma by twisting sideways through dimensions and following her soulprint. I'd followed Aphros the same way. Was it possible I could do the same thing to get into the heart of Sanctuary?

Nothing else to try. Before I could think it over any further, I tightened my grip on Gemma and her soulprint, and twisted.

Nothing happened.

I frowned. For a split second there, it had felt like it was going to work, but then something had... caught. Like there was a glass floor between us and the power of Sanctuary, and part of us had passed through, and part of us had been trapped by the glass.

I frowned at Gemma's soulprint. I was pretty sure I had a good enough grip on it; it had to be something else.

My eyebrows released their tension as I realised it was the Valley-cord that had squirmed away from Sanctuary's warmth. If the fairies weren't going to let Gemma into Sanctuary anymore because of her taint, how did I expect to be able to pull the taint directly into the magical heart that made Sanctuary what it was?

I scrunched up my face. *Stupid, stupid.*

I allowed myself one long inhale, followed by an explosive exhale.

Right. Now we solve this. I am going to save Gemma, and you, Valley, are not going to stop me.

I'd gotten around the Valley's power before. I could do it again.

Okay. But *what* could I do? Together, Aphros and I had been able to separate Scott from the Valley's power, restoring the balance between Sanctuary and the Valley. But how did that help with Gemma? The whole point was that I couldn't just cut her free. I chewed my lower lip. I was missing something still, something obvious.

Gemma's grip on my fingers shifted, a casual movement that drew my eyes back to her soulprint, the glorious pattern of diamond-like stars studding velvet of the deepest night. The Valley's cord hadn't thickened since we'd gotten onto the roads, but its feelers had spread, integrating itself further through the warp and weft of her identity.

If the darkness spread, my best friend would die.

Abruptly, loneliness consumed me. Only I could see the beauty of the roads around me, feel the pulsing of the heart of the Valley, see the soulprints of my friends and the truth of who they really were—but not their faces.

And here, not a single person could see me. I was invisible, non-existent except for a tenuous touching of fingers, and I was alone. No one else could help me.

I bit my lip again, small, rapid bites that worked the threat of tears away.

My road mastery drifted around us, scanning, and I felt myself being drawn into the roads again.

No, I told myself. *You have to stay focused. You have to do this.*

But I couldn't do it alone. Once again, I wished Aphros was here. Wishfully, I tugged at the strange soulprint connection I had with her.

An answer came back, faint and distant. *Hello?*

I stiffened. *Aphros? Is that you?*

What do you need? I am... occupied.

The twins. I squeezed my eyes shut and hoped they'd be okay. *I found the heart,* I told her. *But I can't get in using my road mastery.*

Seeds, she sent back. *Use their magic.*

The connection lengthened and drifted.

Aphros? Aphros, can you hear me?

Nothing.

I took a deep breath. Okay. Seed magic, I could do that. I dug into my pocket—and fear caught at my throat. My seeds were gone. Some time in all the running and trudging and twisting, the packet had fallen from my pocket, and now it was gone.

I slumped.

Scott rippled along my fingers again. *Move.*

I squeezed back, two squeezes and one good long one that I sunk as much *wait* into as I could.

His soulprint shifted impatiently beside us, a flicker of cold starlight licking at the vast emptiness within him.

Darkness. He was so full of darkness. No wonder the Valley had found him convenient prey. No wonder he'd taken so well to death magic.

My breath caught. Death magic. No, what had Scott called it? Shadow magic. Because you didn't have to kill something to use it. You just had to make a sacrifice.

I'd done it once before to get into the Valley, when Scott was nearly lost to the shadows for good. Instead of killing anything else, I'd used myself—my own blood.

I turned and stared at the heart of Sanctuary. Could I do it? I'd used life magic inside the heart of the Valley; logically, then I should be able to use death magic inside the heart of Sanctuary.

If I dared. Did I dare?

Scott had used death magic—*shadow* magic—earlier in Sanctuary, and the world had rocked. Had that been because he'd used shadow magic in Sanctuary, or because of the clash between shadow and seed magic?

If I didn't dare use shadow magic, could I sacrifice some of *my* life, perhaps? That would still be life magic, wouldn't it? But try as I might, I couldn't think of a way to do that which didn't involve blood—which was shadow magic.

I sighed. It didn't matter whether using death magic in the heart of Sanctuary was right or not; it didn't matter whether using it at all made me a terrible person or not. All that mattered was that it was the way to save my friend.

With no other way to draw blood, I took one fingernail between my teeth, braced myself, and tore. My heart thundered in my chest and I cried out around the broken nail: it *hurt*.

The sound of rain rose around me, the smell of water, the feel of clean, fresh droplets running down my face.

I closed my eyes, tightened my grip on Gemma's hand, and let my road mastery flow into the blood that dribbled down my finger. Then I twisted. And this time, it worked.

20

"WHERE... WHERE ARE we?"

Gemma's faint voice made me realise my eyes were still closed—it was easy to forget, considering the roads looked pretty much the same either way—and I opened them.

Wow. The roads might look the same either way, but the heart of Sanctuary definitely did not. Where the heart of the Valley had been pretty much the Black Sinkhole of Doom, the heart of Sanctuary was like standing in a round chamber full of sunshine; the curved walls glowed and the floor was so bright it was like walking on light.

And even better, Gemma stood next to me, now visible, blinking bewildered at the golden light around us.

I shot Scott a look of relief, which he promptly returned. We'd made it.

Calmness infused me, and the golden light glowed more intensely than ever before; this was the heart of Sanctuary, and we'd made it in. I squeezed Gemma tightly.

"I can see you," she said. "Why?"

A smile lit my face; it felt even brighter than the golden fire of Sanctuary's heart. "We're here," I said. "We're in the heart of Sanctuary."

Relief softened her shoulders and the lines of her face. "We... made it." She closed her eyes and swallowed. "What... What now?" she asked.

I took her hand again. "Now we fix you."

"Can... Can I sit down?"

"Of course." Scott and I helped her down, and I squeezed her shoulders. *Here goes nothing,* I thought. Time to save my best friend. "I'm not sure what this will look like," I told Scott. "Or how long it will take."

He nodded and lay down flat on the floor. He must have been exhausted after carrying Gemma for so long. Death magic or no, I wouldn't forget that.

I sat down next to Gem and breathed deeply. The light of Sanctuary's heart seeped in, filling me to overflowing; nothing else could matter right now. I would do this—I couldn't not, not here, not in the very heart of Sanctuary's power. Eyes closed, I drew up my road mastery and examined Gemma's soulprint. There, right where the Valley's power anchored itself in her soulprint, but on the other side; that's where I would need to join her to Sanctuary. "I'm not sure what this will feel like for you," I told her, eyes still closed. "But I imagine you'll need to agree to it in some way, like you did with the Valley. Is that okay?"

"Of course," she murmured.

I squeezed her hand instinctively, then rolled my neck and exhaled, focusing. *Thank goodness I don't have to try to do this on the roads,* I thought. The distractions there had been almost impossible to ignore, but here Sanctuary's warm light drowned everything else out, and it was easy to concentrate. I reached toward the heart. Somehow, I would need to spin it into a cable, like the Valley, and attach it to Gemma.

A loud pop echoed around the golden chamber.

I whirled toward it—as did Scott, leaping to his feet.

I gaped. There, in the middle of the round chamber, was Sanctuary's Keeper, eyes closed, an intangible wind ruffling her hair.

A smile crossed her face, and when she opened her eyes and saw me, it turned vicious. "Hello, Emma Tanning."

My pulse thundered. Would she try to shoot more magic at me? I couldn't assume Scott would have another convenient mouse in his pocket.

(Oh, so *now* the mouse was convenient?

Shut up, self, I commanded. *Shut. Up.*)

"Hello."

Energy crackled around her fingers, lightning silver and sunray gold. "I suppose you know why I'm here."

I nodded, throat dry.

"How, though?" Scott asked. His voice was level and calm, but his fingers twitched at his sides.

And he had a good point.

The Keeper's smile became a shark-toothed grin. "Oh, come now. You are smart children. What else would I be Keeper of, if not the very heart of Sanctuary itself?"

That... made annoying sense. I stood, fuelled by rage at her selfishness. "You... You cow," I spat. "You knew there was a way to save Gemma. You knew this place was here, and instead of helping, you kicked us all out! Why?" I clenched my fists. "Did it make you *feel good*?"

The Keeper scowled, a fleck of lightning sparking at me. "No," she said as I ducked. "I'm not doing this because of how I *feel*. Unlike everyone else in this room, *I* am an adult. No." She raised her hands and power arched between them. "I did it because Gemma made her decision when she agreed to the Valley's bargain. You all made your choices," she sneered. "Gemma chose her path. She must be made to live with the consequences. Or," she added as the lightning concentrated over her right hand, "she can die with them."

The lightning speared toward us.

Gemma screamed.

"No!" Scott leapt forward, straight into the path of the lightning. It hit him square in the chest and he crumpled to the floor.

I cried out and stretched my arm toward him, torn between protecting Gem and making sure he was okay.

His chest rose and fell. Thank goodness.

He'd taken a bolt of lightning for us. Scott, bane of my existence and one-time embodiment of the Valley of Death, had *taken a bolt of lightning* for us. The world was quite possibly ending.

The Keeper pursed her lips. "Not my intended target," she said casually, "but hardly a great loss."

I shook my head. "I don't get it. If you have all this power, why let him get involved with the Valley in the first place? Why let it go as far as it did? Ambergris died, and you did nothing! If I hadn't broken your precious rules, he'd have been possessed by the Valley and the shadows would have been free!"

Pop.

Abruptly, there were two fairies in the centre of the room, the newcomer a dark-haired fairy with glimmering blue wings—Quoise.

I gasped.

"How in the world..." said The Keeper, beginning the question that I was also wondering. How had Quoise gotten here? She couldn't travel the roads, and she wasn't the Keeper—so how?

"I followed you," Quoise said to the Keeper. She raised a sceptre from behind her back and gave a wicked grin. "You left the Forbidden Chamber open and I came through after you. I've always wondered what was in there." She shot me a defiantly proud wink.

A Forbidden Chamber? My chest burned with pride. Good for Quoise.

The Keeper eyed the sceptre warily. "Put that away before you hurt someone."

Quoise's face lit up. I had to give her that: usually the meekest and mildest creature imaginable, she could pull off terrifying glee when it mattered most. "That's the point."

The Keeper sneered at her. "Put it away, and go home. As your Keeper, I command it."

"No," Quoise replied. "You banned me. You're not my Keeper anymore."

"Then you have even less right to wield the magic. Put it away!"

Lightning sparked and crackled as Quoise lifted the sceptre over her head. "Oh," she said. "Didn't I mention? I found something else in the Forbidden Chamber."

The sceptre swirled over Quoise's head.

Magic leapt and crackled, and dread prickled my neck. Something was going wrong.

"The Book of Laws was there," Quoise said softly. "The *original* version. Any fairy may wield the lightning in a state of emergency."

"Not when the state of emergency is that fairy's doing!" the Keeper snapped, dodging a flash from Quoise's sceptre.

"Exactly," Quoise said, any trace of humour dropping away as she squared off against the Keeper.

Around us, the walls creaked and groaned. I quested out with my road mastery—and withdrew immediately. Too much magic. The entire heart of Sanctuary was overloading.

The balance. Any moment now the balance would crumble, taking this place—and us—with it.

"And this emergency is your doing," Quoise was saying to the Keeper. "I read the book, Viri. Someone's been breaking a lot of rules lately. But it wasn't us. It was you." She hefted the sceptre.

"Quoise, no!" I shouted, lunging at her too late.

Lightning flashed, silver and gold, and under the deafening roar a whine began, building, building, higher, louder.

The lightning hit the Keeper just as she released a stream of energy from her hands. It shot past Quoise's lightning arc. The walls shook.

I flung out my road mastery at the fairies and found the thread that connected them back to Sanctuary's real world.

With all the strength I could muster, I pulled at the connection.

"Come on," I muttered. "Come on!"

I pulled harder, straining as magic whirled around the room, a giant storm of pressure and power and light and sound.

Come on!

21

SNAP.

The connection broke. The fairies disappeared. I collapsed back onto the floor, panting—and realised that Gemma was lying still and silent.

Across the room, Scott stirred.

"Come on, Gem," I said, brushing her hair from her cheek.

She blinked with exaggerated slowness; some of my tension eased. Alive. Time to do this then.

Gripping Gemma's hand firmly in mine to anchor myself, I stretched for the heart of Sanctuary. My road mastery sank deeper and deeper into the light, and my worries fell away as Sanctuary's magic filled me to the brim with peace and joy and light.

But there seemed no way to hold it all, nothing to grab onto. How could I spool it out into a thread like this? How could I connect it to Gemma? The Valley had been sentient when Gemma had joined herself to it; did Sanctuary need to be sentient as well? And if so, how on earth was I supposed to do that? All I could sense was vague, gentle light.

I stretched further. Something soft brushed against my awareness—feathers or fur. Then nothing but more golden light.

Scott said the Valley had been leeching his life, using his life to feed itself.

A tiny seed of fear surfaced through the peace and calm of the golden light. I swallowed hard. It made sense. It was logical. And I couldn't think of anything else to try. I had no way to catch the light, no way to drag it to Gemma; I needed it alive so that it could be persuaded to do it itself.

This... was going to hurt.

Gritting my teeth, I turned my road mastery upon myself. I couldn't see my own soulprint of course, but I knew where it was, and I could sense that I was there, alive, a thing, a source of life. Slowly, one tiny piece at a time, I drew on that life force, reeling it out into my road mastery. It didn't hurt as much as I'd feared; it felt a little like using shadow magic.

When I thought I had enough balled up to make a start, I pushed it further out, away from me, away from my road master sense, and feeding it into the light of Sanctuary's heart.

I winced. Okay, so that part hurt. A lot. It felt like I was tugging on a nerve connected deep inside my body, one sharp, shooting pulse of pain that travelled out into the light ahead of me. But Sanctuary was responding; the flutter of feather and fur brushed against my road mastery again, more solid this time, more real. *Come on*, I told it. *Take it. Take my life force.*

It nibbled tentatively—at least, that's what it felt like, tiny bumping contacts like a small, toothless fish.

Slowly, carefully, I fed out some more. Each breath tore raggedly at my throat, and my chest burned like a needle of molten lead had been stabbed through it.

But it was working. A shape took form in front of me: wings; knobbly, golden-furred legs; liquid brown eyes; a glorious golden mane.

I felt it staring at me, curiosity burning in its gaze. *Not me,* I told it. *Gemma. You have to talk to Gemma.*

Its gaze shifted. I fed it more life and it solidified as I watched: a winged horse, small, but growing steadily. It took a cautious step toward Gemma—I could vaguely sense her soulprint in that direction, and I encouraged the horse as vigorously as I could. *Yes. Yes, that's it. Help her. You have to help her.*

It snorted, tossed its mane—and stepped toward her.

The pain in my chest crushed me. Somehow I could see my own fingers beneath my eyes, and they were vague and insubstantial. But the horse, the horse was glorious and real and it was going to Gemma, and she was raising a hand to greet it like an old friend. *Yes.*

Tired. So, so tired. I lay down on the floor.

The pain was nearly gone. I just needed to rest for a moment. Then I'd be fine.

Gemma laughed.

I'd missed that sound so much.

She stood up, strong and vibrant. The black tether of the Valley rippled into her soulprint—and directly opposite, a strong, golden cord anchored her to Sanctuary, fine tendrils creeping through her soulprint and binding it back together.

I smiled, and the last of my tension melted away. We'd done it. Gemma was going to be safe.

The horse's great wings flapped. It whipped toward me. Distantly, I saw fear cross Gemma's face. But it didn't matter, because I'd saved her. *I won't forget you,* I promised Gemma. *Never. Tell Mum and Dad I love them. Anna too.*

Gemma's face crumpled. "No! Emma!"

Don't look back, I thought, smiling. *Don't say goodbye. It's okay.*

"Emma, wait! Emma! Don't do this! Emma, no!"

I closed my eyes; every muscle in my body relaxed. I'd done it. It had worked.

I'd saved Gemma, and everything would be well.

Soft violin strings plucking. The gentle motion of a river rocking me to sleep. The smell of blue.

"Emma, no!"

I could barely hear her now. Colours washed around me, soft rain pattering, glowing warmth surrounding me.

Every sense in my body was alive, so much more alive than I'd ever been before, and as I gave in and drifted, I felt myself break away from everything negative, from every doubt, every fear. I floated, blissful, drunk on golden light and peaceful warmth. If this was death, I thought, it was magical, and no one on Earth should be afraid of it.

22

I FELL BACKWARD into nothingness, and everything around me turned gold and warm and soft. For minutes, hours, years, I lost myself in the comfort and beauty of it all, drifting gently on a stream of eternal happiness.

After what might have been centuries, I bumped against something solid—a seed, a kernel, a nut—and it shifted and shook. Touching it seemed like the most natural thing in the world, and as I did, blood from my finger smeared the nut and blackened its shell. Black and gold, life and death.

Green began to grow.

The seed kernel sprouted and twisted and grew, and I saw visions above me of a green land sprouting, light and dark and green blending together in perfect harmony, and I understood: once, the hearts had been bound together. And once, the lands above them had been bound together in harmony too; no Valley, no Sanctuary, just one wide land stretching from sea to mountain ridges, bright and shining and glorious.

Suddenly, I realised I was drawing closer to the representation of Sanctuary stretched over me. Underneath me something stretched and bunched, stretched and bunched, and beside me great wings beat.

Golden wings. Golden soft feathers, and underneath me, golden soft hair; in my hands, long strands—a mane.

A neck, ears and a head; a pegasus horse, brighter than the sun, more golden than ingots, warm as a winter fire.

And in front of us, a golden cord, connecting us to the image of Sanctuary—to a great, pulsing heart, gold and glowing.

We drew closer and closer to the great ball of gold that shone like the sun, and as we drew near, two patches of darkness appeared within the glow, one a starry night with the deep velvet warmth of summer, and one the dark starlight cold of winter—my two best friends.

We flew like an arrow toward them, and around me the dream shattered, and the vision of the land above me dissolved away and everything was gold and warm, pulsing with the wingbeats of the pegasus I rode.

Then abruptly we were in the chamber of Sanctuary's heart, and the Pegasus jerked downward for a moment as weight redistributed.

Arms wrapped around my waist and somebody sobbed against my shoulder.

"I thought you were dead. I thought you were dead!"

Something sparkled in front of us, and before I could figure out what it was, it shattered over us like cold glass, shivering down my spine and through my hair, and then we were flashing forward through time, rainbows arching around us, clouds forming and dissipating, sounds barely hitting my eardrums before we left them behind again as we sped onward, onward, onward.

I held onto Gemma's arms fiercely and cried and laughed and cried because I'd saved her, and she was okay, and the avatar of Sanctuary was a big, beautiful pegasus, and he was flying us home, home, home.

23

WE LANDED ON the beach in Sanctuary, and as we tumbled off the pegasus, we stared around.

"What happened?" Gemma whispered.

Around us, the beach lay cracked and broken. Further on, pine trees stood at crazy angles, some leaning against their neighbours, some snapped and lying on the ground. "It must have been the earthquakes," I replied quietly. But the elation I'd had at surviving, at saving Gem, was sorely rattled. What had we done?

Behind me was still, too still. I turned.

Scott.

I shifted myself around to face him. "Are you okay?"

His face was sharp, eyes narrow, jaw tight, and his gaze slid off the side of my face and landed in the middle distance. "I'm okay."

I fought the urge to just collapse, right there in the sand. All this—*all this*—and now it seemed like maybe Scott was mad at me. "Are you sure?"

For a long moment, I thought he wouldn't answer. A breeze drifted in off the ocean, bearing salt and clean air. I breathed deeply, appreciating the smell of being alive. The roads had been incredible, but at least here I could focus on one sensation at a time. I inhaled again, savouring the smell of salty air and vowing to never forget it.

"You nearly died," Scott said, and suddenly I had the full attention of his gaze, and it was weighty.

I shrugged. "I guess." I remembered feeding my life force into the heart of Sanctuary... My gaze flicked quickly toward the great golden pegasus. "I called it to life," I said without meaning to. *Wow*, I thought, staring at it. The pegasus. Sanctuary's avatar. I'd brought it to life. I blinked rapidly and shook my head a little. *Wow.*

"That was stupid."

The cruelty in Scott's voice sent a chill of discomfort through my chest. "I had to," I said, facing him again. "It was the only way to save Gemma."

"You didn't have to. I thought we'd talked about you not dying for her sake."

I turned my attention back to him, bristling. "It wasn't like I sat there and had a philosophical discussion about it before I did it, you know. It was the only thing I could do at the time, so I did it. And it worked! I saved her!"

Scott stared out at the ocean again, hands fisting. "You nearly died!"

Sadness and frustration welled in my chest. I clenched my teeth, tossing my head to stop the tears before they could start. "But I didn't, so I don't know why you're so upset! It's all fine! What is your *problem*?!"

That weighty gaze again, pinning me in place.

I refused to squirm.

"Really?" he said, softly, but full of something dark, something heavy—regret? Anger? "You can't see what really happened?"

I frowned. "What—" I cut off and squinted at him. Something... Something else was going on here. Something in the way he sat, or looked, or sounded...

Oh. I sat back, eyes wide. *Oh.*

He nodded fractionally. "So you do see it. I thought you must."

I reached hesitantly for him with my road mastery wide, wide open so I could examine his newly-changed soulprint. "Does... Did it hurt?"

He shrugged. "No. Actually it was pretty nice, compared to the Valley."

I ran my fingers down the side of his face, right where I could see his soulprint glowing—because now instead of cold, vast starlight on the top of a darkened mountain, Scott's soulprint glowed gold: the same mountain top, the same vast sense of distance, but now a dawning, the blush of sunrise on the horizon burning away the stars and filling up the darkness. "What did you do?"

He turned away sharply, breaking contact with my fingers. "You were dying."

I was dying. I'd fed all my lifeforce into the heart of Sanctuary, and I'd left nothing in reserve for myself. I was dying, and he'd come to save me. "What did you do?" I repeated, softer this time.

"The same as I did for the Valley. I... submitted to it. Let it draw on my life force. The same thing you did," he added, eyebrows quirking upward as he glanced at me.

"But how did you know what to do? That I was dying?" How did you wake up in time? I didn't add, remembering him just starting to stir as I'd begun that final stage of the journey.

His breathing was too fast, his fingertips white as he gripped his biceps. He rocked back and forth, once, twice, then doubled over, right down to his knees, and drew in a great, shuddering breath.

I reached for him, but he lifted his head and met my eye. "I knew, because I'd done it once before. Only that time I was too slow, and she died right in front of me."

My stomach did complicated things, and this time I didn't even try to stop the tears from making shining tracks down my cheeks. "But this time, it worked," I said quietly—so quietly. "I'm not dead, Scott. You saved me. Thank you."

He drew in a long, shaky breath. "Yeah. So we're even now, okay?" He said it lightly, but the way his hands fisted at his sides betrayed the weight of it.

I half-smiled, half-sighed, and rubbed away my tears. "Yeah," I said. "I guess we are."

The waves shushed in against the sand. When we'd first arrived, before the roads, it had felt like they were asking a question: Where? Where? Where? I still had the lingering sense of questioning, but the focus seemed to have shifted: When? When? When?

"So..." I said, facing Scott again. "We're all connected to Sanctuary now?"

He shrugged. "Ask it." He tilted his head at the pegasus, who had turned and was regarding us curiously.

I swallowed. "Are... Wait." I scrunched up my face and shook my head. "What do we call you?" I asked the pegasus.

It bowed, head touched to one bent knee. "Helios," it said. "For I am the sun."

I bowed my head in return. "Uh, I'm... Edge. And this is... Scott?"

Helios tossed his head. "I know who you are. You are the ones who gave me life, and for this, I thank you."

I glanced at Scott, then licked my lips. "Are... Are we still giving you life? I mean, are we still connected to you now?"

"He is," Helios said. "You are not. You nearly gave me too much as it was. I tried to break the connection with you, but you had given me life and so it was like trying to separate myself from myself; I could not do it." He bowed his head, sad or thoughtful or maybe both. "But Scott, he was able to assist. Our connection is stable. It is slow. I will not draw his life away from him. You gave me too much, Edge," Helios added solemnly. "It would not have been good for you to die in order to give me life."

Not you, I didn't have the courage to say. Not you.

I took Gemma by the hand, and Scott took my free hand, and together we led our newfound avatar back to Sanctuary—to his home.

24

WE HEADED BACK toward Sanctuary, uncertain of what we would find. The land was quiet and empty, like it was sleeping—or maybe recovering. On the other side of the line of trees, we all paused in shock: a giant chasm had opened, separating the meadow from the entrance alcove.

Mrs Caro and Aphros appeared at the stables, and as soon as they spotted us, came hurrying over. There were hugs all round—even for Scott—and then we arranged ourselves in some sort of cluster and headed back to the stables.

"The twins are fine," Mrs Caro told us.

"I thank you for your assistance," Aphros said, bowing her head solemnly at Mrs Caro.

There was a really great story there, at some point.

My jaw cracked as I yawned. Yep. At some point.

"So," I said as we reached the stables. "What are our chances of being allowed in Sanctuary again, now that we're all connected to its avatar?"

Aphros snorted. "If that fairy of yours has her way, I would judge them to be extremely high."

"*Our* fairy."

"She was not like this until she met you, that much is certain," Aphros said, and through our connection I could sense her amusement.

I pulled a face at her.

"Look, here she comes now," Mrs Caro said, pointing upslope as Quoise sped toward us.

"You're alive!" Quoise squealed as she joined us, flying in a whirling circle, surveying first Gemma, then Scott, then me. She turned to Helios and bowed in the air. "Greetings, denizen of Sanctuary. You are welcome here."

"Greetings, Keeper of the Heart," Helios replied, bowing also.

I raised both eyebrows.

Gem giggled. "She's not the Keeper."

Mrs Caro, Aphros and Quoise exchanged glances.

"What?" I demanded. "What's going on?"

Mrs Caro cleared her throat. "She challenged the leadership of Sanctuary."

Quoise grinned madly. "By the book," she said. "No wonder Viri hid the Book of Law. Not that I've been accepted," Quoise added quickly. "My claim is based mostly on the fact that Viri has been lying to everyone to hold onto her power, but not everyone believes me, and lot of them still believe *her*."

Mrs Caro nodded. "I can't imagine them appreciating the implication that the Valley and Sanctuary used to be connected."

Quoise snorted. "Not so much, no."

"But why?" I asked.

Scott answered, plunging his hands into their usual place in his pockets. "Fear of the Valley," he said simply. He stared at me, but when I remained confused, he continued. "If the fairies stay scared of the Valley, she holds onto her power. But if there's even a hint that the Valley used to be part of Sanctuary, it means the Valley isn't evil—it's something they can fix. *Pfft* goes her control."

Quoise nodded. "Exactly."

I rubbed my hands over my face. "Okay. So, what do we do about it?"

"First," Mrs Caro said very firmly, taking first my hand, then Gemma's, and indicating with her head for Scott to join the line. He did, and she inclined her head approvingly. "Good. First what we're going to do is this."

I waited eagerly for her plan of action, pleased not to be the one concocting it for a change.

"We're going to have this wonderful pegasus here fly us down to the alcove, and then we're going to go home, all of us. And then we're going to have hot showers, and a good meal, and we're going to sleep. *All* of us. For a long time. And then, in a few days, when everyone is feeling better and we've gotten used to all of these recent *changes*..." She eyed us all significantly. "Well, then perhaps we can meet together and decide what—if anything—we should do about this."

Part of me was disappointed with her advice—but a larger, more sensible part of me was really, really *tired*. How many hours had I been up now? A rest sounded really, really good. So did dinner and a hot shower.

And a few days without worrying about friends dying or about saving the world? That sounded like the absolute best of all.

So we held hands, and Mrs Caro got us back to Earth before eight, and as we pushed our way through the tea tree scrub and past sweeping eucalyptus boughs to the crunching gravel of the path, I lifted my face to the dark, cloudy skies of home and breathed deeply, because my friends were safe, and my family was safe. And even when the clouds broke as I headed up the steps through the boulders toward home, I laughed, because the raindrops were fresh and cold and electric, and they washed everything away.

I walked through my back gate and into the house, and there was Dad in his armchair reading, and Anna's music blared from her room and Veve's tail thump-thump-thumped on the floor before she got up and came to greet me, and Mum was in the kitchen baking cookies.

"How's Gem?" she asked, raising her head sharply as I entered, and I laughed, and hugged her, because we'd made it, and I'd saved Gemma, and Scott had saved me, and everything was perfectly, brilliantly fine.

SANCTUARY - BOOK 3

WHEN WORLDS COLLIDE

AMY LAURENS

1

THREE WEEKS.

Three. long. weeks, as long as the trails of rain-drops that streaked down the smudgy windows of the old school bus, racing each other on and on and on until it seemed impossible there was any rain left in the drop.

I picked at a worn patch on the corner of the once-bright-blue bus seat, where the fabric had worn away and the yellowed foam was showing. Three weeks. That's how long it had been since I'd healed my best friend Gemma, since Scott (bizarrely, now also someone I could sort of call a friend) had destroyed Sanctuary.

Well, the magical, multi-dimensional home of the fairies was a little more robust than that. He hadn't *destroyed* it, but he *had* severely damaged it. Using death magic in a place where you're only ever supposed to use life magic will—apparently—do that.

I shrugged as the tag of my uniform dress itched my clammy back. Behind me, kids shouted and hooted, and someone way down the back of the bus had music blaring from their phone, only half-audible from the front over the chatter and the pattering rain. I leaned against the window as a car shushed past, its tyre kicking up spray that still managed to glitter, even though neither it nor I had seen the sun in two days.

The traffic in front of us eased, and the bus hauled itself around the corner onto the main road just a couple of minutes away from school, indicator clicking time as we went. Outside, the grass had shot up to nearly mid-calf on the side of the road, vivid green in the wet, grey light, exactly the kind of lush that would snap and crunch when you snatched a handful of it. Even the gum trees seemed livelier, their usually dull grey-green more vibrant, deeper, the orange-brown sap stains down their trunks bright— almost as bright as the one broad-leafed street tree that was starting to think about winter, the very topmost leaves tinging reddy-orange around the edges.

I glanced up as someone across the row from me clunked the bus's top window open to let in some air; the windows were starting to fog, even though the aircon was blasting. The smell of wet dirt and wet asphalt percolated through the bus, and I inhaled deeply as we turned the final corner into the school, bottle-green gates pegged wide open for the day. The smell reminded me of Sanctuary—not because it was similar, but because it was almost the opposite of Sanctuary's salty, jasmine-scented air—and my stomach twanged with longing.

The bus juddered to a halt, hydraulics hissing as it tilted, the left side lowering to minimise the step to the footpath. The student horde around me rose as one, chattering, waving, school bags slinging onto backs and shoulders and in other people's faces, squashing toes in their careless stampede.

I sighed heavily and slung my navy backpack over my shoulder.

Three weeks.

I schlepped off the school bus with the horde, girls in our blue-and-white summer dresses, boys in their crisp white shirts, and made my way up the footpath to school, once again cursing myself for trusting Mrs Caro, Gemma's mum.

Not that she was an untrustworthy sort of person, of course, but she was an adult, so her sense of priorities was... different. I wanted Sanctuary fixed—*needed* it fixed, because it was my second home and the thing that had taught me to love small-town Nowra after being dragged here unwillingly from big-city Melbourne. But Mrs Caro was more concerned about keeping everyone safe.

Which, yeah, okay, I admitted as the student horde thinned, clusters heading in different directions to the lockers spread throughout the school buildings, safety was pretty important. Been there, learned that one the hard way.

But Sanctuary was important.

Sanctuary was home.

And Mrs Caro had promised we'd try to fix it. And in the last three weeks, she—and we—had done nothing.

I turned the corner around the orangey bricks of H block and glanced ahead to the bay where my locker lived, an alcove of laminated sky-blue lockers stacked double high, the concrete floor stained by decades of locker detritus.

My stomach twisted. Gemma stood in front of my locker, books already clutched to her chest, lip between her teeth as she held her ground against the tide of students swooping in and out to visit their own lockers. Her dark hair seemed even darker in the overcast light, like a cap of shadows pulled back into a ponytail, her thick, sweeping fringe nearly hiding her equally dark eyes.

But as I scanned her with my road mastery—the special ability I had to read and manipulate people's soulprints, a kind of multi-sensory aura unique to each person—I breathed.

Three weeks ago, the connection she'd accidentally developed with the Valley, Sanctuary's bloodthirsty counterpart, had started growing, consuming Gemma's soulprint in an attempt to take over her body. There had been no way to break the connection without risking her life—I'd managed it for Scott before that, but he'd been nearly dead anyway. So for Gemma, I'd gone the safer route: with Scott's help, I'd connected her to Sanctuary, and the two connections balanced out, holding her soulprint steady in between.

I still got a wave of anxiety every time she seemed particularly serious or sad.

Right now, though, the Valley was behaving itself, and Gemma's soulprint was perfectly fine: the same midnight blue, studded with stars and with the texture of velvet, all accompanied by a faint, high-pitched whine and the feeling of being about to remember something important.

I hesitated for a second, wondering if I could avoid her for a little longer. I missed Sanctuary. I needed to get back there and *do* something, and I didn't think I could stand another day of ignoring it, pretending everything was alright. But she saw me and tension melted from her shoulders.

Sighing, I wound my way through the throng of kids to my bottom-tier locker and gave Gem a weary smile as I dumped my bag on the concrete next to it. "Hey."

"Edge!" she said, practically bouncing on her toes. "You'll never believe what's happened!"

I glanced sharply at her. "Sanctuary?"

She deflated a little as pity filled her eyes. "No. You know Mum said we have to wait."

"Mm." I rolled the combination on my school-issue lock, popped it open, and busied myself prepping my books for the day. Gem hesitated a second before launching into some meaningless chatter about a kid named Sally, but I mostly tuned her out. There'd been a time when Gem would have been just as eager as me to fix Sanctuary, and her mother's instructions to wait wouldn't have bothered her a bit. Would have made her *more* eager, even.

It wasn't like I missed the old Gemma, or didn't appreciate this new one who wasn't trying to convince me to break the rules every five seconds, but... I shook my head as I gathered my English and art books into my arms. I kicked my locker shut with my bag inside, snapped the lock closed, and nodded vaguely as Gemma paused for my input. "Uh huh."

She beamed at me and tucked my free arm into hers. "Oh, Edge! Thank you! I knew you'd understand! Come on," she added as the warning bell rang.

Great. Now I'd just agreed to something she'd obviously thought I wouldn't, and I couldn't ask what it was without admitting I hadn't been listening at all.

Something bumped my other shoulder.

I glanced over to see Scott falling into stride with us, blond hair up in its usual ruffled spikes, black-rimmed knock-off designer glasses in place, and—yup, tie-knot loosened to the precise balance between getting in trouble, and making a statement. "Hey," I said.

He didn't look at me. "Hey."

It still felt a little weird to be walking around the school with Scott like this. I'd moved to Nowra at the end of the last school year, mid-November with only three weeks of school remaining before summer break. The first week had been okay—but then Scott had decided he liked me, and that the most appropriate way to try to get my attention was to tease me in front of his mates.

School had started up again in February after the holidays, and it seemed like I'd be in for more of the same—until Gem and I discovered that Scott had gotten himself tangled up with the power of the Valley, Sanctuary's magical counterpart—the one you used death magic to get to, the one that had been leaking awful, soul-sucking shadows all over the place and destroying Sanctuary.

The only way to save Sanctuary at the time had been to fight Scott—but then Gemma had gotten tangled up in the Valley too, kind of accidentally, and a few weeks later—three weeks ago, in fact—Scott had helped me save Gem. In the process, I'd learned that it had been his mother who'd introduced him to death magic—and who he'd been trying to save when he'd gotten connected to the power of the Valley.

I gave my head a little shake as we neared the science block where Gemma and I had roll call first thing every morning.

After I'd convinced him to help me save Gemma, and he'd revealed that he'd only become entangled with the Valley in a last-ditch effort to save his mum's life (an effort which failed, and nearly led to his own death), Scott had demonstrated that he actually had the capacity to act like a decent human being.

And since healing Gemma had involved Scott connecting with the heart of Sanctuary (saving *my* life in the process), he now had a vested interest in its wellbeing. Besides. When there were only three of you who could travel to a secret, magical land, some sort of group bonding was inevitable.

So Scott had ditched his old mates to become a third member of our friendship group. I still wasn't one hundred percent sure I could trust him though.

We slowed to a halt behind the small crowd of my roll call, and I glanced over at Scott to ask if he'd been switched into our class or if he just didn't care about being late to his own—a rhetorical question, of course, since I knew he didn't care, and he tended to shepherd us to our roll call most mornings anyway.

I blinked. He seemed fainter than usual, faded somehow.

I turned to Gemma—but she was the same, slightly faded—and, I realised abruptly, not moving.

Neither was Scott.

My heart raced and the edges of my books dug into my fingers. The last time Gem had vagued out like this, it had been the Valley's connection with her strengthening—prompting the rescue mission that had resulted in Scott kind-of-sort-of mostly breaking Sanctuary.

I bit my lip and leaned close to Gem.

This seemed different, though. The faint fadedness... That was new. And, I realised, looking around more carefully, it applied to everyone. The whole walkway of students seemed faded... and I could smell jasmine, and salt water.

My pulse leapt again, this time in anticipation. Sanctuary! The hall was fading away and everything smelled like Sanctuary.

I stared eagerly around, waiting for it to materialise—but it didn't, and I realised that no one else was moving at all, it was just me, and I hadn't planted a seed to power the crossing to Sanctuary anyway.

I slumped, exhaling heavily.

The world returned to full colour and people began to move again.

"Did either of you feel that?" I asked softly.

Scott and Gemma stared at me.

"Feel what?" Gemma said.

"Sanctuary," I murmured. "Everything just... faded. For a moment. I could smell Sanctuary."

Scott and Gem exchanged glances over my head. I tried not to let it bother me.

"Edge," Gem said carefully, and now I *was* bothered, though I tried to keep the irritation from my face. "Are you sure you weren't just imagining it?"

I tossed my head. "Oh, yeah, you're right, I have no clue at all what Sanctuary really feels like and I was totally hallucinating."

"Edge!" Gem said reproachfully. "You know that's not what I meant." She glanced at Scott again, who gave a tiny shrug.

"What?" I said. "What are you both not telling me?"

"Nothing," Scott said, holding Gemma's eye.

Gem sighed and bumped my shoulder. "He's right. We're not hiding anything. It's just... Well, I know you're impatient to try to fix Sanctuary, but Scott and I can sense it. It's not safe to be there right now. If we crossed over—"

"Then maybe we'd have a chance of figuring out what's going wrong," I snapped. "And fixing it before there isn't a Sanctuary left to fix."

Gem shook her head calmly. "If Sanctuary had been here just now, however that might be, we'd have felt it," she said. "The connection."

I ground my teeth. I knew I was the only one in this party not boasting a magical connection to a magical land. She didn't have to rub my nose in it.

"I'd better go, I'll be late to class," Scott said.

I rolled my eyes. "Yeah, because being on time is *so* important to you, we know."

He patted the top of my head and I was tempted to growl and snap at his fingers. *This* little doggy was not tame. "See you round," he said.

He disappeared into the crowd and I rolled my eyes again. "I really think—" I turned to Gem as the teacher opened the door to our roll call room and students began to file in.

"Later," she murmured as students packed close. "There's no rush."

I clenched my books in my arms. Easy for her to say. I was tired of being the only one who couldn't get answers just by closing my eyes and weighing up a magical connection, tired of people telling me to wait, to not worry about the best home I'd ever known, about the fact that it had been fractured, decimated, last time I'd seen it.

And now they were trying to convince me I'd imagined feeling it just now.

That was it. Everyone else could like it or not; I was going to Sanctuary this afternoon without anyone else, and I was getting some answers.

2

I WALKED UP the driveway with my backpack straps heavy on my shoulders and the sound of traffic humming out on the main road. The clouds were finally starting to sweep away, and the air closed in like a damp rag. I'd always thought Melbourne summers were bad, but man, they had nothing on Nowra, where the humid days seemed to go on and on and on. Urgh.

I dragged the back of my index finger over my temple to wipe away some sweat. Nearby, a few shrieking cockatoos provided a discordant melody to the baseline of the traffic, punctuated by the slamming of a door somewhere.

The sound that was distinctly lacking, however, as I tromped up the stencilled-concrete driveway toward the old brick house, was Veve's barking. Usually our chocolate Labrador couldn't wait for me to get home. But today, there were no frantically excited barks and yips and whines greeting me as I let myself in through the front door.

Frowning, I listened carefully for the sound of anyone else who might be home. "Anna? Mum? Dad?" But it was still too early for Mum and Dad to be home—Dad never got home before six, and Mum had been working back late this week. And it was Wednesday, so Anna would have stayed back at school for maths tutoring.

And yet, no Veve. Weird.

I dumped my bag, then crossed through the house to the glass sliding door in the family room. Maybe she was asleep in her kennel, dreaming so deeply of swimming and chasing rabbits that she hadn't heard me.

I grinned. There was one thing that was sure to wake her up, no matter how deeply asleep she was. I clicked the lock of the door.

Nothing. I frowned again.

I slid the door open and stepped out into the yard. The splintered, grey-wood fence pails were beginning to turn gold in the afternoon light and the lawn was cooling as the shadow of the house stretched over it. Somewhere, someone was mowing their own grass, and the smell of it drifted over the yard. Ants scurried across the pale apricot-beige paving to my left in a rush to get stocked up before the weather started to cool off for the year, and cicadas screeped in the tall, scraggle-footed gum trees down in the reserve behind the house.

But there was still a distinct lack of furry brown Labrador in the yard.

I checked her kennel. Empty.

Anxiety clawed at my chest and I circled around to the left of the house, peering behind the hot water cylinder, under the old pailings, and around the back of the compost bin to make sure Veve hadn't gotten stuck. Nothing, except some old, matted fur and damp dirt. Biting my lip, I headed to the other side of the yard, where it opened up to a raggedy lawn bordered by various small yard trees and ugly, lanky shrubs crouched atop silvering bark chips. Still nothing.

I turned away, thinking that I might give Mum a call and see if she knew anything.

A low noise sounded. I stopped, craning my neck, and listened for it again. There: a low, groaning sort of whine, coming from the awful prickly bushes that grew against the side fence where it met the front one—the same bushes where the Valley's shadows had once dragged Gem and Veve away in the middle of the night.

Heart in my throat, I hurried over and crouched.

Veve gazed back at me, eyes wide, tongue lolling. She tried to stand, tugging backwards, but she couldn't move—some of the lower branches had twisted through her collar, tangling her so tightly she couldn't get out. She'd obviously tried; the collar was up around her ears and thick salvia glopped to the ground as she panted.

I exhaled loudly through my nose. "Frogging elephants, Veve." She must have crawled under there trying to keep cool. You'd have thought she'd know better than to try to hide right where the stinking Valley had captured her.

"Alrighty then," I said as I got down on my knees. "Let's get you out of there, beastie."

Veve's tail flopped twice, as though she was too exhausted to wag it any more.

"Aww, poor Vevey-skin," I crooned as I belly-crawled in next to her. "It's okay. You'll be out in just a sec."

She took the opportunity to plaster some of her salivary goo to my cheek and I screwed up my eyes.

"Thanks, mutt-brain."

Sticks scraped at the skin on my arms as, wincing, I wound my hand up over Veve's head. The branch that had hooked her collar was gnarled and spikey, and I gasped as a thorn pricked the soft flesh between my thumb and forefinger. Gritting my teeth at the awkward angle, I squeezed the branch tight, exhaling in relief as it snapped. I fed it back through Veve's collar and dropped it.

"Come on," I said. "All done."

I wriggled backwards, one hand twined in Veve's collar, the other pressing into the cool mud. My legs, bare in my school dress, fried in the sun, and for a second I thought I could understand the appeal of this prickly underworld. Then a stick stabbed me behind the ear. "Urgh!" I said, clutching the offended ear. "Frogging elephants. What *possessed* you, Veve? Seriously!"

Her tail thumped again as she crawled towards me, claws digging into the dirt as she sought purchase.

The smell of rotten fruit and stagnant water drifted past, and I gagged, heart racing. That was the smell of the Valley, and this was where Gemma and Veve had been stolen by the Valley's shadows in the middle of the night.

But as I lay frozen in the mud, the smell drifted away. I shrugged my shoulders, trying to ignore the unease. The Valley had been quiet ever since we'd connected Gemma to Sanctuary. It was Sanctuary that was leaking all over the place this time, not the Valley. Of course it smelled rotten; who knew what disgusting things had rolled under here and been trapped and rotted away. Probably mice.

Urgh. I shuddered.

Veve lolloped her tongue all over my face again. Whatever. I could think about this later. After a cold shower, for preference.

Everything was perfectly fine.

At last, both Veve and I were extricated from the awful bushes, and I scowled at them—right as Veve collapsed on the grass, eyes rolling, and saliva frothing at the corners of her mouth. My heart raced into overdrive as I flung myself down next to her. "Veve? Veve, what's wrong?"

Her breathing was thick and heavy, and as I stroked her head I noticed that her ears were hotter than I'd ever felt them before. Heat exhaustion, maybe?

I glanced up at the sun, finally showing amid the tattered rags of clouds. Surely it hadn't been that hot today. Muggy, yes. Gross and sweaty, sure. But... heat stroke?

If the Valley had done anything to my dog, someone was going to pay.

"Come on, beastie," I said, shooting a glare at the bushes again. "Let's get you inside." Crouching, I drew her to me and hauled her upwards. She moaned, but I couldn't help it. "It's not my fault you're a heffalump," I told her. As quickly as I could manage while carrying a dog that weighed more than a third of my body weight, I made my way to the sliding door, kicked it open, and got inside. I set Veve down on the tiled floor and switched the air conditioning on just in case before heading to the kitchen.

I snatched up the house phone and hit speed dial, tucking it between my shoulder and ear as I grabbed an old ice cream container from under the sink and filled it with water. "Mum? Hi, it's me. Listen, there's something wrong with Veve." Carefully balancing the container of water, I described what had happened as I made my way back to Veve.

"Call the vet right away," she said when I was finished. "I can't make it home for at least another forty minutes, but call me back and let me know what the vet says."

I agreed and hung up, dropping the phone on the floor for a moment as I put the container of water by Veve's head.

She stretched to sniff at it, nostrils flaring slightly, but didn't move.

Her nose was dry and leathery. I blinked back tears as I scooped up some water in my fingers and let it dribble into the corner of her mouth. She licked feebly and swallowed, tail twitching in the shadow of a wag.

Eyes prickling, I hurried back to the kitchen with the phone and swiped the vet's business card off the fridge. Even if it was the Valley's fault, a vet could probably help me treat her.

My gaze lit on the old towel lying on the kitchen floor that Anna had used to wipe the tiles yesterday, and I snatched it up, wetting it in the sink while I dialled the vet.

"Hello? Yes, hi, it's Emma Tanning here, there's something wrong with my dog Veve." I listed off the symptoms as I carried the wet towel back to Veve and laid it over her belly.

"Do me a favour," said the vet's nurse. "Can you check the colour of Veve's tongue and gums, please?"

I lifted up a flap of jowl and peeked inside Veve's mouth. "Her gums are pretty pale," I said. "But her tongue's really bright."

"Okay. But she hasn't vomited or lost consciousness?"

"No, I don't think so." A tear broke loose and streaked down my cheek.

"Okay, that's good. It sounds like Veve has heat stroke," the nurse said. "It's really important you cool her down as quickly as you can, but not so quickly she goes into shock. Do you know how long she's been like this for?"

"No," I said, struggling to steady my voice. "I got home and she was stuck under the bushes outside. It... It wasn't *very* hot under them, but I guess she'd been stuck for a while, and..." I trailed off as a sob rose in my throat. Veve was five and a half, and one of the only constants I had left from my old life after our sudden interstate move. If she died...

"Hey, Emma, it's going to be okay. Tell me what you've done so far."

I knelt beside Veve and let her lick some more water off my fingers. "Um, I brought her inside to the air conditioning, and she's lying on the cold tiles. I tried giving her some water but she won't drink, so I'm just letting her lick it off my fingers. I have a wet towel on her, too."

"Okay, that's really good, Emma, you did the right thing. Make sure you don't leave the towel on her for too long or her body will think it needs to try to stay warm, okay? How's her breathing?"

I moved the towel and ran my hand down Veve's side, dislodging dust and fur in the process. "Um, actually, I think she's breathing a bit more steadily than she was," I said.

"Good, that's really good. You can probably leave the towel off now. See if she'll have some more water."

I scooped some more water into Veve's mouth and she licked and swallowed, this time her tail giving a good solid thump-thump-thump on the tiles.

"She wagged her tail," I said. "She wasn't doing that before."

"Okay, that's really good, Emma. It sounds like she's doing better. Now," the nurse continued. "Do you have a thermometer in the house at all?"

I thought for a second. "Yeah, I think we have one somewhere."

"Do you know how to take her temperature?" said the nurse.

I nodded, then realised she couldn't see me. "Yeah, I know how to do it."

"Okay. I'll wait while you do that. Let me know what it is."

I nodded again and didn't bother to correct myself this time as I put down the phone and headed to the laundry. I rummaged around in the cupboard below the sink. Why couldn't Mum keep the thermometer somewhere sensible, like with the bandaids or something? But after a minute or so I found it, and ran back to the lounge room.

I grabbed the phone as I uncapped the thermometer. "I have it," I said into the phone. "I'm just taking her temp now."

Veve winced as the thermometer invaded her private places, but I soothed her with a shush and waited with my breath held for it to beep.

It beeped.

I whipped it out and stared at the numbers. "Thirty-nine point three," I said, hoping it would mean more to her than to me.

The nurse sighed in unmistakeable relief. "She's fine, Emma. Her temperature's borderline where we'd usually be worried, but it sounds like you've got it coming down. Good job."

My voice shook as I spoke. "So she'll be okay?"

"Yes, it sounds like it. Bring her in for a check-up as soon as you can just to make sure, but I think she'll be fine. Just keep doing what you've been doing until she feels well enough to get up, and call us back if anything changes or if she seems worse."

"Thank you," I whispered, then said goodbye and hung up. I burst into tears and buried my face in Veve's neck. Her tail flopped and she strained her head to reach me, sniffing.

"I'm okay," I said as I sat up, fur clinging to my tear-dampened cheeks. "You're okay." I squeezed her front paw and noted that it felt hot.

I moved the water container around and dipped Veve's foot in it. "Everything's okay." I hugged her gently, laughing softly as she licked my cheek. "Yeah, yeah," I told her. "I love you too."

3

AFTER DINNER, AS the sun began its drop toward the horizon, I hurried down to the glade by the creek that ran through the reserve out the back of my house, all senses on high alert. The chances of Gem or Scott being down here right now were slim-to-none, but my ears still strained for the crack of twig or rustle of leaves that might mean someone else was coming, and my road mastery senses scanned the bush around me.

But the little clearing amid tall, straight gums and scraggly tea tree thickets remained quiet and empty under the still-overcast skies, the tea-coloured creek burbling along, fat, swollen and happy after all the rain.

I took a packet of seeds out of my pocket: everlasting paper daisies, this week.

In the first month of school we'd been crossing to Sanctuary practically every day, and between us we'd managed to plant a veritable garden. A row of sunflowers bobbed their sunny heads just before the edge of the no-grow zone at the gum trees' feet, and below them the feather-fronds of carrots waved. After three weeks of neglect, I was surprised they were all still thriving—it looked like most of the carrots were ready for harvest.

We'd been talking about introduced species in science class this week, though, and I'd decided the glade needed some natives to balance things out—hence back to the paper daisies.

So I pulled the packet out, tore it open, and gently shook a seed out onto my palm. I tucked the packet away and pinched the seed in the tips of my fingers.

Closing my eyes, I visualised the Sanctuary entrance alcove in as much detail as I could: soft, thick, emerald grass with a circle of gleaming glass wishstones marking the arrival point; rough, white wall enclosing an area the shape of a jellybean about thirty paces end to end, with the archway leading out to the meadow halfway along the scoopy side; the little rockery over to the right inside the wall, with dark grey boulders the size of wombats dotted through a field of smooth, white pebbles and studded with fire-red bushes with long, leathery leaves that smelled like cinnamon.

Once I was confident I had it exactly right, I pushed the seed down deep into the soft dirt of the glade. As I did, my genetic ability to travel kicked in, harnessing the energy stored in the seed to transport me across into Sanctuary—and leaving behind a flower that would grow to almost full maturity in a matter of minutes.

A soft, salt-water breeze kissed my cheeks, and I inhaled joyfully. Sanctuary.

Then I opened my eyes.

When I'd left here last time, a giant rift had been slashed across the middle of the meadow beyond the alcove wall, and the pines along the left edge that separated the meadow from the beach had stood at crazy angles, some snapped in half and some uprooted completely like a drunken giant had passed through. But then, the entrance alcove itself had been perfectly intact.

Now? Not so much. Cracks snaked over the white walls; in places the white had chipped away, showing dark rock underneath. The grass was tipped with yellow, and the little rockery was in disarray, the careful swirling patterns disrupted. It was a wonder I'd been able to get here at all, with it looking so different from what I'd imagined.

A snort interrupted me, and I glanced towards the entrance to see Aphros's white equine head peering around the corner, golden horn glimmering softly in the dusk light.

Instantly, my chest felt lighter and I rushed toward Sanctuary's resident unicorn. "Aphros! I've missed you."

She put her nose over my shoulder and hugged me close. "And I you."

"It's been three weeks since I saw you last," I said. "How long has it been for you?"

Aphros drew back, grave. "Three weeks? But that is not typical." She snorted and tossed her mane. *Here it has been two months*, she sent through our magical, non-verbal connection, the one we had because we'd once joined soulprints in order to save the world—and my life.

Is that normal, I wanted to ask, but she'd already answered that. I'd only been visiting Sanctuary for the last couple of months, but I'd never yet known time to slip that randomly. The worst I'd ever experienced was a couple of hours, and that had been crossing out from Sanctuary back to Earth (although a few times I'd had random side effects that lasted up to a couple of days, like seeing my own body doubled, offset to my left by a few inches). "What's causing it?" I said instead, and she tossed her mane again, indicating the meadow with her gleaming horn.

I glanced out at the meadow that ought to have been gently sloping up to the fairies' Lodge at the top of the hill, and adrenalin twanged in my stomach. The fissure across the meadow had almost doubled in width, now something like five or six metres across. The pines still stood drunkenly about, and a strange kind of shimmery steam seemed to be coming from the fissure, blurring the air and making it hard to see the Lodge, or Aphros's stable.

"What *is* that?" I asked.

The blur intensified for a fraction of a moment, and I glanced back at Aphros—only she was gone.

My eyebrows knotted and I peered around for her. "Aphros?" *Aphros?*

Edge? Is that you?

I turned to my right, and there she was, appearing around the outside curve of the alcove's wall.

It is good to see you! she sent as she approached. *It has been a long time. Are you well?* She neared and drew me into a hug under her chin, just as she had when I'd arrived.

"Um, what just happened?" I asked, face pressed against her soft cheek, hands pressed firmly against the strength of her neck.

Her mane fell over my right wrist, the coarse hair tickling.

"What do you mean?" she said, stepping back so she could eye me.

"You were just here," I said. "I was talking to you. Asking how everything was. Then I blinked and you vanished, and then you were coming out from behind the wall again."

Aphros stamped her hind foot. "Oh dear," she said. "I had hoped that they would not affect you."

I opened my mouth—and the ground rumbled. I darted a glance back up the slope at the fissure, distracted. "The quakes haven't stopped?"

"No," said Aphros sadly.

My hands fisted by my sides. When we'd been here last, Scott had used death magic to protect us against the life magic the fairies were using—but the two magics had clashed, and the ground had rocked—and apparently, it hadn't stopped since.

I still had no idea whether the giant fissure in the meadow was a result of the earthquakes, or if it was something I'd done when I'd been in the heart of Sanctuary—the physical source of all Sanctuary's magic, and the birthplace of—

My lips twitched as a giant, golden pegasus swooped into view over the trees.

The heart of Sanctuary, birthplace of Helios, the great golden pegasus who was the embodiment of Sanctuary and its magic.

He glided toward the ground and landed at a run, cantering toward us before propping to a stop, huge wings flaring to slow him. My breath hitched a little in my throat at the sight.

Helios bowed. "Greetings, Road Master."

I nodded back. "Hi, Helios."

A hiss like steam caught my attention for a second, and my gaze flicked over the fissure—more of the pearly, shimmering fog erupted from it, and the world flickered again.

Nerves thrilled through my stomach, and sure enough, when I turned back, Aphros had gone. Helios, though, had remained. He stood stock still, regarding me gravely. "You see," he said simply.

Throat dry, I nodded.

"The fairies are trying to fix it," he continued. "Well. Some of them. But they too are fractured, just as the land is. It must be fixed."

His gaze bored through me, even as I nodded. "Of course. That's why I'm here." Obviously I was going to fix it. I'd fixed it before, I'd fixed Gem, and now I'd fix Sanctuary again.

Helios tossed his head, great wings half flapping before he resettled them over his back. "No."

My stomach dropped. "No? What do you mean no?" Anger stirred in the depths of my chest. The fairies had tried to stop me once, too, but with a little illicit help from Quoise, my favourite fairy, I'd done it anyway. I was totally prepared to fight the fairies again—though knowing what they were capable of now, this time I'd be a lot more careful. I hadn't expected Helios to stand in my way, though. My nails bit into my palms.

"It is not for you alone to fix," he said, as though pronouncing a weighty blessing—or a curse.

My nails bit harder and I jutted up my chin. "I fixed it all last time."

"No." He shook his head gently and ruffled his wing feathers. "But this time you must."

"That's why I'm here," I ground out. "I already said that."

He nodded. "You must. But you cannot do this alone."

Scott and Gemma's faces as we'd waited outside the classroom swam to mind, skeptical and cautious, sharing information over my head that only they knew. I shrugged. "I'm the only one who wants it fixed," I said. "There isn't anyone else."

The steam from the fissure hissed again, but I kept my gaze firmly fixed on Helios, determined that he wouldn't get away so easily. But despite that, he began to fade. "It is possible, of course," he said, "to follow good rules badly. But it is just as possible to follow bad rules all too well."

Riddles! I didn't need riddles, I needed *answers*.

But before I'd even opened my mouth, Helios had gone. Instead, midway down the slope, on the close side of the fissure, a small flock of fairies had appeared—led by a green-dressed, emerald-winged fairy slightly taller than the rest.

I spun around back into the welcome alcove and headed to the circle of wishstones. I needed answers, and I needed to figure out what in the world was going on with Sanctuary—but I couldn't face a confrontation with the Keeper right now. And besides, I needed to get home.

I slipped back into the yard while the crickets screeped and the dying light of dusk lingered on the horizon. Veve met me, tail now wafting gently and gums no longer deathly-pale. I tussled her ears, my chest tight. "No more getting stuck, okay Veve?"

She licked my arm with enthusiasm, and I didn't even flinch at the slime.

I headed around to the side of the house where the awful prickly bushes skulked in the dying light. My skin crawled as though covered with tiny spiders and Veve leaned up against my leg. "Yeah. Maybe we'll just look from here," I told her.

Pressing my back firmly against the bricks of the house, I closed my eyes. The bricks' warmth seeped into me, a steadying, calming presence. In front of me, though...

I flicked my eyes open again to check that what I was seeing hadn't suddenly come to life. Still just a bunch of shadowed prickly bushes by the fence. Good.

I closed my eyes again, controlling my breathing carefully to keep it even, digging my fingers into Veve's warm fur. A patch of darkness darker than the rest floated in front of me, and a fetid stink of overripe fruit and rotten leaf litter smogged past, something unsensed by my nostrils but perfectly real none-theless.

Veve sneezed.

I chewed twitchily on the inside of my lip and stared at the bushes until dusk faded to twilight, considering my options. I had a few, and none of them involved standing around in the dark with probably-malicious bushes, so I headed back inside. Sanctuary had done something a lot like leaking earlier today, and was suffering through random time skips—and now it looked the Valley might be too.

I made a fist with my non-Veve hand. Helios had said I couldn't fix this alone—but how was I going to convince the others to help?

4

I THOUGHT MY biggest problem on Thursday morning was going to be facing Scott and Gemma again at school and trying to convince them that they really, really needed to help me figure out what was going on with Sanctuary.

When the alarm rang at seven, I left the dim comforting cocoon of my bedroom, and headed into the kitchen for breakfast. Here, sunlight splashed across the walls and over the glossy white floor tiles, turning the pale grey of the laminate benchtop to something slightly gold.

Mum and Dad stood together at the sink, Dad's arms wrapped tightly around Mum as she nestled into his shoulder.

I barely glanced at them as I stooped to grab a bowl from under the bench—but something made me look again, and I saw the tear tracks down Mum's face.

"What's wrong?" I said immediately, straightening, white Corel bowl clutched in the tips of my fingers.

Mum inhaled deeply as Dad smoothed her wispy, light brown hair back off her face, making her seem even more wild than before, like she was trying her best to impersonate a dandelion.

But it was Dad who turned to me, dark eyes sombre, shoulders tense—or was that just from holding Mum still?—and said, "The police from Melbourne called."

In my head, the bowl I was holding crashed to the ground and shattered. Shards spiralled across the shiny floor, spinning under the fridge, up against the skirting, out into the hall.

In reality, I just swallowed hard and placed it carefully on the bench by a scarred, dark-wood chopping board. "Why's that?"

It could have been for something good. It *should* have been. It had been four months since we'd been whipped away into hiding—nearly two since the police had arrested one of the major players in the case my father had been a witness for and told us we didn't have to be quite so secretive anymore.

It could have been something good.

But Mum was wringing the tears out of her eyes with the tips of her fingers, slowly, deliberately, as she leaned back from Dad against the sink, and his shoulders were still tight, and my stomach danced like spiders.

In my head, the face of a random girl—I swallowed again—Georgia, her name was Georgia, I couldn't let myself shy away from that, not if I wanted to move on, the police psych had been crystal clear about that—a face crusted with blood, blackened by fresh bruises, lay on the white tiles of the train station bathroom floor where I'd found her on my way home.

"What's wrong?" I whispered.

Dad calmed himself visibly, flowing in an instant to the crinkle-eyed joker that was the only face of his most people ever saw. "It's okay," he said. "It's all going to be okay." He scooped me into a hug.

I resisted, stiff and straight armed. "Tell me what they said."

"What who said?"

As one, we pivoted to my older sister Anna, who had just walked into the family room. Dark-haired and light-eyed, she looked as different from me as two siblings could get—but just like Georgia, the girl who was dead. My gut clenched.

She read the situation in an instant, hands fisting at her sides, eyes tightening. "What did the police say, Dad?" Her voice came out low, quiet— the deliberate tone of someone used to moving mountains.

Dad stopped trying to hug me, ran a hand over his head and smiled a smile that didn't reach his eyes.

"Just tell them, David," Mum said, gripping the sink behind her with white knuckles. "It's not like they won't find out eventually." She met my eyes with something knowing.

I resisted the urge to toss my head.

Dad sighed, and finally looked like himself. "The police called," he clarified for Anna. "It seems that they've intercepted a threat to us, something that suggested to the police that Romano knows where I am."

Bile rose in my throat.

Last year, back in Melbourne, Dad had witnessed something shady going down—he still wouldn't tell us exactly what—and had been called on to testify. The police had been hoping it would be enough to let them finally get to Antonio Romano, a mob boss, or whatever the proper word was. Did we even have mobs like that in Australia? I had no idea.

But alack. They'd rounded up some important middlemen, but Romano had remained, as ever, untouchable—and a couple of weeks later, I'd been on my way home from school, and Anna had had to hang back at school for something and I'd gone into the public bathrooms which should have been teeming at that time of day—only they weren't, and there was the girl Georgia on the floor, dead and broken and looking so, so much like Anna.

My hand slipped off the edge of the bench from where I'd been leaning, cutting against the corner of the cupboard handle. I winced and lifted my hand up heel first, inspecting the line of chafed skin on the inside of my wrist. Tiny beads of blood were forming along it, like dewdrops along the jagged edge of a rose's leaf.

Two days after I'd found Georgia, we'd been moved to Nowra under witness protection.

I sucked at my wrist.

"So, what," Anna said, crossing into the kitchen with the rest of us. "We have to move again?"

My stomach fell through the floor. I hadn't thought of that.

"I don't know," Dad said. "The police are investigating still."

Anna folded her arms, shrugged, then swung her arms down by her sides again. "Nice of them to get their info sorted before calling us, then."

"Anna." Mum cut a sharp glance at her then took a deep breath. "Look, we're all a bit freaked out by this, I know."

She straightened, shoulder to shoulder with Dad. "But we don't know too much yet, so there's no point worrying. We just have to keep doing what we've been doing, lying low and keeping our heads down. Unfortunately," she added, this time glancing at me for just a fraction of a second, "it means we're back to the old rules, which means straight home from school every day, no wandering around, and no excursions on weekends unless they're strictly necessary."

"What?!" Anna shrilled, exactly as I bolted upright and said, "But *Sanctuary!*"

Ignoring Anna, I ploughed on. "Mum, you *know* there's something weird going on with Sanctuary, you know I have to help Aphros and Quoise fix it, and—"

"No, actually, I don't know that," she said, turning to me with her arms folded tightly across her ribs. "And to be honest, knowing that something strange is going on there, I'd be happier all round if you stayed away anyhow. I'm sorry. I know that's not the answer you want to hear, but I refuse to believe that you are the single only person on the planet capable of saving Sanctuary." She lifted her chin, amber eyes fixed and determined.

"But Mum—"

"No."

It was stifling in here, like someone had turned the heating on prematurely, and my heart was thudding in my ears, and my stomach clenching in on itself.

I might not be the only person *capable* of saving Sanctuary, but it seemed a whole lot like I was the only one who cared to.

"What about maths tutoring?" Anna chimed in. "And my art classes at tech? How long is this going to go on for, what do they mean they *think* he might know where we are, what are they *doing* about it?"

Dad shook his head like a horse irritably dislodging a fly. "I told you, Anna, they didn't say much. I'm not holding out on you. I don't know how long this will last, no one does, but you're not the only one it impacts and the family would have it a darn sight easier if you'd grow up and keep your theatrics to yourself." He threw his hands in the air and stomped out of the room.

Anna opened her mouth as he passed, but thought better and closed it again.

I stared at the spot where Dad had vanished into the hallway. I'd never heard him speak to Anna like that before, not even back in February when Anna had gotten a parcel from her Melbourne boyfriend, the one who wasn't supposed to have our address.

That made my throat go dry, and I looked carefully at Anna, hair twisted up in a messy bun, one strap of her baby pink pyjama singlet slipping from her shoulder as she shrugged and headed to the fridge.

Anna, the one who didn't care about what anyone else thought or said or did.

She'd given Kade our postal address. Granted, that was a couple of months ago now, but... How long would it take Romano to make the connections, to track Kade down and—I swallowed—apply some pressure?

Something inside me crumbled, and adrenalin followed hot behind it. We couldn't spend the rest of our lives running. We just couldn't.

5

MUM HAD GIVEN Anna and me a lift to school, something she hadn't done since we'd first moved up here last year. I guess in the long term it made her feel better or safer or something, but in the short term all it did was make all three of us cranky—and late.

I edged open the door to my homeroom (a science lab-slash-classroom the rest of the day, with bays around the outside for experiments and rows of two-person desks in the middle), scowling and clutching my books—and my late pass. Frogging elephants. Of *course* Mrs Johnston had picked today to be actually engaging with the class, some sort of obligatory-fun, rather than mostly ignoring us for the fifteen minutes of roll call like usual.

Gritting my teeth, I headed toward my usual seat near the front with Gemma, making sure my bright yellow late slip was clearly visible.

Mrs Johnston nodded curtly as I sat, piling my books on the pale-wood laminate desk.

"What's up?" Gemma murmured, barely moving her lips.

"Later," I said, still scowling.

She nodded, and nudged my shoulder affectionately.

Later, as it turned out, wasn't until recess. Scott found us in our usual corner of lawn, tucked between two bricked garden beds just off the footpath in the walkway between the senior common room and the Maths building.

I cracked the top on my banana and peeled the skin down in four equal strips as Scott folded himself down to a cross-legged sit. He leaned back against the bricked edge of the garden bed and tipped his chin up to the sky, this morning a deep blue with clouds scudding across it, the sun playing hide and seek as they did.

Gemma was already sitting to my right, legs curled up under her school dress, carefully plucking purple grapes from their stems with tiny little popping sounds.

We hadn't had grapes around home for nearly a month now; summer was over and they were all overpriced and mostly past their best.

Scott, of course, didn't have a snack, but his butt had hardly touched the ground before the unpeeled half of my banana and a little cluster of Gemma's grapes landed in his lap. He lifted them with his eyes closed and picked the grapes off the stem with his teeth, stuffing them into his cheeks like a cartoon chipmunk. He didn't say thanks, but that was how it went: we pretended he didn't really need our food, he pretended he wasn't really grateful.

A light breeze wound around the buildings, setting the leaves of the creeping, vining ground cover in the planter boxes shivering, and the drier leaves of the dark-trunked gum tree rattling. I grabbed up a fallen leaf from the ground and folded it in my fingers, lifting it up to smell the eucalyptus scent. They were always stronger in hot weather; it was nearly the end of term, and after the Easter holidays the temperatures would cool off, the days would turn grey and short, and even though there'd be plenty of eucalypt leaves whenever I wanted them, they just didn't quite smell the same when they hadn't been baked by thirty-degree heat for weeks on end.

"So why were you late this morning?" Gemma asked, tipping the grape stems off her skirt then picking up the biggest pieces and tossing them into the garden bed.

I frowned as she did. She raised her eyebrows, prompting.

This morning's nerves flooded back, ice settling in my stomach, and I lowered my gaze again and shoved the last mouthful of banana in. I chewed slowly, as slow as I could, but she never took her eyes off me all the while.

"The police called this morning," I said when the banana had gone and I'd licked my slightly sticky fingertips and wiped them on the grass.

In my peripheral vision, Scott tensed, though he kept his head tipped back and his eyes closed as he chewed (banana now), and an outsider wouldn't have caught anything wrong.

On my other side, Gemma was frowning. "The police? Why? Did Anna do something?"

I sniffed. Of the four of us in my family, Anna was definitely the most likely to be in trouble with the police—but in the end, I was pretty sure she was more stubborn than stupid. "No. Not the Nowra police, the Melbourne police."

Something electric ran through me, and both Scott and Gemma caught it. Gem leaned in closer, reaching for my hand, while Scott sat bolt upright, fixing me with his assessing gaze.

"The mob boss..." I swallowed through a suddenly-dry throat. "They think the mob boss guy might know where we are, or something. We're back to school-and-home-only rules. No Sanctuary."

"Oh, Edge!" Gemma launched herself at me, practically landing in my lap as she clasped her arms around my neck. "Is everything alright? What are you going to do?"

"It's fine," I said, Dad's words echoing in my thoughts: *I don't know how long this will last, no one does ... you're not the only one it impacts and the family would have it a darn sight easier if you'd keep your theatrics to yourself.*

I breathed deeply. "We're all fine. It's just a bummer, right? And I have no clue how we're supposed to fix Sanctuary now, since I can't go and—" *And you two won't.* I sighed and gave Gem a squishy hug.

Accidentally, I caught Scott eye: his look was all too knowing, and I narrowed my eyes back at him. So what if he knew I wasn't saying everything. Neither were he and Gem.

"Anyway," Gem said, righting herself and pushing hair out of her face where it had come loose from her ponytail, "it's not like you're *supposed* to be going to Sanctuary at the moment. I know, I *know*," she said, waving her hands as I tried to interrupt. "But I've told you. We've told you," she added with a quick glance at Scott. "It's not safe to be there right now."

I stilled. Okay, so the time skips had been weird, and there was always the Keeper to contend with since she was utterly determined that the three of us were still banned from Sanctuary, even though Gem and Scott practically *were* Sanctuary now, what with their magical bond with the pegasus Helios and all, but... it hadn't seemed *dangerous*, as such. And Helios himself had said I needed to fix things—that *we* needed to fix things. "Please," I said quietly. "Please just tell me what you know." I buried my face in my hands. They still smelled faintly of eucalyptus.

In the silence—which of course wasn't silence so much as awkwardness; the sounds of other students chatting and laughing and shouting still ebbed and flowed around us—I remembered something else I hadn't told them.

"Veve," I said, rubbing at my face before looking up. "You know how I said yesterday that it felt like Sanctuary had, like, faded in on top of us or something?"

Gemma made as if to protest, but Scott silenced her with a tilt of his head and a cutting look.

"Well," I said, ignoring them both, "I got home and, you know those awful prickly bushes around the side of the house?" I raised my eyebrows at Gem and she nodded. "That's where the Valley snatched Gem and Veve," I added for Scott's benefit, oddly gratified when his eyes widened, knuckles blanching as he made fists at the mention of the Valley. "Well, I got home yesterday and Veve was stuck under them. She had heat stroke, and..." I shrugged uncomfortably, as though the Valley's shadows were lurking behind me. "I'm pretty sure she'd been taken by the Valley."

"Taken?" Gemma's voice was thick with scepticism, and she rocked back, lifting one knee and wrapping her arms around it. "Edge, the Valley doesn't just give things back once it's taken them. You know that."

I did—we *all* did—but I also knew what I'd felt.

"And anyway, how do you know it was the Valley? She might've just been stuck. Goodness knows it was hot enough yesterday."

"Not really," I said. "And I'm *pretty sure* I know the Valley when I sense it." My sarcasm could have cut steel. I was used to people questioning me, questioning my abilities—road mastery was rare, so rare that even Gemma's mother and father, who had been visiting Sanctuary for a really long time, didn't know any road masters as strong as I was—but Gem was my best friend, the one who'd always believed me. I busied myself staring at the grey-green leaves of the gum so I had the excuse to look up and blink rapidly a few times.

Something bumped my knee.

Scott. Or his knee, anyway. I stared at it. Somehow, it had never struck me how hairy boy's knees were before—or maybe that was a new thing, because we were all growing up.

"I believe you," Scott said in a low voice, as though he didn't even want Gemma to hear—which was ridiculous, of course, she was right there. Right... there.

I inhaled deeply, and salt water and jasmine filled my lungs while the world around me faded to foggy grey, Scott and Gemma and the plants and the clouds all unmoving. And underneath it all, a different smell, something sweet and sharp that made me want to sneeze, something like sugar and pepper, or fairy floss and sulphur.

I climbed to my feet, peering around through the fog.

But abruptly, the world returned to normal, colour and sound snapping back into place within the space of a heartbeat. I touched the vine leaves in the planter box, heart-shaped, yellow-green leaves on a plant that flowered lilac in the spring: real, cool and slick and waxy to the touch.

"What are you doing there?"

I turned, and saw on Gem's face an expression that was probably a dead match for my own confusion when Aphros had disappeared in Sanctuary. "The time skips in Sanctuary," I murmured to myself.

The Valley had leaked shadows, once. Could Sanctuary be leaking time skips? Urgh. I'd give my right foot to know whether this was just because Scott had used shadow magic in Sanctuary, or because the shadow magic had actually touched the fairies' life magic, or because of something else altogether—maybe something I'd done in Sanctuary's heart.

"What do you mean, time skips in Sanctuary?" Gemma said, quietly, stiffly.

There was a trail of ants just inside the rim of the planter box. You couldn't see them unless you looked closely; they blended in with the dirt and the bark, and were mostly hidden by the viney plant, but they were there, scurrying in their messy row, on their way to who-knew-where.

"Have you been into Sanctuary?" Gem added quietly when I didn't answer.

"Just leave it," Scott murmured, and a burst of good-feeling toward him swelled in my chest.

"No," she said, and I heard her get to her feet. "I want to know. Did you go to Sanctuary alone, Edge? After we'd told you not to? After we'd told you it was dangerous?"

A tendril of vine waved up in the air. I yanked it, and the tip snapped off. "I didn't realise I needed your permission to visit Sanctuary, Gemma. Or," I continued, turning toward her, "did Quoise finally manage to unseat the Keeper, and you convinced them to make you the replacement?"

She paled, but she didn't back down, or look away. "Edge, we told you. Why didn't you trust us? Why didn't you tell me?"

"I'm telling you now, aren't I? Yes, I went to Sanctuary, on Wednesday, after school, and it's a good thing I did, because Sanctuary is breaking, and Helios himself said we need to fix it." I stripped the leaves from my stretch of vine in a single movement and let them drop to the ground. "And besides, why should I trust you when you guys clearly don't trust me? I told you Sanctuary had appeared yesterday, I told you! And it did it again just now, that's why you thought I'd suddenly reappeared over here"— subconscious alarms sounded—*remember this, remember this*— "and inside it time keeps skipping, and the Valley *is* leaking again, and it took Veve, I know it did. So why"—I threw the vine on the ground, snatched up my banana peel from where Scott had discarded it, and prepared to walk away—"won't *you* trust *me*?"

6

I'D AVOIDED GEMMA for the rest of the day, and honestly, it hadn't even been hard. We'd only had one class together, and given it was English in the final period on a Thursday, the teacher just let us read for the lesson. Gem hadn't even come to find me at my locker at lunchtime, so I'd headed out and sat at the edge of the playground alone, trying to look like I'd chosen to deliberately.

Scott, in his defence, did come to find me, but talking to him civilly without Gemma around as backup still felt weird—so as soon as I spotted his blond head weaving toward me through the playground throng, I gathered up the last quarter of my sandwich and ducked around the back of H block, which was *tech*nically out of bounds, all dry, wild, yellowed grass and scrubby bushes and tall scraggly gum trees that were mostly smooth and white trunked, except for the skirt of orangey-brown rough bark around their feet. But here, I could hunker down against the orange, sun-warmed bricks of the humanities building and eat my sandwich in peace. The wind had picked up from recess, too, and it rustled the trees loudly enough that the shouts and cries of the playground faded to white noise. My own little world.

Which would have been super comforting, had I not already *had* my own little world, a.k.a. Sanctuary, and had that particular 'own little world' not been in danger of self-destruction. Or me-destruction. Or Scott-destruction. Whichever.

But I did at least manage to get through the rest of the day uneventfully, and Mum was giving in to her paranoia (okay that wasn't *entirely* fair, it wasn't paranoia if she had a really good reason to be worried) and drove me and Anna home before she went back to work—so I didn't even have to sit with Gemma on the bus.

I mean, I'd have to talk to her soon. She was my best friend. Fighting with her was like, like... Actually, I didn't know what it was like, I thought as scraggy suburban homes with roofs in shades of brown flashed past, their gardens gone leggy and wild from all the rain we'd been having. I'd never been close enough to Anna to fight that badly with her, and my friends back in Melbourne... Well, I'd kind of been conditioned to just go along with whatever they wanted. So no fighting there, either.

Fighting with Gemma sucked, though, that much was sure.

I laid my head against the car's window, which was cold from the air conditioning and buzzing from the thrum of the engine so that my cheek vibrated along with it. More than anything, I wanted to go see Aphros, to talk to her and ask her advice—about Gemma, about Sanctuary, about the police, all of it. But even if Sanctuary had been perfectly safe, I wasn't allowed outside the yard.

Which is how I ended up in the backyard, sitting on the concrete path with Veve, in an old, sky-blue t-shirt and my favourite denim shorts, worn to softness because I'd barely grown in the last two years anyway, staring at the ugly, prickly bushes that skulked against the fence.

Veve lay next to me, face smooshed against my thigh as I idly rubbed the base of her ear between my fingertips, groaning and grunting occasionally as I hit the right spot.

"What do you think?" I asked her, still contemplating the bushes. They stood about chin-height on me, which was to say about a foot-and-a-half shorter than the palings of the fence, and took up about four metres of space along the eastern side of the yard—rather a lot of room for the world's ugliest plant. From here, with my back to the side of the house, I could see the street to my right through the metal railings of the front fence—but we lived in a quiet cul-de-sac; the chances of anyone wandering past and seeing what I was doing—if I did it—were slim. "It's not like we'd be leaving the yard," I added.

Veve sneezed on me and rolled onto her back, wriggling for a moment before tipping her head back, tongue lolling out and flapping drool onto the ground.

"You're equal parts gross and no help at all," I told her, scritching her elbow where the skin was loose and the shape of her bones showed through. "I'm glad you're feeling okay again. But," I continued, "that's exactly why I need to go. I have no one to ask for advice, Vevey. I can't just do nothing. I know it's the Valley, but we've survived it before, right?"

I considered the bushes again with my lips bunched to one side. They had tiny, eye-shaped leaves that tinged to dark red—burgundy, really—on the edges and down the veins, and wicked thorns, some nearly half as long as my thumb and thick as a house nail. Just the kind of place you'd expect a portal to the Valley.

Of *course* I couldn't have a connection to Sanctuary in my yard. Of frogging course.

But... there were no shadows that I could sense. And our excursion into the Valley while trying to save Gem a few weeks ago had suggested that maybe it was just the shadows that were dangerous, not the actually Valley—and that maybe, just maybe, the Valley wasn't *actually* the same thing as the evil, soul-sucking shadows like everyone had thought.

The whole relationship between the shadows and the Valley and the Valley and Sanctuary was kind of murky, and I was pretty sure there was a good story there that the fairies weren't telling—and I was also pretty sure that the Valley wasn't as evil as the fairies tried to claim.

Aphros could cross there, for a start; and Quoise hadn't died when I'd accidentally dragged her there three weeks ago, even though everyone said that fairies would basically spontaneously combust if they went into the Valley.

And I'd used death (Shadow? Death? I couldn't settle on a term that felt right) magic a couple of times now, and nothing terrible seemed to have happened to me so far because of it.

I mean, there was the fact that the sentient power at the heart of the Valley had killed Scott's mother, possessed *him* nearly to the point of death, and worked hard at trying to do the same thing to Gemma... But they had all had to agree to accept the bargain of the Valley's power for that to happen: a soul for power, power for a soul.

"It's not like I'm actually using death, though," I told Veve as she snapped at a passing fly.

The wind exhaled through the garden, and the soft-leaved garden plants wafted happily. Even the lawn rippled a little—but the stiff-branched, waxy-leafed prickle bushes that covered the portal to the Valley didn't stir.

All at once, I sighed. "I'm practically becoming Scott," I muttered as I scrambled to my feet and moved over to the bushes.

Veve leapt up to follow me, tail wagging frantically, making her whole butt wiggle.

"Yeah, yeah, Hairbrain," I said fondly. "Of course I'll take you with me." I made her sit on the ground next to the bushes.

I wriggled my toes in my sneakers—at least I had decent shoes for this trip for a change—and opened the pair of kitchen scissors I'd borrowed from the drawers. This particular pair had three sets of blades to chop herbs into small pieces, and they were super sharp—I'd sliced my fingers on them a couple of times trying to get stuck bits of herb out from between the blades.

I might not have spent the last three weeks planning this exact moment—honestly, I'd hoped never to have to visit the Valley again.

Well, that wasn't quite true; a teeny part of me was actually dying of curiosity over here: rumours that Sanctuary and the Valley had once been part of the same place? Suggestions that the shadows weren't actually a natural result of the Valley? Quoise living through the experience? Urgh. So much curiosity.

So yeah, okay, fine: I'd thought about crossing over to the Valley again. And there were only two ways to do that: one, procure a unicorn-hair ward, because unicorns were the only creatures who could freely cross the border between Sanctuary and the Valley, and walk over from Sanctuary; or two, offer a death sacrifice, which usually meant the literal death of a small animal...

Only I'd figured out a way to make it work by offering my own blood instead.

And in contemplating a theoretical return to the Valley, I'd also thought a lot about how hard it actually was to draw blood on purpose when you wanted it sometimes, and about how the resulting injury tended to sting quite a lot, and how it would be best to have that in as practical a place as possible.

So I opened the scissors, took a deep breath, grabbed Veve's collar with my left hand, and with my right, drew the blades of the scissors over the back of my left shoulder muscle, just about where they jab you with immunisations.

People seriously underestimate the willpower it takes to hurt yourself deliberately. It took a second go before I actually broke the skin, and when I did, I inhaled sharply. Tears sprang into my eyes, but I closed the scissors and laid them carefully on the ground before squishing the tears away with my index knuckle. It didn't really hurt any more than a paper cut—the scissors were razor sharp—but it felt like a shocking thing to have done, and that made the pain seem worse.

"If there was any way but this," I told Veve. "I'd do it." I closed my eyes, imagined the smell and feel of the Valley, and the world slipped sideways.

7

I GASPED, AND fell to the ground, wincing as my palms hit the dry, spiky, straws of dead grass. A wave of nausea crested over me and I swayed on all fours for a moment, waiting for the tussocks and fallen leaf litter to come into focus. The nausea was mostly a by-product of using death magic, but the sudden, overwhelming stench of rotting, overripe fruit, sickly sweet and thick, accompanied by the smell of fetid drains definitely didn't help.

You had to love the Valley. Ha.

Veve slurped at my ear, wet snuffling noises of concern.

I sat up, shielding my face with one hand and wiping slobber out of my ear with my shoulder. Around us, trees that looked almost like some of the shorter types of gum trees gnarled and twisted their way to the sky, their leaves a little less long, a little less dry and grey-toned than any gums I'd seen before. Some had dark red stains down their dark bark, like old blood—and on some, sap still bubbled out, looking an awful lot like new blood.

I'd begun to sweat the second I'd arrived, beads popping out on my forehead and running down my temples, and I winced as sweat made its way into the small cuts on my shoulder. I fished around in my shorts pocket for the bandaid I'd brought and ripped it open. Carefully, I ran my thumb over the cuts, then licked off the smear of blood.

Salty, from the sweat. Ick. I wiped away the sweat with the sleeve of my t-shirt so the bandaid would actually stick, then pressed it on and carefully tucked the tiny bits of rubbish back into my pockets.

The heat pressed down like a wet blanket, thick and stifling. By my side, Veve panted, huffing like a steam train as her tongue lolled. I tussled her ears. "So, how far away is Sanctuary, do you think?" I asked her.

I closed my eyes and looked around with my road mastery, but either I was too far away from Sanctuary to feel it, or the border between it and the Valley blocked my road mastery.

Urgh. There was still so much about the magics of Sanctuary and the Valley that we didn't know. Or, well, that *I* didn't know. The fairies obviously knew a lot more than they were saying, and who knew what Gemma and Scott could now tell through their special connection.

I sighed.

Edge, is that you? Aphros's voice drifted toward me, inaudible but clear as mint nonetheless.

I smiled. *Yeah, I'm in the Valley.*

I could practically see her tossing her mane impatiently. *Stay there, I will come to you.*

Yeah, okay.

I sighed, glancing around at the hot, bright sky that always seemed to feel like midday even though this place had no sun. Not exactly my favourite place to hang out, I'd be honest. But Aphros was right: at least here we wouldn't get interrupted by the Keeper or her lackeys. And Aphros was quick: I wouldn't have to wait too long.

I found a log to perch on, Veve flopped down in the shade right behind me, and we settled in to wait.

Sure enough, before too long—although it was long enough that I'd begun to wish I'd thought about water, not just a bandaid—Aphros's voice flashed into my head again. *I am nearly there.*

I stilled, listening with all my might, and after a moment caught the rhythmic drumming of her hooves somewhere away to my left and a little behind me. I closed my eyes and cast outward with my road mastery; she should be within the fifty-or-so metre range of my ability to detect people any moment now.

And there she was, her soulprint a bright flare of gold and pale green, suffused with the smell of mint—and with her, another soulprint I recognised: deep turquoise blue, rippling in the exact way that sunlight would if you looked up at it from underwater, the smell of rain, and the sound of soft, tinkling fairybells.

Quoise. I grinned so wide my dry lower lip threatened to crack, then pushed my fingers and palms over my cheeks as though I might be able to hold my happiness in.

Veve fish-flopped to her feet in the manner of all startled sleeping dogs, barking delightedly as Aphros appeared.

I hurried over and wrapped my arms around Aphros's neck, inhaling the equine-and-hay smell of her, wiping my face against her neck to get the thick, tickley wisps of her mane out of my eyes and holding tight in case she vanished at any second.

Are you well? she sent.

I'm great. Truth, because I was completely great *now*.

Above me, Quoise giggled. I held my wrist up above my head for the handspan-sized fairy to alight, and brought her in close to my face so she could join in the snuggle. She laughed and wrapped her arms as far around my neck as she could, deep blue wings edged in black and matching her wafty, gauzy dress, fluttering in excitement.

"How did you get here?" I said when the hug-fest finally quit. Although Quoise hadn't been affected when I'd travelled us all to the Valley a month ago, as far as I knew no one but Aphros could walk across from Sanctuary into the Valley—well, Aphros and anyone with a unicorn-hair ward.

"I came with Aphros," she said. "Her presence allowed me to cross from Sanctuary."

"That's great!" I said. "How *is* Sanctuary? What's been happening?"

Aphros tossed her head and stamped a hind foot absently. "You saw how the crevice is affecting things, I think."

"The time skips?"

She nodded.

Quoise held her chin in both hands, heels of her palms meeting in a neat V under her face. "Oh, Edge," she said, eyes wide. "It's terrible. Viri's trying to play things down as much as she can, of course," she continued, referring to the Keeper and ruler of Sanctuary, "but it's hard not to notice that things are getting worse when you can barely finish a sentence these days without the person you're talking to suddenly vanishing."

I frowned. "But that's not happening here?" I waved at the Valley around us.

Quoise and Aphros exchanged glances. "Not as badly," Quoise said. "The main crevice is in Sanctuary, and although the Valley is getting some of the effects, like the quakes and things, overall it seems to be holding up alright. Only..." She bit her lower lip.

There were any number of ways that sentence could plausibly end. "Only Viri still says you all can't come over here without dying?" I said, picking the most obvious.

For as long as the fairies could remember, they'd been told unconditionally that to set foot in the Valley was to die; even the Valley itself had believed that. But for reasons none of us had yet figured out, Quoise hadn't spontaneously combusted when she'd ended up in the Valley nearly a month ago, and if her appearance here today was anything to go by, she'd come over again more than once in the interim.

Quoise nodded. "Of course. She won't let them listen to anything I have to say." She scowled, and it was so adorable I nearly laughed. "But, there are other problems. I might not be dead from being here in the Valley, but it's still dangerous. The shado—"

In the space of a syllable, both Quoise and Aphros disappeared—and Veve.

Panic gripped at my chest for a moment before I cast around and spotted her sleeping behind the log, right where she'd been before Aphros and Quoise had arrived.

Aphros, there was a time skip. Where are you?

Coming to you in the Valley, she responded. *We are nearly there.*

I sighed heavily, shoulders dropping, and folded myself down to the ground to wait.

"Things are definitely getting worse," Quoise said as soon as she arrived this time. "Aphros said there was a time skip?"

I nodded. "Let's skip the polite stuff and list out the important things, in case it skips again."

Aphros tossed her mane, exactly as before. "The fissure is widening. The time skips are getting worse and, obviously, are now spreading to the Valley. Shadows have been sighted. Quoise has a small but loyal core of fairies who believe her and are willing to move against the Keeper should circumstances allow."

She cast a questioning glance at Quoise, who nodded.

"I think that about covers it," Quoise said, hovering near me.

She tugged on her dark braid. "I need that Book of Laws. You know the one," she said, flicking a glance at me.

I nodded. "The one you found before following us through to the heart of Sanctuary."

"Yes. Only, of course, Viri's locked up the Forbidden Chamber again so no one can get at the book." Another tug on her braid. "If I had it, I think I could persuade the others to join me. It would answer so many—"

I blinked, and they'd vanished again. Rubbing at my face, I sat back down on the log next to Veve and tipped my head back against the tree behind me, closing my eyes. *Aphros? Are you there?*

No answer.

I sighed. Shadows. That definitely wasn't good. Might explain why Veve had been pulled through to the Valley though, I thought, reaching out to run my fingertips through her fur. The shadows had done that last time, at the start of the year, when both Veve and Gem had been sucked through. But that time, the Valley had been strengthening. This time... I glanced around. This time the Valley was quiet.

Still. I shuddered as adrenalin pulsed through my body. Shadows. Not good. Not good at all.

A strange noise, rhythmic, whoomping, sounded over the clearing where I sat.

I frowned and looked around, and then, when I couldn't see anything through the trees, up.

My tension melted away as I spotted Helios, glowing golden in the sky like a horse-shaped sun, great, pale gold wings beating the air as he angled himself to land.

He dropped fast, legs windmilling, wings spread wide—and at the last second before his hooves touched the ground, he flared his wings with another feathery noise, and landed at a trot.

I watched through slitted eyes, his mane and tail rippling out light bright enough to cast sharp shadows behind everything, my hand over my forehead to shield my face.

"Hi," I said as the physical embodiment of Sanctuary's power drew close and halted beside me. "What else has broken?"

Helios snorted and flicked his tail, nearly blinding me in the process. "The fairies have closed the ways to the circle," he said. "Quoise does not yet know, nor Aphros."

"The ways?" I wrinkled my brow as Veve yawned to her feet, saw Helios, and lay back down so she could belly-crawl toward him adoringly. Cute.

"The ways." He tossed his head impatiently. "To the circle. Where those who travel to Sanctuary may enter."

My frown deepened. "What, you mean... the alcove? The... circle?" In the white-walled alcove where everyone who travelled to Sanctuary began, clear-glass wishstones drew a circle in the thick, emerald grass: the place where everyone arrived in Sanctuary, no matter where they'd travelled from (unlike the Valley, where travelling over at different crossing points meant you arrived at the corresponding point in the Valley, wherever that might be). "You mean... no one can cross to Sanctuary right now?"

Helios nodded. "That is correct. The fissure grows worse, and Sanctuary is beginning to fracture. The fairies do not want to risk the lives of anyone else."

I snorted. "Big of them." They didn't seem to care too much about other people's lives when the shadows were roaming around trying to devour everything.

Helios stamped suddenly, firmly, and I jerked away a little. "You must find a way to fix this. If Sanctuary fragments, the middle worlds will die."

The middle worlds. *You can get to anywhere from Sanctuary—* Quosie had told me that on my very first visit. I guessed the 'middle worlds' must be Sanctuary and the Valley, then, the worlds in the middle of all the others.

Helios could barely hold still, flitting his wings, rustling feathers, swishing his tail, stamping... His ears flickered up and down, constantly alert.

Another thought took hold. "Helios, if Sanctuary fragments..." I took in a long breath, right as Veve rolled onto her back, offering her belly to the great pegasus. "What will happen to you?"

He stilled, as instantly and completely as though he'd been turned to stone. "I will be torn apart also."

"Oh," I said softly, so softly. "I'm sorry." I rubbed my hands over my face again, fingers sliding up my cheekbones until my palms covered my eyes. "I don't suppose you have *any* idea where to start with this, do you?"

"Only that you might look in the one place where time does not matter."

I blinked. "The roads? You want me to go on the roads again?"

He made a movement that could have been a nod, or could have been tossing his head.

I narrowed my eyes and leaned forward over my knees. "Helios, how much do you really know about what's going on? Is there more that you could just *tell* me? It would save a lot of trouble, you know."

His back feet danced sideways. "I have not the words, and here, I cannot show you."

I straightened, lighter. "You want me to meet you in the heart so you can show me what's wrong? Okay. Okay, that I can do." I stood, wiping sweaty hands on my shorts, shrugging away the trickle of sweat behind my ear. "Roads. No worries. I can do roads."

Veve did her fish-flop movement to her feet again, and trotted to me, tongue still flapping like a wet, pink flag, tail wafting vaguely.

"No, Vevey-pup," I said, rubbing her ears, "you can't come with me on the roads."

Urgh. Which, problem: who was I going to get to come on the roads with me? Gemma definitely wouldn't approve, and Scott... My stomach flipped. There had to be another option.

I ran my lip through my teeth. There *was* one other option. It was totally crazy, utterly bizarre, but... maybe. Maybe it would work.

"I'll get there as soon as I can," I told Helios. "How will you know I'm there?"

"I will feel it," he said, bowing his golden head. "Hurry, Edge. The world is cracking, and you and your friends are needed."

I sniffed. Me and my friends. Yeah. All those hordes of friends. Never mind. I gave my head a shake and wound my fingers through Veve's collar. The other option would work. It had to.

8

"SO REMIND ME what we're doing again?" Anna said, shifting her weight as we stood in the yard staring at the prickly bushes.

I'd managed to convince her to change, but even wearing almost exactly the same outfit as me (old, fitted jeans and a loose tee—she'd foregone shorts when I'd emphasised how much walking would be involved), with her hair pulled up in a messy bun trailing wisps of untameable hair all over her shoulders and round her face, she still managed to look glamorous.

It was something in the way she carried herself, I decided, something that transmitted loudly that she didn't care for your opinion, that she was perfectly happy rocking her own thing, thanks very much.

I rubbed my hands down the front of my shorts—they weren't sweaty, but the feel of the denim against my palms steadied me a little. The sun was inching its way ever closer to the treetops, and although Mum and Dad wouldn't be home until well after dark (apparently the cinemas were still considered safe if you were over twenty, ha), I had no idea how long it might take to get to the heart of Sanctuary and back again.

"Magic," I said, nudging Veve away with my knee. "We're doing magic. It's complicated."

"Yeah I got that by the lack of logical explanation, thanks."

I squinted at her in a mock glare, then inhaled and exhaled firmly. "Okay. Look. How much do you trust me?"

She shrugged. "I dunno, a lot?"

My eyes widened. "Really?"

"Uh, yeah?" She flung her head exaggeratedly to one side and raised an eyebrow at me. "Miss Goody-Two-Shoes? Never been in trouble at school," she said, checking off on her fingers, "barely ever in trouble with the parentals, most organised student on the planet, probably not even human... uh, *yeah* I trust you. Besides. I wanna know what kind of weird crap you and that Gemma kid have been getting up to. I haven't forgotten you 'falling down the boulders', you know," she added, putting actual air quotes around the words.

I squirmed a little. That had been the day I'd been dragged into the Valley by a mysterious force I'd later learned was Aphros. I'd set Aphros free from the shadows, but the Valley's trees had sprung to life and attacked me when *I'd* tried to escape.

Quoise had patched up the worst of it, but I hadn't exactly been in mint condition when Gemma had finally brought me home.

It occurred to me that tonight might end with me bringing Anna home in exactly that state.

Urgh. "Look," I said, rubbing my forehead with the back of my hand, "maybe this isn't such a great idea. This is dangerous, An, and you really have no clue what I'm getting you into, and..." I took a step back so I could flop against the bricks of the house. "Urgh."

Anna surveyed me with her arms folded, one hip cocked, lips pursed, while Veve gave up on us both and headed back to the main part of the yard. The sloshing noise of her drinking sounded a moment later.

Traffic whooshed past on the main road one street over to the right; to the left, the last few cicadas of summer were enjoying the reprieve from the rain, singing their hearts out in the bush reserve that stretched all the way down to the creek and up the other side, nearly to my school.

"So why isn't Gemma doing this with you, by the by?" Anna quirked that eyebrow again. "You two were inseparable for a hot minute there, but you've been moping for the last couple of weeks. Did you break up?"

Something anxious leapt in my chest. I scowled. "No, we did not 'break up'." My turn to do air quotes. "It's just actually dangerous, is all, and she..." I cut off and sighed, pressing two fingers over my right eye. "She's had enough of danger for now."

And, frog it all, that was probably fair enough. I'd been attacked by zombie trees and chased by soul-sucking shadows, sure—but Gemma had been *caught* by the shadows, and possessed by the sentient magic of the Valley.

Urgh. Of course she didn't want to rush to go fix Sanctuary, not when she could kind of tell how it was anyway through her connection to Helios.

Frog it. Frogging frog it all.

"Look," I said, raising my gaze to Anna as though it were weighed down by lead, "I need you. Sanctuary is breaking—they've shut everyone out—and the only way I can talk to Helios to figure out what's going on is by travelling the roads, and to do that, I need another person. If you don't want to help me, I can't make you. But I literally have no other options right now."

Anna's jaw worked, but after a moment she exhaled huffily and swung her arms loose by her sides. "Great. Nice to know I'm the bottom of the barrel."

"I didn't—"

"It's fine." Her mouth smiled without her eyes. "I get it. Let's just get this done, okay?"

"Yeah." I inhaled. "Let's."

I pushed off the wall and walked to the bushes, with Anna following at my side.

Once I was close enough that my hip brushed the spiky tendrils of the bushes, I gave her a brief recap of what to expect—she'd get to skip the momentary nausea and dizziness that went along with using your own blood to travel between Earth and the Valley (which, interestingly, was the exact opposite if you killed something else and used *its* blood instead of your own: *you'd* be perfectly fine, but any passengers you took with you would be treated to some good ol' fashioned bone-crushing pain and agony, *thanks* for that experience, Scott)—took her hand firmly, and broke out the scissors.

I figured a second injury was wasteful, and used one of the blades to pick the new scab off the cut I'd made earlier—but even so, Anna tensed, white around the lips and knuckles as I squeezed my shoulder to make it bleed a little more.

"I know," I said, flicking her a brief glance and an attempt at a reassuring smile. "It's gross. But I'm not going to kill an innocent animal instead, so..." I twitched both shoulders in the tiniest impersonation of a shrug. "Eyes closed."

In an instant, we were in the Valley.

I leaned down over my knees, breathing slowing through my mouth to calm the nausea, staring unfocusedly at the ground.

"Whoa." Anna let go of my hand and out of the corner of my eye I watched her do a slow circle. "You weren't wrong."

I eased myself upright, cradling my stomach.

"This place *stinks*." She grinned.

I rolled my eyes and wiped hair out of my face. "Yeah." I inhaled deeply to steady myself, and wrinkled my nose at the rotten-fruit-and-stagnant-water smell. "It does."

Anna wandered a couple of steps away, eyes wide, face tilted upwards. Even in her denim-and-tee, even at five-foot-seven, you could have strapped a pair of wings on and mistaken her for one of the fairies, like travelling had sparked something inside her—like she belonged.

In thirteen years of living, I couldn't remember Anna looking like she belonged anywhere. People looked at her, were drawn to her, precisely *because* she stood out. Being Anna was the opposite of belonging.

I tilted my head, brow wrinkling as I tried to pinpoint what had changed. It was more than just her blissed-out expression, or the wonder in her eyes. Something, something else... I blinked, a normal blink, only a fraction of a second long—but it was enough to catch the change with my road mastery.

Her soulprint was different.

Usually, her soulprint looked and smelled like strawberries-and-cream, a faint blush of berry pink and cream the colour of the palest skin, accompanied by the sound of clacking keys, like a spider running over a laptop keyboard—and equally as squicky and neck-pricklingly unpleasant as the one time I actually *had* heard a spider running over Mum's laptop keyboard.

The strawberries-and-cream-ness of her soulprint was still there, but the sound had changed; instead of being slightly uncomfortable, it seemed... purposeful.

"You're a freak, you know that?" Anna said, turning back to me with her arms and smile almost equally wide. "I can't believe this is what you've been doing all those times. This is ridiculous! This is absurd! You're supposed to be the good little human who never breaks any rules!"

I folded my arms and raised my chin, my heart pounding at my ribcage. "Name one rule I've broken so far." Yes, okay, I'd broken some over the last few months, but I'd been literally saving the world, so I figured I deserved a little leeway there, and it wasn't like I'd suddenly morphed into some careless rebel who smashed rules left, right and centre for the fun of it. Rules were there for a reason. I liked rules. Good ones, anyway. They made life sure, and predictable, and safe.

Anna laughed. "Uh, the rules of physics, maybe? Oh my gosh, I can't believe this. I can't believe it! My sister is a freaking magician!" She rubbed at her arms like maybe she had goosebumps, still shaking her head wide-eyed and laughing to herself.

I rolled my eyes. "Come on." I took her hand and began walking; it had taken some quick map-sketching on some scrap paper at home, but I was pretty sure the entrance to the roads was about fifteen minutes ahead and to the left.

I glanced around at the twisted, ghost-trunked trees and wiped a bead of sweat from my temple with a free finger. "This is just the Valley. Wait till you see the roads."

9

"OKAY," I TOLD Anna as we stood at the entrance to the roads—totally invisible to Anna, and nothing more than a faint but persistent drift of out-of-place sensations for me. "So remember what I said: just keep me moving. That's all you have to do. Especially if you see something scary."

She narrowed her eyes at me. "Is that likely?"

"Truthfully?" I said, looking up at her. "Yes."

Her jaw worked for a moment, lips twisting to one side until she nodded curtly. "Okay."

"Just keep me moving."

"Yeah, you said that." She shifted her weight from foot to foot, avoiding eye contact. "Are we going or not?"

I exhaled. "We're going." I put my hand on her shoulder, closed my eyes to get rid of distractions, and felt for the roads with my road mastery.

The faint drift of sensations strengthened, sights and smells and sounds that didn't belong here in the physical world, and I imagined myself catching hold of them and tugging.

The visualisation helped, and the faint sensations immediately became a steady tension as energy coursed through me. I held on tightly, and the energy grew, power billowing to life inside me, a growing lightning storm in my chest. Energy crackled and snapped, and my body strained at the edges; my skin hurt, as though something was trying to explode through it in every direction, and my ribs ached as the centre of power settled in my heart, my pulse ringing my body like a gong with every beat.

Hold it, hold it...

A cry escaped my mouth—and the tension snapped, leaving my body twanging.

I opened my eyes, and my face melted into a smile: the roads.

If a single person's soulprint was like a multi-sensory aura around them, the roads were like everybody's auras combined into one: a massive scramble of sounds and colours and smells and textures, all drifting through time and space.

If you were patient, if you were persistent, you could pick out the threads of related sensory information, piece together something like a person's soulprint, and follow it through the chaos—if you could remember to keep moving, which you couldn't, because it was total sensory bombardment, sight after sound after smell after touch, hot sunset orange like when smoke is in the air, followed by birdsong and rustling leaves, overlaid with the smell of wood varnish and the feel of a minky blanket against your skin.

And that was only one split instant: the next it might be deep, dark, oceanic blue, the sound of keys clacking, the smell of toast, and the feel left behind by a kiss that was too wet on your skin, followed by pale, strawberry pink, the quiet whoosh of traffic on a lazy afternoon, the smell of dirt and hot concrete after summer rain, sand between your toes...

I blinked slowly, and realised that a couple of those things were familiar: sure enough, beside me and a little behind, I could see Anna's soulprint: cream blushed with pale strawberry pink, the sound of keys quietly clacking. I squeezed her hand, and she squeezed back, tightly, a little desperately.

I never could get a straight answer from a non-Road Master as to what the roads looked like to them, but I'd heard it was nearly as overwhelming, and not half so pleasant.

Trying hard to shut out the constant sensory bombardment that could befuddle me even with my road mastery shut right down, I tugged on Anna's hand.

It sprang to life immediately, and I could picture the raised eyebrows that went with it, her expression as she came back to herself and remembered what she was meant to be doing. Four squeezes. *Are you okay?*

Two quick squeezes back from me, then three quick squeezes: *Yes. I see something non-dangerous, let me look a second.*

Gold. Anything gold. I scanned around me. Hot pink, magenta, baby blue, water falling against the back of my hands, the smell of pine trees, polished concrete under bare feet, the startling blink of a projector firing up right as you're looking at it, the background whirr of a fridge, my very favourite hoodie hugging my body, the exact taste of Mum's chocolate chip cookies—and I knew they were Mum's, because I could taste the pepper and the lavender, and who the frog else put pepper and lavender in double chocolate cookies?

Wait.

I reeled. My hoodie. Mum's cookies. They were *my* sensations. But how...?

A loop of anxiety coiled in my stomach, cold and heavy. Scott's diary. He'd said the roads had stolen memories from him, made him forget more and more every time he went on them.

I looked around, the anxiety rising to my chest. All these sensations—water and cars and fridges and rain, synthetic blankets, kisses, my hoodie—did every one of these sensations belong to someone real, a person? Had the roads stolen them all?

Adrenalin crackled out to my fingertips. And, when I got back—would I remember what Mum's cookies tasted like?

Four squeezes from Anna's hand.

I gasped. I was supposedly protected on the roads by my road mastery; it was Anna who was totally exposed. She might have worn my hoodie before, and she definitely knew the taste of Mum's cookies—but now, she might not remember either.

Gold. Find the gold, so I could follow it to Sanctuary's heart.

I turned frantically back to the roads, searching, sifting through the sensations as quickly as I could.

Emerald green—no.

Sausages sizzling—no.

Soft lounge leather under my fingertips—no.

A seam of gold snaking through quartz.

It wasn't how the gold of Sanctuary had appeared before, but I'd take it. Now all I had to do was remember to keep following it. Five firm squeezes to Anna's hand, the most complicated message of all, but one I'd only have to use once: *I'm ready, let's get going, don't let me stop moving for anything.*

Two squeezes back. *Yes.*

I stepped forward, road mastery wound tightly around that impression of gold in white rock as it slipped and flitted between all the other sensations, left, right, up, down—upside down. Like last time, it wouldn't do to think too hard about which way was up—but I didn't have much spare brain power left over anyway.

Canary yellow feathers on my cheek; lime green; the scent of white vinegar; something that might have been octopus tentacles twining around my hands.

A flash of darkness; the shush of the ocean against a gentle shore; a prickle up the back of my neck.

Anna squeezed my hand—four squeezes. *Are you okay?*

I'd stopped. I shook the daze from my head and kept walking.

The rim of a glass, a perfect circle under my finger-tips; a gold-leafed wedding cake; the crisp smell of snow; the colour of deepest night; my neck popping; hungry whispers.

Four squeezes.

Concentrate, Edge. Follow the gold.

The sound of a zip. Golden sunlight streaming through a window. The feel of a pencil moving across heavy cartridge paper. The heat of an explosion. *"Come. Come to us."*

I froze.

Four more squeezes.

I sent her three back—looking at something, no danger, hold on—but my pulse rushed at my ears.

It might be the guardians, nightmarish creatures that looked like fire and darkness to my road mastery, creatures who protected the roads from intruders.

Anna sent four more squeezes, and the pressure of her hand against mine made it clear she was keen to keep moving.

Reluctantly, I sought out the seam of gold again and followed after it.

I *hoped* it was guardians I was sensing.

We followed the gold seam further and further, until my feet were heavy and my tongue stuck drily to the roof of my mouth, like I'd been sleeping. Anna reminded me to keep moving every minute or so, and the prickly, slow-moving dread of being followed remained. In all the sensory stimulus, it was easy to forget the whispers, though—and who knew? Maybe they were just a sensation plucked from the head of someone who'd walked the roads, like all the others.

It didn't have to mean there were shadows here on the roads. Of course it didn't.

In the distance, something gold blossomed, a slow explosion unfolding like bright petals. It hung, motionless at full height, easily several times taller than me—and the thread of gold led to it.

My shoulders relaxed. The heart. It had to be.

Last time, I'd approached it from above, and it had been like seeing something through a glass floor. Obviously this time I was approaching it from ground level, as it were, and—I cocked my head and listened hard—yes, I could hear a rhythmic pulsing that might be the beating of a heart.

Darkness flickered around the edges of my vision.

Anxiety stirred.

My grip on Anna's hand grew suddenly sweaty, and I awkwardly switched hands across my body for a moment so I could wipe my hand dry on my shirt.

My neck prickled.

Colours and sounds still shifted around me, but they'd been random before, and now... Long, echoing pipe noises. The smell of decay. The hiss and pop of a crackling fire. A sense of vast distance, of exposure. Footsteps right behind me, even though— of course I looked—there was no one.

My pulse pitter-pattered. *Just get to the heart. Just get to the heart.*

Swallowing hard, I took a cautious step forward.

Whispers stirred around me. *"Blood. Want to drink your blood."*

I clenched Anna's hand. *Run.*

I had no frogging clue how shadows could be on the roads, but I'd heard those whispers before, and I'd recognise them anywhere, even in my nightmares.

"Your life, want your life, so sweet, so sweet your blood."

Run. The heart couldn't be that far ahead; I knew it was bigger than it looked right now, but it couldn't be that far.

My back broke out in chills, and I risked a glance behind.

My heart leapt against my chest. Shadows raced each other in the middle distance, a pack of hounds gaining quickly and baying for blood. My blood. I squeezed Anna's hand again, hard.

The golden, glowing heart loomed over us, surrounded by a sheer wall, like glass, or perspex, but finely textured.

Oh, frogs. I'd forgotten about the shield.

Last time, I'd needed blood to get through it, and maybe that had only been because I'd been with Gemma, who'd been connected to the dark magic of the Valley, but this wasn't exactly the time to stop and experiment.

I couldn't let go of Anna. And I really, really needed blood.

"Sweet, so sweet your blood. Want your blood."

I actually snorted at the irony of it all. *You and me both, shadows.*

I tried biting down on my cheek as we ran, but I just couldn't convince myself to do it hard enough, even though the shadows were gaining, maybe a scant ten metres behind.

Anna tripped. My arm wrenched backward. I cried out at the pain in my shoulder.

"Want your life. Come, come to us."

My shoulder. I needed to open the cut on my shoulder. My heart pounded, fear electric and bright.

I jerked Anna along—she followed smoothly. I put my head down and ran.

We approached the shield. I tore at the thin scab on the fleshy part between my shoulder and bicep and squeezed.

My fingers came away with a small smear of blood; I had to hope it would be enough.

Three paces.

I held my fingers out in front of us.

Two.

A shadow leapt, catching my heel.

I kicked it away, lunged for the shield.

My fingers made contact; the blood sizzled.

I fell, rolling onto my shoulder, dragging Anna after me.

10

"ARE WE DEAD?" Anna lay on the smooth, golden floor beside me, still clutching my hand.

I lowered my own head back to the floor and worked on catching my breath, staring at the roof above us that seemed to be made out of light the colour of the sun. "No," I said. "Not dead."

My ankle hurt though, the one the shadows had caught, and my shoulder was going to have a bruise the size of Tasmania from where I'd landed on the floor.

Still. Not dead.

I exhaled loudly.

A flutter of wings responded. I let go of Anna's hand and rolled awkwardly to a sit, cradling my sore shoulder. The walls curved around us, forming a perfectly circular chamber that glowed like we'd found the heart of the sun, instead of the heart of Sanctuary.

I squinted a bit as my eyes adjusted, already breathing more deeply and evenly. Just like Sanctuary itself, the heart contained some magical property that worked to calm you down; minor aches and pains fell away, my chest lifted, my lungs filled right to the bottom with pure, clean air.

In the middle of the chamber stood a small dais, round, like the room, and about five paces across. My stomach twisted. Last time I'd been here, Viri, the Keeper of Sanctuary, had appeared on that platform and tried to kill us.

I scrubbed my eyes with my fingers, not wanting to see Scott slumped deathlike between me and the platform, or Gemma huddled next to me, breathing raggedly, unevenly, like each one might be her last.

Long, slow inhale, smooth, controlled exhale.

Scott and Gem weren't here. Neither was Viri.

I felt more than heard the flutter of feathery wings again, and hauled myself to my feet. "Helios? Are you here?"

"Who's Helios?" Anna dragged herself semi-upright, crossing her legs and leaning back against the wall.

"The..." I waved my hands. "The embodiment of Sanctuary's magic. He *is* Sanctuary's magic. Kind of. It's complicated."

"Sounds like."

My pulse quickened. "But he told me to meet him here, because he can show me what's happening, so he'd better frogging be here or else..." Or else I had no idea what to do. I chewed on the inside of my lip.

The flutter of wings came again, and I turned toward it, eyes closed, road mastery opened.

I relaxed into a smile: the great, golden pegasus was definitely here: I could sense his soulprint, even if I couldn't see his body. *Hello?*

A breath of wind across my face. *Greetings.*

"This is probably going to take a sec," I said, turning back to Anna. "And it might look really weird. But we're pretty much safe here, so feel free to, like, rest or something."

"Sure thing," she said, and tipped her head back against the wall, eyes closing. "Take your time."

So can you show me? Can you show me what's wrong now I'm here? I sent to Helios.

A snort. The sense of something pulling at me, at my road mastery.

Carefully, I spooled it out, a tiny thread of energy that came from either my head or my chest—I couldn't tell which—and extended toward Helios.

He took it, redirected it—and the world exploded into light. In front of me, I saw the great, seething ball that Aphros had shown me once, immense, hanging like the moon in an empty space. Gold and black intertwined with one another, writhing and twisting and flashing, surrounded by a minty green glow. Aphros had told me it represented the balance between Sanctuary's life magic and the Valley's death magic, and at that time, there'd been a lot more darkness than light.

The image changed, and I had the sense of falling backwards—not through space, I suddenly realised, but through time. And the further I fell, the lighter the darkness in the ball in front of me became, until eventually, it was actually a ball of wriggling, flashing green and gold. Not a trace of black to be seen.

I fell a little further, and the wriggling and flashing stopped: the ball was a uniform colour, mostly gold but with that same minty glow around it, and deep inside it, kind of like the way new leaves glow in the sunlight.

What is this? I sent to Helios. *What am I seeing?*

This time, I felt like I was falling forward; I flung my hands out to protect my face from impact—but I hadn't actually moved. The massive ball of light changed, green and gold separating first, and then gradually, the green turning darker and darker, until it was black. The black began to grow, overtaking the gold, until it looked like it had when Aphros had first shown it to me—exactly like it, I realised: Helios was showing me the history of the magics of Sanctuary and the Valley.

A blinding flash engulfed the ball for a fraction of an instant, and the black began to recede until it occupied about half the space again, and I thought that would be it; we'd rebalanced the magics after saving Scott from the Valley, cutting away the extra power from the Valley and forcing it to diminish. But the falling sensation persisted, and the ball continued to change: an extremely slow outward explosion, black and gold separating entirely as the ball ballooned in size, cracks appearing all over it, nothing but void inside.

Abruptly, the connection snapped and I regained my usual senses, blinking rapidly at the sudden change to the round chamber of the heart.

"Whoa."

"What?" Anna shifted against the wall, looking up at me.

I pinched my forehead between my thumb and two fingers, screwing up my face and blinking, trying to make sense of what I'd seen. "Okay," I said. "So. I think what I've just seen is that once, the Valley was green, and not black—I guess that's where the mintiness comes from?—only hang on, back at the beginning they were both the same, which fits with what the book suggested, only then the green went dark somehow?" I slumped. "And now it's all just fracturing."

But I hadn't needed to see the magics to know that. So it must be the other stuff that Helios thought was important?

"Okay in English, this time?" Anna quirked an eyebrow. "Unless, you know, you don't actually want me to know, because you're doing a super job of being incoherently cryptic right now, just saying."

I scrubbed at my forehead with two fingers and winced. "Right. English. So. If I'm interpreting this correctly, which honestly, I don't see how else you could interpret it, so I have to assume that I am—"

Anna cleared her throat pointedly.

"Right. Yes. Okay. There are two places, right? Sanctuary and the Valley? Sanctuary is the home of the fairies, you use life magic to get to it."

"Life magic?"

"Plant magic. You plant a seed."

Anna nodded. "Sure, seems legit."

"And then there's the Valley, which you use death magic—blood magic—to get to, which we did earlier."

She nodded again.

"For as long as most people know, the two places have been... like... opposites of each other. Life versus death, happiness versus terror, good versus evil, that kind of opposite."

"Antithetical."

I furrowed my brow. "Anti-what?"

Anna grinned. "Antithetical. The word you want is 'antithetical'. Not just opposites, but, like, totally incompatible opposites, absolutely contrary, that kind of thing. Antithetical."

I stared at her. "First of all, who are you and what have you done with my sister, second of all why on earth don't you actually use your brain at school, and thirdly, yes, antithetical, sure."

She turned her grin up by several notches, blazing with smugness. "You're welcome."

I rolled my eyes. "Okay *anyway*, Sanctuary, Valley, antithetical," I said, barely stumbling over the new word. "But. There are rumours that they used to be the same place. And we discovered last month that even though everyone *thought* the shadows were coming from the Valley, like, a natural result of it or something, actually they're two separate things: Valley," I said, waggling my left hand, "and shadows." I waggled my right.

Anna frowned. "Shadows like the things that chased us out there?" She gestured roughly to where we'd entered through the wall of the heart.

"Yeah." I stretched my mouth in a frown without moving my eyebrows. "Shadows like those."

Rubbing her upper arms, Anna got to her feet. "You were saying something about colours."

I nodded. "So, Sanctuary's magic is gold. Obviously." I twirled a finger at the glowing gold chamber around us. "And the Valley's has always been black when I've encountered it. But there's always been this weird thread of green everywhere too, pale, like mint green, on everything to do with Sanctuary, and it's there when you look at the combined magics." And, I realised with a jolt, in Aphros's soulprint.

Anna shook her head a little. "I'm going to pretend like 'combined magics' made sense. But I get Sanctuary gold, Valley black, mysterious green."

I nodded again. "Helios, the physical body that holds Sanctuary's magic, showed me a vision just now, backwards and forwards in time. The two magics are usually just intertwined, in a great big ball." I meshed my fingers together and held my hands in a ball shape. "But from what I could see, it didn't always used to be that way. Firstly, there was originally only one colour, which suggests that the theory that Sanctuary and the Valley used to be the same place is right—which the book on road mastery agrees with, so that's cool. But the other weird thing is that the black of the Valley used to be green—that minty green that keeps showing up everywhere."

"Okay," Anna said slowly, drawing the word out. "And this information is useful to you somehow, I assume? We, like, risked our lives and now you got the info you need and all's well that ends well, etc?"

I screwed up my face. "Sure. Let's run with that theory."

"Edge?" Suspicion laced Anna's voice.

I sighed. "I'm sure it's useful information," I said. "I just have no idea what to do with it." I slumped to the floor and buried my face in my hands. "I wish Aphros was here." She *sort of* was, in that I could reach her through our internal connection so long as I was in the heart—but the communication was faint, distant. Not great for trying to have a technical discussion.

She's green and gold, just like the Valley and Sanctuary used to be. There has to be something in that. I wished I could talk to her *now*, while this was all still fresh. Not that I was likely to forget any of it, but just... I sighed again.

"Uh, Edge?"

I lowered my hands. My eyebrows twitched downward as I saw the concern on Anna's face. "What?"

"I, um, I know you said we're safe in here, but... is that normal?" She tilted her head toward the wall, eyes wide.

Adrenalin spiked through my stomach. The circular wall of the chamber glowed gold everywhere else, but where Anna had gestured... I swallowed, fingers gripping my knees whitely as I stared at the patch of darkness that pressed and roamed against the wall. The shadows, looking for a way into the heart. "No," I said, heart pounding in my ears. "No, that's not normal."

"Right, yeah, I thought so. And..." She licked her lips, hands fisted at her sides. "It's not good, is it."

Shadows on the roads, Sanctuary and the Valley fracturing... No. No, it was all very *ungood.*

"What will happen if they get in?" Her voice was barely audible.

I stood up, strode over, and took her hand. "If they get in—"

Frogging elephants. If they got in, they could corrupt Sanctuary's magic entirely. Was that what had happened to the Valley? Was that why it had gone from green to black? Fear erupted in my chest and I fought to keep my breathing level.

"If they get in it will be bad," I said briskly, squeezing her hand. "But they're not going to get in, so it's fine."

A faint, barely-heard crackling punctuated my words—and fine lines appeared in a fracture pattern across the wall of Sanctuary where the shadows pressed.

I swallowed. "But just to be on the safe side... I think it's time to go."

The instant we reappeared in the Valley, I took off, heading toward Sanctuary. *Aphros!* I called, tugging on the connection between our soulprints. *Aphros!*

"Wait, where are we going?" Anna said, jogging to catch up. The sweltering heat of the Valley had already closed down on us, and Anna looked damp and sweaty. "I thought we were going home now."

I glanced up to my left, back in the direction of the connection with home. "We are. But there's something I need to get first."

Edge? Is that you?

Aphros, I need you. I need some things from you. And I think I'm going to need a few of them.

I am coming, she sent back. *I will see you soon.*

11

WE TUMBLED BACK into the yard a fraction of a second before Mum came around the corner, Veve skipping at her heels. Hastily, I pressed my forefinger over the cut on my upper arm, while Anna tugged her shirt straight.

The sun had vanished behind the treeline, dusk lighting the sky in pink and orange. The pungent smell of the Valley faded away, replaced by the more mundane smells of the suburb: distant smoggy smells from the main road, eucalypts still hot from the day, clean grass and warm pavers from the yard.

Even though it was still warm and a little humid, it was nothing compared to the dripping, cloying closeness of the Valley's heat, and in the light breeze the sweat on my forehead began to dry.

Mum narrowed her eyes. "What have you two been up to?"

Anna shrugged. "Nothing much."

Mum turned her gaze to me, eyebrow lifted.

"Mum, I swear, we haven't left the yard." *It's not a lie,* I told myself. *It's not a lie.*

Mum pursed her lips, scrutinising us.

I forced myself to breathe. We hadn't left the yard, and the only reason we were on lock-down was because of the stupid mob business, and they weren't exactly going to follow us over to the Valley—or, even more ludicrous, the roads—so we really hadn't done anything wrong. We'd been totally safe.

Well. Apart from the shadows.

"Come inside," Mum said at length. "I had a call from the police on the way home."

Anna and I exchanged glances and followed Mum. Veve pranced along beside me and I ruffled her ears. "Hey, Hairbrain."

She licked my fingers and I gave her a half smile, awfully glad she was okay. Impulsively, I reached down and hugged her around her middle as Mum and Anna disappeared inside. She thrashed in protest, and I released her, straightening and blinking furiously. "Love you, puppy."

Inside, Dad had melted into one of the armchairs in the family room, lines of his body shouting fatigue, his fingers barely gripping the glass bottle of expensive soda water whose top tilted precariously.

Mum leaned a hip against the kitchen bench, arms tightly folded.

"So, the police?" Anna said, sliding onto one of the wooden barstools at the bench near Mum.

I stayed near the sliding door, hands behind the small of my back, gripping the door handle, shoulders pressed against the cool glass.

"There's been a reported sighting of some men known to be intimately connected with Romano in Canberra." Mum flicked a glance at Dad. "There's no confirmation of why they were there, of course, and it could be anything. It's probably not related to us."

"But it could be," Anna said, nodding.

"It could be."

I swallowed, tightening my grip on the door handle. "If they're in Canberra," I said carefully. "Then it's only a two or three hour drive to here. They could be here literally at any moment."

Dad raised his bottle at me in a silent salute, then chugged down half the soda water.

"Yes," Mum said, nails bloodless at the tips as she gripped her arm. "The police officer I talked to doesn't think they're aware of our specific location yet, only that we moved north. They seem to be setting up some kind of base in Canberra and the police there have placed them under constant surveillance. But unless they do anything wrong, there's no legal reason to arrest them at this point. The police will call us immediately if it looks like they are moving our way," she added as something of an afterthought, releasing her arms dramatically and striding to the pantry. Jerking the door open, she crouched, then rummaged in the vegetable box.

"There's nothing we can do?" I said softly.

"Are we going to have to move again?" asked Anna.

Mum reappeared with a handful of potatoes, snagged a knife from the magnetic strip above the bench, and started chopping a little more vigorously than necessary.

"No," Dad said when it became clear that Mum wasn't saying anything else. "And possibly."

Mum snorted at that, and Dad cut her a sharp glance. "Liv, it *is* 'possibly'. The police are well trained, and they have them under surveillance. For all we know, they could do something stupid and get themselves arrested in the next hour. We don't know."

And that was the clincher, really, wasn't it: we didn't know. Our whole world could come crumbling down again in the space of a heartbeat—and we just didn't know.

12

MUM DROVE US to school again on Friday morning. Instead of letting us out in the drop-off zone, she turned right into the carpark, found a spot down the far end where the asphalt turned to grey gravel and pale, washed-out dirt, and parked the car.

We walked back up to the main entrance together, Anna towering half a foot over either of us.

I clutched the straps of my backpack so tight I knew I'd have red creases in my fingers for a good while afterwards.

Mum parted from us at the front office, heading in to make an emergency meeting with the principal.

Anna and I walked through the grassy quad together as the breeze rustled the leaves of the huge gum that towered over it, branches tossing, loose strips of bark flapping.

Overhead, misshapen clouds chased each other across the sky. I glanced at them, jealous of their ability to simply disappear. Something heavy curled in my chest, my stomach, and Anna nudging my shoulder with hers in farewell as she split off toward the senior common room did nothing to help.

Everything seemed too bright; even the bushes that lined the hall on the right glinted, with their thick, glossy leaves that felt like palm leaves, but that were long and thin, growing straight out of the ground like a giant's grass tussock—or a clump of swords.

Sun chased shade chased sun as the clouds raced over the sky; the flickering quality of the light and the way the wind snatched people's voices away, muffling them even though the quad wasn't more than about twenty metres across, made the whole school seem slightly unreal, out of place somehow.

I tried to shake it off as I neared H block and headed for my locker—but the sense of unreality only heightened as I realised it was Scott hovering by my locker, instead of Gem.

"Hey," I said, giving him a fraction of a second of eye contact before dumping my bag and crouching over it. "Where's Gem?"

"Geography trip, remember?"

Right. Half the year studied geography in first semester, while the other half—my half, Scott's half—studied history. Midway through the year, we switched. That explained why the quad had seemed a little empty.

I shoved the books I'd used for homework back into my locker and pulled out what I'd need for the first few classes, before cramming my bag into the bottom half. I stood, kicking the blue door closed, and stared at Scott, hugging my books to my chest.

"Uh, what?" he said, taking half a step back and rubbing awkwardly at his nose. "Is there something on my face?"

I exhaled, closing my eyes and hugging my books even tighter for just a second, curling around them. I couldn't do a thing about my family's safety right now. But I could do something about the safety of Sanctuary. If I had time. "Look." I opened my eyes again and straightened. "Gemma won't listen to me, for whatever reason, but you said you believe me, so you have to believe me about this. I've been on the roads again—"

Scott's eyes widened. "You what?"

"I took my sister, it was fine—"

"Your sister? Edge, what the hell?" He ran a hand through his hair, tugging up the spikes. "Are you insane?"

I narrowed my eyes at him. "Look, shut up, okay. Stop freaking out: it was fine. But, well, it's not fine, that's the point." I sighed and let my face drop to my books for a moment. "Scott, I talked to Helios in the heart of Sanctuary. Mrs Caro was right: Sanctuary and the Valley *did* used to be one place, and not only that, but the Valley was corrupted somehow. I'm guessing that's where the shadows come in, given..." I swallowed. "Given there are shadows on the roads right now."

Scott's eyes widened even further, practically owl-like. "*What*?"

"I need to investigate that somehow, try to figure out how and why they got there. They were trying to break into Sanctuary's heart too, but..." I pressed my forehead into the heel of my hand. "I can't take Anna for that. If there are shadows on the roads, I need..."

I let my hand drop to my side, and mentally listed off all the reasons why Scott didn't have to help, why he wouldn't want to help, why it would be stupid for him to offer. I sighed. "You know what? Never mind. I'll figure it out." I turned away.

Before I'd gone two steps, Scott caught my elbow. "Hey, where are you going?"

I shook my head, staring at the white plastic buttons on his school shirt. "You don't have to come," I mumbled. "It's fine. I'll figure it out."

"Don't be ridiculous."

Inside of my lip between my teeth, I looked up.

"Of course I'll come," he said, gaze flicking back and forth between my eyes. "I owe you, anyway. I was a complete ass to you last year, and at the beginning of the year, and I can't pretend that all of it was the Valley. I... I'm sorry."

He had a tiny fleck of yellow in each of his otherwise brown irises.

"Yeah," I said. "You were."

"Sorry." His voice was barely audible this time.

I shrugged, sighing. "So you owe me. You'll help, then?"

He nodded. "Of course. Least I can do. You want me to meet you after school?"

I stared at him for a second longer before it clicked: Scott believed me. He was going to help.

And I was *not* going to cry about that, urgh.

"I can't leave the house, remember?" I said. "You'll have to come over."

His hand dropped away from my elbow as he straightened. "What, to your house?"

"Is that a problem?" I jutted my chin up and lifted my eyebrows. "There's a crossing point to the Valley in my backyard, remember."

His gaze raked my face again, left eye, right eye, back to the left again. "No," he said. "That's not a problem at all."

"Good." I gave him one quick, jerky nod, and turned. "See you after school," I said over my shoulder as I headed off to class.

He didn't reply.

Which was good, because then I didn't have to think about whether to turn and look at him again or not, or whether to try trusting my voice again or not, and meant I was free to inhale dramatically like I'd just been about to drown, and blink furiously as my body decided it was tears that I should drown in.

We'd fix this. Somehow, we'd find a way. I might not have a say in protecting my Nowra home, but Sanctuary? That was my home too, and that one, I could definitely try to protect.

13

SCOTT ARRIVED BEFORE Mum and Dad got home, but just in case I thought I'd managed to escape any awkward questions, Anna decided to step into parent role for them.

"Who's this?" she said with narrowed eyes as I let him in the front door.

I turned to where her head was poking out from her room down the end of the apricot-tiled hall. "Scott."

Her fingers appeared around the wooden doorframe, followed by the rest of her. "Is he your boyfriend?"

"No, Anna." I rolled my eyes, pretending I hadn't noticed the way Scott had gone rigid where he stood, not two paces from the front door. "He's a friend. He's..." Urgh. While I totally approved of honesty in theory, the whole talking-to-my-family-about-Sanctuary thing was still weird: first Mum, now Anna.

Magic. Totally messed your head up.

"He's here to help with the roads."

Anna's gaze sharpened. "You're going on the roads again?"

I nodded, brow furrowed, lips slightly pursed. "I have to." *Please, Anna. I have to do this. Please understand. Please.*

She sighed explosively. "I suppose there's no point telling you to take your phone."

I shook my head. "No reception."

"Or telling you to be careful." She folded her arms and leaned against her doorframe.

"Of course I'll be careful."

She sniffed. "Yeah. Right." She rubbed at her chin with one shoulder, spreading the lock of hair that had fallen there over her ear. "Going anywhere near those shadows isn't being careful, Edge, it's verging on suicidal."

I stared at her, hands fisting by my sides. "It's not. You know I have the ward."

Scott moved to my shoulder. "Ward? Is this something I should know about?"

"I got a couple of unicorn-hair wards from Aphros. They have limited use, but they can protect us from the shadows in a pinch."

"Nice of you to tell me this now."

I raised an eyebrow at him. "You said yes anyway, didn't you?"

"Well sure, but—"

"Pssh." Anna rolled her eyes. "If you two are done, I'm pretty sure you have, like, a world to save or something." She tilted her head meaningfully to the family room.

"Right." I exchanged glances with Scott. "Yeah. Let's do that."

I led him through the family room and out the sliding door to the yard.

Veve greeted us both with her usual buoyant enthusiasm, licking and slurping and pushing through Scott's legs in an effort to get him to scritch her back. He staggered, arms flung wide, and I grabbed his forearm to steady him. He laughed, shook me off, and bent over to snuggle Veve's face in between his hands, running his thumbs over her ears.

It was easy to forget sometimes that his mother had basically made him her slave in her quest for darkness and power, that he'd watched her die, that he'd been possessed by the Valley as a literal agent of darkness and had nearly been taken fully to be used as the Valley's body.

Mostly, that made him kind of wary or haughty, depending on the company, and prone to using the fastest means to get what he wanted, moral or not.

Occasionally, just occasionally, moments like this reminded me of exactly how much he'd missed by not having a normal childhood.

"Okay, I'm sure Veve would follow you to the end of the world and back now," I said all of a sudden, wanting to stop thinking about Scott's Tragic Past™, "but can we get going?" I worked the moisture back into my mouth and rubbed self-consciously at my left shoulder where the cut (and bruise) was. Scott had done some pretty horrible things in his past, some of them directed at me, and I didn't particularly feel like hosting a pity party for him right now.

"Lead on, boss," Scott said, straightening and gesturing at me.

I rolled my eyes, but led him around to the side of the yard where the prickly bushes skulked. "Portal of darkness," I said, waving at them. "As advertised. Here," I added, fishing a braid of thick, wiry, cream hair out of my pocket and passing it to him. "Tie it on." I stooped to tie my own unicorn ward around my right ankle, and Scott, after hesitating for just a second, copied. Veve, naturally, was delighted that we were getting down to her level, and shoved herself into my face, demanding attention. I nudged her away and stood back up. "I don't think you'll be able to activate it yourself," I said to Scott, "but I'm pretty sure I can activate it for you with my road mastery if you get into trouble."

He nodded curtly, and held out his hand.

With just the tiniest bit of my inner lip between my front teeth, I took it, dragged him closer to the bushes, and reached up to peel away the scab on my shoulder.

Man. This was seriously going to leave a scar.

I ignored Scott focusing intently on my shoulder, closed my eyes, and made the crossing.

We tumbled out into the Valley and I squished my face up, swallowing repeatedly to fight down the nausea. I leaned over my knees, resting on my forearms, and forced myself to breathe slowly.

"I could have done it, you know," Scott said quietly.

I glanced at him. He'd barely moved from where he'd entered, which, if I'd been in the mood to be impressed, might have been impressive. The crossing was smooth, but most people still staggered on re-entry. "What," I said, my voice thin and gaspy. "And killed another mouse for me? Thanks. I'm good."

His jaw twitched. "I didn't mean that. I meant—"

"I know what you meant." I straightened, inhaled, stretched my arms up, and exhaled firmly. "I'm fine. Really," I added, making the fleetingest eye contact I could manage. "I am. Fifteen minutes that way." I pointed ahead and to the left.

He looked like he wanted to say something, but I turned to go and he thought better of it, following me silently through the twisted, blood-stained trees.

Within minutes, we were both dripping with sweat. "So why did you agree to come?" I asked to take my mind off the humidity. "I thought it wasn't 'safe'." I sketched air quotes around the word.

"Gemma and I have slightly different definitions of 'safe'," Scott said, copying my intonation.

I glanced over my shoulder at him. "So why didn't you come before? Or say something? When Gemma was going on?"

He shrugged awkwardly. "Sanctuary is your guys' place. What would I do to help? Kill another mouse?" He smiled wryly.

I got the feeling that that wasn't the entire story, but I let it drop and plodded on, ducking under a low branch that tangled in my hair for just long enough to send adrenalin pulsing through me.

I shoved the anxiety aside. No zombie trees. Just normal twigs and branches. Well, normal for the Valley, anyway. I exhaled heavily and rolled my neck.

"Edge?" Scott's voice was funny, a cautious note it didn't usually hold, a little higher than usual.

"Mmm?" I said without looking back.

"Edge?" he said again, and it seemed like he'd fallen a bit behind. "You know that unicorn ward?"

I turned, bracing myself for melodrama, and eyed him where he stood still in the shade of the trees. "What about it?"

He swallowed heavily and tilted his head at the ground. "Might be a good time to use it."

My brain finally caught up with what I was seeing: that wasn't just any old shade pooled around his feet. "Shadows," I hissed. *Crap*, I thought as adrenalin flooded back again. *Crap crap frogging elephants crap.* "Hold on. Don't move."

"Wasn't planning on it," he said shortly.

I closed my eyes. My stomach flipped as the soulprint of the shadows hit my senses, dark and terrifying. I extended my road mastery out, just as I'd done in the heart of Sanctuary, aiming for the tiny sliver of green and gold wrapped around Scott's ankle. But to get there, I had to dodge through the shadows without touching *their* soulprints, or who knew what might happen.

Slowly, slowly...

"Eat you, drink you, give us your life..."

"You doing something there, Princess?" His voice sounded steady, but he hadn't called me Princess in a very long time.

"Working on it."

Closer, closer...

"Sometime today might be nice."

"It'll be faster if you stop interrupting me."

"Come, come to us, give us your blood, your life..."

Urgh, I'd lost about a foot by stopping to answer Scott. I squinched my face up tighter—as though it might help me concentrate—and wove my way through the shadows again. Left, right, left again, over that bit, under through there...

The shadows shifted, constricting the thread of connection I had with my road mastery. *"So sweet, so sweet your blood, your power, your life..."*

I gasped as though someone had thrown a bucket of cold water over my head; it was suddenly hard to breathe.

I gritted my teeth. Just a little bit further.

I forced my senses onward. Closer, closer... There! I snagged the ward, feeding my road mastery into it.

Nothing happened.

Panic squeezed my chest even tighter.

What had I done last time to activate it? I couldn't remember, I couldn't remember...

"Edge?" Scott whispered. "Please hurry."

The shadows had twined around his legs and hips, and were reaching for his chest. *"Sweet, sweet life, sweet power, drink your blood, your life."*

How do I do it, how do I do it? I fed more of my road mastery into the ward. *Come on, work!*

I had a vague memory of silver light and discomfort, drawing on some deep part of myself that wasn't road mastery.

My soulprint. I had to feed out my soulprint.

A burst of silver light momentarily drowned out the soulprint of the ward. Nausea heaved in my guts and I doubled over, pressing my fingers against my mouth.

Frogging elephants, it was like looking at my own body opened out on the ground in front of me. No wonder we weren't supposed to know our own soulprints.

The smell of roses. Another blinding flash of silver. Soft bells tinkling in an unearthly melody. The ward flared to life, green and gold billowing through the dark.

The shadows screamed.

More power, more.

They screeched, a high-pitched noise that grated against my ears.

More power.

The shadows began to retreat.

I kept up the flow of power, hands knotted, sweat pouring down my face.

The shadows backed away. Further, further...

I collapsed to the ground, knees too weak to hold me up any longer.

But the shadows had fled; Scott was safe.

I closed my eyes and curled up on the ground, planning to sleep for a short eternity.

"Thanks," Scott said, settling on the ground beside me.

"No worries," I said, and my voice hardly shook at all.

"This," he said, and I waited patiently for the rest of the sentence—only it never came.

"This what?"

"This," he said, waving his hand in a vaguely circular motion. "You asked me why I didn't come before."

Suddenly the grass in front of him was utterly absorbing, and he stared at it like he might die if he blinked. "You saved my life just now," he said in a voice so low I hardly heard it. "I was waiting to come with you."

Ten minutes later I could move without feeling like I was dragging my limbs through concrete, and I forced myself to sit up. "Okay," I said, screwing up my face and shaking my head. "Roads."

Scott pursed his lips. "I'll be honest, I'm not sure that's such a great idea right now."

"What?" I cut him a filthy look. "That's the entire reason we're here! I have to investigate the shadows!"

He sent a flinty glare back. "We've burned through one ward already, and it took all your focus to do even that. *Don't* brush me off," he snapped as I opened my mouth to protest. "I saw how much effort that took. How many of those things do you even have? How do you expect to fight a whole *mass* of shadows on the roads?"

"I can at least track them down, find out where they're coming from—"

"How? How are you going to track them down? Wander aimlessly all over the roads until you find something? Because I'm no genius, but that doesn't exactly sound like the greatest plan."

"Fine! What do you suggest we do, then? Give up?"

He stared levelly at me. "No. Gather more information. Hasn't it ever occurred to you to wonder why the unicorn wards work, for instance? If it's unicorn power that affects them, what if Aphros could do something that would get rid of the shadows for good?"

"You think we should go talk to Aphros?"

His jaw worked as he chewed on his inner lip. "As a start, yes. Remember... Remember that book you told me about? The one about road mastery?"

My pulse skipped. Of course I remembered the book Quoise had found in the fairy library that explained how road mastery worked. I'd been kicking myself ever since for not taking it with me so I could read it cover to cover. "What about it?"

"I think we should go get it."

"But it's right in the middle of the fairies' Lodge, we can't just walk on in and ask for it."

He grinned impishly, and I remembered that despite everything that had happened to both of us, we were really just thirteen-year-old kids.

"I didn't say we were going to ask."

I stared at him a moment longer, mulling it over. I really, really hated to admit it, but he was right: heading back to the roads wasn't guaranteed to give us any more information, and it would definitely put us into danger with the shadows. On the other hand, sneaking into the fairy Lodge was also risky—Viri had tried to kill us before, and I pretty much had to assume at this point that she'd do it again, maybe even that she'd given the other fairies orders to kill us on sight—but really, I'd take fairies over shadows any day of the week.

And I really, really did want that book.

I sighed heavily and rubbed my hands up my face. "Fine! You win. Let's go break and enter." I fished out another of the unicorn wards from my pocket and handed it to him.

Scott grinned again as he wrapped the ward around his wrist, fixing it with a simple over-under knot. "I always knew you weren't as prissy as you seemed."

"Shut up." Go in, get the book, get out. This was totally going to be fine.

14

WE CROSSED THE invisible boundary between the Valley and Sanctuary warily, peering in all directions for any sign of fairies.

I'd had a brief conversation with Aphros while we'd walked, via our soulprint-connection, in which I'd learned that she basically had no idea about anything: no idea why she could cross between Sanctuary and the Valley while others couldn't, no idea why the unicorn-hair wards worked.

That was one thing she did agree with, though: it seemed very likely that 'Valley' did not equal 'shadows', and that, given what Helios had shown me, the shadows were a latecomer that needed to be vanquished before they could corrupt Sanctuary as well.

On the whole, the conversation had not been much use at all, and that, together with the sweltering humidity of the Valley and the rotting stench had combined to leave me in a fantastically grumpy mood.

But now, as Scott and I stepped into the dim coolness of Sanctuary, dripping sweat from our forty-minute trek through the Valley, we both inhaled deeply. Scott jumped a little as the unicorn hair ward around his wrist sizzled and imploded into ash; I'd forgotten to warn him about that.

Usually, the border between Sanctuary and the Valley was impenetrable; the unicorn hair ward enabled us to cross without a blood sacrifice, and it could survive a trip *into* the Valley, but for whatever reason, returning the unicorn hair to Sanctuary always made it fizzle and die. I handed him a new one, and this time he wrapped it around his ankle and covered it with his sock like the first one had been.

As I glanced around, eyes peeled for the slightest glimpse of fairy wings through the trees, the distinction between the Sanctuary and the Valley couldn't have been more obvious.

The border itself may have been invisible, but it was still clear: behind us, twisted, stunted trees almost like alpine gums, with yellowing leaves and sap stains down their trunks; ahead, cluster-leafed, soft things that stood tall and graceful, leaves vibrant and healthy, trunks smooth and grey-brown. (I had no idea what kind of trees they actually were, but they looked something like how I'd always imagined ash trees, so in my head that's what they were.)

"Come on," I muttered, grabbing Scott's arm and steering him over to the right where the trees were thicker. "We don't want to be seen."

Immediately ahead, the tall trees thinned, and after about ten or fifteen metres ordered themselves into a long promenade carpeted with thick, crisp grass that led to the fairies' Lodge, a white-stone single-storey building that sprawled higgledy-piggledy in every direction like a maze.

Its walls glowed faintly in the dim light of Sanctuary, making it look almost like a moon in Sanctuary's grey-blue sky. Vines crawled all over it, glossy, waxy leaves twinkling in the dusk, tiny, white star-flowers pulsing gently as they emitted their own silvery light.

Pretty, but right now, it was pretty in the same way a tiger was: one wrong movement, and it would eat us alive.

"Do you know another way in?" Scott murmured.

I nodded and kept moving, watching where I stepped, avoiding fallen twigs and dry leaves, detouring around low-hanging branches that looked like they might swish. Thankfully, there was basically no undergrowth; we made it around the first point of the Lodge in only a couple of minutes.

I glanced around. Still clear. "In here." I skipped the six or seven paces from the treeline to the wall, pulse in my throat. Scott followed and copied me as I spidered my fingers through the vines over the wall, hunting for the hidden door.

"What am I looking for?" he whispered.

"Edges," I said.

"There are more than one of you?"

I shot him a Look. "So. Funny. Shut up and search, will you?"

He smirked, but resumed shuffling through the vines, picking them aside and feeling his way over the seamless wall of the Lodge.

My fingers snagged on something. I pulled a pale, new tendril of vine aside and squinted. "Over here."

Scott moved to my side.

"Help me clear the vines from the door," I said, tugging at a strand as thick as my finger, woody and tough. "Try not to break things," I added when he started snapping vines. "We don't actually want the fairies to know this is where we got in."

He rolled his eyes in response, but did as I asked, bending and shifting the vines instead of breaking them.

"What are you doing?"

We both jumped at the high-pitched voice behind us and whirled around, backs pressing into the wall, my hands convulsing around the vines at the small of my back.

The fairy hovering at head height a few steps away crossed her arms and frowned at us, turquoise-blue wings fluttering.

I slumped forward and clutched at my chest, remembering how to breathe. "Quoise. Frogging elephants, you terrified me."

"Good," she said. "Imagine what would have happened if someone else had come to investigate."

I straightened, gaze sharpening. "Is anyone else coming?"

"Not yet. I sensed your soulprint here, though."

The most dangerous aspect of trying to sneak into Sanctuary: all fairies were—well, not Road Masters, exactly, they couldn't *do* things with their road mastery like I could, but they had the basic ability of sensing people's soulprints, and they could sense the print of any and all visitors in Sanctuary at any given moment, across all of Sanctuary's multiple dimensions.

"I assume you got in from the Valley?" Quoise said, eyebrows raising. "Given we've *apparently* stopped all visitors through the portals?"

I nodded. "Aphros gave me some wards."

"Good." She nodded once and folded her arms. "Don't use—"

She was gone.

"What just happened?" Scott said, still staring at the spot where she'd been.

I sighed, puffing air out over a fat lower lip. "Time skip."

"Time skip?"

"The big fissure that opened up through the meadow, yes?"

He nodded.

"There's some sort of pearly steam or something coming out of it, and every time a new puff is released, time skips weirdly and the fairies—and Aphros—all zip to wherever it is they were, or wherever they will be, or... something." I raised my eyebrows, forefinger pressing against my temple.

"But why is this affecting time?"

"I don't know!" I closed my eyes and forced myself to continue calmly. "If I knew," I said, voice still tight, "don't you think I'd have explained?"

"Is this what happened the other day at school?"

I glanced at him. "Which one? The first time, no. I mean, I guess it could have: everything went all grey and foggy, I could smell Sanctuary, and everyone else seemed frozen although I could still move, so I guess I could have moved and it would have looked like a time skip to you guys when the fog lifted. That's what happened the second time."

He frowned, gave his head a shake, and went back to shifting vines. "But that's not what happened here."

Irritation flared in my chest. "How do you—"

"For one we're already *in* Sanctuary," he said over top of me, hands moving on autopilot. "So it's not like some sort of fog is coming over us or anything."

"But the steam—"

"And for *two*," he continued, "what you're talking about is essentially a skip forward in time. You moved, we didn't, and when we woke up—or whatever—you'd gone ahead without us. Ish. Right?"

Despite myself, I nodded.

"But here," he nodded to where Quoise had been, "they're moving *back* in time. Not the same."

Frog it all, he was right. "Well, so what?"

"So, different mechanisms," he said. "Probably. Just something to keep in mind," he added as he pulled a final strand of vine away and stepped back. "It that enough?" he asked, nodding at the wall.

I glanced over it. "Yeah. Should be." I stepped close to it, and felt around the edges of the hidden door for the latch. Nope, nope, nope... Ah ha. I picked at the little catch, and the heavy white stone door swung inward. "Welcome to the Lodge," I said, gesturing Scott in.

He glanced at me with slightly widened eyes, then ducked into the hallway, long and straight as far as the eye could see, walls made of the same stone as the outer wall of the Lodge, except mid-grey, and the floor glowing with golden light.

I followed him in, adjusted some of the vines so they wouldn't get jammed, and closed the door. It latched with a satisfying *thunk*. "Come on," I said, taking the lead. "It's not as long as it looks."

Frog it all. Scott was right about the different time skips; on Earth, it was like everyone there was freezing except me, and I could continue forward without them.

Here, it was like everyone was reverting backwards, and I was staying still—well, and Scott too, and Helios, so probably everyone who hadn't actually—what, been born? Come from? What was the proper term here? Whatever. Here, the time skips were affecting everyone who wasn't a native. On Earth, it was affecting everyone but me, and the only thing special about me was my road mastery.

One set of skips affecting everyone from Sanctuary, not visitors; the other affecting everyone from Earth, but not Road Masters.

I shook the idea away and concentrated on navigating us safely to the library. I could have an existential crisis later. Like, age thirty or something. Right now, I had more important things to do.

15

WE ENTERED THE library and Scott paused, drinking in the room.

I had to admit, it *was* pretty grand: I swept a glance over the towering stacks, easily seven or eight meters tall, every one stuffed to overflowing with books in all sorts of sizes and colours and bindings. That could have been any super large library back on Earth, though; what made this one really special was that instead of floor space, the fairies used the void above the shelves to congregate.

Raw-hewn tables and stools hung from the roof, draped in ferns bursting forth from gilded pots, the whole aesthetic like something out of a home style magazine for rich minimalists—a style only emphasised by the huge expanse of white ceiling, splashed with gold and intersected with twining vines and intricate floral motifs. One day, I'd have a bedroom exactly like this.

My lips quirked into a tiny smile and I grabbed Scott's wrist. "Come on," I said, and dragged him down the row in front of us.

Since the fairies used the void space to read, relax and socialise, the ground area was entirely filled with shelves and rows, each row about twenty or thirty metres long, spliced by an aisle down the middle that was easily a hundred meters end to end. Every third or fourth row ended in a door like the one we'd come in—a handy feature, no doubt, but one which made it im-frogging-possible to figure out where I was now in relation to where we needed to be.

The road mastery book had been off to one side, tucked against a wall, but where that bit of wall was exactly... We reached the aisle in the middle of the row and I paused, bottom lip to one side between my teeth.

"You do remember where it is, don't you?"

The doubt in Scott's voice grated against my nerves and I clenched my fists. "Of course I do." Randomly, I turned left. "Okay. Bright yellow-green book about yay big." I held my hands up to indicate something about the size of a small paperback. "Cloth bound, lots of gold all over it, title is Through Roads Between."

Scott nodded once and picked a shelf at eye level. "I'll take this side, you take the other."

"Sure."

Scott and I skimmed shelves back to back, fingers racing over the spines, lips moving as we processed the words at top speed, trying to find something useful before the fairies found us.

"Edge?"

"Mm?"

"Where did the unicorn babies come from?"

I shot him a quizzical look. "You're seriously thinking about that now?"

He shrugged—"Care and Feeding of Unicorns"—and tapped the spine of a bright red book at his eye level.

I sighed with an exaggerated shoulder-heave and let my hands rest on the books in front of me. "Well, Scott, when a mummy unicorn and a daddy unicorn love each other very much..."

He smirked, eyes crinkling. "That's just it, though, isn't it." He leaned towards me. "Where's the daddy unicorn?"

My mouth opened as though it had an answer, and then when it realised it didn't, my tongue curled around my front molars and my lower jaw jutted out.

"Good point, isn't it."

Frog him, his eyes practically gleamed in the dim light. I rolled my own in response and resumed my search. "Sure. It's a fantastic question. But it's so not relevant to what we're supposed to be doing right now. You know?"

He shrugged and shoved his hands deep into his pockets, still grinning. "Hey, I don't ask for inspiration, it just arrives."

"Yeah," I muttered, scanning the spines in front of me with both my eyes and my fingertips. "Sure. Can you put in an order for something relevant next time, though, please? We have a world to save, remember."

He sagged like a puppet with its strings cut. "You're no fun."

"As advertised. Come on, I'm done with this shelf."

I ducked around into the next row. It had to be around here somewhere—unless the fairies had moved it, of course, or *re*moved it.

I bit the inside of my lip. If they'd removed it...

Scott kept trying. "Oh hey, here's a book about dragons! I knew they had to be real somewhere!" he'd say, or else, "Whoa, why would you want to read about that?"—clearly fishing for my attention.

But it wasn't until he made an exaggerated, full-body shudder and said, "Ew, come on. I used shadow magic on a regular basis and even I think that's gross. I know everyone thinks the fairies are supposed to be nice and all, but why isn't this kind of thing in a restricted section or something?" that I snapped upright, left hand gripping the soft bit at the top of the spine on the hardcover I'd been scanning. "Restricted section!"

Scott glanced at me. "You really want to check out the restricted section *now*?"

I shook my head a little. "That's where the road mastery book will be. Come on."

I led the way back down our current row, heart tripping in my chest. Restricted, restricted... I supposed all the signs for the stacks would be up high, where the fairies could see them. If I was designing a library like this, where would I put the restricted section?

We reached the aisle—and my heart stopped as a red-winged fairy appeared at eye-level from around the corner.

I froze, forgetting how to breathe, and Scott stumbled lightly against my back before he too saw the fairy and tensed.

The dark, lithe fairy simply stared at us, her red dress some sort of fabric that shifted colours in the light, sometimes the colour of bright, healthy blood, sometimes the colour of the dark sap on the trees of the Valley.

My spine crawled.

But something about her seemed familiar, and she still hadn't said or done anything; I risked a breath, remembered to blink.

"Ruby?" I whispered.

Months ago, on my very first visit to Sanctuary, another fairy had drawn Quoise aside to talk about the shadows. Her presence had led to the discovery that I was a Road Master. I'd never spoken to her, or seen her since, but I'd gotten the impression she was Quoise's friend.

She blinked, a slow, exaggerated movement like time had slowed right down. "Run," she whispered, eye contact never wavering.

Time skipped.

Ruby vanished.

I frowned, opened my mouth.

Scott frowned back. "Well that was—"

A gentle chime rang out through the room, as though someone had tapped a triangle. The note hovered in the air for a moment, swelling instead of softening.

Our frowns deepened. I opened my mouth again.

A rushing sound: quiet, louder, loud.

I swivelled, looked down the aisle to my left.

My eyes went wide.

A huge wave, tall as the shelves, roared toward us, sloshing and angry, tearing books from shelves and tossing them into the air.

I snatched at Scott's wrist. "Run!"

We pelted down the aisle, and I fought Scott as he twisted to look behind us.

"Wait!" he said.

I ignored him and dragged him onward.

My shoulder nearly broke out of its socket as Scott stopped suddenly.

"Wait!" He braced against my tugging.

Closer, closer.

"Scott!"

"The ward," he said, turning slightly to clench my arm.

"What?"

"Use the unicorn ward."

"I know what you meant!" I snapped. "Why am I using a ward"—I dug furiously in my pocket—"instead of running like a *sane human being?*"

He lifted his chin at the wave, staring it down, the roar of it so loud we had to shout to be heard. "It's not real!"

I looked between him and the wave, eyes wide. "You're kidding me, right?"

His jaw twitched. He let one hand drop from my arm so he could face the tidal wave square on.

I guessed not. Pulse hammering at my chest, body bursting with adrenalin, I clenched the ward in my hand in front of us, gripping the braid part, loose, bristly hair sticking out the top and bottom.

"What exactly do you want me to do?" I shouted, angling my head toward Scott without taking my eyes off the ward.

"Just activate it!" he shouted back, grip still firm on my upper arm.

I could feel the spray as the wave roared closer, twenty paces away, fifteen, ten. The smell of salt water, spray spitting on my face...

I closed my eyes, gasping for air, and forced my road mastery toward the unicorn hair.

Please let this work. Whatever Scott's seen, whatever he's thinking... please let it work.

The pre-surge hit us; my legs were soaked.

More road mastery, more power...

"Edge, hurry!"

The bright flash of silver and the smell of old roses; the smell of mint.

The darkness behind my eyelids turned gold, like I was staring at the sun through closed lids, the veins of my eyelids visible.

Nausea gripped my stomach in its fists.

Scott grabbed me by the shoulders, spun me to him, held me tight.

The wave crashed over us, roaring like a freight train on loose tracks at high speed.

I cringed, waiting for the blow...

But it never came.

"Come on," Scott shouted in my ear. He felt around for my wrist, laced his fingers through mine, and by the time I'd opened my eyes was dragging me along the aisle in the direction the wave had come from.

I stared in wonder at the back of the wave, still crashing its way through the library, wreaking chaos on the books—only, I realised as we ran, the books were perfectly fine. Once the wave had passed, the library had returned to normal, although the roar still echoed through the high-roofed room and the smell of salt water still overpowered the smell of old books.

"Where are we going?" I asked, a stitch starting in my side.

"Elsewhere!" Scott said. "I don't know about you, but I feel like that was one heck of an intruder alarm."

I glanced back over my shoulder just as the wave hit the far wall and vanished with a final, impressive splash.

Non-water sprayed from one side of the room to the other in the wake of the impact, settling, sloshing to the floor, a foot-deep ocean that slowly began to drain away.

"Come on," Scott said, tugging me gently to a stop in front of a tall, brown door, like all the doors that led out of the library, this one at the end of the aisle.

He pushed the brass handle down and slipped through the doorway.

"Shouldn't we try to find the book now that the defence systems are down?" I whispered as I followed.

He shook his head. "What if they just set it off again? How many wards do you have left?"

"Two." I ran my fingers over the bumps of the braids in my pocket.

Scott shook his head a second time and set off down the dim hallway, thick green carpet muffling his footsteps, strip lights in a lip around the roof barely bright enough for me to read his face. "Not enough. We'll have to try again another day."

My chest ached—and not just from the frantic run. I skipped a couple of steps to catch up, and bumped his shoulder with mine as I fell into step.

"Thanks for coming with," I said. Who knew what the wave would have done if I hadn't used the ward.

He flicked me a half-smile, glanced around, and ducked left as the hallway widened briefly into a square landing.

"Wait," I said, jerking around to follow. "Where are you going?"

"Trust me," he said. "I have a feeling about something."

I halted, leaning over my knees, trying to get the stitch in my side to let go.

Trust him?

I watched as he snuck further down the hallway in the gloom, practically bouncing on light feet. If the whole high school thing didn't work out for him, he could definitely consider a career in cat burglary.

That sparked an uncomfortable twinge in my guts, but I shoved aside images of Georgia on a white-tiled floor in a bathroom in Melbourne, forced the kernel of worry over mob bosses closing in on my family back into the closets of my mind.

Trust Scott? Well, first of all, he'd trusted me when no one else did, and although we hadn't gone to investigate the roads (yet), he'd come here to help me look for my book.

I straightened and took a deep breath. Secondly, he'd pretty much just saved our butts.

I guessed I could trust him for a little while longer.

16

"YES!" SCOTT HISSED a few minutes later. "I knew it!"

I glanced around under sceptical eyebrows, working my mouth. This landing looked pretty much identical to the last two we'd crossed: dim, boxy, and moody with all the dark wood and mossy carpet. Except this time, the left-hand option ended in a door. "What did you know?"

He turned to me, eyes alight, and bounced once on his toes. "That defence system in the library. That was one heck of a magic trick, don't you think?"

"Uh, sure?"

"Lot of power behind that. Big magic."

I wrinkled my brow. "Yes? And?"

He grinned, although it looked like he was trying hard not to. "Magic that big needs a source, right? It's not like there were dozens of fairies hovering around conjuring it up. It seemed more like an automated thing, an in-built defence."

I shook my head as though dislodging a fly. "Scott, I know you're enjoying this, but will you just get to the point already?"

"Permanent defence system," he said, holding up an index finger. "Really big power source to run it." He held up the other. "If they are way apart"—he stretched out his arms—"the power drains before it gets where it needs to go. They need to be close." He lined his fingers up side by side.

"So," I said, still frowning, "you think there's a big power source nearby. This helps us how?"

Now he really did cut loose with the grinning, teeth gleaming in the light reflecting off the roof. "What's the biggest magical power source you've seen?"

My eyebrows drew even tighter. "The big ball of Sanctuary-Valley magic."

Scott huffed, eyes rolling. "Second biggest, then."

My lips twitched as I finally glimpsed where he was going with all this. "Tie between the heart of Sanctuary and the heart of the Valley," I said deliberately to annoy him.

He narrowed his eyes at me like he knew. "Well *obviously* the fairies aren't drawing on the Valley to power their little death-wave, are they."

"Obviously."

He stepped aside, pointing at the door behind him, the one blocking the way to the left. His head dipped, eyes gleaming and wide. "Look!"

He was pointing at a door that at first glance looked like yet another clone of the ones we'd seen so far: tall, brown, and wooden.

Which—I tilted my head, frowning—why *were* all the doors here so tall? Surely a building designed for fairies should have fairy-sized doors, not these towering over-sized human ones?

Though granted, I realised, looking more closely, this one did have a fairy-sized door cut into it in the middle at the very top.

Something tickled at my subconscious, and I squinted.

Oh, road mastery. Right.

I shut my eyes and focused my road mastery—and sure enough, the door flared to life in the darkness behind my eyes as though it was a living thing. "That's weird."

Limey leaf green swirled through a golden haze, the smell of something fresh and sharp filling the air—almost like mint, but not quite, less sweet, more *green*-smelling.

"What can you see?"

"A soulprint," I said, looking at him again. "What can *you* see?"

His eyebrows twitched upwards and he pointed higher up the door.

This time, I saw the tiny line of gold script on the fairy door at the top. I stepped closer.

My breath caught. The Forbidden Chamber.

I glanced back at Scott. "You think...?" It made sense. He was right: *something* had to be powering that wave, and a direct connection to the heart of Sanctuary would definitely do the trick.

The million-watt smile was back, and he nodded, bouncing on his toes again. "Let's have a look."

Immediately, I frowned. "Scott, it's forbidden. Like, it's literally there in the name. And just because the current Keeper is a nasty piece of work, that doesn't mean that there isn't a good reason for the chamber to be forbidden."

"Quoise went in."

"Quoise is a fairy."

He tugged on my sleeve and tilted his head toward the door, eyes wide, chin tucked so he peered through his lashes at me. "Please?"

If the fairies caught us there, we could kiss our freedom goodbye—and maybe our lives. On the other hand, it did seem like a good place to start getting some answers. I sighed. "I hope I live to regret this," I whispered furiously.

Scott beamed. "Oh, don't worry," he said. "You will." He gestured for my hand, flicking his fingers impatiently when I took my time. The instant he had a firm grip on me, he grasped the door handle. "Ready?"

"No." But my pulse quickened, and despite my best efforts, my own eyes were probably just as alight as Scott's.

"Three-two-one," he said quickly, and pushed down on the handle.

It didn't budge.

"Well, it is forbidden," I pointed out. "You couldn't exactly expect them to keep it unlocked so anyone could waltz in."

"There's got to be a way," he muttered, releasing my hand and skating his fingers over the wood.

I inhaled to speak, thought better of it, and bit my lip to one side again. The door had a soulprint. As far as I knew, only people— fairies, humans, unicorns—had soulprints. People, and the magics of Sanctuary and the Valley. Why would a door have a soulprint? How? Tentatively, I let my road mastery brush against it.

The soulprint twisted to life, twining around me in the same way Veve wound through my legs when she was after a pat.

Instinctively, I scritched at the door.

It arched against me like a cat.

"What are you doing?" Scott asked, and I felt him pause next to me, curious.

"It's alive," I said softly, eyes still closed, fingertips skimming in circles over the polished wood.

"The door or the chamber?"

"The door."

"You don't... You don't think it's another alarm, do you?"

My hands stilled. Scott, being the cautious one. Had the world ended without me noticing? "It might be," I said. "I don't know."

More than that: I had negative five-billion clues. Since when did doors have soulprints? Either the wood had been alive somehow to begin with—alive differently to a tree, because I'd seen plenty of those, and even the zombie trees that had attacked me hadn't had soulprints—or someone had put the soulprint there somehow. Which was impossible, at least as far as I knew. You couldn't just make something and stick a soulprint in it.

Almost instinctively, my fingers resumed skimming over the surface, the soulprint of the door arching with delight where my road mastery met its soulprint.

The connection between us strengthened, and I could feel the pulse of power feeding back through my fingers, like the door was purring.

My fingertips began to sting. I tried to let my hands drop to my sides—but I couldn't tear away from the connection with the door. Like a strong magnet, it held me tight.

My breath caught in my throat and my eyes flew open as I sought out Scott's face.

"Are you okay?"

"It's holding me," I said, voice breathy, adrenalin like ice through my chest. "I can't let go."

Scott took half a step back, staring wide-eyed at the door. "It's a trap."

"Please don't leave me," I whispered. *Look at me. Look back at me. Please don't leave me here.* My heart trilled.

He glanced at me, unease vanishing in an instant as he straightened, shoulders square, chin high, eyes soft. "Of course not."

The sting intensified until it overtook both hands, skin burning like a thousand tiny cuts rubbed with lemon juice, tendons and ligaments aching at every joint like they strained to keep my hand bones together.

I gasped.

Immediately, Scott put a hand on my shoulder, warm and firm. "Hey, I'm not going anywhere," he said.

"It hurts," I bit off, jerking my chin at my hands, stuck to the door at shoulder height.

He grabbed my forearm and tugged.

"Hey, hey! Ow!"

"Sorry," he said, releasing me. "I had to try."

"Yeah, well it *hurt*."

"I said sorry."

I closed my eyes and reminded myself not to breathe so fast. I took a long, slow breath, trying to force my pulse to slow down too. It didn't work.

The pain crept up to my wrists.

Why? I thought at the door. *Why are you doing this?*

The power thrummed like purring again—*ow*—and the door's soulprint arched against me.

I didn't understand. Not just that the door had a soulprint, but that it seemed genuinely friendly. *You're hurting me,* I told it. *Please stop.*

The door's soulprint stilled, the restless shift of green and gold pausing in its movements.

My breath hitched. *You... You didn't know you were hurting me?*

Slowly, the pressure on my wrists began to ease.

Thank you, I breathed. *It still hurts,* I prompted when nothing happened.

The door didn't speak, as such, but I got a clear sense of conflict: it was supposed to hold me here for its masters, but no one had ever talked to it before, petted it before; no one had paid it attention in a very, very long time.

If you let me go now, I told it, hoping desperately I wasn't falling into old habits and promising things I had no intention of keeping, *I'll come back and play with you. I... I promise.*

"What's going on?" Scott whispered.

"Shh!" I snapped as the door's soulprint tensed. *It's okay,* I told it. *He's a friend.*

Frustration, a darkness like total blindness. The door couldn't sense him.

No, I agreed. *He's not... like me. Or the fairies. Do...* Froggity frogging frogs. This was either about to be genius, or the dumbest thing I'd ever done—and that was saying something. *Do you want to meet him?*

It leapt back to life at once, stirring and twirling and twining, impatient, restless, excited.

"Scott," I murmured. "You know how you said you trust me?"

"Yeeeees…"

"Touch the door."

Suddenly, raised voices sounded down the hallway behind us. Fairies. My pulse raced again.

"You sure that's a good idea right now?"

"Please trust me," I said. "Please." The pain had reduced to that first initial sting in my fingertips. Just a little bit more, and I'd be able to rip my fingers away—and even if Scott was stuck, I could probably do something with my road mastery to get him free.

He stepped shoulder to shoulder with me as the voices behind us grew louder; no one was shouting yet, just talking urgently between themselves. Holding my gaze, he reached out slowly and let his hand rest next to mine against the door.

The door's soulprint sharpened its focus, homing in on him.

Frustration. Still blind.

Let this hand go, I said, tugging on the hand closest to Scott. *I can help.*

My hand dropped away. My eyes rolled up and my shoulders sagged a little. Halfway there. I laid my hand gently over Scott's, partly covering it, partly touching the door.

"What are you doing?" he whispered.

I kept my eyes closed. "The door wants to see you." Slowly— but not too slowly, because those voices were getting loud now— I reached for Scott's soulprint, letting it take up all the space behind my eyes until all I could see with my road mastery was the bare hilltop under early morning stars, the dawn just kissing the horizon.

The door hissed.

I didn't realise it was audible until Scott reacted. "What was that?"

I gave a mute shake of my head. *What is it?* I asked urgently.

The door's response was pure, golden light—the same colour as Sanctuary's power, the same colour as the dawn.

Yes, I said quietly. *Yes, he is connected to Sanctuary's heart.*

"Two of them!"

I glanced left, back down the hallway, and fear prickled through my whole body. Three fairies, silver, copper and green—but not Viri, I realised, and remembered to breathe again. *They're coming*, I told the door. *Please. If you don't let us go right now, if they capture us, I'll never be able to come back and play with you.*

"Please tell me you're doing something," Scott murmured from my right.

My jaw twitched as the fairies came closer.

"Oh ho!" said the copper-winged one. "It's none other than Emma the Breaker herself. Viri *will* be pleased."

Please. He is tied to the heart of Sanctuary. Please help us.

Pain burned through my hands again—and Scott's, I assumed as he hissed.

"What do you think Keeper Viri is going to do with them?" the green-winged fairy asked the others casually. "The lightning?"

"Maybe to start," silver-wing said, grin like a wolf showing all her teeth in her pale face.

Please. He practically is *Sanctuary. At least help him.*

A gentle click echoed through the landing. The door to the Forbidden Chamber swung open.

Scott and I stumbled forward, dragged with the movement—then, suddenly, we were sprawling on the floor as the door disconnected us.

"No!" screamed a fairy. "You can't be in there!"

"Get them, hurry!"

The door swung shut with a thump.

In complete darkness, I felt for Scott, finding his leg, his knee—then his hand as he reached for me and wrapped his fingers tightly through mine. I could hear his breathing, could hear my own—and my pulse.

Scott shifted. "Edge?" he whispered.

"What?"

He lifted my arm up, stretching forward until my fingers met cold rock.

Stomach sinking, chest constricting, breaths coming hard and fast, I whirled around on my knees.

The Forbidden Chamber was about a metre and a half squared, walled with solid rock, and pitch dark.

"We're in a tomb," I whispered, and clenched Scott's hands.

"We'll find a way out," he said. "I promise."

17

"IT CAN'T JUST be this," I whispered in the dark that smelled of stone.

"Where's the book, for a start?" Scott replied.

I felt him shift against my right arm. After the first few moments of panic when we discovered the Forbidden Chamber was little more than a five-foot box of stone and darkness and that the door wouldn't—or couldn't—speak to me from this side, we'd ended up sitting against the wall shoulder to shoulder so we could at least feel that someone else was there with us in the dark.

I had my knees up and splayed against my elbows, hands clasped in front. "Or the connection to Sanctuary's heart," I said dully, letting my head tip forward to my chest. I didn't know what I'd expected of a 'forbidden chamber', but it had definitely been something more impressive than this.

Scott gripped my arm. "Did you see that?"

My head snapped up. "See what?"

"Look up."

I did. Darkness yawned above us, a storey, two, three—there was no way to know; the darkness was absolute. "I don't see anything."

"Keep watching."

Seconds ticked by, but the tense anticipation between my shoulder blades slowly dissipated. There was nothing but breathing in the dark, Scott's warm skin against my left arm, and the mineral smell of stone.

Plus, it was starting to feel cold in here. I rubbed my arms briskly. "I still see nothing."

"It will come again, just wait."

I sighed, and decided to ignore the desperation in his voice.

I tipped my head back again, letting it fall sideways onto Scott's shoulder as I stared up at the infinite black. I was too tired to care about the way he tensed for a moment before letting out a careful breath. It had been, what, four thirty when we'd left home? We'd walked all the way through the Valley, crept through Sanctuary to the library, spent some time searching, had come looking for the Forbidden Chamber... It had to be at least six thirty according to my body, maybe close to seven.

And I hadn't eaten a thing. No wonder my energy was fading.

"There, did you see it?"

I jerked upright, blinking rapidly; I didn't even remember closing my eyes. "Where? Where?"

"There!" he said, pointing—not that I could see it, but I felt his arm lift.

But regardless, I didn't need his gesture: this time, I'd seen it myself, a flash of gold high, high up above us. "Of course!" I stood up, running my hands over the walls as I traced out our tiny space.

"Of course what?" Scott said. "Where are you? What are you doing?"

"Feeling the walls," I said. "Get up and help."

The scrape and shuffle of him standing sounded, then, "Okay, what are we looking for?"

"Handholds. I mean, I can't guarantee there will be any, the fairies can all fly, but if they have human-sized doors, why not a way for humans to get up there?"

Scott was silent for a second. "Oh, right. Flying."

I nodded, remembered he couldn't see me, and paused with my hand resting in a cupped hole in the rock at about shoulder height. "Right. Of course the entrance here is nothing much. They can just fly straight on up to wherever it is, and it's an extra barrier for people who shouldn't be here."

"Like us."

I grinned. "Like us. Here, give me a hand will you?"

Shuffling footsteps, then Scott's hands patted my back and shoulders an instant before he walked into me. "What?" he said.

"I've found a handhold." I grabbed one of his hands and directed it to the handhold in the wall. "Hold onto that for me for a sec." I crouched and searched the wall below, and sure enough, there was another one around knee height. "Got it. You going first, or am I?"

"Feel free, by all means."

I rolled my eyes and began to climb, one dark handhold after the next. For a moment I was suspicious of Scott's motives, but the concentration it took to climb, feeling out each handhold, slowly shifting my weight up, reaching for the right spot with my feet, soon drove everything else from my mind.

It felt like forever, my limbs getting shakier and shakier as the golden light flashed intermittently above us. Realistically, it was probably only about ten minutes until we reached the top and clambered out into a circular chamber, like Sanctuary's heart but smaller.

This chamber also glowed gold, but whereas in the heart the light seemed to come from everywhere at once, here it was a twisting, twining pillar of light on the opposite side of the room that lit the circular, brown stone walls—and where the heart of Sanctuary was blinding in its brilliance, this room was barely brighter than a cave with a fireplace.

I crossed the room in ten easy steps to the foot-high semi-circular dais jutting out of the far wall, which the pillar of light stood on. A waist-high lectern stood between me and the pillar, a heavy, ornate book resting on it, looking like a relic out of the sixteen hundreds.

The pillar flickered, light flaring.

"That's the light we saw," Scott said.

I glanced back over my shoulder at him, still standing by the chute. "Yeah," I said. *Obviously*, I didn't say. "Here, come look at this." I leaned over the book and squinted, trying to make out the lettering. The lectern tilted away from the light, leaving the book's cover in shadow, and part of the gilt letters had peeled away, making them even harder to read than they'd been originally, in their heavy, gothic font.

Book... My heart skipped. *Book of Laws.* "Scott," I whispered urgently, fingers hovering over the cover without quite touching. "This is it."

Scott reached around me and lifted the cover. It brushed against my fingertips, soft and firm, little dints where the letters had been pressed in for the embossing.

I shifted aside, and Scott flipped a couple of the marble-edged pages gently.

"Wait," I said. "Flip back. What was that?"

He flicked back a bit until I put a finger down to stop him.

"There. World Creators," I read from the heading on the page. I didn't know what it was talking about, or what had snagged my attention, but something about it seemed vaguely familiar.

Scott skimmed the page with his finger. "Here," he said, stopping about two thirds of the way down and tapping the page. "This is what Gemma did."

I read the paragraph he was pointing at, then looked up at him, wide-eyed. The first time we'd been on the roads all together, when we'd been trying to take Gemma to the heart of Sanctuary to link her to it and save her life, the guardians of the roads had attacked us. Or, well, they'd appeared menacingly, anyway; I still didn't know exactly how dangerous the guardians actually were, and if they *would* actually attack. But either way, they were pretty darn terrifying, and I'd tried to distract them with my road mastery, which had worked for a little while. But in the end, it had been Gem who'd saved our butts: we'd fallen off the roads into a strange, grey world, completely empty of anything except ourselves. It had only been a few paces square, and the sky, or roof, or whatever, had been low enough that I could brush it with my fingers.

A whole new world, one that Gem had created in a hurry and had transported us all to without a seed, without blood, fuzzy and small because that was all she'd had time to imagine.

It was exactly what the book was describing.

I drew my eyebrows down, thinking. The fissure in Sanctuary was definitely a problem, but shadows getting into the heart seemed like the most pressing issue we were dealing with right now. "So could we, like, create a new world to shove the shadows into?"

Scott bounced on his toes. "I don't know. Let's go try!"

"What, now?" I cut a glance at him. "I thought you didn't want to go on the roads with the shadows there."

"Yes," he said, bouncing again, "but this is new information. This is something we could actually try to fight them with. We have to at least figure out how to make the new worlds, and we can't do that without going on the roads." He tilted his face up and fluttered his eyelashes. "Come on. Please?"

I rolled my eyes and worked my mouth. On the one hand, I was tempted. On the other, it was getting late back home, and I really didn't want to stress my parents out any further than necessary. "I'd really better not," I said. "I need to get home."

Scott sighed, but didn't say anything, which was pretty decent of him.

"Come on." I turned to the entry chute, leaving the book open behind me.

Scott strode ahead. I watched as he walked to the chute and turned to face me so he could begin the climb down. "What?"

I hadn't moved from by the dais.

"What is it?"

"Quoise said she wanted the book," I said, looking back at it for a moment. I met his eye again. "That if she had it, it would make things much easier."

Scott raised his eyebrows. "You think we should take it?"

"I don't know." Rules were rules. Viri wasn't the one who'd invented these rules, who'd created the Forbidden Chamber... But what was it Quoise had said weeks ago when she'd decided to help us save Gemma, going against Viri's wishes? Neither of us broke rules until we met each other; maybe we'd never met rules that needed breaking until then.

"Well, I do," Scott said with a curt nod. "Anything that will help Quoise get rid of that cow Viri is alright by me." He grabbed the book off the stand. His grip fumbled, and it slipped.

I cringed as the page we'd been looking at tore.

"Sorry," he said, guilt flashing over his face. He smoothed the page out and closed the book carefully. "Come on. Let's go."

Green light flashed through the chamber, and when it died away, Viri fluttered over the dais, silver and gold lightning crackling around the ball-shaped head of her golden sceptre, tiny gold tiara glittering in its light, viridian-green dress dancing and snapping in a wind generated by her magic. "Emma, Scott," she said, dangerous smile glinting behind the lightning. "I'm so glad you've come."

Lightning crackled toward us.

We dove to the side, Scott grabbing my sleeve, the seam tearing as we tumbled to the ground, me hugging the book to my chest.

"Get that book!" Viri pointed at us as three other fairies—oh look, it was our friends silver, copper and green again—appeared behind her.

They separated and flew toward us from the left, the right, from above.

I curled my body around the book; it probably wasn't worth my life, but I definitely wasn't giving it up without a fight.

"Edge!" Scott grabbed my arm and hauled me off the ground. "Get up, we have to get out of here!"

"How?" I shouted back over the crackling of the lightning; the acoustics in here amplified it until it took on a life of its own, stabbing my eardrums, disorienting me.

"Come on!"

I got my feet under me and ducked as Viri sent another bolt of lightning our way. "Where are we going?"

"The only way out!" He leapt, dragging me with him toward the dais.

Lightning sizzled past us again as Viri screeched. Behind her, the connection to the heart pulsed.

The heart. Scott was going to jump straight into the heart.

"You're not a Road Master!" I screamed at him as he dove to the right to avoid being caught between a bolt of Viri's lightning and the copper-winged fairy.

"You are!"

Urgh! I dodged left, leapt over another lightning bolt, and flung myself behind Viri toward Scott.

"Get that book!" Viri screeched.

Something jerked my arm.

The silver-winged fairy had the back cover of the book in her hands, and somehow her magic was strong enough that I couldn't pull her through the air. She dug her heels in like the air was solid, wings buzzing, jaw set, and yanked white-knuckled on the cover of the book.

"Edge!"

In the corner of my eye, Scott dove toward the heart. "You'll die!" I screamed.

Book, Scott; book, Scott.

Pulse thundering, limbs burning with adrenalin, skin tingling from the magic-thick air, I gave the book one last solid yank, and launched into a sprint.

With an angry growl, the book tore in two, suddenly lighter in my hand. The abrupt release gave me an extra burst of speed that sent me stumbling.

I tripped.

Scott reached for the glowing pillar of light.

"No!" I scrabbled across the ground.

His hand stretched closer.

To my right, Viri flung the sceptre toward us.

"Look out!"

Scott dodged to one side as the lightning sizzled into the heart.

The heart's next pulse boomed through the chamber like an explosion of light.

I collapsed to the floor as it passed over me, my free hand clapped over my head, light blinding even through tightly shut eyes.

"Quick, now!" Scott fumbled at my arm.

I raised my head. Viri and the other fairies had been blown backward by the force.

I got to my feet, doubled over, and grabbed Scott's hand.

We ran for the heart, leapt—for a moment it felt like jumping into a window, too solid to let us through.

I flung out my road mastery. *Let us through!*

Light shattered around us. I screamed as it sliced my skin—face, arms, legs.

Scott shouted too, grip on my hand tightening.

Thud.

We hit the ground.

Instantly, the light and sound died away, and all I could hear was the two of us panting and gasping.

I tensed, fingers gripping at the floor, my hip bone aching, waiting for Viri to follow us.

Nothing.

My cheek was wet.

I touched it, and my fingers came away bloodied. They matched the scores of tiny cuts up and down my arms, each one releasing a couple of pinpricks of blood—and the ones on my legs, and on Scott's face and arms.

I closed my eyes, shoulders sagging, tension draining, and collapsed back against the floor. We made it. We only had half the book, but we'd made it.

Scott shook my shoulder. "Uh, Edge?"

"Mm?" I contemplated exactly how long I could get away with lying here. If I slept for a few hours… I sighed. Quoise could only get us back at the right point in our personal timeline, and it was already probably late enough that my parents were going to freak out. Guilt twanged through my gut.

"Edge, you'd better take a look at this."

I took a long, slow breath and hauled myself upward so I was sitting.

Scott stared at the wall of the chamber to the left of us, tense, rigid.

I followed his gaze—and froze. The walls of the heart usually glowed gold, filling the room with light and warmth.

The wall to the left of us was black, the chamber partially dim.

As we watched, the darkness crept along, spreading in both directions. In the centre, the wall had cracked, and shadowy tendrils wafted toward us.

"I think," said Scott, licking his lips, "we'd better go."

I glanced down at the Book of Laws—or the half I had left. It felt like sacrilege, what I was contemplating, but on the other hand, it was pretty much desecrated now anyway, torn clean down the spine. I set my jaw, gripped the pages in one hand and the hard front cover in the other, and tore.

The cover came away surprisingly easily. I tossed it on the ground, rolled the rest into a tight cylinder, and shoved it into my back pocket. I had a feeling I was going to need both my hands free.

18

WE CREPT OUT of the heart on the opposite side to the shadows, where the heart was still golden and glowing. I halted as we exited onto the roads, overwhelmed as ever by the mass of sensations: sweet roses and honey, musty carpet, stiff bristles, the sound of pages flicking, the long scrape of a pen over thick paper, soft fur, a warm hug, the feel of a toenail on the tips of my fingers, flashes of emerald, magenta, fire-engine red.

Scott tugged at my hand.

Right. Moving. I blinked away the disorientation and took a few steps. But what was I supposed to be following? Where were we going?

This was no good.

Sighing, I tugged Scott back the few paces to the wall of Sanctuary's heart. With a quick flick, I pulled the scab off my shoulder, and walked through the wall, the golden light melting over me as I did.

"What are you *doing*?" Scott dropped my hand like it had gone red hot and stared at me.

I eyed the shadows on the opposite wall. "Listen. There's no point going on the roads without a plan. It's not like we're following them to Sanctuary or anything; we're already here! So where are we going? And since we're here..." I inhaled. "Since we're here we should try the world creation thing."

His jaw worked for a second as he considered it, darting glances at the shadowy tendrils snaking their way into the heart on the other wall.

They didn't seem to have sensed us, or to care about us if they had.

"Fine. You're right. Something needs to be done, and soon by the look of it. Do you want to try first, or do you want me to?"

I took a depth breath, a little tension releasing with the knowledge that he'd agreed. "Okay, here's what we'll do. We'll head back onto the roads, go about fifty or sixty paces away so we're not so close to the shadows, and then you have a go. Remember, Gem said it was just like travelling, but she imagined a blank world instead."

"I know."

I nodded. "Good. You have a try, and if that doesn't work, then I will." While it would be super cool to be able to just create my own worlds from the roads, if only one of us could do it, I actually hoped it was Scott. I already had road mastery, and that was enough to be solely responsible for.

"How will you know I've tried?"

"I don't know, six squeezes," I said impatiently.

"Six?"

"One through five are taken."

"I thought we only—"

"Do we really need to talk about this now?" I said, nodding pointedly at the drifting tendrils of shadow.

Scott's mouth became a line. "You're right. Let's go."

The second entry to the roads was no less overwhelming, but Scott got me moving quickly again, and kept me going for a good minute until he tugged me to a stop.

Then, nothing.

Well, nothing from Scott. From the roads, I caught the sound of a boat motor, a baby crying, the smell of oranges, the feel of shopping bags heavy in my hands, a soft cheek against the back of my hand, sunlight off steel, magenta light, tangerine, the smell of new leather shoes.

Six squeezes. He must have failed.

I inhaled deeply and blew out through my lips like I could blow the nerves away. *Okay. Just like travelling. Just like travelling.*

A sharp tug on my hand; pressure on my shoulder.

I turned—and my chest clenched. Shadows, closing in fast— inasmuch as it was possible to tell distance in a place with no fixed landmarks, anyway.

Okay Edge, this is it. Travelling time.

I closed my eyes—not that it made any difference—and tried to clear my mind—an impossible feat on the roads at any time, let alone with shadows bearing down.

Scott's grip tightened.

I know. I know!

Think of nothing. Greyness, that's where Gemma took us. Just think of grey.

The sound of clinking china. The colour red. An upbeat, pulsing drum. The smell of coffee.

The shadows, whispering: "*Sweet, so sweet your blood. Want your blood, your life.*"

Scott's grip on my hand.

Nothing. Think of nothing!

For an instant I was able to blank everything out and make it grey. I twisted almost instinctively, as though it might help the travelling.

"*So sweet your blood.*"

I yelled as the shadows swarmed around us, tendrils darting in close, jerking away before I had time to do anything.

Travel, frog it all! Think of nothing!

Emerald, crimson, the smell of wet dog, corn chips crunching in my teeth.

Nothing! Nothing!

There! Grey nothingness!

I grabbed onto the sensation, twisted, gripping Scott's hand like death.

A shadow darted forward, latched onto my thigh. I screamed as ice-cold pain shot up it, trying to push the shadow away.

But it was too late. We were falling sideways—travelling! We were travelling!—and the shadow gripped my leg like jellyfish tentacles, hooking into my skin, dragging along with us. Wind roared around us in darkness.

Light flashed around us again and spat us out into my new world—not nothing at all, but something, somewhere, some sort of room. Something about it seemed vaguely familiar—but there was no time. No time to concentrate on anything but the shadow, rearing behind me, drawing on my leg, the wind still roaring and snapping around.

My thigh. The ward. In my pocket, right near the shadow.

Frantically, I shot my road mastery into it, faster, faster, harder, until—

Flash!

The world burst into silver bells and roses for an instant, and the shadow shrank back, shrieking.

"Get it out, get it out!" Scott shouted.

I whipped the final unicorn ward from my pocket and brandished it at the shadow. "Get back!"

"Eat your soul, your blood, drink your life."

The strange wind roared.

"Get back!"

I poured power into the ward—more, more, more—and it too exploded in a flash of light and roses, crumbling to ash in my hand.

I blinked frantically, trying to clear the afterimages from my sight. The shadow. Where was the shadow?

But the hall was bright and clear. The shadow had gone.

I slumped against a nearby wall, head nearly falling off my shoulders.

"What in the..."

The voice sounded familiar. I mean, it made sense that if I was going to create a world of my own, it would be similar to what I knew—but Anna? Could I create *people* for my new world too?

"Edge, was that a shadow in our hall?"

I looked up, chest still heaving as I fought for breath. Strange. This new world looked exactly... like... our front hall. With Anna, emerging from her bedroom, and Scott standing by the front door.

"Princess?" Scott said though equally gaspy breaths, one hand knuckling his side. "I don't think this is a whole new world."

19

A STRANGE, PEARLY shimmer flickered over the hall around me, obscuring the apricot tiles and warm-toned walls. I frowned, blinking rapidly as the momentary shimmer disappeared. New... world? What was he *talking* about? "What?"

Scott opened his mouth, then frowned down at it as though it had decided to speak without him. He looked back up at me. "What what?"

"Edge?" Anna was still watching us from around the doorframe. "Was that seriously a shadow in our front hall just now?"

I stared at her, brow wrinkled. "Why would there be shadows in the hall?"

She rolled her eyes, then inclined her head at Scott. "Who's he?"

I turned from her back to Scott, still frowning. So was he. "Scott."

Anna's fingers appeared around the doorframe, followed by the rest of her. "Is he your boyfriend?"

"No, Anna." Something about the familiarity of Anna's teasing melted away the strange confusion. I pretended I hadn't noticed the way Scott had gone rigid where he stood, not two paces from the front door. "He's a friend. He's..." Urgh. This whole talking-to-Anna-about-magic thing was really weird. "He's here to help with the roads."

Anna's gaze sharpened. "You're going on the roads again?"

I nodded, brow furrowed, lips slightly pursed. "I have to." *Please, Anna. I have to do this. Please understand. Please.*

She sighed explosively. "I suppose there's no point telling you to take your phone."

I shook my head. "It doesn't work over there, you know that."

"Or telling you to be careful." She folded her arms and leaned against her doorframe.

"Of course I'll be careful."

She sniffed. "Yeah. Right." She rubbed her chin with one shoulder. "Going anywhere near those shadows isn't being careful, Edge, it's verging on suicidal."

I stared at her, hands fisting by my sides. "It's not. You know I have wards." I stuck my hand in my pocket to feel for the bundle of unicorn-hair wards Aphros had given me.

My stomach jolted.

My pocket was empty, except for something silty that felt suspiciously like ash.

Scott moved to my shoulder. "Ward? Is this something I should know about?"

"Never mind," I muttered.

Anna had shifted as Scott had stepped to my shoulder, her chin jutting up, arms tighter. "She gets hurt, you pay," she said, staring Scott down.

He nodded. "We'll be careful."

"Pssh." Anna rolled her eyes. "Sure you will. You're using your own blood to cross over to a weird world that stinks so you can travel roads that screw up your brain so you can fight shadows that want to suck your soul. Super careful."

I opened my mouth to protest, but Anna cut me off with a wave. "Why are you still here? Don't you have, like, a world to save or something?" She tilted her head meaningfully to the family room.

"Right." I exchanged glances with Scott. "Yeah. Let's do that."

I led him through the family room and out the sliding door to the yard. Veve greeted us both ecstatically, licking and slurping and pushing through Scott's legs so he'd scritch her back. He staggered, arms flung wide, and I grabbed his forearm to steady him. He laughed quietly, shook me off, and bent over to snuggle Veve's face in between his hands, running his thumbs over her ears.

Touching, but we had more pressing matters to deal with. The warm sun of late afternoon beat down on us. I glanced at it, trying to judge the time as I steered Scott by the forearm around the corner of the house. I checked the windows. No Anna. Good.

"So where's the crossing?" Scott said.

"Doesn't matter, we're not going." I halted abruptly against the side of the house, just under the cool shade of the eave on the edge of the footpath, facing the prickly bushes across the grass.

Veve tried to weave through my legs, but I pushed her away. "What?"

"We're not going." I took a depth breath and turned to him, ignoring Veve as she nudged my hand. "Scott, there was a time skip."

"What? What are you talking about?" He shook his own hands free of Veve's slobbery attentions; she finally gave up and flopped on the grass at our feet, panting like a train coming into station.

"You know how I told you time kept skipping in Sanctuary?"

He narrowed his eyes. "Yeah...?"

"We've just been through a time skip. We went to the Valley, we did stuff, and then we got skipped back here."

He blinked, as stunned as if I'd just punched him. "How do you know?"

Chewing the inside of my lip, I pulled a tight roll of paper out of my back pocket. "My unicorn wards are gone," I said. "And..." I held the roll of paper out to him. "I didn't have this in my pocket when we walked in my front door."

"What is it?" He took it and began flicking through the pages of what seemed to be a pretty mangled book. A few pages in, he gasped, and locked gazes with me. "Edge, we didn't just visit the Valley. This is Quoise's Book of Laws."

My eyes transformed instantly into saucers. "The Book of Laws?" I said, voice hushed as I huddled shoulder-to-shoulder and elbow-to-elbow with him so I could read it too. "No way! How the frogging elephants did we get away with the Book of Laws?"

"Half the Book of Laws," Scott corrected, flipping to the end of the section we had.

I glanced at him, eyebrows way up. "So who has the other half?"

Scott exhaled heavily and leaned against the bricks. "We don't remember a thing. All that"—he flapped the book—"and we have no idea what we did."

"No, Veve. Down." I shooed her away from the temptingly-flapping book with my knee, then shoved my hands into my pockets and joined Scott back against the bricks, one foot up against the wall to keep my balance. "I don't know," I said as my fingers traced out the empty space of my pocket again. "But it wasn't a fun trip."

"How do you know that?"

I let my head fall back against the bricks and stared past the eave at the endless depth of the vivid blue sky. "I had six unicorn wards in my pocket when we got here."

I turned my head, met his yellow-flecked brown eyes, pulled out the linty lining of my pocket. Black dust drifted to the ground, dusting my shoe on the way. "Now I have none, and this?" I flicked at the top of my right sleeve, where the fabric had torn away from the body of the shirt. "My shirt was perfectly fine when we walked in the door of the house. I know that a hundred percent for certain."

He glanced down at the blue-and-black-stained cotton of my pocket lining before meeting my eyes again. "I don't get it. What are the wards?"

"Unicorn wards," I said, stuffing my pocket back where it belonged. "Aphros's hair. They let you cross from Sanctuary to the Valley without a blood sacrifice, and I can activate them with my road mastery as protection against the shadows."

"That's pretty cool."

"We burned through six of them, Scott. Six. That means that, on average, each of us just risked our lives *three* times." I turned to him again, searching in his eyes for some glimmer of understanding. "We just nearly *died, three times each*, and we have exactly zero memory of how, or why, or where."

His mouth twitched like he might be biting his inner lip. "Okay, yeah, that's not so cool."

"Not so much, no." I bumped the back of my head gently against the bricks a couple of times. We had the Book of Laws, or at least part of it. We'd burned through six unicorn wards. And Anna had asked me if there had been a shadow in the hall.

Frogging elephants, we were in so much trouble right now. I exhaled with a huff.

"Wait," Scott said. "Thick, itchy unicorn hair?"

I wrinkled my eyebrows at him. "Yes?"

Lifting his foot up, Scott peeled his sock back to reveal a braid of Aphros's creamy hair. "I guess we only went through five."

Good, but hardly enlightening. "I guess so."

Adrenalin drained from my chest, dragging uncertainty in its wake. I let my head fall back against the bricks. Of all the frustrating things in the whole wide world...

"What do we do now?" Scott said quietly.

I shrugged, a half-hearted twitch of my shoulders.

Veve, who'd been resting on her belly on the grass, grunted and flopped sideways, legs and tail fully extended. I've never taught her to play dead, but if I had, it would have looked just like that.

I sniffed. Even Veve agreed the situation was hopeless.

"Why unicorn?" Scott said after he'd finished fixing his sock.

"Why unicorn what?" I didn't exactly snap at him, but honestly, I just wanted him to leave and let me be miserable in peace—miserable about something I didn't even know the size or shape of, about lost memories and whatever it had cost us to get the book.

"Why unicorn wards?" he said, shifting his hips against the wall and propping one foot up, mimicking my posture. "Why not, like, fairy wards, or, I don't know, shadow wards?"

I stabbed a quick glance at him. "You really want to wear bits of shadow tied around your ankle?"

He shook his head, not a no, but a dismissal. "Why *unicorn*? Why Aphros? Why can she cross the border but no one else can?"

I bounced the inside of my cheek between my molars; this conversation tickled something in the depths of those locked up memories. I danced around the edges, trying not to force the memory... but it slipped away regardless, water through sand. I sighed.

"I don't know," I said. "And she doesn't know. Her soulprint," I added, realising I hadn't told him yet, "looks like the combined magics of Sanctuary and the Valley before the shadows arrived, though."

Aphros had seemed genuinely surprised and intrigued when I'd told her that her soulprint matched that of the Sanctuary-Valley magics before the Valley had been corrupted, presumably by the shadows, so there'd been no help to find there, either.

He drew his eyebrows down.

I watched for a second, but when no revelation was forth-coming, I switched to watching Veve instead, her sides huffing, ear twitching as a fly landed briefly. No point crossing to the Valley now anyway. We had no more wards. I'd have to sneak over at some point and ask Aphros to make some more, but that would take her an hour or so, and there was no point Scott hanging around that long. "We'll have to try again tomorrow," I said, right as he said: "I know that that's important, but I have no idea how." We exchanged glances and half-smiles, and he pushed off from the wall. "Tomorrow, then?"

I nodded. "Come over whenever. I'm not going anywhere," I added with wide-eyed, head-waggling irony as I remembered the reason Scott had to be here in the first place. Urgh.

"Sure," he said. "See you then."

I should have walked him to the gate in the front fence; instead, I stood motionless and watched him unlatch it, shift Veve to one side with his knee, and slip through, latching it closed again behind him. He looked up at me once, but he didn't speak, so neither did I, and then he'd disappeared off toward the neighbour's house, toward the end of the cul-de-sac, toward the path that led down to the creek, and the crossing to Sanctuary.

I rubbed the centre of my forehead with three fingers. I'd thought we were making progress, with our plan to check out the shadows this afternoon. Now, it felt like I'd slammed into a brick wall instead, and at high speed.

Well. Not quite. Scott had left me the Book.

I stared at the curling font of the title page for a moment—Book of Laws. *Book* of Laws. Book *of* Laws. Book of *Laws*.—and exhaled. I couldn't check out the shadows, but—apparently—I had some reading to do.

20

"EMMA?" MUM'S VOICE cut through a half-formed dream of feathery wings and shadows. "You might want to get up, your friends are here."

I rolled over blearily in the dimness of my bedroom just in time to see Mum withdraw. As the door clicked closed, I let my eyes do the same; holding them open felt too much like scouring them with sand. I must have only been asleep, what? Four, five hours? Urgh. Carefully, I unpeeled my tongue from the roof of my mouth and swallowed a couple of times. Really should have cleaned my teeth before bed.

Now that I was semi-awake, the room felt oddly warm around me, given how early it was. I exhaled and snugged my doona up around my chin. Way too early.

I cracked an eyelid open. Oops. I'd fallen asleep with my lamp on last night. I stretched up to the low bookcase by my bed and felt around for the switch.

Wait, I'd been reading. If I hadn't turned the light out before I'd fallen asleep, I probably hadn't put the book—the Book—somewhere sensible either.

I flailed for a second in the sheet, untangled myself, and sat up. Book. Where was the book? I hunted through my covers. I hoped I hadn't slept on it and wrecked it.

But the book wasn't on my bed.

I peered over the edge, but it wasn't on the floor either.

Urgh, fine. I flumped down onto the floor, dragging half the doona down with me, and felt around under the bed. My bed had one of those heavy bases that were practically another mattress, only solid, so there wasn't much room between it and the floor; the book wasn't there.

I shoved away the anxiety knocking at my chest. It had to be in the room somewhere. I sat for a second, staring around the room. Not on the white bookcase next to the bed. Not on the bed, now definitely the most dishevelled part of the room. Not at the foot of my bed near the laundry hamper, or peeking out from the gap in the wardrobe's sliding doors. And the rest of the floor was clear. Urgh.

Something tugged at my consciousness and I glanced out the window. The sky was bright and blue. I frowned at it. Why was it so blue this early in the morning?

I crawled my way back onto the bed and leaned on the sill. Ah. Right. Despite what my body was telling me, it was *not* early in my room; it was late. Quite possibly after-midday late. Whoops.

Someone tapped at the door. "Edge? You in there?"

Gemma! Right, Mum had said friends. "Just a second!"

Ah ha, and there was the book, wedged down between the wall and the bed. I scooped it up, stumbled my way across to the wardrobe, shoved the left door open (it flew aside with a zzzzzzh, landing against the wall with a satisfying *thunk*), and snatched some clothes out of my drawers.

Dressed and semi-presentable, I went to the door opposite my bed and yanked it open. "Hey," I said, trying to look like I'd been studying or reading or something.

Gem's lips twitched. She reached out and smoothed the frizz of my bed-hair down. "Big night?"

"Funny," I said, still blocking the doorway with my body, door handle firmly in my left hand. "What are you doing here?" It was strange, the way my heart was still pounding in my chest. It wasn't like it was unusual for Gemma to be here. But after this week, I didn't know.

She gave a half smile and wry eye contact that suggested she was feeling a little awkward too. "Scott said you guys found something important."

My eyebrows lifted, then lifted further as she stepped aside a little to reveal none other than Scott himself behind her. "Okay..." I let my door swing all the way open. "Come in then, I guess." I stepped aside while they did, Gemma making herself comfy on the bed with the messy doona, Scott sitting on the floor right by the door, leaning against the wall, knees up and encircled by his arms as though he was trying to take up as little space as possible.

"It's okay," I said to him, sitting against the window on the bed, next to Gem but a little way apart.

He flicked me a quick glance then resumed staring intently at the carpet by my bed.

I didn't *actually* roll my eyes, but I imagined doing it.

"So what's going on?" Gemma said.

I rotated my left wrist slowly in my right hand and inhaled slowly. "See that book on the bookcase by the lamp?"

Gem raised an eyebrow at it. "You mean the one that looks like Veve's been mangling it?"

I nodded. "Take it."

She did. I caught the exact moment she realised what it was by the widening of her eyes and the little intake of breath—and the way her fingers suddenly became gentle as they traced the title on the first page. "No way," she murmured.

"Yeah," I said, stretching back against the window. "There's only one little problem. We have no idea how we got it."

"What?" Gem's eyebrows knitted together. She looked at Scott, and when he only shrugged a little, looked back at me. "What do you mean you have no idea how you got it?"

"Time skip," I said, then remembered I'd never actually explained properly to her what they were. I did, and she rocked back a little, blinking.

"So let me get this straight," she said. "You two went into the Valley, planning to get on the roads to investigate why the shadows are there—which, can I just say, is monumentally stupid, even if you did have unicorn wards—and sometime during the trip you just *happened* to take a detour, where you just *happened* to find the Book of Laws, which you just *happened* to be able to steal... Then time skipped and you ended up back here with a shadow?"

Scott shifted on the floor, loosening up a little, but didn't say anything.

"Yeah," I said. "Pretty much. Only," I reached over and took the book from her, holding the spine in my left hand and running my right fingers down the edge of the pages, feeling for the rough spot I'd found, "there's more. I think I know why we took the book."

My fingers snagged on the tear that made one of the bible-thin pages stick out just a fraction, and I flipped open to it. "I read the whole thing last night," I said as Scott scooted closer until he was kneeling by the bed.

I lay the book down on the bed between the three of us. "The book's pretty roughed up—I'm guessing it's torn in half because the fairies tried to stop us taking it, either that or the shadows, but why would the shadows want the book?" I shook my head. "There's stuff in here that will definitely help Quoise's bid for Keeper, I can see why she wanted it. But anyway, this section here," I said, tapping the page, "is the only part with a torn page. I think this might be what we were reading when we were interrupted."

"World Creators?" Gemma said, reading the title aloud as she and Scott bent over the page to read.

I closed my eyes and leaned back against the window, arms wound around my legs, fingers knotted.

She'd see it. Of course she'd see it. How could she not? And then, maybe then...

I worried at the inside of my lip.

Even with my eyes closed, I could still see them both: two visions of the night sky, one diamond stars studding the velvet darkness, the other the silhouette of a dark, treeless hilltop high above rolling hills in the dimness just before dawn.

"Scott," I said without really meaning to.

"Mm?"

"Why has your soulprint changed?"

Silence. The kind of silence that was utterly without pages scuffling, or people shifting, or even the sound of breathing. My pulse quickened and I tried to ignore the burning sensation of being scrutinised.

"When... When did it change?" His voice was low and husky, and he had to clear his throat.

"Right after you connected with Sanctuary."

"Has mine changed?" That was Gemma.

I hesitated. It wasn't a big change, not like Scott's, not something that changed the whole feel and character of her print. Still. "A little," I said softly. "Around the same time."

I'd always thought of soulprints as kind of a shortcut for someone's personality; Scott had been filled with emptiness and darkness when I'd first met him, a lingering sense of disquiet and vast, open spaces. But it was true: since he'd connected with Sanctuary, some of that metaphorical darkness had begun to fall away. He even seemed actually happy sometimes.

Gemma's soulprint I'd always taken to mean that she was bright and sparkly and a little annoying at first (that was the high-pitched sound on the edge of hearing and the feeling of being about to remember something important), but with hidden, comforting depths. And it was true that she'd been a little less sparkly of late, a little more cautious.

But surely that couldn't be everything. That felt too… small. The roads were full of the kinds of sensations that made up a soulprint, sights and sounds and smells and tastes and feels; there were so many possibilities, so many combinations.

That someone's soulprint could just… change, that it wasn't a fixed piece of something that uniquely identified them…

Could people really just change like that?

Gemma gasped, derailing my thought train. "No *way*."

"You said that," I said automatically.

"You really think Gemma's a world creator?" Scott said, and I didn't even have to open my eyes to know the exact tilt his head would have, part curiosity, part contemplation.

I opened them anyway. "Yeah." I rubbed the back of my neck. "And… The unicorn wards. We burned through five of them. I figure I must have used one back here to get rid of the shadow Anna said we brought, but… If we'd been on the roads just to check out the shadows, and they'd come, we wouldn't have hung around. We'd have used a ward each to get free if we had to, and we'd have left. I think…"

I swallowed and closed my eyes again. It was easier if I could pretend they weren't both staring at me hungrily, like I'd received a special revelation that they needed or something. "I think we went to the roads *after* reading this, to see if either one of us could make a world. Like Gem did."

"And could you?" Gem asked, and I felt the shift of her weight as she leaned forward.

"We don't know," Scott said levelly. "The time skip."

I heard him inhale, and when he didn't speak, opened my eyes to see him chewing consideringly on the inside of his cheek.

"What?" I said. "Just say it."

He lowered his brows. "You told us about the time skips the other day at school."

I frowned back at him. "Yeah?"

"They didn't affect you. You were in Sanctuary, you saw the time skips, and they didn't affect you."

My chest lifted and my frown cleared as I saw where he was going. "We *must* have been on the roads," I said, "because time skips in Sanctuary and the Valley didn't affect me."

He nodded, while Gemma glanced back and forth between us as though we were a particularly riveting tennis match. "So we were on the roads. We were probably trying to create a new world, but the shadows interfered. Has..." He paused to breath in, gaze flicking from one of my eyes to the other and back again. "Has it ever seemed to you like we could take the shadows with us when we travel?"

My eyebrows twitched down. "I don't think so. Gem?"

She shook her head.

Scott exhaled loudly. "I think we were trying to create a new world to put the shadows into, but either we couldn't make new worlds at all, or something went wrong and we shoved the shadow back here, instead."

My eyebrows lifted. "Actually, that makes perfect sense. Which means..."

I turned to Gem, adrenalin squirting into my stomach once more; if she said no, I wasn't sure I could bear it. I wasn't sure our *friendship* could bear it. "Gem," I said softly, searching out her eyes. "I know you don't want to go into Sanctuary while it's dangerous, and I'm not going to lie and say the roads are safer, because they definitely aren't. But the shadows are breaking into Sanctuary's heart, and Quoise has seen them in the Valley again. We can stop this," I said, leaning toward her. *Please. Please say you'll help.* "But we need your help." I glanced from eye to eye. *Please.*

She took in a deep breath and exhaled slowly through her lips. "Yeah," she said. "Yeah of course." She shook her head gently, blinking. "This is bizarre, you know. You're supposed to be the one with fancy powers," she said, nudging my knee with hers.

I was so relieved I could only give her half a smile; a full one would have blinded her. "Funny." Ah, what the heck. I launched myself at her and tackled her backwards, squeezing her tight.

She shrieked, but hugged me back.

"Thanks," I mumbled into her shoulder.

"Duh," she said softly.

"When you two are finished rolling around on the bed," Scott said pointedly, standing up and striding to the door.

I laughed and sat up, pushing Gemma off the bed with my legs.

She squeaked, flailing, but clung to the doona and managed to avoid thumping onto the ground. She got her feet under her and joined Scott at the door.

I bum-shuffled to the edge of the bed. "There's one other thing," I said, breathing deeply, filling my lungs right up, stomach tingly.

Anticipation washed over me, and I felt my eyes light up as Scott and Gem paused, looking at me curiously. "You guys," I said breathily, "the roads are *alive*. Like, sentient-alive. The roads can think. They can *communicate*."

I pressed my fingers to my cheeks. Sentient roads. Roads we could communicate with. The whole concept was so magical, my chest was going to explode.

"Alive?" Scott leaned forward, two tiny vertical lines marking the inner edges of his eyebrows.

Frogs. I'd forgotten about the roads stealing some of his memories. A lot of his memories. Glow thoroughly diminished, I nodded. "The book says so, anyway."

He nodded, just once, tightly. "So let's go talk to them." He vanished out into the hall.

"Yeah," I said softly as Gem exchanged glances with me. "Let's."

21

"AND WHERE ARE you three going?"

My heart sank as I paused halfway out the sliding door to the yard and turned back to Mum, who was in the hallway on the other side of the family room, a couple of steps away from my bedroom door. "Just outside," I said. "We'll stay in the yard. I promise." Scott and Gem busied themselves greeting Veve, trying hard to feign innocence.

Mum narrowed her eyes at me, lips pursed. "Is this the kind of 'staying in the yard' you did with Anna the other day?" she asked, sketching out the air quotes with two fingers.

Be cool, I told myself. *Don't lie,* my conscience told me. As a compromise, I just kind of stood there, heart hammering, forcing myself not to chew on my lip.

Mum snorted softly, closed her eyes with a wobble of her head, and pressed two fingers in between her eyebrows. "I am going to regret this," she muttered, before letting her hand drop and looking at me again. "Fine. I don't want to know, but fine. Stay in the yard. I am going down the road to pick up some groceries with your father, and if you are not physically, bodily present in that yard when I get home, I swear, you won't leave this house for a week apart from school. Okay?"

I nodded, little tiny bobs of my head.

Mum stared at me a moment longer, like she was wondering what exactly had possessed her to say what she had. Just as I was wondering if I should maybe go, or maybe say something, she deflated, shoulders rounding, and headed off down the hall toward the front door, her bedroom, and Dad.

I slipped out the sliding door, breathing out through rounded lips. "We're good," I said as Scott and Gem shot me questioning looks. "We have an hour, an hour and a half tops though."

Scott nodded briskly. "Let's get this show on the road then." He led the way around the corner of the house, striding purposefully.

I hung back for a second so I didn't have to walk right next to Gemma. I wasn't quite ready to forgive her for not believing me sooner.

We congregated by the prickly bushes in an odd triangle-circle-thing, and Veve tried to push her way into the centre. "I'm sorry," I told her as I shooed her away. "The roads aren't a good place for a dog."

Gemma snorted. "They aren't a good place for a person, either."

I ignored her. "You'll be safer here," I told Veve as I made her lie down on her mat on the edge of the paving. "And I'll take you for a nice big walk when we get back."

I rejoined Scott and Gem and lifted the sleeve of my shirt.

"I can do that," Scott cut in quickly.

I rolled my eyes. "Don't be ridiculous. I have a scab here ready to go."

"So do I," he said, and showed the back of his left wrist.

I would have placed real money on the fact that that scab hadn't been there when we'd got back from our little excursion yesterday. But before I could protest, Gem grabbed his elbow and he grabbed mine.

"We don't know how dangerous it is," he said. "We should share the load around." Without waiting for my reply, he flicked the scab away and closed his eyes.

I barely had time to close mine before we were in the Valley—and I had to admit, although it wasn't like I *needed* Scott to do the crossing for me, it *was* nice to arrive in the Valley without the usual swamp of nausea and dizziness. The decomposing smell was bad enough without adding the need to vomit to the mix.

I watched as Scott bent over with his hands on his knees, drew in one long breath, and straightened, shoulders square.

If I hadn't spent the last few months watching him closely, I wouldn't have seen the tightness around his eyes. I knew exactly what he was feeling, and how long it lasted—and he was doing a frogging good job of hiding it.

"Come on," Gem said, totally oblivious, having never done the crossing herself. "Time's a-wasting."

"Oh, so now you're in a hurry," I muttered, falling into line behind her as she set off through the trees, footsteps swishing in the yellowed tussock grass.

"Hmm?"

It wasn't worth a fight. "Never mind."

The muggy heat of the Valley seeped into our clothes, our hair, our shoes as we walked; before long we were all wringing wet and gleaming with sweat.

The still air was stifling, a thick pillow over my face, and yet again I cursed my lack of forethought: when all this was over, I was going to convince Mum to buy me one of those big, twenty-litre containers of water from the supermarket, the ones with the built-in tap, and I was going to stash it here near the entry point from my yard. I flicked a few strands of hair off my face and sighed.

"Never gets any comfier, does it," Scott said, glancing sideways at me.

I shrugged, staring mindlessly at Gemma's back, the way her shoulder blades moved as she walked, the shape of the sweat patch forming on her shirt. *It is what it is,* I would have said, if I could have been bothered moving my mouth.

The real problem, as I saw it, was how we were going to make sure we were back in the yard when Mum got home. Gem's mum, Mrs Caro, was a Time Master, like I was a Road Master: for most of us, travelling back to Earth meant a random time skip that might get us back on time, or late, or even earlier than we'd left (although that was far less common). In Sanctuary, if we got a fairy to manage the crossing for us, they could guarantee getting us back 'at the right point in our personal timeline', as they called it: if we'd spent half an hour in Sanctuary, they could ensure we got back to Earth half an hour after we left.

Mrs Caro, though, being a Time Master, could control the timing of the crossing perfectly, up to about five hours either side of travelling into Sanctuary (or the Valley, I assumed, though she'd never been there to help us travel back out of the Valley again). Mastery powers seemed to be at least a little genetic:

Gemma was a Time Master too, although not as strong as her mother; despite several years of practice, she could only control the timing of the crossing within about two hours.

Which meant our clock was now ticking: we had two hours, max, before Gemma would lose control of crossing back home, and we'd be subject to the totally random whims of travelling. We might arrive back before Mum got home—or we might not.

I frowned.

"What?"

I glanced over at Scott, who was looking curiously at me. "Just thinking," I said. "You know how when we travel back home, the timing can go off?"

He shrugged, pouting out his bottom lip. "Sure."

"Time skips," I said, twirling a finger around in the air to indicate the general vicinity.

He also frowned. "Maybe?"

Gemma halted abruptly, causing both Scott and I to crash into her. "*Probably*," she said. She glanced back at me as I rubbed the hollow of my shoulder. "Sorry. But it's a pretty big coincidence, don't you think?"

"Yes," I said, a littler snappier than I'd intended. "That's why I said it."

"Hmm." She set off again and, rolling my eyes, avoiding Scott's pointed looks in my peripheral vision, I followed.

Fifteen minutes later we were at the entry to the roads, and only a handful of seconds later, the muddled, glorious chaos surrounded me. I blinked slowly, even though I saw the same things with my eyes closed as open: flashes of tangerine in darkness; the bright light of early sunrise; a gleaming silver reflection.

As ever, other sensations bombarded me too: the sound of a car pulling away; the gentle, inconsistent knocking of someone rummaging around a floor above your head; a flock of screechy birds heard from far away.

The taste of a perfectly ripe mandarin; the cloying feel of rancid oil on my tongue; the way cold, winter air tasted as you breathed it in.

Rough wool tugged past my fingertips; the warmth of a fire; the chill of a shadow.

That chill slithered down my spine and I shivered, gripping Gem and Scott's hands tightly.

I steeled myself with a breath. "Hello?"

I'd never spoken on the roads before; there'd never been anyone to speak to. Talking into the middle of the chaos of sensation felt about as useful as calling down an empty corridor at night—with the same prickly, not-quite-real feeling of being watched. I shrugged my shoulders back in circles, trying to get rid of the prickling.

Through the overwhelming sensations, a breath of air brushed against my cheek, so real I lifted my hand to touch it—only to be pulled back by Gem, gripping firmly.

The air smelled fresh, minty—like Aphros.

Hello? I sent.

Nothing.

"Hello?"

The breath of air again, amid the smell of sausages barbecuing, the feel of soft, freshly moisturised skin, the exact colour of the roses we'd had outside our house in Melbourne.

Well. It was as good a direction as any, so I set. off, following the breath of air, Scott and Gemma clutched tightly at my sides.

It was as impossible as ever to keep track of passing time on the roads, but with Scott and Gemma prompting me every minute or so to keep moving, before too long—twenty minutes, maybe?—we reached a place where the sensations of the roads seemed to dim a little, as though being filtered through fog that grew denser and denser as we walked.

The path we were following began to climb steeply; although you tried hard not to think too much about 'up' and 'down' in this place, it was impossible to ignore the sharp angle when your knees and thighs protested with every step.

It dawned on me that I could see a little of Scott and Gemma on either side of me: not just their soulprints, but their actual, physical shapes. "Hello?" I said, pressing one hand against the stitch in my side, a little breathless. "Can you guys hear me?"

They turned toward me, Gemma beaming and throwing her arms around my neck, Scott half-smiling and running a hand through his hair.

"But what does this mean?" Gem said when she'd finished impersonating my collar. "Why can we see you? How?"

"I don't know," I said softly, staring around. I detached Gemma's hands from my arm and took a few steps forward. The strange, grey fog had gathered thicker around us, muffling the overwhelming sensations of the roads, creating a kind of curtain around us. "Hello?" I ventured again.

Hello.

The answer was soft, barely there, and, I suspected, mostly in my head. "Did you guys hear that?" I murmured.

They shook their heads.

An overwhelming sense of shyness flooded over me, and it took a second before I thought to question it. Why was I shy all of a sudden? What was I shy *of*?

Oh. It wasn't me feeling shy; it was me sensing shyness with my road mastery.

Carefully, I separated the feeling from my own thoughts, reminding myself that I was feeling perfectly okay, that it wasn't me that was worried or nervous, drawing in a long breath and slowly letting it out through pursed lips. My heart still knocked at my chest regardless. "It's okay," I said, for the benefit of whoever it was that was feeling nervous. "We won't hurt you."

The sense of something peering at me from around a corner, or up from under a table, or out from under a blanket, or possibly all three sensations at once.

I rubbed my temple with two fingers.

"What is it?" Gemma said softly.

"I don't know," I murmured back. "Might be the roads."

Yes, came the reply. *Yes, we are the roads.* A bundle of sensations accompanied the thought, a dim, scaled-down version of the experience of actually being on the roads. *Why are you here?*

I took a deep breath. "To help." I hadn't meant to say that, but it was the answer, truth at its most simple.

The roads recoiled a little. *With what are you here to help?*

"The shadows," I said. "The shadows are taking over again, and we think there might be a way to stop them."

"This is really weird," Gemma muttered behind me.

"Shh," said Scott.

The shadows, said the roads. It shivered, grimacing, horrified. *Please. Please get rid of them.*

"We want to," I said. "But we're not sure how. Do you think we could create a new world to put them in? Would that contain them?"

Yes! the roads said, leaping forward hungrily. *Yes, the other, the one with you, she is a World Dreamer, she is stronger than the ones before, she can do it!*

"Roads confirm you're a World Dreamer, Gem," I murmured. "And they think you're strong enough to dream up a new world to stuff the shadows into."

Her grip on my hand tightened. "I'm afraid."

I squeezed her hand back. "Me too." Because sure, okay, Gemma could create a new little world just for the shadows; but how would we get the shadows *in* there? I had a sinking feeling it would involve me, and my road mastery, and using myself as bait.

We were going to need a *lot* more unicorn wards.

The roads shuffled nervously—or at least, my road mastery received the sensation of nervous shuffling, again with that sense of having multiple images of a similar-but-not-identical concept thrown at me at once. *The shadows...*

More nervous shuffling.

"What about them?" I said, trying to keep my voice kind without slipping into 'older person talking to a small child' voice.

They're... they're breaking into Sanctuary.

"I know," I said, and even though I did, adrenalin still stabbed my chest. "We saw."

You have to hurry, the roads whispered. *Please?*

Maybe a small child wasn't such a bad comparison after all. I rubbed my temple again as the roads' multiple layers of imagery squished my brain into a pretzel. "We need to get home first," I said. "Prepare properly. I need more unicorn wards."

No!

I cringed as sensations drowned me, anger and pain, terror, desperation, dark shapes looming over me, branches threatening to hit me.

No, the roads repeated, gentler this time, a loving touch on my cheeks, a tight, sweaty grip on my hands. *Please. You must do it now. Otherwise it will be too late, and Sanctuary will be gone.*

"We have no wards," I said. "No protection." But my chest ached at the desperation the roads were projecting, and tears born of a frustration that wasn't mine threatened to fall.

Please. We'll help you. We can keep the shadows from eating you. We can. But please. Please help us now. Please.

The tears fell.

Wordlessly, Gem wrapped her arm around my shoulder.

"Are you okay?" Scott asked in a low voice.

I nodded, fighting back the heavy misery of the roads that weighed down my chest like a rock. "We have to try," I said. "Now."

"Now!" Gemma squeaked. "But—"

"Please," I said, and I didn't know if the word was mine or if it came straight from the roads through my mouth. I sagged. "Please."

That one was mine. I took a deep breath. "The roads say they can prevent the shadows from eating us." Eating us. Great terminology, thanks for that image there, roads. I sighed. "Let's just do this and get it over with." I gave Scott and Gem the best smile I could manage, a thin-lipped thing that never reached my eyes. "Please."

Gem stared at me a moment longer, her own eyes tight, afraid. She swallowed; she nodded. "Okay." Her voice was hoarse.

"I'm with you," Scott said, lacing his fingers through my free hand.

I squeezed it gently. "Thanks."

22

MY PULSE FLUTTERED in my chest like a bird, so fast I might as well have sprinted the whole way here from Sanctuary. But the roads had said that it was nearly too late for Sanctuary—and we'd seen that for ourselves. I exhaled slowly and shot Gem a tight smile. "You ready?"

She nodded, thin-lipped and serious.

"Do you even remember what you did last time?" Scott said quietly.

I nearly snapped at him—the last thing we needed right now was buzzkill negativity—but seeing the concern in his eyes, I realised he hadn't meant it like that.

And anyway, Gemma nodded. "Yeah," she said, hands fisting at her sides. "I think so."

I exhaled firmly this time. "Okay. So here's the plan: a few steps away from here, I'm going to lose sight of you guys. Scott, you're on communications. Gemma's going to be too busy to keep me moving if we do need to move—or, you know, run, if it doesn't work. Whatever you do, don't let us get separated."

I waited until he nodded, then turned to Gemma. "Gem. I don't think it's going to take long for me to attract the shadows' attention, so maybe get started right away. How long is it going to take you to create a new world for me to throw them into?"

She frowned, then scrunched her eyes closed, mouth bunching side to side as she thought. "Less than five seconds."

I nodded. "Good. Okay. So maybe wait for my signal then, because there's no point you being ready too early."

"But Edge," Gemma said, eyes round. "From what I remember of last time, there's no real difference between imagining the place and travelling to it. How are we going to draw all the shadows with us at once?"

I bit the side of my lip. "We can't, I guess. We'll have to do it in waves. I'll grab as much of the shadows as I can to drag through with us, and we'll just have to keep doing it till it works. I'll... I'll squeeze once when I see the shadows, and then a good, hard squeeze when it's time to go."

Gemma nodded, though her eyes were still too round.

Scott shook his head. "I don't like this. We should go see Aphros first, get more wards—"

"We don't have time," I said, cutting him off with a sharp look. He'd given the last one we had to Gemma; I had my road mastery, and Scott had insisted that he was disposable, whereas if Gemma was taken by the shadows, we'd have no hope at all. I didn't like it, but I had to admit his reasoning was sound. "The roads said Sanctuary could fall at any moment," I continued. "We have to do this now." I inhaled deeply and held it.

Scott nodded.

I breathed normally again. "Okay," I said. "Let's go." I Scott's hand, and together the three of us stepped forward.

Within three paces, Scott and Gemma were misty outlines at my sides, and the sensory stimulus of the roads began knocking against my senses.

Cold wind. The sound of traffic. Horse's hooves clopping on a stone path. The smell and taste of dust. Baking sunshine as insects chirped and whirred.

I squeezed my eyes shut. Another step, two more, three. I couldn't see the others now, but their soulprints were there: twinkling stars in a velvet night, the high-pitched whirring noise overlaying it; dawn over rolling hilltops, grassy silhouettes all the way to the end of night.

I turned my attention forward. Somewhere out there were the shadows.

A hot orange sunset; rippling emerald satin; a waterfall, pattering into a limestone pool; the sweet taste of purified water; the smell of bitter coffee grounds.

Scott squeezed my hand.

Shadows. I needed the shadows.

Once before, I'd sent my road mastery out away from me on the roads; maybe that would attract the shadows, if I could make it noisy enough.

Slowly, carefully, breath light and shallow, I eased my awareness forward and away from my body. The world spun for a moment. I pushed forward as the dizziness subsided, something silvery and transparent crinkling and crackling around me, like pushing through cellophane.

Yes. This was what it had felt like last time, and that had been noisy enough to distract the guardians of the roads. Hopefully... I pushed further forward, my body somewhere behind me reeling and swaying.

There: a patch of darkness, the sense of being stared at.

I pushed toward it.

Somewhere, bile rose in my throat.

Come on, shadows. Come and get me.

The darkness mounted in front of my road mastery, like slow clouds boiling. A tendril of shadow broke away and waved toward me.

I darted back before it could touch me—touch my road mastery.

The shadowy tendril hesitated for a moment, then followed, bolder, more confident.

I eased backward further, closer to my body one hair's breadth at a time.

The tendril stretched and lengthened, keeping pace with me—but the rest of the shadows stayed away, and I had the sense that they weren't too interested.

I had to *make* them interested.

But how?

If only I had a ward on me. Even though the shadows didn't like the wards, they definitely *reacted* to them.

But then, it wasn't the ward so much as me activating it; could I mimic that, somehow, with just my road mastery?

I braced myself and *flowed*, the same way I did when I was flowing my power into a ward—only this time, I just flowed *out*.

Silver light surrounded me and nausea gripped my stomach in a vice like I was vomiting out my insides—but I had the shadows' attention, for sure.

Their susurrus began: "*Eat your life, so sweet, so sweet your life, want to drink your life.*"

I hauled my road mastery toward me as they closed in. The smell of roses and the tinkling, other-worldly melody filled my senses.

Shadows leapt toward me.

My road mastery collided back into my body with the force of a two-storey drop. I gasped, then gasped again as I saw with my eyes rather than my road mastery the shadows leaping over and over each other, a pack racing toward me.

I swallowed hard, and tugged on Scott's hand.

Five.

My heart pounded.

Closer, closer.

Four.

Sweat trickled down my temple. Scott's hand was slippery against my palms.

Three.

I swallowed, trying to wet my mouth. Just one. I only had to grab one shadow.

Two.

That one, the one at the front.

How the frogging elephants had I grabbed onto it last time? And why the froggity frog-frog couldn't I remember?

One.

The shadow touched my outstretched hand.

I closed my fingers, and my road mastery, hanging on with all my might.

The world spun.

There was a brief flicker of a grey-fog world like the one Gemma had made last time.

The world lurched.

My stomach emptied, burning my throat and sinuses with acid. We were back on the roads, the shadows a little way from us but closing the gap again fast.

Three.

Two.

One.

I grabbed the lead shadow again and clamped down with my road mastery, forcing a connection between us.

The world spun.

Grey.

A lurch.

More vomit.

Back on the roads, the shadows ahead once more.

Time skips. Somehow, instead of staying in Gemma's created world, we were bouncing back onto the roads, and it was causing a brief time skip.

Thank goodness, I added, swallowing down stomach acid again as the nearest shadow made contact and the cycle began again. Because if it wasn't for the skip, the shadows would have us.

Grey.

Lurch.

Retching this time, my stomach too empty to bring up anything else.

I wiped my mouth with the back of my free hand, panting as the roads appeared again, shadows a little way ahead and gaining.

We were alive, but for how much longer? I only had to slip once, miss a shadow...

Gemma only had to miss the timing once, and the shadows would be on us for good.

My heart was going to break my ribs in a second.

Shadow contact.

Squeeze Scott's hand.

World spinning.

Grey.

Lurch.

Retch.

Breathe for five seconds until it starts again.

I couldn't keep this up much longer.

The lead shadow reached me. I reached for it. We connected— and something slipped, like I'd overbalanced, lost my footing.

The shadow leapt up my arm, triumphant. *"Your life, so sweet your life!"*

That's it, I thought, exhausted, detached. *We're done for.*

Stop! A voice shouted through the chaos, piercing my eardrums. *Stop!*

The voice was in my head, even though my ears hurt. Was it me? Was I screaming?

This is how they died! the voice screeched. *This is how they died! We can't let you die too!*

Ah, I thought, watching the shadow envelope my elbow. Not me. The roads.

Trust me, I sent back. *I'd stop it if I could.* But all I could do was keep watching, chest aching, throat burning, as the shadow gulped at my shoulder.

Vaguely, I realised it was cold.

23

FIRE BURNED OVER us, so hot in comparison to the shadow my skin felt immediately crisped. I shrieked, ducking, arms shielding my head. Scott and Gem did the same.

But the fire was only warm, not blistering hot, and as I peered out through slitted eyelids, I realised I had my arm back. The shadows screamed, fleeing as fast as they could, leaping over each other and away.

When they were gone at last, the fire vanished. Grey fog thickened around us.

The air felt suddenly cool.

I stood up, heart still pounding as the adrenalin worked its way through my system. I opened my mouth, but it was dry; my tongue wouldn't work. So I swallowed, worked my mouth, swallowed some more, and when I could finally speak through cracked, split lips, I said, "What do you mean, you can't let us die *too*? Who else has died trying to do this?" *And why didn't you tell us before?*

The fog thinned and sensations from the roads out there began to leak through: chocolate sponge cake on my tongue, teal green plastic, air-conditioning humming, a shout.

"Go keep watch," I muttered to Scott and Gem. "Let me know if anything comes."

They nodded and headed off behind me, one left, one right.

"Roads?" I said.

Still nothing.

I tossed my head, straightened to full height. "Answer me!" My hands clenched at my sides.

The firsts, came the hesitant reply. *The firsts died trying to save me.*

"The first what?"

A deep breath, like a rush of air before storm, or the tide sweeping in through narrow rocks. *Many people have stumbled upon us,* the roads said, and visions of hundreds of thousands of people of all ages and heights and ethnicities and builds swept over me, leaving me reeling like I'd been plunged into the middle of a bottomless crowd. *But only for a short slice of time. They come, they vanish, and while they are here, for only an instant, we see what is in their head, what is in their minds.*

"And you take it," I said. "You steal people's memories."

The roads gave simultaneous images of cringing and shaking heads. *No! No, we do not steal! We borrow! Only borrow.*

"But they don't get them back again," I said, thinking of Scott's diary, with all his missing information recorded in it. "Once you take the sensation from them, they don't have it any more, and they never get it back."

They can regain it, the roads pleaded. *They can experience these things anew. How can they, who have so many of these experiences, who are always gathering new ones, constantly, forever... How can they begrudge us one or two, when we have nothing, when we go nowhere, when we experience nothing that is not brought to us by others?*

I scrunched my eyes tightly. "They can't get all of them back," I said. "Not the important ones." First kisses, parents or friends now dead, or even just moved away, favourite childhood memories... There were plenty of things you couldn't repeat again.

I swallowed. "Who died? Who were the firsts?"

Nodding, eagerness. The roads continued: *Many people visit, but only fleetingly. From all lands they come. But then came the one, the first one, and we could not draw memories from him. And then he brought another, like him, and together they travelled our lengths until finally they found us here, and met us, and talked with us, and from them we learned many things.*

But then the third one came, and although we could draw memories from him, he was different. We didn't know how until one day, they stepped from us to return home, and landed... somewhere else.

"Sanctuary?" I asked, imagining it as clearly as I could in case the roads were sensing what I was thinking.

Agreement, longing, sorrow. *Yes. The place you now call Sanctuary. The... the place where they took the shadows, and hid them.*

"But someone broke the rules," I said, recalling conversations with Quoise, with Viri—and the Book of Laws. "And the shadows were set free."

Yes. Pregnant silence; a blank wall. The roads were hiding something—presumably the identity of whoever had broken the rules.

"The firsts," I said instead, heading back toward something it seemed like the roads might actually discuss. "How did they die?"

Because... because they locked away the shadows, and when the containment broke, the shadows took them first. Because they were angry, the shadows, for being contained.

So, two road masters and a world dreamer had travelled the roads that first time, whenever that had been, and had dreamed up Sanctuary, then trapped the shadows there.

Plausible, I supposed, but it felt like a key piece of the puzzle was still missing. I frowned. "So where did the shadows come from?"

The fog around me froze; I stood in a grey cocoon, sightless, soundless, alone.

"Roads?" My heart hammered in my chest, as though it knew the answer. "Where did the shadows come from?"

The fire flashed around me again, burning bright. Anger lashed at me, hot and terrible.

My heart pounded, my nails bit my palms, adrenalin shook me and tears leaked down my cheeks—but I stood steady, chin raised, waiting for the roads to calm.

At last, the maelstrom subsided.

Us, the roads sent, tiny, forlorn, hopeless, abandoned. *The shadows are ours.*

"Yours?" I said, wide-eyed, hands hanging loose as I tried to process what the roads were suggesting. "But how can they be *yours?*"

In the beginning, the roads said, *we were not careful. We did not know to be careful. We took any sensations, all of them, anything we could find. We were...*

Hunger filled me, the kind of deep-seated ache and longing that came from living half-starved your entire life. I nodded. "I understand," I said quietly. "And then?"

A battery of sensations assaulted me: bad experiences, pulled from the heads of the people who walked the roads: grief, regret, longing; prickling of the spine, someone watching from behind, echoes in an empty hallway, a presence in the dark, creaking floorboards, a bloody face, a body more meat than human—

"Stop, stop!" I hugged my head, covering my ears and eyes. "Please! Stop!" I had enough images like this of my own; I didn't need to add any more.

The bombardment stopped, a tentative apologetic feeling drifting toward me.

"It's fine," I said, still breathing heavily through my nose, letting an imaginary river wash away the thoughts of blood and death, just like the police psychologist had taught me. The river turned red in my thoughts; I made it deeper, stronger.

I exhaled slowly. "You stole bad thoughts from the others," I said, eyes still firmly closed, hands pressed against my cheeks. "And they overwhelmed you." Dots connected in my head, understanding lighting me up. "The shadows are the bad thoughts?"

Affirmation.

"And you tried to lock them all away in Sanctuary, or the Valley I guess, but they... got out?"

Yes, was the barely-audible reply.

I sighed. I knew a thing or two about those kind of thoughts, and it wasn't too hard to imagine them taking over and becoming just like the shadows. Thank goodness I'd had the psychologist to train me. I rubbed the centre of my forehead. I was *pretty* sure I remembered how she'd taught me, but I hadn't memorised it or anything; it wasn't like I'd expected to one day have to teach someone else.

You... you have to get rid of us, the roads said, but the images that accompanied the thought read more 'murder and destroy' than the bland 'get rid of'.

"No," I said. "No. I can help you. We can find a way to deal with this. I can teach you how to deal with the shadows. If you want me to," I added belatedly.

It is too late. The shadows have nearly pierced the heart of Sanctuary. We can hold them off a little while longer, and the heart is strong... But you are running out of time. We are running out of time. You must destroy us.

"But what about putting the shadows into a new world?"

It will not hold them, not forever, and when they break out again they will be stronger than before. The roads' echoing voice was heavy with despair. *The rules will be broken. They always are.*

"I can help you," I said, throat tight. "Please, just let me help you."

You cannot. You cannot help us.

Someone tapped my shoulder. I jumped. "It's been nearly two hours," Gemma said in a small voice.

Frogging frog it all. Frogging elephants. Elephanting frogs, too, for good measure. Urgh. I clenched my fists. "I can help you."

Darkness flashed over us, thick and absolute—but just as suddenly, it was gone.

"What was that?" Gem asked.

Well? I asked the roads.

The heart, it replied, with golden light and warmth. *The heart has fallen.* The golden light dimmed to shadow-black.

I inhaled sharply. "Sanctuary?"

A chorus of heads shaking. *Not yet. But soon.*

"How soon?"

"Edge, I don't know what they're saying, but that darkness wasn't good," Gem said.

"What's going on?" Scott had rejoined us, peering intently around.

I exhaled in exasperation. "I know it wasn't good!" I said, holding up my hands. "The shadows have reached the heart of Sanctuary!"

"What?"

"Oh no! Are they in Sanctuary yet? Can we stop them? Edge, we don't have long until they take over entirely," Gem said.

"I know!" I said. "Just shoosh for a second, will you?"

They subsided and I turned away from them, back to the roads.

"How long do we have? Until the shadows take over completely?"

A storm building on the horizon; the whistle of a kettle growing louder and louder; a pin, drifting in slow, inexorable motion into the skin of a balloon.

"I *know*," I said. "How *long*?"

Confusion; uncertainty; the sense of time as an infinite, unravellable loop.

Hesitant fingers on my shoulder. "A few hours, at most," said Gem quietly.

I turned to her. "How do you—" My road mastery took her in. "Oh." The dark cord that threaded away from her soulprint, her permanent connection with the power of the Valley, was steady—but, I realised, with a jolt of panic, the glowing gold cable that signified her connection with Sanctuary was dimming.

I swallowed. "Okay," I said hoarsely. "Okay." There was no way I'd be able to convince the roads to listen to me in only a few, short hours, no way I could try to teach it everything the psych had taught me—and it had taken me weeks of practice for the techniques she'd offered to start working. It was too late. *We* were too late.

I should have come three weeks ago.

How do we destroy the shadows? I sent to the roads.

The only way you can. A pause, a sense of vast horizons, time unravelling. *You must destroy us.* A sense of floating, flying, freedom. *Please*, the roads said. *Please promise you will help.*

I set my jaw. *Yes*, I sent. *Yes, I will help.*

So. A few hours to figure out how to completely destroy the roads, in order to destroy the shadows, in order to save Sanctuary—and the Valley—and, assuming the shadows would try to leak out and corrupt the Earth as well, the world.

Three hours to save the world.

It had been nearly two hours since home; regardless of anything else, we had to head back first so Gemma could control the timing of the crossing.

Home, then three more hours. I just loved deadlines involving actual death.

2 4

MY BACKYARD FADED into view and I searched the sky frantically for signs of the time.

But there were no shrieks from the house, no one waiting to pounce on us and cling to us and tell us desperately that they'd been looking for us; the sun was still midway up the sky, and it looked like we'd beat Mum home after all. Gemma had done it. I sagged with relief.

"So what now?" Scott asked, running a hand through his hair with a wide grip.

I frowned, though not at him. There was still someone who should have noticed our return. "I don't know," I said. "Wait here a sec, I just need to check something."

I left him and Gemma at the prickly bushes, and ducked around to the back of the house. "Veve?" I called. "Puppy?"

Nothing. I slid the door to the family room open and stuck my head inside. "Veve?"

Anna strolled out of the bathroom, hair wrapped up in a towel, heading toward her bedroom. "Not in here," she said, frowning. "I thought she was out with you."

"Yeah," I said. "Of course." I closed the slider, heart hammering at my chest. "Come on, Veve," I muttered. "Where are you?"

But she wasn't around the far side of the house near the laundry, or in her kennel, or anywhere else in the yard, and by the time I got back to Scott and Gem, my chest was tight, icy adrenalin zipping through my veins.

"Veve's gone," I said before Gem could speak.

"She might just have got out the gate, though," Scott said, eyebrows drawn.

I closed my eyes and nodded, swallowing hard against the lump in my throat.

"I'm sorry, Edge," he said, stepping closer and squeezing my shoulder awkwardly. "But we have to stay focused. You know what the roads said: we only have a couple of hours to fix this, or we lose Sanctuary for good."

"I told you we had to hurry," I said blindly. I swallowed again until I was sure the tears wouldn't fall, then glanced at Gem. "We should have been working on this weeks ago."

Gem shrank. "I know. I'm sorry. I was afraid." She straightened and lifted her chin. "And with good reason, look what's happened to Veve. I suppose you're just sad it wasn't me this time."

"Don't be ridiculous," I snapped, right as Scott said, "We don't even know the shadows have got her."

"Of course we do," I said, glaring at him. "The gates are shut, Anna thought she was in the yard." I tensed as our car pulled into the driveway. We were back on time, but what would Mum say when she found out Veve was missing again?

"That doesn't prove anything," Scott said, while Gemma cut in: "It doesn't matter. We have to save Sanctuary."

"I know!" I shouted, stepping back with my hands fisted. "I told you that! I tried and I tried to tell you that, but you wouldn't listen to me, and now we only have a couple of hours left and Veve is gone, and I'm not sad it wasn't you, I'm just sad that you wouldn't *believe* me! But if you still don't want to help, then fine! Go! Just go!" And despite my best intentions, I burst into tears.

"Um, Edge?" said Gem. She pointed at the prickly bushes.

Veve's dark red leather collar, snagged, still buckled, in their thorns.

Scott stiffened—but not at the collar, he was facing the house still.

I turned toward him and realised why: Mum was emerging from around the corner, pale and tense. "They're coming," she said before I could speak. "We have three hours at most before we have to be packed and gone."

"Who's coming?" I said stupidly, dazed. Veve. I had to find Veve.

Scott stepped forward, shoulder to shoulder with me, as Gem gripped my other arm painfully tight. "No," she said. "No, you can't go."

"I'm sorry, Gem," Mum said. "But you know we have no choice. I'm so sorry." She stared at the three of us for half a second before shaking her head. "You two need to get home. The police will come to see you soon to talk you through things."

Scott's jaw twitched.

"We can't go," I said, stomach clenched, chest tight.

"Emma, don't do this," Mum said, voice steady, but nostrils quivering. Her bottom lip trembled as she stopped, then twisted as she jutted out her chin and worked her mouth. "You know we have no choice. Your friends—" She drew in a breath. "Scott and Gemma need to go. And you need to come in to pack."

Dizzy.

The edges of my vision blacked, but I clenched my hands and stared at Mum. "Veve's gone," I said. "The shadows have her. I have to find her."

Mum's breath hissed inward. She shook her head, face crumbling. "Edge," she whispered. "We don't have time. I'm sorry. We have to go."

Was I doused in ice, or burning in fire? Both at once, it seemed. *"I am not going without my dog."*

Mum swiped the corner of her eye, jaw twitching as she fought for control. "Gemma," she said, and I turned to Gem in surprise.

"Yes?" she breathed.

"Is it true? That you can get Emma back before she leaves? When you cross to Sanctuary, I mean."

Gemma knit her brow, lips stretched and thin. "No," she said. "That's my mum. I can get us back an instant after we left, though, if I'm concentrating hard and everything goes right."

Mum focused Gemma in a laser-beam stare. "Then make sure it all goes right."

I inhaled sharply. "You mean...?"

"Go," she said, turning on her heel and stalking back to the house. "Be safe," she threw back over her shoulder. "Find Veve."

I exchanged glances with the others.

"Two hours," Gem said. "I can only control the crossing within two hours."

"We only have two hours anyway," Scott said. "Or the shadows will have won."

I whirled to face the bushes, grabbing my friends by their shoulders. "Two hours," I said grimly, "is enough. Let's go destroy some roads."

2 5

APHROS, I CALLED as we hiked through the Valley toward Sanctuary's Lodge. *Veve's missing. I think the shadows took her from my yard. Have you seen anything?*

Silence for a moment, except for the swish-crackle-thud of our footsteps through the yellowed, brittle grass clumps, then, *You are right. The shadows have her. She is alive, but they have her trapped. I am sorry, Edge, but the only way to save her is to vanquish the shadows, and I am not certain that can be done again this time. Already they have taken over the heart of Sanctuary.* She sighed. *We will fall. I can hold them at bay for a little while, but unless a more permanent solution can be found, Sanctuary will fall for good, and Veve with it.*

I bit my lip. No. Veve was not going to die. Not here, not today. And neither was Sanctuary.

Everything rested, really, on figuring out a way to get rid of the shadows. The roads had told me that the only way to destroy the shadows was to destroy the roads themselves, but honestly, I wasn't sure that was even possible.

And even if we did get rid of the shadows, what about the Valley's glowy heart? The pillar of light might not have caused the shadows, but it certainly didn't hesitate to use them, and it killed Scott's mum and nearly killed him, and it had tried to suck the life right out of Gemma.

That didn't match with the sense I'd got of what the Valley had been like back when it was green, and not black.

I tugged on the tips of my hair in frustration. I was missing something, some jigsaw piece of information that would snap the picture into focus for me—and I had two hours to figure it out. Maybe less, if Veve was in physical danger right now, though from what Aphros had said, I didn't think she was.

My frustrated reverie was interrupted by Scott and Gem stopping abruptly in front of me.

"Shhh," Gem said to me, even though I'd stopped and hadn't made a sound. "Look."

Through the trees right at the border of the Valley, right where the leaves that tickled my ear began deepening to fresh green, we peered through to the grassy avenue that led up to the Lodge. My heart pounded in my chest: thick swirls like sooty smoke spiralled up from the roof of the Lodge, and the usually white walls were greyed and dim. Instead of Sanctuary's usual smell of jasmine and salt water, everything smelled of ash.

"Is it burning?" Gem whispered near my ear.

I shifted, trying to get a clearer view. "I don't think so," I said, wiping a bead of sweat from my temple as my body cooled from the trek through the Valley. I tried my road mastery—and recoiled. Yup, definitely not smoke. "It's shadows," I said softly. "They're here."

Gem inhaled sharply, and Scott tensed. "Look," he said, indicating upward with his eyebrows.

I gasped. A ring of fairies had exploded out of the Lodge's roof, right where the spiral of shadows was most concentrated. The fairies circled the thickest branch of the shadows, wings flashing emerald and ruby and sapphire and magenta in the twilight of Sanctuary—even darker than usual because of the shadows.

One fairy cried out, and at her signal the others raised their arms, and I caught the flash and sparkle of the silver sceptres they'd wielded against us last month.

Another cry. Silver lightning shot from the sceptres.

The shadows shrieked, twisting upward, sucking inward, pinched at the waist where the fairies attacked them.

"I don't think we can help here," Gem said, then bit her lip.

Much as I hated to admit it, she was right. It was unlikely that Veve was in there, given she'd been taken through the portal to the Valley from the backyard, and there was little we could do to attack the shadows like the fairies were.

My stomach flipped. We couldn't attack them, yet somehow we had to get rid of them entirely. What in the world were we thinking?

The world shifted, a pearly sheen rolling over everything for the barest of instants, and the fairies disappeared, the shadows winding back to mere exploratory tendrils. A time skip.

I chewed the inside of my lip. If we could find a way to predict the time skips, or even cause one, it could be a serious advantage in our fight against the shadows—because although the roads had said that the only way to get rid of the shadows was to destroy the roads themselves, I was still pretty sceptical that a) we could even do that, and b) that it was really the only way.

I mean sure, the roads might have caused the shadows—sort of, without meaning to—but that didn't mean we had to kill the roads to destroy the shadows, did it?

Bad memories.

You didn't have to kill yourself to erase bad memories.

A shiver slid down my spine as I saw Georgia again, face bruised and battered, lying in her own blood.

I'd give quite a lot to be able to time skip back past that one. Which... The time skip just now had rewound the shadows' take-over of Sanctuary a little. Could we skip back far enough to erase it entirely?

Tempting, and probably full of complications. But regardless, even a small time skip could make a difference.

I exhaled through pursed lips. "The fissure," I said. Gem and Scott glanced at me. "If we can figure out how it's causing the time skips..."

Scott nodded grimly as Gemma inhaled. "Yeah," she said. "And I'm positive there's a link between them and the fact that time skips randomly when we travel between home and here." She nodded emphatically. "We need to know what's going on. Let's go."

I didn't smile, because the shadows had still taken over Sanctuary, and my dog was missing, and somewhere back at home literal, actual bad guys were hunting my family down... But my chest did lighten, because Gemma was with me, in every sense of the phrase—and it felt good to know my best friend had my back again.

26

THE FISSURE THAT cleaved the meadow in two had widened even further since I'd seen it a week ago, now easily six good, long paces across, its edges crumbling to reveal dark dirt and large rocks with veins of silver.

Well, probably not *actual* silver, but something that glimmered silver in Sanctuary's twilight. I tiptoed cautiously to the edge and peered in.

"Please be careful," Gemma said fretfully behind me.

"I am," I said. It was hard to tell in the dim lighting, but as I leaned over the crack in the ground, it looked like it was maybe— six, seven, eight—I tried to measure it out—maybe ten feet deep, narrowing toward the bottom in a V that meant it didn't really have a floor.

Possibly, I decided, the crack ran much, much deeper, and only as it widened would we see how deep it really went.

Hissing filled the air, and I leapt back, Scott grabbing my shoulder, Gemma snatching at my arm as pearly white fog issued from the crack like steam from a train funnel and a sweet, sharp smell enveloped us.

Around us, the world shifted a little, and even though there was no one nearby to measure it against, I was sure Sanctuary had just experienced another time skip.

"That was close," Gem said.

"Yeah," I said, shaking her off and stepping back to the edge of the fissure as the fog drifted away.

Time skips. Sanctuary had only started experiencing them since we'd returned from the roads with Helios, since the fissure had opened in the meadow—or maybe since Scott had used death magic—blood magic—there, clashing it against seed magic.

Before, we'd assumed that because the clash between blood and seed magic had caused big, booming earthquakes, it had caused the fissure too. But the fissure was clearly connected to the time skips, and maybe so was travelling, and...

Something niggled at my mind. The roads. The roads had seemed confused when I'd asked them how much longer we had until Sanctuary fell completely; they'd given me that sense of time as something cyclic, something looping, rather than something linear.

And.

Before Gem or Scott could protest or stop me, I sat down on the edge of the fissure, my feet hanging into the crack, my fingers digging deep into the thick, moist dirt of Sanctuary to make sure I didn't fall. But I had to get closer, because it was almost like I could hear something, or feel something, deep in the heart of the fissure.

"What are you doing?" Gem squeaked, but Scott shushed her gently.

"Trust her," he said, and I glowed just a little.

I closed my eyes and let my road mastery spool out around me, becoming gradually more aware of my surroundings, like tuning into background noises you hadn't realised were there until you stopped and made yourself listen.

Sure enough, the faint tug of sensations grew stronger—and it was coming from the bottom of the fissure.

I bounced my inner lip between my teeth. Did I dare? What if I was wrong?

"Gem," I said carefully. "You know how you said before that travelling was probably related to the time skips?"

"Yes," she said, matching my slow, careful tone as she sat down to my right, far enough back from the edge that I couldn't see her in the corner of my vision as I stared into the fissure.

"Elaborate," I said.

A waft of fog rose from the fissure, deep below my feet, pearly white and rising in a puff. It swept over me in an instant, cool and dewy and sweet-smelling, while the tug of sensations down in the fissure grew stronger.

I leaned forward a little, raising my chin as the fog lifted, as though a little of my stress and fear had gone with it.

Gemma released her painful grip on my shoulder and exhaled. "Are you okay?"

"Perfect," I said without turning to her, letting the corners of my mouth soften upwards. "Travelling?" I peered back down into the crack and watched as fog played down below. "Time skips?" I was so sure I was right.

Dirt bounced off the wall of the fissure as Scott sat beside me, peeling my the fingers of my left hand up out of the dirt and lacing them one at a time through his.

Gem cleared her throat. "Um. Yeah." She took a noisy, steadying breath. "Right. Well, obviously, every time this fissure does its... thing, Sanctuary skips back in time, maybe randomly, maybe in proportion to the amount of steamy stuff released, I don't know. And when we travel from Earth to Sanctuary—"

"Or the Valley," Scott added, and out of the corner of my eye I could feel him staring at our hands.

"Or the Valley," Gemma repeated. "When we travel from Earth to *here*, time is, I don't know, fluid. It's like the trip doesn't have a fixed length of time it should take, like the, the path we're taking to get from there to here changes length, or like there are multiple options for a path, different ways to get here." She shuffled forward to sit beside me, legs tucked firmly up underneath her as she risked a quick peek into the fissure and then straightened. "When I use my time mastery, it's like I can sense different paths in front of us, all going to the same place, and I can choose the shortest one. But the longer it's been, the fainter they become. And the stronger *I* get, the more paths I can sense."

I nodded. "Thanks," I said, using my free hand to unlace my fingers from Scott's. "That's what I hoped you'd say." I braced my hands against the dirt, tensed, and jumped into the fissure.

27

AS I FELL, I closed my eyes and twisted, the way I'd done in the heart of the Valley when I'd been twisting through dimensions looking for Gem. Only this time, I was twisting toward the roads.

I thudded to my feet—and sure enough, the roads whispered around me, my vision lighting up with tea-tree green, chocolate brown, autumn-leaf red, umber orange; my ears full of the sound of distant, rolling thunder, the faint drone of a TV, the keening, haunting cry of a black cockatoo; my skin prickling with ice-cold dread, a frost-laden breeze across my cheeks, the blast of an opening oven; my mouth full of the feel of melted butter, thick with the cloying sweetness of store-bought pastry cream, burning with the heat of a dry curry.

A smile spread slowly across my mouth, and then, before I could forget myself, I threw myself sideways, twisting again just as I'd done when I'd moved between dimensions—and, I suspected, exactly how I'd twisted when I'd fallen off the roads back into the front entryway of my house.

The cool twilight of Sanctuary washed over me, salty air breathing in from the ocean across the meadow, the calming nature of its atmosphere flooding my senses.

My smile widened.

Fifteen paces ahead of me, Gemma and Scott leaned over the edge of the fissure, Gemma sobbing so her shoulders shook, Scott gripping her arm, eyes tight, body rigid.

"Hey," I called. "Looking for something?"

They whirled, surged toward me, and as Gemma crashed into me, holding me tight, and Scott hovered for a split second before giving up and wrapping his arms around the both of us, regret surged through me.

"Hey," I said, wiping tears from Gemma's face. "Hey, it's okay. I'm fine."

Gemma flung herself away. "Why would you *do* that?" She scrubbed at her face, then glared. "We thought you were dead!"

Scott folded his arms around his chest, jaw set. "It was a pretty dumb thing to do."

"I'm sorry," I said in a tiny voice. "I didn't mean to scare you."

He nodded once, a jerky, upward movement. "I hope you found something worth risking yourself for."

I did a quick inhale-exhale and gave myself a mental shakedown. "Yeah," I said. "Yeah, I did. The fissure connects to the roads."

Gem's forehead wrinkled. "The roads? But then how did you get back here?"

I couldn't help it: I grinned, because this was our secret weapon, our trump card, the one thing that meant we actually stood a chance against the shadows. "Time skip." And it was now under our control, and we'd find Veve and find a way to beat the shadows, because we had all the time in the world.

"What do you mean, time skip?" said Scott, brow furrowing to match Gemma's.

"It's like Gemma said," I said, pacing back to the fissure. The others waited a second, then followed. "When we travel, we're not just skipping straight from Earth to here. We're using the roads. All of us, even if you're not a Road Master. That's probably why we have to use a sacrifice to travel, in order for it to work properly for non-Road Masters. Or maybe everyone who can travel is a Road Master," I added as the thought came to me. "Only their abilities are too weak to get on the roads properly, so instead they can just do a sort of slide, where they cross in and out again in an instant, getting onto the roads in one place," I said, gesturing to my left, "and getting off in another." I waved to the right.

Gemma nodded. "But what about the time skips?"

"Right." I grinned again. "So we know that when we travel, time can slip randomly. While I was talking to the roads, they showed me something. I asked them how long we had, until Sanctuary was lost, and they were confused, like they didn't understand what I meant by 'how long'. They showed me a bunch of images of time as a circle, or a loop. You know how the fairies say that you can get anywhere from Sanctuary?"

Gemma nodded, little enthusiastic bobs, while Scott continued his serious eyebrows.

"In all your years of coming here, have either of you ever met someone from another world? Have the fairies mentioned specifically other worlds? Like, individual, identifiable ones?"

My grin broadened further as they both shook their heads.

"The roads don't connect all *places*, you guys. They connect all *times*."

Gemma's eyes went saucer-wide, and even Scott looked a little awed. "No way," said Gemma. She pressed her fingers over her mouth. "But that makes so much sense, though. What you said." She shook her head. "It fits."

"Can we prove it?" Scott said.

I raised my eyebrows. "Do we need to? Isn't it enough that it works?"

"If we're going to use this to fight the shadows, no, it's not enough. We need to know what the limits of this are. How..." He stopped, clearing his throat. "How far back we can go, what we can change, what... impact it will have."

Oh. My chest constricted and tears prickled my eyes. I dug my pinky nail into the tip of my thumb to stop them spilling over.

I very much doubted that we'd be able to go back and save his mum, just like I doubted we really could rewind Sanctuary to a time before the shadows—and he probably did too. But I knew he needed to know if we could try.

Impulsively, I hugged him tight, pinning his arms against his body as he stood rigid.

He flashed me half a smile, though, as I let him go. "Yeah."

I nodded, screwed up my face to make sure nothing was going to leak, blinked a few times, and inhale-exhaled. "Right. What we are going to do is this. Someone is going to go fetch Mrs C so she knows what's going on, and in case we need backup. You guys can flip a coin. The other two of us will go back on the roads and try to figure out how we can force the time slips; I can't create a new world off the roads like Gemma can, but I can slip us off them back into the real world, and I need to see how much I can control that."

Gemma tossed her hair. "Well I'm not going back, you need me to handle the timing of the crossing."

Scott turned to her. "That's exactly why you need to go. What if I try to go back and get your mum and I end up hours late? That's not going to help anyone."

"But that's not fair! I—"

"Wait." I held my hands up at them. "There's another option here." I closed my eyes so I could concentrate and called. *Aphros? Are you there, can you hear me?*

Cool fog shushed out of the fissure again, lifting a stray hair off my face. Sweetness, like walking into the kitchen while Mum was making something with lots of icing sugar, with a hint of something sharp and sneezy underneath.

Aphros? I sent again, in case the time skip had erased my call to her.

Edge? Why are you here? It is not safe! You must leave Sanctuary, leave at once!

Aphros, we think we have a way to fix this, I sent, focusing on her mint-and-gold soulprint. *The fissure in the meadow is causing the time skips, and it's linked to the roads. We've found a way to control the time skips.* Sort of. *Aphros, we can do this. We can beat the shadows.*

Somehow. Without stuffing them into an alternate world, or destroying the roads. A somehow that would likely involve hunting down the shadows and destroying them one by one—for as long as it took.

Silence, my pulse thrumming in my ears.

What do you need from me?

We need someone to fetch Mrs Caro while we try to figure out how exactly this all works.

A snort. *I cannot fetch her.*

No, but could you find Quoise, and send her? And... I set my shoulders. *And we're going to need a lot of wards. As many as you can make. And fast.*

Gemma clutching at my arm tore my concentration away from my conversation with Aphros, and I opened my eyes. "We need to hurry," Gemma said in a low voice.

I followed her gaze up the slope to the Lodge—and my heart skipped. Dark shadows oozed out through every crevice, through every door and crack and window, the vines and blossoms that covered the Lodge withering, crackling to dust. The shadows drifted out of the Lodge, inexorable, unstoppable—and heading for the stables.

28

THE LODGE. DID that mean all the fairies were... That the shadows had them all? My jaw twitched. *Aphros, where's Quoise?*

She is well, Aphros replied. *I have her. She will get Maria. Please, hurry.*

"It might be time to try your escape route, Emma," Scott said from just behind me.

I glanced back at him, his mouth tight and eyes strained as he watched the shadows drifting slowly toward us down the slope. "Yeah." I said. "Let's go."

"Wait!" Gem clutched at my arm again, pointing away with her other hand. "The stables! Lily and Filibere!"

Adrenalin pumped through my stomach. "What are we going to do?"

"We can't do anything!" Scott said, trying to haul Gem and I back—but he was too late, and we were already sprinting toward the stables where the baby unicorns lived.

"Aphros says she and Quoise are in there with them," Gemma gasped out.

I flicked her a glance; I'd forgotten for a moment that she was connected to Aphros too. "Quoise is supposed to be going to get your mum."

"Fine," Gem panted. "She'll be safer back on Earth for now. Aphros reckons she can hold the shadows off them, but they trapped her last time. What do we do?"

I really did not remember this slope being so long. A stitch was burning in my side, and my throat hurt as I tried to gulp down air.

"I don't know." I'd seen Aphros hold the shadows at bay before—heck, we used her hair as a ward against them. But I also remembered clearly the very first time I'd seen Aphros, before I'd even known who she was, the time she'd dragged me over the border to the Valley and I'd cut her soulprint free from the shadows. She'd been trapped, and scared, and helpless. And yes, afterward, once her soulprint was detangled, she'd saved our butts—but while her soulprint was trapped, she'd been entirely at the shadows' mercy.

And Lily and Filibere were only babies.

We stumbled up to the darkened doorway of the stables, and I pressed my hand against the rough, wooden doorframe, leaning down as I fought for breath.

Gem pushed past me, brushing aside the grey cloth that functioned as a door.

I straightened so I could follow her—and Scott stopped me, gently pressing the back of his hand against my upper arm.

"We have to save Sanctuary," he said, eyes round and serious.

My gaze flickered between his eyes, left, right, left, right, noting again the flecks of yellow in the deep, woodsy brown.

"I know," I said. "But we have to save Aphros, too." And Veve, frog it all, but Scott was right, there: my best chance of saving Veve now was to save Sanctuary. Aphros, though, was right here. Her I could save right *now*. I turned and entered the stables.

Warm air full of the green sweetness of hay greeted me, soothing and comforting.

A large stall lay to either side of me, and at the end of the aisle, fifteen or so steps away, was the biggest stall of all, partially lit where the light drifted in through a gap in the corner of the roof.

Gem was already down there, palm pressed against Aphros's nose, face buried in Aphros's neck, while Quoise fluttered nearby, arms folded, blue wings flashing in the dim light.

The twins, Lily and Filibere, were curled up in the far corner, golden limbs entangled with each other, one foal's nose over the other foal's flank—asleep, I thought, until I drew close enough to see their wide, brown eyes staring up at us.

With my road mastery, I caught the flash of blue that was Lily, and the streak of copper that was Filibere. Otherwise, the two golden foals with their nubby, fuzzy horns looked identical.

"We have about five minutes," Scott said from just inside the door, arms crossed firmly over his chest. "The shadows are heading this way, but not too fast. Yet."

I drew in a deep breath, full of equines and hay and straw and dust. "Quoise is going back to Earth to get Mrs Caro," I said firmly. "You'll be safe there," I said directly to her. "Obviously come back if you can, but if you can't, we'll meet you in the glade."

I stepped up to Aphros, leaning my head against her neck on the opposite side to Gem. "Aphros," I murmured. "I know you can hold the shadows back for a while, but what if they trap you, like last time? What if they trap your babies?"

She trembled. "We will be fine."

But I caught the hesitancy underlying her words, and Gemma must have too, because she reached under Aphros's chin, searching for my hand.

I clung onto her fingers, my other hand twining through the roots of Aphros's mane. I took a breath and held it, scrunching up my face, searching for some alternative. But the plan I'd come up with was the best I could think of, and I couldn't see any other options. "Aphros," I said carefully. "You can stay here and try to fight them off. Or you can run somewhere else in Sanctuary, or the Valley." She could run fast, that was true. But would it be fast enough? And could she stay away for long enough?

Gemma's fingers tightened around mine.

"Or," I breathed into the soft, white hair of her neck, "you could come with us on the roads."

I'd been whispering, but the tension in the stall was so high that everyone had been quiet as a pin-drop anyway—and everyone tensed as they heard my suggestion.

"I know the shadows can get there too," I said, "but if we stick together, our chances are better. And Gemma and I can both twist us on and off the roads. We can get away. I need you," I added, and my fingers tightened in her mane. "I need you to help me figure out how to use these time skips to end the shadows once and for all."

Because I couldn't destroy the roads, and I meant that in two senses: one, I had zero clue how to even accomplish that, and two, how could I? How could I destroy them now, knowing that they were the only thing that enabled us to get to Sanctuary in the first place? If I destroyed the roads, we'd never see Sanctuary again.

And Sanctuary was a dreamed world anyway; it seemed at least possible that destroying the roads would mean Sanctuary would be destroyed forever as well. I was trying to *save* my second home, not endanger it further.

Which meant destroying the shadows somehow, which meant figuring out how to leverage the time skips to our advantage.

Scott was right: we had to figure out how far back we could go, and what we could fix.

I needed to get to the heart of the Valley, and I needed to get to it before the shadows did—the *first* time. "Please, Aphros," I whispered. "Come with us. Help us."

She snorted and shook her mane, brushing Gem and me aside. "Fine," she said. "I do not even know if it is possible, but for you, for them"—she pointed her horn at her foals—"I will try."

29

WHEN THE GREAT heart of the Valley appeared before us as we trekked along the roads, I thought at first that I'd done it, that I'd taken us all the way back in time before the shadows had appeared—but as we drew closer and the foals began to prop and start, nostrils trembling, tails and ears flicking uncertainly, I realised I was wrong.

The shadows weren't here, for sure, but that was because they weren't here *anymore*, not because they weren't here *yet*; the heart was black and silent, with no trace of green at all.

"I will wait outside," Aphros said as we reached the outer barrier of the chamber, curved round like that of Sanctuary, but grimy and charcoal grey instead of glowing gold. "With Lily and Filibere."

It had turned out that getting the unicorns on the road was no more or less complex than getting ourselves on the road—with the added bonus that I could actually see them as we walked. It was strange to have someone else visible, and not just as a soulprint, and we'd made excellent time with Aphros able to keep me moving. The whole thing was practically social, since Aphros could see not only me, but also Scott and Gemma, and so relay conversation back and forth between us.

But as we'd drawn nearer and nearer to the heart of the Valley, conversation had lulled, and even Scott and Gem reported feeling uncomfortable and grim.

"Okay," I said to Aphros, ignoring the way my heart pattered at my ribcage. No shadows here, nothing to be frightened of.

Memories of the glowing pillar of light swirled in my mind, the way it had sucked at my thoughts, my willpower.

But Gemma said the Valley's heart was quiet, and the connection she had to it through her soulprint didn't look any stronger than before to my road mastery.

I gripped Gemma's hand (and presumably she gripped Scott's), peeled the scab on my shoulder free, and stepped through the barrier into the heart of the Valley.

Thick, acrid smog covered me for an instant as I passed through, burning my sinuses, my throat. I emerged, coughing, into a round chamber about the same size as the heart of Sanctuary— about twenty or so metres across. Gem and Scott, also covering their faces and coughing, were right behind me.

"Cozy," Gem noted.

I took a few steps around the chamber, running my fingers over the wall next to me, watching as black smoke or paint or something flaked away. Odd. Sanctuary's walls had always seemed to be made entirely of light.

"It's dead," Gemma said. "Empty."

Scott pushed past us and strode to the centre of the room, stepping up onto the dais that took up about a quarter of the floor space. He closed his eyes, face tense, hands fisted.

But after a moment, he sighed and opened his eyes again. "She's right," he said simply. "There's nothing here."

My back crawled. This was weird. Way too weird. "Are you still connected, Gemma?"

She shifted her shoulders experimentally. "I'm connected to *some*thing."

"But there's nothing here. No shadows, no light," I said striding around the perimeter. "And no power." I glanced at Scott. "How is the Valley still there?"

He frowned. "The power source must be hidden. There's something here, Gem says she's connected to it, and as you said, the Valley exists. So there has to be something here still. Something we're missing." He stared around at the walls, all in similar condition to the one I'd touched, with flaking, fading paint, or whatever it was like paint that was flaking off the smoky barrier.

Aphros, I sent. *There's nothing here. It's empty. What are we missing?*

"I'm going to tell Aphros to come in," Gem said.

I nodded, half smiling that we'd both had the same idea.

A second later, her gleaming golden horn appeared through the grimy wall, followed by her white nose, brighter than ever in this gloomy room.

She entered fully, flicked her tail once, and stopped dead, the foals on either side of her peering around wide-eyed, noses still trembling, tails still twitching.

I gasped. Around Aphros, the floor was turning green.

Mint green.

The colour of Aphros's soulprint—and the Valley, before the black had corrupted it.

Gem clutched my arm and even Scott inhaled sharply as the minty green spread, black flaking off the walls faster and faster and faster and faster until the black flecks spiralled upwards in a kind of reverse tornado, up into the roof of the chamber, through it, away, beyond—leaving behind walls of pristine minty green.

I breathed deeply, and the room smelled of mint. "Aphros," I said, a hundred speculations colliding in my head. "Why does your soulprint look like the Valley before it was corrupted? Why do unicorn hair wards repel shadows? Why are you the only one who can cross into the Valley without a sacrifice?"

"And Aphros," Scott said softly, stepping up to my side. "Where do unicorn babies come from?"

That jagged something in my memory; he must have mentioned it before, once, in passing.

It was Gemma who broke ranks first, running to Aphros, laughing, arms wrapping around Aphros's neck.

The babies shied away, snorting at this sudden outburst.

"It's you," Gemma said, running her hand down Aphros's nose. "It's you!"

Scott shook his head, and despite the happy adrenalin thrilling through my stomach, I had to agree. "But how?" I said. "How could Aphros be connected to the Valley? Her soulprint has the same green, yes, but Aphros, you told me yourself that you're made of both Valley magic *and* Sanctuary magic. And what about the glowing light?"

"And if you're the avatar of the Valley," Scott said in a strange voice—I glanced over: his eyes were oddly tight, too—"why didn't you stop the light when it took my mother? Or me? Or Gem?"

Point. No wonder his voice sounded strange.

I realised Aphros hadn't moved, even though the twins had drifted away to sniff at the floor, the walls, the dais. "Aphros? Are you okay?"

She began to shiver.

Slowly, one hoof at a time, she backed away—then the shivers became shakes, and she was swinging her head, her horn scribing a glimmering arc in the air. "No," she said. "No, no, it is not I. No!"

"Aphros, wait!" Gemma flung herself around Aphros's neck, hugging her tight. "It's okay. It's all going to be okay." She burst into tears—which at least stopped Aphros.

Aphros tucked her nose over Gemma's shoulder, hugging her back. "Oh, Gemma," she said. "Oh, Gemma."

Lily and Filibere crept back to Aphros's side, nuzzling at her in concern, tiny gold ears trembling.

Scott's jaw twitched. "I need an answer, Aphros," he said quietly. "Why didn't you help us?"

Aphros raised her gaze to meet his, liquid brown eyes wide. "I did not know," she said, just as soft. "I still do not."

I sighed explosively and swung my arms. "Right, well, there's only one way to figure this out, isn't there. Scott, get down."

I motioned him off the dais, and he glared at me, but obeyed. "Aphros, over here. Gemma, hold the twins back, please."

"Help me out," she said to Scott, and they took a foal each, hugging them firmly but gently around their shoulders.

Aphros hesitated with her front hoof suspended over the dais, the step a mere half-foot high but with the heady significance of a skyscraper.

I crossed to her and placed a hand on her neck. "Come on," I said. "It's going to be okay."

She snorted and gave her mane a little toss, but put her foot down—then the next one, and the next, and the next.

Nothing.

I let out my breath. Fine. We'd do this the hard way.

I reached toward her again, road mastery at the ready—

Green fire swept up through the room, blinding, glittering, and I raised my arms over my head as the wave of light flashed from floor to waist to ceiling.

I stood for a long moment, head tipped back, staring at the place where the light had vanished into the ceiling.

"Whoa," Gemma breathed—and the spell was broken.

I giggled. "Well, I think it's safe to say you're *something*, that's for sure." I glanced back at Aphros. "You sure you don't know anything about this?" I asked curiously.

She shook her head, one hind foot stomping.

A pop echoed through the chamber, and a puff of darkness dissipated over the middle of the plinth. My heart leapt to my throat—shadows, what were we going to do?

But as the smoke cleared, my eyes went round: it was Viri, green wings glittering, her face just as surprised as mine.

30

"YOU!" VIRI CURSED, face narrowing to hatred.

But unusually, it wasn't directed at me; she was glaring at Aphros.

"You cannot be here!" she snapped, practically crackling with anger. "It is not allowed!"

"Well why not?" Scott snapped back, arms still firmly wrapped around Lily's shoulders. "It's clear she belongs here, definitely more than you do. Why *shouldn't* she be here?"

"Yeah, what else have you been hiding?" Gemma added.

"That is not for you to understand!" Viri tossed her hair, eyes spitting metaphorical fire at us all.

Aphros stamped a hind foot. "I disagree, Viri," she said carefully. "I think it is exactly for us to understand. For me, in particular. You cannot be unaware of how this chamber has reacted to me. Perhaps that is even what called you here." Her ears lay back flat against her head and she stamped again. "In point of fact," she said, voice still level, "I demand an explanation."

"Oh, you demand, you demand," Viri sneered. "Well I hate to break it to you, *horse*, but it's none of your business. The fundamental rules being broken were bad enough. I won't tolerate them being flouted again." She raised a hand, and lightning crackled over her fingertips. "It's for your own safety, you know."

The lightning zapped from Viri's fingers, straight toward Aphros.

I didn't consciously think about it—I just sort of twisted sideways, and immediately back the other way again, and all of a sudden I was standing right behind Viri as she raised her arm—and I simply reached out and stopped her.

Her eyes widened so much they practically swallowed her face.

I smiled, a small, terrifying little thing. "I don't think so."

She remembered to breathe again. "No," she said, shaking her head in tiny, frantic movements. "No, you haven't."

"Haven't what?" I said, the smile still curled on my face like a waking lion.

"You can't have." She fluttered backward a little—and bumped into my other hand.

It had never really hit me before just how much *bigger* I was than the fairies—and Viri, it seemed, was having that same realisation, eyes darting this way and that as she realised I had her trapped.

"You were about to say," I told her, "that this is for Aphros's own safety. Something to do with the rules. I *think*," I added gravely, "that it's just about time you told us the truth. For once."

"Or what?" Viri sneered.

I shrugged. "Or nothing. We'll figure it out whether you tell us or not. Look at how much we already know. How much we can already *do*." I paused, holding her gaze for just long enough that I'd be able to make a point.

I twisted sideways and back again, landing on the other side of Viri just as she finished hearing the word 'do'.

Viri squeaked.

I smiled without my teeth. "What do you think?"

She held my gaze for a moment. Abruptly, she sank to the floor.

I moved with her, ready to slip back and catch her at the slightest hint she was up to something—but instead, shoulders slumping, head bowed, she stroked the minty-green floor of the dais. "I am sorry," she whispered. "I have failed you."

She vanished in a tongue of green flame and a quiet 'puff'. I jumped back as greenish-grey ash rained to the floor, forming a small pile—just small enough to have maybe weighed the same amount as Viri.

"Did she just...?" said Gem from the side of the chamber.

"I think so," Scott said back in a hushed voice.

Frantically, I skipped back.

But although I could see her, I couldn't touch her, couldn't interact with her—couldn't stop her from dying, even though I skipped, and skipped, and skipped.

I stopped, shoulders heavy with defeat, and tears prickled my eyes. Yes, fine, she'd tried to probably-kill us all last month when we'd been saving Gem, but this... This was too sudden, too unexpected.

I couldn't help it. I crumpled to the floor, face crumbling too, shoulders shaking as I cried. It wasn't fair. The whole thing just wasn't fair. If the stupid roads had just guarded themselves in the first place, not taken the awful memories from people... If they hadn't been so *selfish*, then none of this would have happened.

Aphros's soft nose touched the back of my bowed head, and she snorted gently, ruffling my hair.

I sat up, wiped my arm across my face with a great, sniffly inhale, and sighed. "I know," I said. "I know. We have to keep moving."

I stared at the pile of ash that, only a minute or so ago, had been Viri—alive, and annoying, and bright and sparkling. And alive, had I mentioned that?

I clenched my jaw against thoughts of Georgia. At least this death was clean. No blood, no bruises. I stared at the pile again. Just a little heap of ash, green and grey and—

I tilted my head. Green and grey and something shining metallically. Holding my breath, I reached for it with a single finger.

"What are you doing?" Gemma gasped, right as Scott said, "Ew, Emma, no."

But they couldn't see what I did. Gently, I brushed the ash aside—soft as butter, light as air—and underneath was a shining, metallic, greeny-gold stylised acorn, fat and round like a walnut shell, but definitely, from the little cap on top, supposed to be an acorn. I pick it up; it fit perfectly in my hand, and it reminded me of something, something I'd seen.

I inhaled sharply; the acorn was growing warm.

Hurriedly, I set it back down—and the cap popped open, and a tiny seedling made of nothing but green-gold light began to unfurl.

And that reminded me of where I'd seen it before: as the seedling became a sapling became a small tree, I remembered the first vision Helios had given me, of the kernel I'd discovered floating adrift in his power, and how when I'd touched it it had sprouted into a tree, showing that the Valley and Sanctuary had indeed once been whole.

The tree reached the ceiling and stopped growing up, instead putting out more branches and widening its trunk, until the whole chamber felt less like a room and more like the natural circular space created under the canopy of a tree.

The trunk widened and twisted until two people could have easily fitted inside—three people, four.

An arch began to glow in the trunk, and while the rest of us stood transfixed, it was Aphros who dared approach, one careful footstep at a time.

The arch widened to a doorway.

Aphros drew closer.

"Be careful," Scott said, and the trance jarred loose, and we all blinked and looked around to see how everyone else was reacting to this magic tree. He flushed, staring at the floor, one arm still draped around Lily. "Sorry. But it is the Valley."

"My babies," Aphros murmured, looking back at them, then at the tree again, then back to her babies. She tilted her head, ears flickering wildly. "I see them here, and yet I hear them within the tree." She stepped toward it again, nose outstretched, trembling.

Be okay, I thought, hands knotted at my sides. *Please let this be okay.*

Aphros stepped into the light of the tree.

The tree rustled, shivered—and in a flash of gold edged with sooty black, the whole tree sucked inward, shrinking in an instantaneous whirl, zipping back down to nothing—inside Aphros.

Aphros swayed.

"No!" Gem cried, reaching for her. But before she could make it, Aphros swayed again and fell to her knees.

Lily and Filibere whinnied and raced for their mother. They only barely beat the rest of us.

I sat, scooping Aphros's head into my lap while Gemma clung to her shoulder, sobbing.

"Aphros," Gem sobbed. "Aphros, get up."

I looked up as Scott knelt next to me, his eyes wide and serious and fearful.

"I should have stopped her," he said.

For the second time, my face crumbled. I swallowed and shook my head. "You warned her. We didn't know. You tried."

But as he reached for her face, his hands shaking, Aphros inhaled dramatically.

I dodged as her horn waved wildly, nearly skewering me, then Gemma, then Scott as she thrashed her head back and forth.

She stood, oblivious to us, and we scrambled aside as she shook violently, mane and tail flying, horn scribing a figure eight in the air.

Her eyes flew open; she stilled, statue-like.

Another great inhale—but this time she exhaled normally, and peered around. "Gemma? Scott? Edge? My babies!"

They flocked to her, nuzzling against her side and making little crooning noises, and she sniffed them over nose to tail, assessing them in a blink before tossing her head high and exhaling again. "I remember," she said, voice full of wonder. "I am made whole, and *I remember*."

31

APHROS STOOD. THERE was an almighty *floomp*, and two great, white wings suddenly unfurled from Aphros's sides, the wind of them knocking the three of us backward, though the babies stayed nuzzled against their mother's side.

I stared, wide-eyed, lips parted.

Aphros snorted and shook her head, her mane, stamped her front feet, danced on the spot—and flapped her massive, feathered wings, each one easily as tall as I was.

Lily whinnied.

Aphros swung around to nuzzle her, folding her wings neatly at her sides.

"What... What's happening?" Gem said, hesitantly. "Why... I mean... *How*? What's going *on*?"

Aphros snorted again. "That, Gemma, is an excellent question. But the real question is, what are we going to do about it?"

Scott hissed through his teeth impatiently. "Aphros, we're on a deadline to try to save the place. Riddles aren't going to help anyone."

I stepped toward her. "You're... You're the Valley's avatar, aren't you," I said. "Like Helios is for Sanctuary."

Gemma clapped a hand over her mouth. "The twins!" she mumbled.

Scott glanced at her curiously. "What about them?"

Gemma pointed. "They're gold. Like Helios. I always wondered why they were gold!"

Scott raised an eyebrow at Aphros. "But the twins were around before Helios, right? Unless they've been around forever, since Aphros"—he waved vaguely at her—"you know. Forgot. I mean, babies don't just actually spontaneously appear, right?"

"They appeared to me," Aphros said with a hint of amusement. "One day, I went home to the stables, and there they were, and I knew that they were mine, but I did not know how or why they came to be there."

I sniffed. "Mum'd *love* that."

"But I see now: they have come to me through the roads, through time." She nuzzled them again, first Filibere, then Lily. The two foals shook their heads and danced. "They have not yet been born," Aphros added. "And yet, on the roads, time is fluid. And so, here they are."

"Fascinating," Scott said with a strange expression, "but what does this mean? Edge is jumping back and forth in time on the roads, you're apparently the Valley's avatar... What happened to the glowy light? What happened," his hands fisted at his sides, "to the people it devoured?"

Oh. Right.

"I'm sorry," I murmured. "I don't think I can go back far enough." It was sort of like Gemma had said: I could sense the options stretching around me, and could feel where they stretched into the distance, beyond my reach.

And even if I could go back that far, the skips hadn't let me save Viri.

He shrugged me off. "I wasn't talking to you. I'm talking to Aphros, and I'm wondering why, if she's the literal embodiment of the Valley's power, she didn't do something to prevent all this happening in the first place!"

Lily and Filibere hid from the shouting under their mother's wings, peering out through the feathers and looking adorable, and tiny, and vulnerable.

I stepped to Lily's side and placed a reassuring hand against her flank.

"The rules were broken," Aphros said sadly.

"Yes, so we've heard. But are you going to tell us what those rules *were*, and why this *matters*, or are you going to just keep hiding things, like the fairies?"

"Scott," Gemma said reproachfully.

But personally, I thought he had a point. "What rules, Aphros? What happened? Helios showed me that the Valley used to be one with Sanctuary, and then they were two places but they were healthy, and then... then the black. Was that the shadows? Did they break the rules?"

Aphros was trembling. *Edge*, she sent softly. *Edge, I am sorry. I was not there, I could not help. I am sorry. I am sorry.* She hung her head, and I lay my free hand on her shoulder, and Gemma came to her other side.

"Hey," I soothed. "Hey, it's okay."

A gentle pop sounded behind me.

I jumped.

Quoise fluttered over the middle of the plinth, her arms clutching a spring-green book to her chest. "Aphros?" she said, peering around. "I couldn't get out of Sanctuary to find Maria. What's going on?" She saw Aphros and her new wings, and her mouth dropped open. "Oh my goodness," she said, her hand covering her mouth. "But, the rules!"

"Yes," said Aphros gravely. "But I rather think we are past that now, do you not think?"

Scott stamped his foot and flung his hands up in the air, whirling to pace a few steps away and then back again. "Will someone tell us what is going on?"

It wasn't like him to lose his cool like that, but I was glad he had, because it saved me from doing it.

"You haven't told them?" Quoise said, wide-eyed.

"Obviously," I snapped.

There was a moment of intense eye contact between Aphros and Quoise, and it struck me that perhaps Gemma and I weren't the only ones who could talk to Aphros without speaking.

Quoise sighed and fluttered over to perch on Aphros's head, trying to find somewhere to balance the book before giving up and hugging it to her.

Aphros twitched her ears as Quoise landed, but stayed still.

"I'll tell you," Quoise said.

"Thank goodness," Gemma murmured. "One of us was going to pop any second now."

My lips twitched, and I let myself down to sit cross-legged on the floor. Gemma came around to join me, and after a moment, Scott did too.

"A long time ago," Quoise began from up between Aphros's ears, "Aphros was the Valley's avatar. All the fairies know this, but until this happened just now"—she waved a hand around at the green room, the same colour as sunlight filtering through a soft-leafed forest—"Aphros didn't remember."

Aphros stamped her foot at that, and I realised that it wasn't just the humans here who were upset—with good reason. I'd been upset at the thought of the roads taking *one* of my memories; how would I feel if they'd taken all of them, and I'd had to start over again?

"We didn't remember as far back as the Valley and Sanctuary being one," Quoise clarified. "That was in the Book of Laws, which only Viri was allowed to read. Until, you know. Last month. But we knew about Aphros."

Last month Quoise had entered the Forbidden Chamber for the first time in order to save us from the Keeper, Viri—all while we tried to save Gemma from the power of the Valley.

"Wait a minute," I said. "If Aphros is the avatar of the Valley, the"—I waved my hands vaguely—"you know, it's body, then why did it have the weird glowy light thing that kept trying to take over people?"

"I'm getting to that," Quoise said. "So. A long time ago, Aphros was the Valley's avatar. But then—well, I told you the rumours about Sanctuary and the Valley being created, didn't I?"

We nodded, Gemma and I more agreeably than Scott.

"It's true," she said. "It's in the second part of the Book. The very first people to use the roads created Sanctuary and the Valley, and somehow set the land up with its own power source so it would continue to run after the creators died. Created worlds usually die with their creator," she added.

"I read that bit," I said. "About being able to create worlds. Gemma can do it."

Quoise nodded. "That may come in handy," she said, but instead of elaborating, she continued with her story. "Unfortunately, the roads became corruptted with the shadows. The only thing the creators of Sanctuary could think to do was to seal them within the Valley, sacrificing one half of their land in order to protect the other, and the roads.”

“Bad memories,” I said.

Quoise looked puzzled.

“The shadows came from the bad memories the roads skimmed from the people who travelled them.”

“Ah,” she said, brightening in understanding. “That makes a certain kind of sense.”

She rubbed Aphros’s ear, which had been twitching rapidly in front of her.

“Shhhh,” she soothed. “It will be okay.”

She looked back at us. “So. They tried to trap the shadows in the Valley, but the shadows were too strong. The hearts of both Sanctuary and the Valley are weak spots, thin places where it’s easier to reach the roads than anywhere else. And the shadows broke through into the Valley’s heart. The creators were there, but the best they could do was use the power of Sanctuary to cut Aphros free from the Valley in order to save her, and pen the shadows back into the Valley’s heart.” She bit her lip. “They...”

I nodded jerkily. “They died doing it,” I said. “We know.”

Quoise sighed heavily. “Aphros was connected to Sanctuary as a source of life for her, the shadows were trapped in the Valley. It lasted a good, long time. But then your mother arrived,” Quoise said, nodding at Scott, “and she was a stronger Road Master than we’d had in centuries. She found the roads, and the Valley’s heart, and...” She bit her lip again, eyes round.

Scott twitched his shoulders uncomfortably. “Yeah,” he said. “They used her to get out.”

Quoise nodded. “They did. They sucked her dry creating their own avatar, the glowing pillar of light, and when they’d used up all her power and still didn’t have a proper body, they... came after you. And then Gemma.”

Gemma shivered and pressed her knee close against mine, leaning her head on my shoulder.

I tipped my head over and hugged her with my cheek.

Scott’s fingers twitched, and although he was fighting it, tears welled in his eyes.

I took his fingers and squeezed them so they’d stop, and he shot me a grateful look.

"There's one thing missing, though," I said, looking back up at Quoise. "What were the rules that were broken in all of this?"

Quoise hung her head. "That," she said, "is the greatest failure of the fairies, for it is we who broke the rules and failed Sanctuary." She took a deep, steadying breath. "The fairies were also created," she said. "Imagined as a later addition to Sanctuary by the world creator, and given life by the Road Masters, who took sensations from the roads to give us soulprints—and life."

My eyes grew round as saucers.

Scott edged his fingers out from where I was crushing them.

"It was our duty to protect the hearts," Quoise said. "Especially from the shadows. When it became clear that Aphros wouldn't be able to hold the shadows back alone, we were created to help her, to push back against the shadows from Sanctuary. But we failed.

"Viri... One of us listened to the shadows' pleas, felt sorry for them, trapped and penned. They convinced that fairy to let them out, and she agreed—only for a moment before she realised what she'd done and changed her mind, but it was long enough to break Aphros's hold on them."

She hung her head. "We failed, and the shadows escaped, and the creators of Sanctuary died to buy us time, and Aphros was sealed away from everything she was ever supposed to be in order to save her life."

32

I INHALED DEEPLY, the smell of mint filling my lungs, the taste of it sharp on my tongue. It felt good: fresh, and clean, and energising.

"Okay," I said, and everyone looked at me from where they'd drifted around the chamber, Quoise and Aphros in deep conversation just off the edge of the dais, the twins curled up asleep at Aphros's feet, Scott examining the wall where we'd entered in minute detail, and Gemma lying sprawled on the dais next to me.

I shifted slightly so I could see everyone. "We need to do something. While we've been sitting here, the shadows have probably taken over the heart of Sanctuary entirely, and I know we have the advantage of using time skips now"—probably, assuming I could always get them to work reliably—"but I really think it's time to move."

Scott raised an eyebrow. "And you have a plan for said movement, which you're going to share?"

I grinned. "Of course. Here's what we're going to do. Everyone?" I paused until I was sure I had their complete attention. "We're going to re-imagine Sanctuary."

Gemma sat up next to me. "Edge, I can barely imagine a twenty-foot grey box. How am I supposed to re-imagine the whole of Sanctuary?"

My grin didn't waver. "With help." I pointed around the room. "We have here the avatar of the Valley. We can get the avatar of Sanctuary no problems. You have a Road Master to help"—I pointed at myself—"and someone who knows how it was done before." I pointed at Quoise.

Gemma's gaze slid toward Scott, who I was studiously avoiding looking at.

"It's fine." He shrugged. "I'm sure I'll come in handy somewhere. Or not."

I chewed at the inside of my lip. I felt sorry for him, sure, but not enough to jeopardise my plan to save Sanctuary. Like he said. Priorities, right? "I'll need to figure out exactly how the time skips will work—"

"Oh," Quoise interrupted. "Here. This should help with that." She held out the green book she'd arrived with.

I took it, blinked—and a smile blossomed over my face. "The road mastery book!" I waved it at Scott. "This is the one I was looking for in the library!"

"There's a section in there on using the roads to time travel," Quoise said. "I tracked the book down the other day when you two disappeared from the library without a trace."

Scott and I exchanged glances. "Uh, yeah, we may or may not have, um, found the Forbidden Chamber that day," I said.

"You *what*?"

"Um," I said, "is this a bad time to tell you that the first half of the Book of Laws is currently on my bedside table at home?"

"First... *half*... Table? At *home*?" Quoise said faintly. She fanned herself and closed her eyes dramatically. "Well," she said. "I hope you at least had the good sense to *read* it, though you must actually have less than half if you didn't get to the bit about Aphros and the creators and the shadows."

I nodded. "Probably. I do have the bit that proves that Viri's been overstepping her role as Keeper, though." I tried hard not to grin, I really did. "I'd say our shiny new re-imagined Sanctuary might be just the cue everybody needs for a new person to take on that role."

Quoise giggled behind her hand. "Oh, Edge."

Gemma shook her head. "Edge. You know this is madness, right? You get how impossible this all is? Create a whole new world out of nothing? But one which is exactly like another world that already exists?" She shook her head. "Impossible." But her tone was one of wonder, not defeat. Still, she added, "Couldn't we just try locking the shadows away again?"

I shook my own head at that, and emphatically. "Gem, the original creators of Sanctuary, the firsts, they died trying to make that work, and Scott's mum died because it didn't."

"It worked for a little while," she said, sighing.

"Do you really want to be responsible for any future deaths the shadows might cause?"

"No," she said, and sighed again. "You're right, of course. You always are. I..." She darted a glance at me. "I'm sorry I didn't listen to you. Earlier. When you said we had to come do something."

I shrugged. "If we had, we might not have uncovered all of this." I gestured broadly at the room. "After all, we definitely wouldn't have brought Aphros here unless we were desperate."

"I'm going to need help," Gemma said, firmly this time. "I believe that what you're suggesting is possible, but it's too big for me to manage on my own. I can't keep the whole of Sanctuary in my head at once, and you have to do that to build the world—it's like travelling, only you have to keep the *whole thing* in your mind, not just the entrance alcove."

"Aphros," I said. "And Helios. You're connected to both of them. You can talk to Helios long range, too, like you can with Aphros, right?"

She nodded.

Aphros tossed her head. "We can help you with this," she said. "Helios is made of Sanctuary, and I of the Valley. If you stay connected to us, we can hold the vision of them in your mind for you."

"See?" I nodded firmly. "Great. So that's that part organised. Quoise," I said. "What did the Road Masters have to do to help?"

She pointed at the book in my lap. "The last chapter in there suggests you'll need to work with Gemma to infuse a soulprint into her imagined world, in order for it to function effectively without either of you around. The creators made the hearts, remember, so that Sanctuary and the Valley wouldn't die with them."

My heart pounded at my chest. "So... You're saying Gemma needs to re-imagine Sanctuary, and I need to re-imagine the hearts?"

No wonder they'd needed two of them to do it. Oy.

Quoise nodded. "Not quite, though. You only need to connect the hearts that already exist; you won't need to make entirely new ones."

"And the fairies? They were created too, right, so..." I trailed off. "How do we do this without erasing you all?"

She smiled gently. "You'll need to re-imagine us, too. Just like the first Road Masters did."

"But I don't know how to do this," I said too quickly. "What if I get it wrong? What if one of you comes back different, or doesn't come back, or—"

Quoise waved dismissively, grinning. "The last chapter." She nodded toward the road mastery book. "All you need is our soulprints."

"Well, sure," I said, "but how many of you are there? A hundred? More?" I shook my head. "I don't have time to learn all your soulprints, and even if I did, I couldn't guarantee I'd be able to remember them accurately to bring you back."

Quoise tilted her head. "Oh, my. If only there were some permanent record we had of everyone's soulprints, something contained and small and portable that you could, I don't know, activate when you needed them."

My face lit up. "You have them saved."

When Gemma had been missing a month ago, stolen by the shadows, I'd needed a way to track her through the Valley and its layers of dimensions. Quoise had taken me to a room with two walls covered in tiny drawers, all locked behind glass that vanished when Quoise touched it with a key.

Inside each drawer had been a glass vial about as big as my pinky, each one containing the soulprint of a visitor to Sanctuary—*every* visitor, and, it appeared, every fairy.

I frowned. "But Quoise. There's still well over a hundred of you. To open and activate every single one will take at least..." I trailed off, trying to do the maths. From what I could remember, I might be able to do maybe two or three per minute.

Which meant... "Thirty minutes to an hour. We don't have that long. Gemma will have the place reimagined in under a minute once she gets going."

Quoise shook her head, grinning. "Edge, you're thinking too linearly. All you have to do is activate one, cycle back in time using a skip, activate the next one, cycle back, and so on. You don't need thirty minutes when you're on the roads and can use the same minute over thirty times."

I hugged her—gently. "Quoise, you're a genius."

"Pshaw." She flapped her hands down from the wrists.

"It's going to be rough," I said though. "That's a lot of concentration, all while I'm on the roads. What if I forget what I'm doing? What if I get distracted by the roads and lose myself?"

Scott stepped up. "That sounds like a job for me," he said. "See? I told you I'd be useful somehow." His face was mostly serious, but I caught the light in his eyes that meant he was joking around.

I bumped him with my shoulder. "You?" I said. "Useful? Pah. Never gonna happen."

I grinned though, and although he narrowed his eyes at me, his lips twitched. I inhaled, shook myself all over, and exhaled firmly. "Right. So Gemma is going to re-create Sanctuary-slash-the-Valley, with Helios and Aphros's input. I am going to connect the hearts to the land that she creates"—somehow, magically—"and then Scott is going to help me re-create the fairies."

I turned to Quoise. "Two things. One, are the portals into Sanctuary still sealed so no one can get in, and is there some way to do that for the Valley as well? The last thing we need is someone appearing as everything's changing."

Quoise nodded. "I can manage that. If I go back through here"—she waved to the centre of the dais—"I'll be well placed to lock down access to the Valley. There are one or two others who can help me."

I nodded once. "Good. And the second thing I was going to say is, Scott"—I turned to him—"I'm probably going to need to be able to see you and speak to you." This whole thing was too complicated, too important, to leave to coded hand squeezes—and I might need both my hands free. "So we're going to have to find that part of the roads again where we can talk."

He gave a tiny shrug. "No worries."

"Gem," I said, "where will you be? We need to sync up our activities somehow so I can do the soulprint thing as you're creating the actual world, so, I don't know; could you work from that place on the roads too?"

She shrugged. "Probably. Yeah, I don't see why not."

I looked around at everyone, holding my breath. Aphros, with her beautiful new wings; the gorgeous, golden twins; Quoise, looking determined and wildly excited; Gemma, just about ready to faint with nerves, I thought, but jaw also set in determination; and Scott, the very last person I'd ever have expected to be here to help us save Sanctuary.

Just look at us all, about to save the world. I snorted softly. "All right, team," I said. "Let's get Helios and get this show on the road."

33

"ARE YOU READY?" I asked Gem, trying not to let nerves waver in my voice. Around us, the grey stillness of the heart of the roads lay silent. I wasn't sure if they'd cottoned on to what we were trying to do yet—I could only assume they had, since they could pretty much pluck things from our minds—but they hadn't responded to my greetings.

Still. So long as they weren't going to interfere, that wasn't really a problem.

"No," said Gemma in response to my question. Her lips twitched briefly into half a smile. "Let's get started, this is killing me."

"And Sanctuary," Scott added.

I rolled my eyes, but he was right: we'd snuck back a little to get into the Lodge and retrieve the soulprint records before the shadows could get there, but the only way to find Helios had been to travel back to Sanctuary in the present—and it was looking pretty bleak.

Darker than ever, it was hard to see even the stables from the Lodge at the top of the slope, and instead of the usual calming atmosphere, I'd spent the whole brief excursion with the back of my neck prickling and my spine between my shoulder blades crawling.

"Okay," I said. "Gem, the timing's on you. Let me know when you're ready for me to pull in the soulprints."

She nodded, brown cheeks flushed, and gripped her hands tightly together in front of her. She shut her eyes. "Wait." She flung her arms down by her sides. "This feels stupid. Here, I'm going to sit down." She sat cross-legged and looked up at me.

I sat, one knee touching hers, the other touching Scott's as he made the third side of our triangle. "I'm not going to be able to stay here," he murmured, gesturing to the three huge backpacks behind him that contained the glass vials of the fairies' soulprints.

I nodded. "Let's just start."

Gemma closed her eyes again.

A breeze began to play over us; strands of hair tickled my cheeks. I swept them aside.

She must be talking to Aphros and Helios, getting her vision of Sanctuary straight.

Frogging elephants, I wished I could hear what was going on. I shifted restlessly.

The breeze picked up to a wind, and I glanced around. Was this Gemma's doing, or an unavoidable side effect, or something else?

Aphros, I sent. *What's going on?*

Shhh, Edge. We are dreaming the world.

I closed my eyes—and inhaled sharply. With my road mastery, I could see dark clouds swirling in a vortex around us—not dark like the shadows, but a darker version of the grey world Gemma had taken us to our first time on the roads.

And beneath it all, a sense of unease, my stomach rolling, shoulders tensing...

It took a moment for me to realise that, once again, these sensations weren't mine, but the roads'.

It's okay, I told them. *We can do this.*

Fear, dread.

Images of projects going wrong—a rocket exploding just after takeoff, someone falling from a wire.

The wind swirled, hard enough now that my hair streamed back and my t-shirt flapped.

A long, high-pitched whine built around us.

Roads, I said sternly, *you have to let us do this.*

A child hiding under a blanket; someone pulling away from a nurse holding a needle; a toddler wailing as firm hands brushed her hair.

Bass notes, pounding, thumping, deep drum beats starting slow, but getting faster, faster, faster.

I'd heard these noises before, seen the same flickering flames and darkness that I could sense out on the very edges of my road mastery: the strange and awful guardians that we'd seen on our first trip into the roads, and never again since.

Acknowledgement.

A sense of curiosity, of someone watching a small group of travellers with interest; then fear, and the creatures appearing like claws out of their sheaths.

The drums beat louder, closer.

Different travellers, in ones or twos or threes, seeing the creatures and falling away, terrified, off the roads, never to return.

Suddenly, I understood: the beasts were just the roads, a defence system, the roads' way of scaring off people it didn't want on them.

At the edges of my road mastery, I felt them draw nearer.

But you let us through, I shouted over the roar of the wind that now whipped over us. *You let us through! You liked us!*

Sadness, a tear rolling down someone's cheek—I could feel it as though it were my own—a sense of loss.

Nothing's changed! I told the roads, shouting now over the noise of the wind and the constant, frantic pounding of the drumbeats. *We're still here to help! We're* trying *to help. Please, let us try this.*

Fear. A body of a woman—one of the creators—lying still on the ground, limbs at haphazard angles, eyes staring lifelessly.

We are not going to die.

Possibilities. Options unfurling like fractals in fluorescent green and yellow and blue in the roaring darkness around us.

My hair whipped against my face, sticking to my mouth.

Drumbeats, faster, faster, until they were nearly seamless.

No, I said. *Not today. Today we are going to save Sanctuary—and you.*

The roads stilled, the thumping beat of the drums cut short, though the wind still swirled and roared.

Please, I said. *Let us try.*

The roads didn't answer—but the feeling of being watched slowly drained away, the flickers of flame faded.

I breathed out, and my shoulders dropped. *Thank you.*

"Okay," Gemma shouted over the wind. "I have the vision stable, I can see Sanctuary, and I can see the Valley, but there's something missing. They're not linking like they should!"

I forced my attention away from the roads and back to the problem at hand. With my road mastery, I could see exactly what she meant: above us, her vision of the new Sanctuary shimmered—but it was two visions, not one, Helios's and Aphros's, with an ugly seam in the middle.

We needed something else, something extra, some tie between Aphros and Helios...

Of course. "The babies!" I shouted back. "Use the babies as a link!"

"Duh, of course!" Gem went silent for a bit, then, "It's working! They're working perfectly as a bridge between the two!"

I grinned, covering my mouth with the side of my index finger. We were really going to do this. Above us, the seam began to blur gold with little streaks of copper and blue, the light diffusing out into the Valley and into Sanctuary, erasing the gap between them.

Gemma tensed. "I've got it," she shouted, melting in relief. "It's nearly there! The babies, they did it! Go Lily! Go Filibere!"

Yes. Yes yes yes yes *yes*.

"Wait!" Gem cried.

My heart jolted as I saw what was happening: power siphoning out from the distant babies into the vision above us, the gold shimmer, the vision growing clearer and sharper—and the sense of Lily and Filibere fading.

"Wait, it's using them up!" Gem shouted. "Aphros, pull them back! No! No, stop!"

She grabbed at my hand, and I held it tightly.

"Edge, I can't stop it! They've connected Sanctuary and the Valley but the connection is draining their life force, they're going to die and I can't save them!"

"I see it!" I shouted back. Frantically, I tried tugging at their connection with my road mastery. "I can't detach them!"

It is alright, Aphros sent, voice eerily calm amid the roaring wind. *They have not yet been born. I will see them again one day soon. Let them help us now as they may.*

"They're still too young to die!" I screamed back, both aloud and internally to Aphros. "If the connection drains all their life force, you might see them again when they're younger, but this will be it for them both!"

"A time skip, Edge," Scott said urgently into my ear. "Can you reach them from here?"

I shook my head—I'd never reached something from so far away before, and I couldn't time skip now, I had to stay here. "I can't leave!"

"But they can!"

Could I send someone away without me? I had no idea—but this seemed like a mighty good time to try.

I stretched my road mastery out toward the heart of the Valley where the twins had stayed with Aphros. Further, further...

It wasn't far enough. I couldn't reach. Not like this, anyway.

The wind raged as I disconnected my road mastery from my body like I'd done twice before and pushed it onward, further.

The green. Follow the green.

I swayed.

My stomach heaved and lights flashed around me.

Further. Further. *Come on! You have to do this.*

Somewhere back near my body, Gemma was sobbing.

It hurt.

I couldn't breathe.

But the twins were *just there*, copper streak and flash of blue.

"Send... them out," I gasped, hoping I was saying it to Aphros. "Can't... quite reach."

Please. Please understand, I begged.

My heart skipped as the two soulprints began moving toward me.

That's it. Closer, closer...

I grabbed them, registered how faint and weightless they were—nearly completely gone—and *twisted*.

At the last possible instant, I let go—and the twins twisted through the roads without me. I had no idea where I'd sent them, but I'd felt a flash of gratitude from them, and a sense of calm.

They were going to be okay.

I stopped straining, and my road mastery snapped back into my body with the force of a speeding car.

Knocked flat on my back, I worked at reminding my body how to breathe.

Beside me, Gemma let out another sob, but she didn't move— I couldn't see exactly what she was doing right now, but I could tell it was taking all the concentration she had.

Scott reached for my hand, and I clung to it, hauling myself back up.

Aphros was right. We'd see them again. They weren't gone for good. I smeared the tears off my cheeks and shuffled to reform our triangle, knees pressing against Scott's and Gem's.

Gemma tensed again, leaning forward, staring intently at something no one else could see. "There's something else now," she said urgently. "I've got the vision whole, but something's preventing it from taking hold."

"Soulprints?" Scott shouted at me, eyebrows raised questioningly.

I nodded. Time to feed the soulprints into the new land, and hopefully blot out the shadows. I took a deep breath, and closed my eyes.

34

ABOVE US, SANCTUARY and the Valley unfurled, dim and ghostly and—from what I could make out—perfectly formed. Gemma had done well.

Now it was my turn, and hopefully I could do her handiwork proud.

The wind raged around us, swirling, biting. Soulprint, soulprint. Somehow, I had to get the soulprints of Sanctuary and the Valley back in there, connecting them to their hearts.

A movement caught my attention—shadows. The shadows were forcing their way through from the roads as they sensed the new world forming, travelling down the connection between Gemma and her imagined world, fading in and out as Sanctuary did. The harder Gemma worked at forming the world into reality, the stronger the shadows became; but if she slackened off and they faded away, so too did Sanctuary. She had no way of making one real without the other.

What could I do?

Well, first things first: I had to try to get Aphros and Helios connected to Gemma's new land. At the moment, they were connected to it only through their connections with Gemma, the cord from Helios bright and gold, and Valley's cord now green instead of the deep black it had been, thanks to Aphros.

No wonder she'd been able to merge soulprints with us to save us when we were in the heart of the Valley. No wonder her hair repelled the shadows.

Wait, there was something in that.

"Scott!" I shouted.

He leaned close, replied—but I couldn't hear what he said over the raging wind and the need to concentrate fiercely on what was going on above our heads.

"The ward!" I shouted. "I need the unicorn ward!"

His knee bumped against mine as he moved. Stillness... And then the rough, wiry braid being wrapped around my wrist, knotted tightly in place.

"Thanks!"

Warm pressure around my arm.

Okay. I had to get the shadows away from the connection to the new Sanctuary—and then do something to make sure they wouldn't come back again, but that was problem two.

I had my road mastery, which could attract their attention, and I had the ward, which could repel them. Now to see if my hair-brained, desperate idea would work.

Carefully, I fed a little trickle of my road mastery into the braid and felt it warm around my wrist.

"Gem!" I called, hoping she'd be able to understand me. "Imagine harder. I need the shadows practically real. And... this might hurt a bit."

I didn't hear her reply, but surely enough, the vision above us intensified, colours brightening, edges sharpening—and the shadows darkening where they climbed the connection between Gem and the vision.

Deep breath.

Keeping the tiny bit of road mastery connected with the braid, I sent the rest out above me, that weird, cellophane noise accompanying the movement. Closer, closer...

The shadows were climbing higher, drawing near to the new Sanctuary.

I moved faster.

Closer. Bit more. Nearly there. Not too close, or I wouldn't have space to get away.

There.

Now the painful bit.

I let the power *flow*, as though it was spilling out of me. Silver light flashed. Bells tinkled, and the smell of vintage roses appeared.

The shadows halted their climb, and I felt them staring.

Come on, I thought, vaguely aware that my body was panting and gasping.

My lungs hurt. So did my head, fire searing from behind my eyes down to the top of my spine.

Gritting my teeth, I forced more power out through my road mastery—and vomited.

Frogs. I hoped it had missed Scott and Gem. Probably, since I could distantly recognise the feel of Scott's arm around my shoulders.

Acid burned my throat and sinuses—but the silver light flashed again, the bells rang louder, and the shadows reversed direction and began leaping down the connection toward me.

I waited until they were just above Gem's head before I let my road mastery begin backing away.

The shadows followed, racing into Gemma's body.

She screamed.

Keep coming! I shouted at the shadows, flashing power through my road mastery again.

The silver light flared, the bells rang, the smell of roses filled the air—and I vomited again, like someone had turned me inside out.

Come on! I told them.

The leaders left Gemma behind and leapt at my road mastery.

I reeled it back toward me.

The shadows drew nearer—almost all of them had left Gemma now, space folding weirdly so that the distance between her and me seemed like halfway to forever.

My road mastery collided with my body.

I rocked, fighting for balance.

The last shadow left Gemma.

"Now!" I screamed through the roar of the wind, the nausea in my stomach, the fear, the adrenalin, the shadows leaping toward me like a train bearing down on me. "Imagine it fully, Gemma! Now!"

The vision snapped to full, glowing colour above us.

The shadows pivoted toward it.

"No!" I shouted, activating the ward in my hand. I retched again and the surreal feeling of seeing my body splayed out in front of me intensified.

Knives stabbed my belly; fire burned in my throat.

I forced my road mastery away from me again, dragging the power of the ward with it, dragging my own soulprint out of my body, the cellophane crackling of my road mastery moving tearing at my ears like it would make them bleed.

The shadows raced at me.

My road mastery leapt over them, my body gasping for air.

I stretched at the top of the leap—and there was Gemma's connection with the new Sanctuary. I wrapped the power of the ward around it, and sent one last immense burst of power toward it, the flashing silver light, tinkling bells, and rose scent of my own soulprint filling the air.

The shadows would get back up through that connection only over my literal dead body.

35

THE WARD'S POWER severed Gemma's connection with her imagined land.

As the two ends of the connection snapped away, I grabbed, hunting frantically for the green and the gold. Hurry, hurry... I was holding onto consciousness by a thread, my whole body pounding.

There, right there.

I latched onto the green and gold with my road mastery, dragged them upward...

And as Gemma's connection fell away, blasted by the unicorn ward so that no more shadows could follow, the strand of green and the strand of gold were left, still connected to the land above us.

I held them for as long as I could, supporting the connection— and as I fell away, my road mastery weak and faint and snapping back toward my body, relief washed over me: it was working. Helios and Aphros's connections to the land was strengthening, their power flowing into the land where it swirled around, strengthening further before returning to them.

At once, I saw how this connection would be able to sustain them; Helios wouldn't need to be connected to a human in order to maintain his body, because his connection with the land would do it.

My road mastery collided with my body. I reeled, landing flat on my back.

After a moment, my vision stopped spinning. "I'm okay," I croaked to Scott, who was feverishly checking for a pulse in my neck.

And it was true. I ached like nothing I'd ever felt before, and my stomach felt like it wouldn't settle for days—but I was okay.

And above us, Helios's gold power and Aphros's green power were merging and mixing, filling up the land with self-sustaining power.

And that was why there had been two of them, I realised, watching the green and gold powers swirling through the land, filling it from the dirt deep beneath the surface, all the way up to the tips of the grass, creeping up the trees, up the mountains, up, up, up until the land glowed. The two powers merged, blending into a unified spring-green glow, like sunshine through soft spring leaves; Sanctuary and the Valley were whole again, with two hearts that beat in unison to power this glorious, imaginary place.

Awe for the first creators filled me, and I stared up at the land in wonder. To have imagined all this alone, that first time, to have called Aphros and Helios into being to sustain the land...

I pressed my hands to my cheeks.

But there was still one thing left to deal with—the shadows. They swarmed hungrily around Gemma's feet, searching for a way in.

The lingering power of the unicorn ward I'd broken over her was holding them at bay for now, but they recognised her as the way into the new Sanctuary, and they were circling like sharks, and they weren't going to give up any time soon.

I could take Gemma away, just step off the roads into her new version of Sanctuary and leave the shadows behind.

But I couldn't leave them here. They'd break through eventually, just as they'd break through from wherever we trapped them.

But what was I going to do with them? Sure, Aphros's wards could hold them at bay, but if she hadn't been able to banish them completely before now, it seemed hardly likely that the wards could do it now.

I bounced the inside of my lip between my teeth. I was missing something.

The shadows were memories. Bad memories. The roads had shoved them aside, they'd grown...

I sighed. That was the key, of course. You couldn't just shove bad memories aside and hope they'd go away. Bad memories festered. You had to learn how to process them, how to let them be without letting them overpower you.

I'd learned that. I still wasn't great at it—like anything, it was a skill you had to practice—but with the police psychologist's help, I had enough skills under my belt to deal with my own dark memories without getting crushed.

I sighed again and pulled myself up into a sitting position, groaning as I met sore muscles I didn't know I had, shoulders heaving.

Scott wrapped one arm around me and drew me against him, helping me stay mostly upright.

In front of me, Gemma had collapsed forward over her folded legs. I reached out and coaxed her toward me, and she curled up with her arms cushioning her head in my lap. I twined my fingers through her hair.

Roads? I sent, exhausted and spent, but surrounded by my best friends in the whole wide world, both lending me whatever strength they had left.

Panic in my chest that wasn't mine.

Please, I said. *I can't destroy you. I don't know how, and even if I did, I wouldn't do it. But I can help you.*

Disbelief, a man scoffing, a woman sniffing scornfully.

Look. I tilted my head toward the newly made Sanctuary above me, still glowing, a spot of calm in the wind that roared like a tornado around us. *I can help you. I know how. I promise.*

Silence, empty of everything but the gale.

Please, I said. *Trust me.*

The wind died away with a snap so sharp my ears rang, and for a moment I shook my head against Scott's shoulder, wondering if the wind had really stopped or if I'd finally gone deaf.

But no: the raging winds were gone, and slowly my mind adjusted to the silence.

I took a deep breath. *This is hard,* I said, assuming the abrupt death of the wind was a good sign and that I had the roads' attention. *Really hard. You're going to have to actually look at the memories.*

Panic; frantic creatures, small and furry, fleeing madly through the dark, tiny, squeaky screams going with them.

Trust me, I said. *I know.* Visions of blood and shadow filled my mind: the shadows, chasing me through the Valley; the zombie trees, snatching at my shoulders, my arms, my hair, roots lifting to trip my feet; Georgia.

Usually, I breathed hard and imagined a waterfall washing them all away; this time, I opened myself up to the roads, slowly, hesitantly.

It recoiled. *I don't want it, I don't want it.*

Please, I said small-ly as my fingers clenched. Distantly, I felt Gemma detangle them from her hair and wrap them in her hands. *You don't have to take it. But please just look.*

The roads' attention came back around slowly, one tiny space at a time. *It hurts.*

Yeah, I said, feeling the panicked nausea well in my stomach. I pushed it down. *It does. It's awful, and it sucks, but*—I inhaled. *But you can't run from it. All you can do is learn to live with it.*

How? the roads begged. *How can you do that? It hurts so much.*

I stumbled as a reel of images flashed past, schoolyard bullying and a car crash victim and bodies in the wreckage of a building and more and more and on and on and on, every horrible, awful thing people had ever done to each other or experienced.

I heaved, but there was nothing left in my stomach to come up—nothing except a little more acid, its burn still less than the horror of the images.

I wiped my mouth with the back of my wrist, wiped my wrist off on the side of my formerly-blue shirt. *Yeah,* I gasped at the roads as Scott clutched my shoulders tighter. *Yeah, it's awful. But what's the alternative?*

The roads shoved the memories it had shown me away so hard I nearly fell. An unreal wall of brick slammed up in front of me, twice as tall as I was and climbing fast.

I reached out toward the vision that seemed so real, so close— and I touched the un-wall gently, just with my fingertips. *I know,* I said. *I know you want to run and hide. I know you just want to cut the memories loose, shut everyone off.* I'd done that for eight weeks over Christmas, mostly by force—but I hadn't exactly made an effort to make new friends, either. *But are you really happy that way?*

Yes. The shushing, multiple voices of the roads were petulant, like a toddler clinging to a point of view they knew was wrong out of sheer spite.

You can't lock yourself away, I said. Like Sanctuary, the real world would always call you back eventually; you couldn't stay hidden from it forever.

Images of the shadows. *We can lock* them *away. Make better rules, so no one will find them.*

I shook my head. *You know you can't. Rules can't keep you safe. They're important, good rules are great, but you can't rely on them, roads. Someone will break them eventually, and you can't keep running forever. The only thing that can keep you safe is you—and trusting someone to help you.*

Ideas whirled in my head about my own life, my own running—our family's running. Maybe, just maybe, I was talking to myself here too.

And maybe—just maybe—there was something I could do.

But I had to solve this problem first, or the other wouldn't matter; the shadows were circling around us now, and I wasn't getting out of this alive if I couldn't convince the roads to listen.

I held out my hand toward the wall in front of me. *Will you? Trust me? Let me help?* I waited, breath caught in my chest, eyes scrunching so tightly closed they hurt. *Please,* I thought to myself. *Please say yes.*

An exhalation; the sense of someone taking my hand. The wall vanished. *Show us.*

36

AND SO I did: for the first time in a long time, I let the memory of Georgia consume me.

The open-air train station bustled with commuters in the after-school rush, the smell of hot concrete and trains mingling with the hot chips a knot of students were noisily consuming further down the platform, their navy-blue blazers rounding their shoulders so they looked like a cluster of formally-attired gulls, licking salt from their fingers and laughing, eyes bright, smiles wide.

They must have been dripping with sweat in this late spring humidity—and indeed, the brown-haired boy cradling the butcher's paper package in one arm had thrown off his blazer, had it slung nonchalantly over his shoulder, and sweat had darkened his light-blue shirt—under his arms, over his back.

The chips smelled good regardless.

I stayed away from the boisterous group, my thumbs tucked into the straps of my backpack, heavy with the weight of my textbooks, and cast them little side glances, longing more for their hot chips than the sense of belonging they exuded.

I had my own friends, my own group, and even though I caught a different train home than any of them, even though they always decided what we were going to do without asking me—Grace especially—it didn't matter, because I didn't know any better, and they were my friends.

I shifted restlessly as a train took off in the opposite direction, hot air puffing against my face like an oven, and glanced at the count-down timer over our own platform. Six minutes until my train.

Six minutes was long enough to pee, right?

Right.

The crowd had thinned with the departure of that last train, and I didn't have to dodge anyone as I made my way back down the gum-stained platform to the awful, dingy toilet block.

I hated using train station toilets—but it was this, or hold for the forty minutes it took to get home.

I glanced around to make sure no one was watching, and used my skirt over my hand to protect me from the grime and germs as I twisted the handle of the toilet door.

Inside, white tiles about ten centimetres square lined the floor and the first foot of the walls—an attempt at something classy that fell way, way short when paired with dingy beige walls with cracked paint, covered in stains and festooned with cobwebs.

Used paper towels littered the floor, damp, scrunchy breeding grounds for disease, and someone had spilled something dark red all over the floor.

I clapped my hand over my mouth as I realised it looked like blood. I'd seen stalls before spattered inside with blood where some woman had clearly been having the period of her life, but this was next level again. Gross.

I hovered in the doorway, unsure if I really wanted to deal with this today.

Hold for forty minutes, or step over some disgusting woman's mess? They'd probably missed the sanitary bin and left a tampon lying on the floor, and it had seeped into a puddle of water or something—because that was an awful lot of blood.

Forty minutes. Eh.

I stepped forward—and my brain registered what was going on before my eyes or body did, because I hadn't even stopped moving when I started to scream, and by the time I stopped dead the scream had already ended, and I was backing up against the wall, hands over my mouth, my backpack crushed between me and the sink, tears stinging my eyes, gasping, stomach heaving—

Breathe, Edge, breathe, remember how to breathe, it isn't Anna, it isn't, it can't be Anna, she's at school, she's still at school, and look, that's not your uniform, it's close but it's not quite right and oh God above, please let this be a joke, this can't be real, she isn't dead, she isn't, she isn't, her *face*.

So much blood.

So much blood.

So much blood.

Screaming, high-pitched and painful, shrieking, and I was sobbing, sobbing, sobbing, and the roads around me screamed and writhed. *It hurts,* they cried. *No, it hurts, please stop!*

But I couldn't, I was there, and it was like the last four months had never happened, and there was Georgia right there, right now, in front of me, and I was shaking and I knew I was supposed to do something to back out of the memory, but I couldn't remember, it was too vivid, too real, she was *right. there.*

"Edge, Edge please, come on!"

"We're here, Edge, it's okay, we're here for you. We've got you."

Someone was holding me, rocking me.

Someone else was in my lap, clinging around my waist.

"Hush, Edge. It's okay. I know. I know. But I've got you."

"Please, Edge. Please come back to me!"

Stop! the roads screamed. *Please, we want you to stop!*

I hurt all over, inside and out. My road mastery felt faint, and ragged. My stomach was rolling in panic, my chest heaving.

But Gemma was here, and Scott, and they were holding me tight.

Around us, the shadows twined.

I forced myself to draw in a long, long breath to cut through the panic.

Please stop, the roads whimpered.

"Like this," I whispered to them, and slowly, slowly, one tiny, baby step at a time, I drew on the steps the police psychologist had taught me.

Acknowledge the memory. *I see you, Georgia.*

Locate it in my body. *My stomach heaving. Chest tight, gasping. Face and hands tight. Spine crawling.*

Take control of my body. *Deep breaths, long and slow. Relax the hands. Untense my face.*

Can't do much about the stomach or the spine, but breathe. Long and slow. Long and slow.

Separate my thoughts from the memory. *There's Georgia, over there.*

Here's me. Separate.

Still panicky, but separate.

I felt the roads watching, focusing intently on what I was doing.

Legitimise the fear. Yep, totally rational to be terrified when you find a murdered body who looks like your sister. This is logic. This is a rational, normal response. There is nothing wrong with this response.

Reassure it. I take this fear seriously. I can take the following steps to address it: stay with my friends in strange places. Keep our location secret. Stay in contact with the police. Let someone know where I'm going. Be on my phone to someone when I enter a strange place so if I get knocked out, someone will know. Use my road mastery to make sure no one dangerous is around.

This is a legitimate fear. I have taken steps to address it.

I remembered how I'd felt when I'd defeated the shadows that first time—like finally, I'd taken control of something I was afraid of, like I'd stood up to it—and won.

I am calm, I told myself. *I am in control. I acknowledge this memory as a part of my identity. I acknowledge that I will never be rid of it, and that it will shape who I become. But memory?* I addressed the image of Georgia in the train station bathroom directly, as an image in my head, but separate and distinct from my own thoughts. *You are not in control. You have made me who I am*—and it had, in so, so many ways, I realised: because of this event, I had Gemma, and Scott, and Sanctuary; because of this, I had grown the courage to stand up for my friends, for my family, to battle the shadows, to fight for what I believed in; I'd learned that standing up for things meant making sacrifices, like my dad had, but that I was capable of defeating the darkness in the end.

Tears rolled down my cheeks.

You have made me who I am.

I wrapped one arm around Gemma in my lap, still hugging my waist, and my other arm around Scott, still holding me tight.

But you are not in charge.

In my mind's eye, I imagined a river, deep and clean and wide, and full of things like love, like friendship, like the people who were there for me over and over and over again, like the smell of Mum's chocolate-chip cookie soulprint, like the sound of Dad laughing, like pleasant dreams and Sanctuary and the smell of Aphros's soulprint, the way I'd felt when I'd realised Gemma was safe, the look in Scott's eyes when he'd realised for the first time that *he* was...

I let all of it spill into the river, and let the river wash over the image of Georgia in the bathroom, sweeping it away.

Around me, another river ran, silver and shining and barely visible to my sorely weakened road mastery—a river created by the roads, washing away the shadows.

Somehow, I knew that we wouldn't be seeing the shadows again—and that the next time I remembered Georgia's face, I'd thank her, because even though I'd much rather she be alive, it was because of her unintentional sacrifice that I was here—and that Anna was.

And while I couldn't skip back in time far enough to stop her dying, I could use the rest of my *future* time to make sure that she hadn't died for nothing.

Goodbye, I whispered as the rivers faded.

And the roads whispered back, *Goodbye*.

37

I BREATHED A deep sigh of relief as Scott capped the last of the vials and tossed it onto the thigh-high pile next to us. It landed with a clink that I barely noticed through the sensations of sandpaper against my fingertips, the feel of hot, tropical, summer sun beating down on me, and the smell and taste of the world's freshest, ripest, most perfect peach in my mouth, juice dribbling down my chin.

Carefully, I rolled all the sensations together, forcing them down with my road mastery, pressurising them, more and more and more until—

Pop.

The fleeting sensation of an orange-winged fairy before she vanished, presumably to reappear in Sanctuary.

"There," Scott said, dusting off his hands. The whole reviving had taken less than three seconds this time; it was amazing what more than a hundred repetitions of something in a short period of time did for your skills. "All done."

I slumped, aching all over.

It was done.

I had a strong suspicion that when we got back to Sanctuary, everything would be perfect: Gemma had done a stellar job of reimagining it, and after a brief rest and with Scott's help, I'd managed to bring every single fairy back alive—even Skye and Ambergris, who'd been taken by the shadows—and even Viri.

I figured everyone deserved a second chance. No one deserved the shadows—and no one deserved to die alone with their guilt, even if it was totally justified guilt.

"Awesome," I said wearily. "I'll take you back to Sanctuary now."

Scott narrowed his eyes. "I feel like there's a definite 'but' waiting at the end of that sentence."

I shrugged—more of a twitch than anything else, I was so bone-tired. "No but. I'll drop you off, and then there's something else I need to do real quick before I join you."

He opened his mouth, but I waved at him to shush.

"Please. Just, don't argue, okay? I have to do this."

He squinted suspiciously at me some more, but nodded. "Okay. Fine. But if you're not back, like, three minutes after I am, I'm coming to find you."

"You can't get on the roads by yourself," I said, grabbing his hand and preparing to twist.

"I don't care," he said, squeezing my hand gently. "I'd find you anyway. I'd never stop looking till I found you, if I thought that you were in danger."

I rolled my eyes. "I'm not doing anything dangerous."

"You're on the roads and you're exhausted. That's like, like, driving home at three a.m. after a party."

"First," I said, "you sound like my parents. And second, when have you ever been to a party that lasted until three a.m., not to mention had to drive anywhere afterwards?"

He shrugged. "I'm imagining, right? It's the theme of the day. Plus," he added, sobering, "I can actually drive. Mum used to make me drive her down to the store sometimes. You know. When she was too, um..." He scuffed his feet against the ground. "Well, you know. When she couldn't drive herself."

I stared at him, horrified. "That's awful."

He shrugged again. "So look, you have three minutes, is all I'm saying, Miss Time Traveller. And then I'm going to assume you're in trouble, and I will find you."

I squeezed his hand back gently. "Yeah," I said. "I know."

And before he could keep staring intently at me, I twisted, popping us out right on the beach in Sanctuary. Immediately, I let go of his hand and twisted back again, reaching for the roads.

Scott grabbed after me, but it wasn't a proper entry point to the roads, and I was the only one who could get through. I smiled a tiny bit as I felt the ghost of his grip on my hand. Three minutes, or he'd tear the world apart to save me.

Deep breath.

This time, as I twisted, I felt the fog of the roads try to come with me.

The image of a puppy, sitting square-upright, desperate to be helpful; a child, bringing slightly bruised and mangled wild-flowers in from a garden with pride and delight.

Can you take me to them? I sent, along with a picture of the people I meant.

A pause, and then agreement, heads nodding vigorously—the puppy, also nodding, its tongue lolling to one side. *Yes.*

I twisted again, letting the fog follow me. It hissed out into the world ahead of me, and I watched as everything froze.

But this had to be the wrong place, surely: I'd expected to come out in the city—one of them, anyway—where I could see what the men were up to. Instead, I'd come out in the middle of the bush, gum trees with olive-green bark and some with white-and-grey trunks and still others with black, rough skin; the smell of eucalyptus everywhere; tussocky grass beneath my feet, and twig-and-leaf matter, and scrubby, tiny-leafed bushes with little orange berries.

This is the wrong place, I told the roads, which were never far away from me, no matter where I was. I sent a picture of what I'd intended.

Heads nodding, so many of them, a whole auditorium full. *Yes, yes. Go on, go on.*

I shrugged—but I walked on, my road mastery protecting me from the time leak—just as it had done back at school when I'd felt Sanctuary descend on us.

My heart nearly stopped as I looked up from watching my step and saw three men just ahead. But they were held fast by the roads' fog, frozen in time, and even though my heart pounded wildly in my chest, I crept closer.

It stopped again as I realised what the men were doing: they weren't just standing around, staring aimlessly at the ground. There was a hole there, at their feet, a hole about four feet across, and—I swallowed hard—just deep enough to hide a curled up body in.

I pressed my eyes closed and steadied myself. *How does this help?* I asked the roads. *I don't even know where we are.*

A vision filled my mind of the bush around us, every hill picked out, every track, and I could see the main road winding back toward the city.

The sensation of a desperate-to-please puppy accompanied it, and I smiled.

Thanks, I said. *That's perfect.*

One more quick stop, and we'd be able to stop running—for good.

I twisted, and the bush disappeared.

38

I LANDED BACK in Sanctuary under the pines near the beach. Nothing looked the same. It was better.

Cool, fresh pine mingled with the salty smell of the sea, and a gentle breeze lifted the small, wispy hairs on my neck.

In front of me, the meadow stretched out like a thick, emerald rug, grass calf-high and crisp enough to crunch, smooth as velvet from the bottom of the slope to the top.

Down to my right, the wall around the entrance alcove gleamed in the dusk light, a jellybean-shaped pearl, the wall smooth and shining.

To my left at the top of the hill, the Lodge seemed to have grown by two or three storeys; now it sprawled *up* as much as it sprawled *out*, and living, breathing vines twined over it, their tiny white flowers twinkling so bright it seemed covered in fairy lights. I smiled. How appropriate.

Directly across from me, the stables had had a makeover, too: they too gleamed white in the low light, walls clean and fresh with wide breezy windows.

But what really made my heart skip were the trees behind the stable. The far end of the meadow was part of the border with the Valley, part you couldn't cross, part where the brush had always been thick and dense, the trees not sickly so much as unwel-coming, like a thorny hedge or a fence.

Only now, it was clear that it wasn't the Valley any longer, but simply an extension of Sanctuary: the underbrush had opened up, and the ashy trees grew tall and straight, tiny round leaves fluttering like confetti, ferns and baby plants swaying at their feet.

And beyond, where the sickly trees had been, twisted gum trees—still gnarled and worn but now smooth-barked and stain-free, friendly trunks with character and personality, waving kindly in the breeze.

And the mountains behind, blue-cast and wholesome, and the air smelled fresh and clean.

A bark.

I whirled around to see Veve bounding toward me from the Lodge, followed closely by the turquoise-blue, fluttering flash of Quoise's wings. I dashed toward her, and we met in the middle of the slope, me falling to my knees to hug Veve, Veve jumping manically around, stomping on my fingers, slurping at my cheek.

I laughed, and smeared the tears from my eyes.

Quoise caught up and launched herself at my neck, hugging me tight. I patted her on the back gently and grinned. "So you like it, then?" I said.

She gave a muffled, strangled sound that I took as a yes.

"You made it!" Gem and Scott joined us from the stables, Aphros following with Helios trailing behind.

"Yeah," I said, standing up.

"Where did you go?" Scott asked.

I ignored him and turned to Gemma. One world might be safe—but I still had to finish dealing with the other one. "How long do we have left?"

She blinked. "Oh. Yeah."

I smiled a little. I wasn't surprised that she'd forgotten about my home deadline in all the chaos. But I hadn't.

She checked her phone, and her face fell a little. "Thirty seconds over time." She glanced up at me. "I'm so sorry."

I laughed, and held out my hand for her. "You're going to have to hold onto her," I told Scott. "I have to take Veve." I wound my free hand through Veve's collar.

"But Edge, we're too late, what are you doing?"

"Roads," I said, grinning. "We'll be back soon," I told Aphros and Quoise and Helios. "I promise."

Helios bowed gravely. "You have done well, Emma Tanning," he said. "You have restored my home and my family to me. I thank you."

I softened, shoulders relaxing as I exhaled. "Yeah," I said. "You're welcome."

Then I grinned again. "Look after those babies, when you find them."

He tossed his head and flared his wings, nodding me away—and an instant later, I was twisting us off again, back to my own yard.

Bright sunshine washed over us, and the smells shifted to the concrete-and-oil smells of town mingling with the green, eucalypt smell of the bush.

Mum exhaled heavily. "You're back." Her gaze slipped to Veve, panting happily at my side. "You did it."

I nodded.

"Sanctuary?"

"Fixed," Gemma said.

Mum's shoulders relaxed a little. "Well done."

I closed my eyes. "Mum," I said. "Do you have your phone on you?"

"Of course. Why?"

I tried doing the maths in my head. I'd gotten it right. I *had* to have gotten it right.

Of course I had.

"You should be getting a phone call in a sec," I said.

Sure enough, her pocket began to trill. Brows lowered in confusion, she drew the phone out and answered it, turning away from us toward the house.

I bounced my inner lip between my teeth and tried to ignore my pulse thundering in my ear. Any minute now. Any minute.

Veve pulled away, and I let her go, the leather of her collar rough against my fingertips. She bounced toward Mum, gave her a sniff which Mum ignored, and went off to find her water.

Mum turned back to us, her eyes round. "It's the police," she stage-whispered, fingers over the microphone. "They've caught them. They think they've actually caught them. And not just them, but *him*, too. Emma, they *actually* think they've *got* him this time!"

Scott and Gemma were lost in a confusion of pronouns, but I knew exactly what she meant, and I could hardly stop myself cracking at the seams with relief. They'd done it. *I'd* done it. It was over.

"They couldn't tell us earlier," Mum said, voice thick with awe as she relayed the information she was receiving through the phone, "but they found a body a few weeks ago in the bush up in the Dandenongs thanks to an anonymous tip. It's taken them this long to finalise it all, but they have enough evidence to arrest them all in conjunction with that murder—and a couple more. We can stay," she said, eyes bright. "We don't have to run."

We'd have to wait and see if they could make the charges stick, but it was a start. A really, really good start.

I pressed my fingers over the grin blooming over my lips.

We'd done it. And now, we could finally stop running. For good.

EPILOGUE

THE DOORBELL RANG.

That doesn't sound exciting in and of itself—and it wasn't, not really. But as I left my cosy-warm bedroom and came out into the icy hall, where the pale, wintry light through the window by the door was dappling the tiles as the leafless trees danced in the breeze outside, I smiled. Veve stood woofing at the door, tail up like a flag, ears pricked.

Mum popped out of her bedroom, bouncing on her toes. "Can I try again?"

I laughed. "Sure," I said, and gestured to the door.

Mum pushed Veve gently aside with her knee and closed her eyes, resting her forehead against the door. "Navy blue," she said. "I hear rain, and... is that loud ticking, like a really big clock?"

"Anything else?" I prompted, even though I was already impressed; visiting Sanctuary hadn't boosted her skills dramatically like it had mine (likely she wasn't all that strong in the first place), but it had given her enough of a push that she could work on developing her road mastery with solid practice— and she was doing well. A month ago, she wouldn't have picked up on the ticking.

Mum inhaled loudly. "Is that... cinnamon?"

I nodded, face alight. "I think so."

She turned to me, beaming with pride.

I held out my fist for her to bump. "We'd better answer it," I added, gesturing at the door with my free hand.

"Oh. Yeah." Mum stepped aside so I could do the honours.

The deliveryman outside nodded. "Parcel." He hefted a small box at me.

I opened the screen just wide enough to grab the box—and not wide enough for Veve to push past—and juggled the box inside, tucking it under my arm so I could sign for it. "Thanks," I said.

He nodded again, and left.

The door closed behind me with a satisfying click, and I checked the addressee. "Anna," I told Mum. She nodded, and retreated to her bedroom to do whatever it was she'd been doing before the opportunity to practise her skills had arisen. "Anna!" I yelled down the hall. "Parcel!"

There was a muffled thumping and then, down the end of the hall, her door popped open, spilling the sound of dance-rhythm pop music into the house. "Here," she said.

I took it over to her. "I'm going to take Veve for a walk," I said as I handed over the box.

"Yeah, sure." She was already flipping the box over in her hands, looking for the return address. "Whatever." She withdrew, her door closing with a little snick. Immediately, it popped open again. "We're still on for this evening though, right?"

I made a confused face. "This evening? Nope, no idea what you're talking about. Totally forgotten."

She threw a sock at me and slammed her door.

I squeaked, hoping the sock was clean. "Meet me outside at five!" I shouted through the door. "Or I'm going without you again!"

She'd be there, of course. The way she'd lit up that time I'd taken her to the Valley was nothing compared to how she was now with the reimagined Sanctuary—especially now that Aphros was finally pregnant. It was that which had made Anna decide to aim for animal nursing next year, since she didn't have the grades to do vet science.

I stuck my tongue out at her door and headed outside.

I might have a date with Anna in Sanctuary this evening, but I had a prior engagement to deal with first.

Outside, the wintry air prickled my cheeks, and I inhaled deeply, relishing the feel of the fresh air deep in my lungs. Nowra didn't have a winter like Melbourne did, but this was a passable substitute.

"Hey, Edge!"

I whirled around. Gemma was on the footpath outside my front fence, bundled up to her chin with a thick, cream scarf under her coat and a cable-knit beanie over her dark hair. "Hi!" I called.

She let herself in through the gate, and Veve went ballistic, tucking her tail under her butt and spinning in mad, gleeful circles all around the yard. "Hi, Veve," Gem said as Veve finally quit and trotted back over to say hi. Gem tussled Veve's ears, then brushed her gloves on my arms to get rid of the brown fur. "Hi, Edgey." Her cheeks were flushed pink.

"It's not that cold," I said. I had a jacket, sure, but I'd come from Melbourne: this was *not* gloves-and-beanie weather.

"Shut up," she said.

"You two losers going to hang out in the backyard all day?"

We turned, and there was Scott, striding across the footpath in a frogging t-shirt, arms swinging like he owned the whole wide world, blonde hair spiked and tousled, grinning wide as the sea.

Gemma rolled her eyes. "No. Of course not."

"So where are we going?" he said, letting himself in—as though there was ever an option.

I grinned. Sanctuary was calling our names.

Gemma tucked her arms through ours, and Veve danced around us, and the corellas flew overhead with their screechy cries, and together with my best friends in the world, I twisted away from one home toward the other—toward Sanctuary.

ANOTHER KIND OF HUNGER

SCOTT WAITED FOR the usual shouts of irritation to greet him as he slammed the front door of his home and kicked his school shoes off. Instead, silence hovered over the house, heavy and cloying. Silence, that was, except for his rumbling stomach. He sighed and schlepped down to his room, dodging the stacks of miscellaneous paperwork and clothing in various states of cleanliness that lined the hallway. Looked like dinner would be beans on toast again.

Scott kicked open the door to his room and crossed the threshold into sanity. The rest of the house was his mother's domain, carpets crusted with dirt and crumbs and ineffectual insect spray, mould growing in the corners where damp had invaded the house, drains stinking like a public toilet block.

In his room, the carpet was, if not clean, at least vacuumed. The array of stains were at least assured to stay where they were, and the walls had been scrubbed down so regularly they were starting to look worn. He closed the door with a heavy sigh and dumped his school bag in the bottom of the wardrobe.

Undressing was an exercise in precision; trousers washed only two days ago meticulously folded for reuse tomorrow, sweat-infused shirt in the hamper, tie over the hanger in the wardrobe. He pulled on trackies that would have crushed his carefully cultivated reputation in one fell swoop if anyone from school ever saw them, and a t-shirt that had sprouted at least two new holes since he'd worn it last time. There was a uniform free day coming up next week; he'd have to raid Mum's wallet again.

Out in the kitchen, three envelopes skulked on the bench, all addressed to his mother, all unopened. Scott glanced at them. Phone bill, electricity and water. He rubbed a hand up his face, under his glasses and over his eyes. Dammit. The welfare payment wouldn't be banked for another ten days. He'd have to call Aunt Sally again.

Whatever. Problem for later. Right now, the most pressing problem was his gurgling stomach. Lunch had been good old air yet again—easy to hide with enough arrogance and a few simpering girls to hold people's attention—and it was nearly half past five.

He opened the panty door and was halfway through reaching for a can of baked beans before his brain registered the shadows. *What the hell?* He clenched his jaw, hands fisted. This was just too far.

Heat settled in Scott's stomach as he stalked into the laundry. The rancid air made his eyes tear, but that was just another fact of life. He scooped a mouse out of the writhing tank in the corner— he'd long since gotten used to the feel of ten mice trying to cling tooth and claw to his arm at once—and shoved the wretched thing in his pocket. It squeaked in anguish as something broke—but he'd long stopped caring about that, too. He had the best role model in the world for not caring, after all.

But shadows, right there in the kitchen? Right where his mediocre dinner was supposed to be? Okay, so the house had more in common with a trash heap than a home. Okay, so she was often caught up in her mindless little schemes and forgot to make food. But *shadows*? In the *kitchen*? His cheek began a little twitching routine as he flung the pantry doors open again and surveyed the damage. God damn it all, he was hungry.

Scott fought down the disgust building in his chest. He should wait, be cautious and sensible, go down to the stream and cross over properly.

His stomach rumbled. Screw sensible.

He grabbed at the mouse, hardened against its pain by years of practice, and set it under his hand on the shelf, right near the edge of the shadows. Did he dare?

His stomach rumbled again, not so much a gurgle of hunger as a tight knot of emptiness. Gritting his teeth, Scott shoved the mouse towards the shadows with both hands. He closed his eyes and at the last instant, just as he felt the first brush of darkness, he snapped the mouse's neck.

It wasn't a terribly difficult thing to do; just about as difficult as breaking a paddle pop stick. And imagining it was just a stick helped with the guilt later. Just a little guilt—four hundred and sixty three mice previously were enough to dull the edges of it—but he added another one to the tally even as he imagined the Valley in crisp detail, eucalypts with their flashing leaves dancing in the wind, the smell of dirt and hard rock, the sharp-edged tussock grass, the heavy, cloying heat.

His body twisted towards the place, and he flung out a hand, catching at the darkness he sensed behind him—and Scott popped into the Valley, dragging a fistful of shadows. He flung them away and wiped his hand on his shirt.

In only took a minute to dig a grave deep enough for the mouse, and then he was off. He knew where she'd be; she never went far and, coming around the corner of a hill, Scott saw the billowing pillar of darkness his mother called home. It still made his neck itch.

Muttering idle threats to himself, he marched towards it, hardly even hesitating as he plunged from broad, sunless daylight into all-consuming black.

"Mum? Are you in here?"

A laugh that was only half delighted rang out. "Scott, darling? What a lovely surprise."

Hands fisting at his sides, Scott marched closer. The pillar, only a couple of paces across from outside, had been steadily growing in breadth every time he'd entered it; now it took him no less than thirty long strides to reach the centre of the darkness, where his mother luxuriated beneath a twisting, spiralling column of light.

"Seriously?" he muttered, glancing up at it.

"Isn't it lovely, dear?"

The look on his mother's face bordered on rapturous, and Scott sighed. "Yeah. Sure, Mum. It's lovely. But—"

Scott Harden? a voice boomed in his head. *Do you also come to me?*

Scott blinked. "Uh, Mum?"

She tittered. "Isn't it simply marvellous?"

He eyed the pillar with suspicion, hunger momentarily forgotten. "What *is* it?"

His mother turned to face him for the first time, eyes alight. "This is the Valley, Scott," she said, voice sharper and more lucid than he'd heard it in weeks.

"I know we're in the Valley, but—"

"No! This *is* the Valley." She turned back to the twisting pillar of light. "This is the heart of its power, made sentient, given life."

Scott eased himself a little further away. *Crazy lady at two o'clock. Okay then.* "That's... That's great, Mum. You did this?"

She beamed, even as the voice lashed out at his thoughts. *Together we have done this thing. I am will, I am power; she, merely the life force I required.*

Scott frowned. Life force? That sounded... permanent. "Uh, Mum? You sure this is a good idea?" It wasn't obviously; her ideas rarely were. But this seemed stupid on a more spectacular level than usual.

"Now, Scott," she chided, taking his hand and tucking it into the crook of her arm. "Don't you want something nice to eat?"

He snatched his hand back. "Funny you should say that, Mum, considering all the *shadows* where the *food* should be in our pantry."

While he'd spoken, his mother had positioned herself behind him, and now she took him by the shoulders and forced him forward, towards the pillar of light.

"Mum, I'm serious! You can't keep messing around with these things. We can barely afford to eat as it is, and if you d—" The word died in his throat and he swallowed down the sudden burn of grief. He shook his head.

His mother squeezed his shoulders and pulled him close to her, hugging her back against her chest. "Hush, now dear. Don't you think I know that? Why else do you think I did this? Can't you imagine what this much power can offer us?"

He tried to face her, but her iron grip held him fast. "Mum, I—"

"Go, son. Make your peace with the darkness, and you will rule it all."

She shoved him forward and he stumbled, trying desperately to fling himself aside. Instead, he tumbled headfirst into the pillar of light. He screamed as it swallowed him, light burning through every pore.

So, you come at last, the voice he'd heard before said with satisfaction, louder this time.

Scott spat blood from his mouth, wiped his lips on the back of his hand, and dragged himself to his feet. "No."

No? The light flared around him. *But Scott*—shivers slid over him at the sound of his name, eerily familiar on the light's metaphorical tongue—*you could have so much.*

Image flashed fleetingly through his head, control, order, neatness, everything clean and tidy and organised. Longing rolled through his body. He shoved it aside and forced himself to sound nonchalant. "Heh. Not unless you've got dinner in there for me."

He reeled as images of food assaulted his senses: the smell of roasting chicken; potatoes crackling in a buttery pan; bowls dripping with jewel-coloured fruits, sweet and lush; cheeses stacked higher than his hips, creamy-coloured and butter-yellow, veined and holed; the smell of rosemary, savoury and fresh; mint, sharp and sweet; cakes laden with icing and cream, swirled through with jam and curd and chocolate.

"Stop!" he cried, cowering with his hands over his head. His gut wrenched. "Please, just stop!"

All of it, crooned the voice. *You could have it all.*

The sensations intensified, his stomach cramping in response. "No," he whispered, curled into a quivering ball. "I am not my mother."

No? the voice whispered back. *Are you sure?*

"I'm sure." The words were barely audible, but given he could hear the light in his head, it probably didn't matter.

You refuse? The light's voice roared like lightning. *You refuse me?*

Scott only had time to tense before the burning began again. Knives of pain shot from every inch of his skin, sharp and hot. "Stop!" he screamed—only he couldn't scream, couldn't breathe. Pain poured down his throat, a liquid fire that set his body ablaze. In his head, he screamed, and screamed, and screamed.

Between breaths, he realised that the shouting wasn't all in his head, wasn't all his. "Mum?" he sobbed. "Mum! Help!"

The high-pitched whine of an insect filled his right ear over the roar of the light. It took a decade of effort to raise his arm, cup his hand, and the whole time he was terrified the mosquito would fly away. But he must have moved faster than it felt, because he slapped his own temple, capturing the creature, and in the instant its life force drained away, he imagined his mother's den in perfect clarity, and twisted away.

He lay on thin, dusty carpet, wheezing and clutching at his ribs as the fire died away. He couldn't tell if the sounds he was making were sobs or groans or maybe even laughter, because the whole thing was insanity; his mother had cracked, finally, gone mad and nearly dragged him under as well. He was going to die, cold and hungry and alone.

Sobs. Definitely sobs.

The doorbell rang.

He staggered upright with a monumental effort of will. His muscles ached and his skin felt raw, but he straightened, exhaled, and cleared the pain from his face. Heaven knew he had enough experience doing that, as well.

A vaguely familiar smell greeted him right before he opened the door, and then he did, and he had to lean against the doorframe to stop himself was falling.

"There's a letter with the delivery," the pizza guy said, holding out one of the cobweb-edged envelopes his mother got specially made.

Pizza. Mum had ordered pizza.

Hand barely shaking at all, he took the envelope. With a crisp, crackling tear, he opened it and withdrew the letter.

"I'm sorry, Scott. It will all be better soon. I promise. I went back a little to get you the pizza—I'm sorry about the pantry—and I'll be home in time for bed. Save me a slice. I love you." The bottom was signed with her initials, and next to it... He let out an explosive exhale that almost sounded like a laugh. She'd sketched a mosquito. It had been her he'd heard after all.

Scott closed his eyes and pressed the note against his chest, not even caring that the pizza guy might see the wetness leaking around the corners of his eyes. He appreciated the pizza more than words could say, and she'd saved him from the light, that was true. But where the shadows had come once, he knew they'd come again, and one day he wouldn't be strong enough to drag them all away. "Dammit, Mum," he told the letter. "It'll never be over. Not ever."

But for now, at least, there was pizza to eat.

FREE EBOOK

Thank you for buying this book!

When you buy an Inkprint Press book in print, we like to thank you by offering you the ebook for free. Please head to:
    http://www.inkprintpress.com/books/books-by-genre/fantasy/sanctuary/
    And use the coupon SANCPRINT to download your free copy in both .mobi and .epub formats. (The coupon will only work once.)

SUPPORTERS

With thanks to my amazing Patreon supporters, Clare, Thea and Bethy <3

https://www.patreon.com/amylaurens

ACKNOWLEDGEMENTS

SO many people have contributed to the making of this series, and while I've thanked each of them in the individual books, I'd like to take one last opportunity to thank them all again here. In no particular order:

Clare, for everlasting support, amazing covers, and incredible, super-human patience.

Liana, for being my writing rock, no matter what bizarre things I come up with.

Daimien, because I literally could not be doing this without you.

Miles, Bethany, Kerryn, Shanna, Kimberly, Renn, Lauren, Michelle, Emily, Anna and Stephanie for typo-spotting, genre-identification, proofreading and general encouragement (any remaining errors are, of course, mine).

Anthea, Lily and Steph for boundless enthusiasm.

Merc Rustad and Ada Hoffmann, without whom the first few drafts of book one probably would not exist.

Belynda for physically helping type in corrections <3

The Pitch Wars mentors who gave me feedback—J.C. Davis, Wade White, Catherine Scully and Juliana Brandt.

Mum and Dad, for hand-selling half a bajillion copies of the first book as they burst with pride over their daughter <3

Carol, who loved this story enough to keep asking for more.

And last, but never least, God, who continues to lead me in this ridiculous journey. Amen.

ABOUT THE AUTHOR

AMY LAURENS is an Australian author of fantasy fiction for all ages. She has never seen a fairy or travelled to Sanctuary (sadly), but she has definitely owned a Labrador almost exactly like Veve (though Amy's Labrador was yellow, not brown).

And while she's definitely not a Road Master (pity), her kids are pretty sure she has eyes in the back of her head and a sixth sense for spotting trouble. She hasn't told anyone this, but actually she has *two* sets of eyes in the back of her head—one because she's a mum, and one because she's a teacher.

You can find out more about Amy and her books at her website, www.amylaurens.com.